DRAGON'S FURY

SERIES

VOLUME IV

★ ★ ★ ★ ★

COMING SOON BY JEFF HEAD

DRAGON'S FURY VOLUME V – EAGLE'S TALONS

(In 2004)

THE STAND AT KLAMATH FALLS

How rural western farmers fought entrenched environmentalism and the Federal Government and won.

(In 2005)

OTHER NOVELS BY JEFF HEAD

DRAGON'S FURY VOLUME I – BREATH OF FIRE

DRAGON'S FURY VOLUME II – TRODDEN UNDER

DRAGON'S FURY VOLUME III – HIGH TIDE

DRAGON'S FURY

VOLUME IV

THE LONG MARCH

JEFF HEAD

www.dragonsfuryseries.com

Published By:

Alpha Connections

Emmett, ID 83716

This is a work of fiction. The events and characters described herein are imaginary. Any similarities to actual persons or events are purely a result of the author's imagination.

Copyright © 2003 Jeff Head

All Rights Reserved.

This work, and any parts thereof, may not be copied, reproduced or transmitted in any form, or by any means; electronic, mechanical or otherwise without prior written permission from the author.

ISBN 0-9715779-6-X

Proudly produced in the United States of America

Dedication

This book, and the entire series, is dedicated to lovers of liberty everywhere, and to the principles upon which true liberty rests: faith, morality, virtue, honor, free will, commitment, valor and eternal vigilance. Most especially, it is dedicated to all of those Americans and their families who have served in defense of liberty and sacrificed their time, their efforts, their very lives and the lives of their loved ones for that cause, whether at home or abroad.

In particular the entire Dragon's Fury series is dedicated to those victims of terror whose lives were so brutally cut short on September 11, 2001, and to those selfless emergency personnel, firefighters, police, National Guard and volunteers who worked to help the trapped and injured, and to recover the victims.

It is also dedicated with great respect and humility to the passengers and crew of United Airlines Flight 93. On that ultimate day of infamy, those heroes resisted their enemies and fought back, resulting in the crash of their aircraft and the death of all involved before it could reach its target, thus saving hundreds if not thousands of more innocent lives. Their struggle and the defeat of terror and tyranny on that day foreshadows on a small scale the ultimate defeat of tyranny and terror by free people everywhere, who when called upon, rise to whatever heights necessary to maintain liberty and virtue, irrespective of sacrifice or cost. God rest the souls of those brave passengers on Flight 93.

Finally, this work is dedicated to those committed and professional service men and women who have been, and will be, called upon to bring about a just and lasting retribution for the attacks of 9-11 that killed and injured so many. The recent successful operations in Afghanistan and Iraq are examples of this. May we honor the sacrifices of all those who go in harms way for our benefit, and may we be prepared to make our own sacrifices for liberty and for our Republic wherever and whenever necessary.

Acknowledgments

As with all of the volumes in the series, special thanks go to my family for their faith in me. In particular, thanks to my dear wife of 25 years for her love and patience with this work and to my sons, Jeff and Jared for their input and suggestions…and to my daughter Katie who has faithfully read all of the volumes, promoted them, and had faith in her Dad. In addition, thanks to my father, A. L. Head Jr., a combat veteran of World War II, for all of his support, and to my mother, Georgia, whose Christ-like love and faith have always been an example and inspiration to me.

Once again, I cannot have a section on acknowledgements without personally thanking those who have collaborated with me.

Thanks to Joanie Fischer of Pennsylvania, for her reviews, edits, faith and encouragement.

Thanks to Chris Durkin of Pennsylvania, for his edits, perseverance, faith and invaluable technical input.

Thanks to Cory Emberson of California, for her edits and her faith and belief in this project.

Thanks to Matt Bracken of California, for his reviews and for his input as a former U.S. Navy Seal platoon leader.

Thanks to Arthur Hines of North Carolina for his input and for his service on the point of the sword in the Special Forces in Vietnam.

Thanks to Matthew Riley of Connecticut, for his reviews and for his input as a former U.S. Navy Seal.

Thanks to Chief Master Sergeant Jack Newton and Master Sergeant John Davis of the 159th Security Force Squadron, Louisiana Air National Guard, for their input regarding security force issues after the retaking of Incirlik air base in Turkey.

To each of these and all others, who have encouraged me and put up with my ramblings, I say again, heartfelt thanks.

Author's Note

Every effort has been made to make Volume IV of the Dragon's Fury series, "The Long March", a standalone novel that can be purchased and read individually. In order to do this, in the introduction of characters and the story line, short paraphrasing of past activities have been included in an effort to bridge the volumes together. Hopefully this will allow first-time readers enough flavor and background to enable them to enjoy Volume IV without having to first read the other three volumes. At the same time, I have attempted to do this in such a way as to also allow those who have already read Volumes I, II and III to pick up the tale with as much continuity and as little redundancy as possible.

Obviously, such an effort is an attempt to satisfy two conflicting interests. I believe I have struck a good balance. I suppose that time, the experience of readers and their comments will tell whether my attempts have been successful or not. In either case, whether you are a new reader of the series, or whether you are returning for Volume IV after having read the others, I hope that the read is an enjoyable, compelling and thought provoking one for you

I say all of this with one final comment and observation. The books are written as a series. Even though I am making every effort to allow the various volumes to be read as standalone novels, they really were meant to be read as a series and I sincerely hope everyone who picks up one volume of the series and reads it, will be inspired by that reading to read them all.

DRAGON'S FURY

VOLUME IV

THE LONG MARCH

www.dragonsfuryseries.com

Prologue

March 21, 2009, 21:50 EST
Death Row
Federal Detention Facility
Outside of Reston, VA

He couldn't get the words out of his mind, even though it had been more than five months.

"Mr. Krenshaw rose to some of the highest positions possible in our free and moral society. As a result of his love for himself, his ambition, his commitment to enemies of this nation and his corruption…as a result of his perusal of all of these things above his commitment to his fellow citizens and the liberty that availed him of the very opportunities he enjoyed…he sacrificed it all and threw it all away.

"David Krenshaw, as great a traitor as this nation has ever known…and it has known a few…has been given the guilty verdict he so richly deserves and it is this administration's absolute hope that he will be sentenced to die for those crimes. An ignoble and dishonorable end to an ignoble, dishonorable, traitorous and murderous life."

When he'd heard those words, the enormity of his situation had finally struck home, deep into his heart and soul. Even more so than the words *"Guilty as charged,"* uttered by the foreman of the jury on that fateful day in October of last year. For some reason those words spoken by the Attorney General of the United States at a news conference after the announcement of the guilty verdict had finally made clear to him the full extent of his situation. Up until that point, he had held out hope that somehow, someway, his many allies and his wealth and influence would retrieve him from the nightmare. But it hadn't worked out that way.

As much as he contemplated those words of the Attorney General, there were still other words, uttered a few weeks later, that were emblazoned even deeper in his mind…and they came back to him now. If the Attorney General's words had finally awakened him to the awful state and reality of his circumstances, those later words punctuated with utter finality what the consequences of those circumstances would be for him personally. They were the words of the judge at his sentencing hearing in late December.

"Mr. Krenshaw, it is never an easy or a tasteful task to sit in judgment of someone's life or liberty. But I must say, in this case the task has been rendered more palatable as a result of your heinous deeds. Those treasonous crimes caused or abetted the deaths of many hundreds, possibly tens of thousands of your countrymen, and helped lead this entire nation to as precarious a precipice as it has ever stood upon in its long history.

"If ever there were a reason for maintaining and administering the death penalty, this is it. Therefore, Mr. David Krenshaw, on Counts 1, 2, 3 and 6 the Court sentences you to death by lethal injection on March 21st, 2009.

"On Count, 4 and 5, the Court sentences you to 20 years in federal prison on each count, the sentence on each count to run consecutively. That's a total of 40 years, but the death sentence I have just imposed renders moot any further explanation of the terms of these sentences.

"The Court also imposes upon you for each of the six counts a fine of $1.5 million for the aggregate sum of $9 million to be paid by your estate.

"The Court accepts the government's recommendation with respect to restitution, and orders restitution in the amount of $40 million to be paid by your estate and maintained in trust for the expected civil suits that will arise out of your guilty verdict.

"These are the sentences that are imposed upon you by this court in accordance with the laws of these United States. They are fair and just sentences that are commensurate with the nature and gravity of your crimes. I only wish to God that the victims of your crimes, indeed all of us, had been treated as fairly and justly.

"We shall rise above the deeds of individuals of your ilk, Mr. Krenshaw and your allies, our enemies. Make no mistake about it, in the end, we will be triumphant. Let this sentence, and its swift execution, be a warning and testimonial to all enemies and traitors amongst us or in foreign places, American justice will not be denied…it will be served."

The finality of that sentence had been punctuated by the swift appeals process that was a result of the wartime conditions. Two appeals had been made. The last had gone to the Supreme Court only yesterday, and the high court had refused to even hear it. Now, here he sat, just over thirty minutes before the sentence was to be executed, and there was no one left to turn to…he was, in the end, alone.

His wife had divorced him less than two weeks after the trial and conviction, claiming ignorance (which, he thought, was absolutely true), and demanding and then receiving from the court a generous support settlement from whatever would remain of his estate. As beautiful as she was, as attached to him and his career as she had apparently been…despite the many years…now she was gone and did not so much as even send him a letter.

After being taken into custody, despite his efforts through back channels with his lawyer, he had never heard from or been contacted in any way by the agents of Jien Zenim, his great mentor. As much as he had done for the man, as supportive as he had been of what he still believed were the man's long term views…never mind the fact that millions of dollars had been paid to him for that support…Zenim and his agents had not come to his aid, had not retrieved him from this hell.

He had been stripped of his vaunted position on the Council on International Relations, the CIR, and the people within those ranks, despite significant movement towards his line of reasoning regarding current world conditions, were also distancing themselves from him as quickly as they could. The prestige and power of that influential body derived from influential politicians from both sides of the aisle, leading media executives like himself and leaders from every part of society all dedicated to their own vision of world governance. He had harbored such great hopes of directing all of that power and influence in support of Zenim's vision. And considering the numerous setbacks to American interests precipitated by the current administration's efforts to thwart Zenim, he had thought he was on the verge of realizing that goal. But that was before his arrest and trial. Now all of them were both unwilling and powerless to help him.

Finally, his former co-workers at WNN, the World News Network, were also distancing themselves from him as rapidly as possible. The place where he had risen to his pinnacle of influence and wealth was now a vacuum to him. None of them had talked to him, none of them had visited him…none of them *wanted* to. Despite all he had done for the individuals he had considered loyal to him, he found that the loyalty was only skin deep…in fact, no deeper than what loyalty he held for them. Now, to a person, they justifiably claimed that their former support of his ideas and policies had been purely innocent, and that they had been completely ignorant of his involvement with the enemies of America.

"They're all backpedaling. They're all abandoning my sinking ship, every one of them," he thought as he sat up on his cot and turned towards the small table holding his last meal.

David Krenshaw knew in his heart that, if the roles were reversed, he, too, would be abandoning this particular sinking ship. So it was hard for him to cast too many aspersions towards his former associates. He was at least honest enough with himself to recognize that truth about himself. But that knowledge did not lend any comfort to him…he was the one here in this cell.

In an effort to try to afford some measure of comfort in his last hours, a priest had been made available to him. But David's complete lack of remorse or repentance had left the priest no room to provide absolution. David had heatedly communicated to the priest that he was convinced that God, if he were even willing to admit His existence, was the one who had caused David to fall from his position of wealth and influence…had in fact turned His back on David.

In the end, despite his recognition of the awful conditions he found himself in, David was unwilling to feel, let alone accept, any responsibility for his own actions. It was all someone else's fault. It would always be someone else's fault to the very end.

Like so many totally irredeemable and depraved individuals, David was only interested in his own perspective and what was in it for him. Now, even when there was nothing left in it for him but the sharp end of a needle, everyone else was an object of blame and an object of manipulation…even, in David's mind, God.

He got up and stepped to the small table to eat. He tried not to view it as a last meal…tried to look upon it as nothing more than a late dinner. In an effort to maintain that perspective, he had even told his guards to select the dish for him when he had been given the opportunity for a last request…whatever they thought appropriate. Now, as he sat down he found that his efforts to treat the meal as any other dinner would also be denied him.

While removing the stainless steel cover from the plate holding the food, he smelled the entrée briefly before he saw it. Looking down, the recognition and the finality of this last meal…and the reasons for it…flooded his mind and he began to sob.

Chow Mein.

March 21, 2009, 22:26 EST
Execution Chamber
Federal Detention Facility
Outside of Reston, VA

Director Andy Syke, along with approximately twenty other individuals in the witnessing room, watched the small entourage as it made its way down the hall to his left and to the door of the small room with the single bed and medical equipment in it. Like the hallway, that room was separated from the witness room by a row of thick glass windows. Audio was channeled into the room through a speaker system built into the walls.

As he watched, Andy could see the warden, a priest, the doctor and four prison officers…and there was David Krenshaw, supported between two of the officers, sobbing uncontrollably, being carried along, his feet dragging, his body totally limp as he was unable or unwilling to support himself.

"What a miserable excuse for a person," the Director thought.

The Director and FBI Agent in Charge (AIC) of the investigation and apprehension of Krenshaw had suspected all along that at his core, Krenshaw was cowardly and totally self-serving, not at all dedicated to the ideology of the cause that had bought and paid for him over the years. Now Sykes was himself witnessing the obvious verification of that suspicion.

Andy turned to Attorney General Hull, who was seated next to him and who had made a point of being present at the execution on behalf of the administration.

"Mr. Attorney General, in all my years I don't believe I have ever seen such a miserable excuse for a human being. It almost makes one pity him."

Dean Hull turned to the AIC who had been so instrumental in bringing the man they were watching to justice.

"Andy, you are right, Krenshaw is pitiful…but I have no doubts that his current *pain* is only because he was caught and is finally having to face the consequences of his actions.

"We can never afford to forget how many good, honorable Americans are dead because of the actions of that totally depraved and traitorous excuse of a human being. He was wholly without remorse throughout the time he was committing these crimes and throughout his trial. I cannot pity him in the least, and though I do not relish what we are about to witness, I am nonetheless gratified that such an individual as this will now have to account for the damage he has caused."

Andy Syke agreed with the Attorney General and was anxious to punctuate that agreement.

"Well, I agree whole-heartedly with that. Perhaps pity was not a good word choice. We surely can't afford to show him an ounce of it, irrespective of how sad an excuse for a person he is, and irrespective of what he looks like at this minute.

"One thing is for sure: he and his handlers did not show us any pity, nor would they have wasted it on us in the future if Krenshaw had been allowed to continue his agenda. Irrespective of his own weaknesses, our enemies used Krenshaw effectively against us, and I, for one, am glad he is soon to be permanently out of play. I just hope that any more like him are deterred by this administration of justice, or that we find them soon and administer a similar form of justice to them."

The Attorney General nodded as Krenshaw was now physically picked up and placed on the bed.

"Well said, Director, well said. Here we go."

At this point Krenshaw, who had been limp and had required help from the guards, began to resist, kicking and flailing his arms and legs wildly in an effort to get off the bed. His incoherent yells and screams could be heard from the other room. The four large guards, one handling each appendage, held him firmly in place despite the struggle while the attending doctor fastened the restraints around his arms, legs, body and head.

Finally Krenshaw was completely restrained. But although he continued to struggle against the restraints, they held firm. The only indication of the continued struggle was Krenshaw's red face, a few very restricted movements around the arm and leg restraints, and his continued yells, which were now muffled by the restraints around his head. An almost eerie, calm atmosphere settled over the room.

Upon a nod from the warden, the doctor placed an IV tube into Krenshaw's exposed arm and attached it to a drip that was wheeled over next to the bed. A small delay ensued as everyone waited for almost thirty seconds until the appointed time. At precisely 10:30 PM, after the warden had the exact time recorded, he nodded again to the doctor who then turned to the medical equipment and activated the drip, allowing the lethal fluid to begin flowing into David Krenshaw's veins.

Within twenty seconds Krenshaw's struggling and yelling had stopped. His eyes remained open and he continued to move his eyeballs around wildly for another minute as the drug continued to take effect. Then his eyes closed and he appeared to drift into a deep sleep. About two minutes later, his entire body experienced two quick spasms, followed by his breath coming short and very quickly for a few seconds. Then he lay completely still.

At precisely 10:36 PM the attending doctor examined his charge once more. When he was finished with that examination, he turned and looked to the warden and the gathered witnesses and pronounced David Krenshaw officially dead.

As Andy Sykes and the Attorney General rose to leave the room, Andy distinctly heard the Attorney General, who himself had been a U.S. Army Ranger in his younger days, whisper the phrase:

"Sic Semper Tyranis."

Chapter 1

"Whether in chains or in laurels, liberty knows nothing but victories." – Douglas McArthur

April 3, 2009, 02:37 EDT
Isolated Training Area
Eglin Air Force Base, Florida

The two rotors were still turning as the eight man team came down the ramp out of the tail end of the modified Osprey aircraft and quickly made their way into the forest next to the small clearing. No sooner had they cleared the back ramp of the aircraft than the Osprey canted its rotors slightly forward, leaned that way and took off, leaving the men to their own devices.

None of the eight wore uniforms or any identifying insignia. All eight of them were using the latest generation night vision equipment and carrying MP5SD submachine guns and other equipment on their backs. They communicated through miniature radios that were fitted to small ear-pieces lodged in each of their right ears and to small microphones that wrapped around their face, positioned near their mouths. All of them were fluent in Spanish.

Despite the lack of official uniforms, if ever captured with the equipment that they carried, that equipment itself would identify who they fought for, whether they were personally identified or not. For this reason, most of their high-tech equipment, except for their miniature and very powerful digital radio, would be cached in a specific area about two miles from their landing zone for later use after they had met up with their point of contact (POC) on the ground. That contact was a long-time partisan and CIA operative who had been working for the United States government for many years. The meeting with their POC and the expeditious caching of their equipment was what the soldiers were practicing this early morning in the Florida woods.

They had been practicing and training for the various aspects of their operation for over eight weeks now. Eight grueling weeks amounting to 14 to 16 hour days and covering every conceivable aspect of their upcoming mission. From the insertion and meeting of their POC, to the caching, to every conceivable alternative for accomplishing their mission in advance of the major U.S. military operation that would follow. Tonight was the last practice run at the insertion. Four days from now, on April 7th, the practice would become reality.

Sergeant Hernando Rodriguez considered all of this as he led the team into the trees. Once completely under cover of the trees and in their shadows, Hernando used hand signals and instructed the others to quickly kneel down and take up defensive positions from which they could observe the small clearing they had just left, and from which they could watch for the signal indicating that their contact had seen them and all was safe.

After the intense fighting in Alaska over the last several months, Hernando had welcomed the call back to the lower forty-eight states. He knew it meant that he would be picking up where he had left off before being called north with so many others to fight the Red Chinese invasion across the Bering Strait in June of last year. That invasion had been spectacularly successful for the Chinese and ominous for America and her allies. Nome had fallen, Fairbanks had fallen, Prudhoe Bay and the American north slope oil fields had fallen, and then been destroyed by the Americans themselves using nuclear demolition devices. It had all finally been stopped right at the outskirts of Anchorage with the use of the new Hail Storm missiles that American forces had employed.

Although the Chinese had not been completely defeated in Alaska to date, they had now fallen back to a strong defensive position well to the east of Nome, which they continued to occupy. American and Canadian forces were now building up for the upcoming offensive in the spring. More AGM-999 Hail Storm missiles were being produced and stockpiled as rapidly as possible for use in that big attack that would hopefully eject the Chinese from North America for good.

Hernando had been called back south just ten weeks earlier, before the big offensive could begin. After an all too short two week leave to visit his wife and new son in Miami, he had returned to Eglin Air Force Base to prepare for this mission with the 1st Special Forces Operations Detachment-Delta (SFOD-D) that he had been assigned to and had been training with before the fighting began in Alaska.

Along with the allied offensive in Alaska, the United States and its allies were also on the offensive in Israel, where American, British, and Israeli forces had used masterful strategy and more Hail Storm missiles to decimate GIR forces surrounding that nation. This had allowed them to break out of the vast perimeter in which they had been contained. Allied forces had now advanced well beyond Damascus on the north, and had retaken the Egyptian capital of Cairo and the Nile River valley in the west.

A similar victory for allied forces near Moscow was allowing Russian, European and American forces in that theater to go on the offensive this spring as well. As a result, allied prospects had dramatically shifted for the good., the allies were moving forward, pushing back the Greater Islamic Republic (GIR) and Coalition of Asian States (CAS) forces in several critical areas around the globe. This included Hernando's upcoming operation where the U.S. leadership was now directing more resources and energies back towards what was viewed as unfinished business in the Caribbean.

The long-awaited move against Cuba was now in the final stages of preparation, and a critical part of its overall success would hinge on the success of this covert mission in which Hernando would take part, and in which he would personally play such a pivotal role. The invasion of Cuba was slated for April 14th, and its prospect of success would directly correlate with the successful completion of Hernando's mission. Those parameters provided for the quickest victory with the least resistance if the Cuban leader was already out of the picture.

Hernando was proud to have been selected for this pivotal role in the overall operation. Having successfully made the transition from the Ranger Regiment to the Delta Force, he was certain that the best of the best would be able to get the job done for the nation. He thanked God and his parents for his upbringing that had put him in such a position. He prayed he would do well, that he would make his wife and son, his parents, his superiors, his nation, and his God proud of him.

…and his prayers were soon to be answered.

April 5, 2009, 14:45 local time
Presidential Residence
Havana, Cuba

Fifteen year old Ernesto Contrerez shut down his personal computer where he had been reviewing the latest data available to him on the war, and got up from his desk. He walked out of his personal, finely adorned bedroom into the large living room of the central air-conditioned mansion to watch his satellite TV in the hopes of catching a WNN report. As he did so, he reflected again on his position in Cuban society. At times like this, it never ceased to amaze him that he lived in such opulence, while so many of his countrymen lived in such poor conditions…even squalor.

His father lived with him here in this wing of the Presidential residence as they had done for several years. His father drew a fine wage from the state for just assenting to whatever it wanted with respect to Ernesto. The two of them often found themselves trotted out before the local and international press, and displayed as a shining example of what the state and its glorious leader could accomplish for the individual.

But at fifteen years of age, Ernesto had formed definite opinions of his own in that regard. Like any teenager, he was prone to question those in authority over him, particularly his parents, and he had a lot of questions for both his biological father and for the individual who acted as his father in fact, his *Padre*. Ernesto knew that the Cuban dictator viewed himself not only as his father, but as the father of the entire nation. In so doing, he made sure that he kept both Ernesto and his father very close to him.

But these questions and thoughts were not something he dared raise openly with either his own father or his *Padre*. If nothing else, nine years of living in near proximity to the mechanisms of the state apparatus had taught him at an early age what he could safely explore openly and what he couldn't…and the questions he had regarding his own position in society, and how that society provided for him and for his countrymen, were definitely off limits.

In the end, Ernesto knew that his biological father was utterly bought and paid for by, and at the beck and call of, the leader of their nation and its apparatus. His dad had found himself in the right place at the right time over nine years ago when events concerning Ernesto had unfolded on the international stage, and he had immediately moved to take advantage of them by being the absolute lackey of the state and demanding complete custody of Ernesto.

"I'm not sure that he had any viable choice," thought Ernesto as he reflected on those events.

"Not to have done so would have probably meant his death."

But as Ernesto thought about the potential death sentence his father would have received for defying the state, his recollection was drawn back to another individual, and the very real death that individual had experienced. His mother had died smuggling Ernesto out of Cuba back in 1999 when he was only six years old.

"She had *given* her life for me on those waters and she had done so freely," Ernesto reflected, "and she had done it in an effort to deliver me out of this hellhole to what she was sure would be a better way of life, a life she felt God had led her to risk everything to obtain for her son."

Now, nine years later, Ernesto had never forgotten his mother, or her faith, even though his father and El Macho himself were sure that they had obliterated any capitalist or other American tendencies left over from those few months Ernesto had spent in America.

But they were wrong, utterly and completely wrong. Ernesto, while at the focal point of that international incident between Cuba and America, had not forgotten the experiences he had while there. He was, to this day, constantly comparing what he was being told by the state with what he had both seen and experienced in America…and what he was being told by the state was coming up very short. He thought back on it again as he sat down in the soft, deep cushions of the couch and turned on the television.

"So much freedom…how could they all be so free?" he thought.

"I can still remember it.

"So much love from my aunt, uncle and cousins. So much prayer to God on my behalf…prayers said openly and without fear.

"So much care from those who saved me from the sea. So much love from so many others–and they helped me in spite of their state apparatus at the time…and not to garner favors from it."

…and the food and material wealth those people had, he still marveled when he thought on it.

"So much to eat and so many comforts for everyone! How could it be…how could so many of them have such positive outlooks, even when their own government at the time was doing all it could to also kiss up to El Macho?"

In his heart, Ernesto knew why.

"It is because they are truly free," he whispered to himself.

And so Ernesto had not forgotten. At first, upon being delivered back to Cuba, he had been too young to recognize the significance of those memories. He had nonetheless locked them away in a quiet, secret place within his mind.

As first the months, and then the years passed, he pulled them out to examine them often, sometimes late at night, sometimes when he pretended to be listening to his tutors and handlers, sometimes when he was taken to the estates out in the country to hunt or fish. He would review them over and over in his own mind, determined not to forget his mother or his relatives, or the things he had seen, heard and experienced there in America. Now, as a teenager, he had developed his own opinions about what it all really meant.

At the time of his mother's death, and his brief stay in America, the experience was whirlwind, and he was so young. There was little time to reflect upon the deeper meaning of it all. Now he was older, and after considering the conditions around him from what he considered to be a much more mature and informed perspective, and after comparing them to the memories emblazoned in his heart and in his mind, those opinions had crystallized. He believed he understood why his mother was willing to pay the ultimate sacrifice to get him to the shores of America. And now he wanted, perhaps more than anything else, to repay her for her sacrifice.

Despite the inherent dangers of harboring such opinions, and the greater dangers of ever expressing them openly, Ernesto knew that life in Cuba was a lie. It was a lie that was being fed to the entire world to justify that which could not be justified…to bolster and support a decadent, weak and perverse system.

It was a lie that to this day sullied the memory, the faith, and the sacrifice of his mother. It could not be allowed to stand, and Ernesto, emboldened by the determination and ideals of youth…and by his own faith in that same God his mother had relied upon…was resolved that he was going to do something about it, do something to turn it around and expose the truth.

…and he already knew who he could count on to help him accomplish it.

April 8, 2009, 14:45 local time
COSTIND Headquarters Facility
Beijing, China

Admiral Lu Pham was genuinely gratified at the report he had just delivered to General Hunbaio, the head of the Chinese Commission of Science, Technology and Industry (COSTIND), and to Chin Zhongbaio, a ranking member of the Politburo and the President of COSCO, the Chinese Ocean-going Ship Company.

Lu had known both men for over fifteen years, ever since they had brought him from Vietnam to China to resurrect the supercavitating models and projections he had developed back in the 1970s as a young officer in the service of the fledgling North Vietnamese Navy. The Chinese had given him all the resource and authority required to bring those old models and designs into full, modernized production and had rejoiced with him when they had ultimately been successfully used to surprise the U.S. 7th Fleet in 2006, over three years ago, at the onset of the World War they were now embroiled in. As a result, naval warfare and the advantages historically held by the U.S. Navy were drastically altered that March of 2006 in the western Pacific Ocean.

Despite that victory, and the others that followed, Lu had never underestimated the Americans. They had quickly developed their own defenses and counter technologies to what Lu had wrought. But initially their efforts had been ineffective in countering the LRASD weapons, or "Killer Whales,:" as they were now called all around the world.

"Until last summer," thought Lu.

That is when the Americans, with the advent of their SUB-CIWS, Submerged-threat Close In Weapons Systems, had very nearly overcome the Chinese edge.

Those new defensive weapons had been, and continued to be, a very real concern for Lu and his engineers and developers...and for the entire Chinese military leadership. The Americans had drastically reduced the effectiveness of the supercavitating weapons by employing underwater supercavitating defenses against them. So successful had these systems been in defending American ships, that they indeed threatened to turn the tide of the naval warfare drastically back in favor of the Americans late last year.

But with the deployment of the latest Batch 4C upgrades to the LRASD weaponry, the Chinese had once again vaulted to what they felt was a secure position. That upgrade had been successfully developed in China and tested in the Yellow Sea in the fall of last year, and then had seen its first combat use in December. That relatively minor engagement had proven a complete success when a U.S. Navy Arleigh Burke Aegis destroyer, equipped with the new American SUB CIWS, had been sunk along with two of the three transports it had been escorting. Had there been more weapons available at the time, the entire convoy would have been sunk, and the large naval forces off of Anchorage could have been attacked and destroyed as well. If enough weapons could be deployed, the destruction of those forces off Anchorage was still a possibility, which would allow the PRC forces in Alaska to potentially stop the American offensive there and maintain a strong foothold in North America.

But large scale deployment was still a problem. The Chinese Navy had literally taken prototypes and used them in combat before full scale production procedures and practices had been developed. There simply had not been very many weapons, outside of what their R&D facilities could manually put together, until full scale production could be instituted, and that time was now very near.

The new upgrade was capable of being retro-fitted to any of the various LRASD configurations, allowing the weapon to approach their targets at supercavitating speeds and then rise out of the water like a missile when approaching the American SUB CIWS effective range. Then, the sea-skimming missile, approaching in excess of 600 knots, would skim the sea and impact low on the vessel within a matter of seconds of taking flight. And it would accomplish this, as had been shown in the case of the sunken Burke destroyer, more quickly than the American missile defenses could react against it in order to prevent it.

As a result of Lu's and his team's innovations, soon the Chinese would begin to retrofit and upgrade about half of the shallow attack, the deep attack, the air-launched, and the intelligent loiter configurations of the LRASD weapons currently in inventory to the new terminal, sea skimming attack capability. The upgrades would begin rolling out to the Pacific next month, then the Indian Ocean, followed by the Mediterranean Sea and Atlantic Ocean.

It was the status of the weapons system themselves and their production roll-out schedule that Lu had just briefed his leadership on. They were very relieved to hear the positive report, and hopeful that the Allied offensives that were currently underway could be contained. These offensives were the allied follow up to the defeats that the CAS and the GIR had experienced late last year.

As he opened up his portion of the meeting for questions, Lu was secure in his own estimation that the CAS naval advantage, even if somewhat reduced, could now once again be firmly re-established, allowing the Chinese and her allied forces to severely threaten and contain their enemy's offensives on the high seas.

April 8, 2009, 18:37 local time
COSTIND Headquarters Facility
Beijing, China

After the meeting, as he departed in his official state limousine for his ultimate report to Jien Zenim and the executive council of the Politburo, Chin Zhongbaio could not help but note that Lu had only indicated that these new innovations would allow the PRC to regain part of what it had lost with the advent of the American SUB CIWS weapons. He never indicated that a complete advantage over the Americans would be forthcoming.

"We will not enjoy the unmatched advantage we experienced throughout 2006, 2007 and half of 2008," he thought. "That advantage was precisely what allowed us to make the gains we enjoyed in that time frame."

He mentally listed the nations and areas that had either surrendered or been defeated and come under CAS control as a direct result of China being able to negate the U.S. Naval advantage, and then drive the U.S. Navy east in the Pacific to Midway Island.

Japan, the Philippines, Formosa, Singapore, Thailand, Cambodia, Burma, Malaysia, New Guinea, the entire continent of Australia and many, many island chains. He mentally drew a line from the west of the Samoan Islands up south and then west of New Zealand and north to the vicinity of Midway Island, and then on up to the Alaskan Coast. All points to the west of that line were now controlled and occupied by the Coalition of Asian States, principally China and India.

As a result of these tremendous gains, the list of nations who were official members of the CAS had continued to grow as more and more of them were officially pacified and brought into the coalition. China and India had been the initial members, followed by the entire GIR (which now included the entire Islamic world). Early on, Vietnam and Cambodia had joined, followed by the induction of first Japan and then the Philippines after their defeat and capitulation. Now Malaysia and New Guinea were official members and it was hoped that within the next eighteen months the entirety of the Australian continent, to be split up into four different *people's republics*, would also be sufficiently pacified to be inducted.

Chin knew that all of this was contingent on the PRC and the rest of the CAS holding their gains and keeping the Americans at bay. He hoped they would be able to do this. He knew that a continued massive influx of military personnel and civilians, particularly throughout mainland Asia, Japan, the Philippines, and Australia, would make it almost impossible for the Americans to ever roll back the clock, despite whatever gains, if any, they were able to make in the future.

"If the GIR forces in Europe, Africa and the Mid East can hold their ground, and if our own forces in Central and South America can continue to keep America and her allies tied up in those areas, then I know we shall prevail."

But Chin knew that those were going to be very tall orders for the GIR and the CIS, particularly now that America and her allies had the taste of victory in their mouths, and most particularly as the United States continued to churn out SUB CIWS equipped ships and the new AGM-999 Hail Storm missiles. This realization focused Chin on another key component that the PRC itself would have to focus on to assist with the overall CAS success.

"Our efforts within the United States are going to have to be stepped up. We have to curtail their production and break their spirit," he thought, and that was precisely how he would summarize his report to Jien Zenim and the executive council of the Politburo the next day.

April 9, 2009, 23:37 local time
35 km outside of Havana
Cuba

Hernando Rodriguez considered what his point of contact had just shared with him. He had been in country for two days with his team. The insertion, caching of his weapons and contact with his POC had gone exactly as planned. Now, if the information he had just received proved to be reliable, it would be a bonanza for American forces and allow him to completely and optimally fulfill his mission.

But the operation was risky.

Apparently, according to the POC, there was a relatively high level official in the Cuban government whom the point of contact had known for two decades and who regularly supplied data to him, which was then passed on to the CIA. That official had been hinting for the last five years that there was a potential to infiltrate the Cuban leader's direct, personal circle of influence. But that potential mole was so politically charged that the official had never been willing to mention the specifics.

Until this week.

Now, the official had come forward and indicated that the potential mole wanted to contact the Americans and arrange for the capture or killing of the Cuban leader himself. What was more, the point of contact had determined who the mole was and the name was a shocker. The story of Ernesto Contrerez was something Hernando himself was personally familiar with. He remembered it almost as if it were yesterday. Hernando had been thirteen years old at the time and, being from the Little Havana area, he had gone with his parents down to Ernesto's uncle's house to stand vigil on several occasions while Ernesto was staying there.

He and his family had been there that fateful day when the INS, armed to the teeth like a bunch of Gestapo secret police, had stormed the house while their superiors continued negotiating with Ernesto's uncle's family for transfer of custody of Ernesto to the government so they could send him back to Cuba and his father. Hernando remembered the heavy handed tactics of those American officers-how they rifle butted their way into the house and held the family at gunpoint while absconding with Ernesto.

"I still can't believe any American administration, even one as corrupt and leftist as the one in Washington at the time, would send that little boy back to the tyranny of Cuba," Hernando thought.

But they had, and within a few months, the stories regarding Ernesto had faded from the public view, except within the Cuban community where his basic status was tracked through the Cuban grapevine as Ernesto was inducted into a life of propaganda, reprogramming, and state-sponsored opulence.

"Now, here I am, contemplating contacting a fifteen year old Ernesto to have him help my team capture the leader of Cuba and bring him to justice in America."

But Hernando was by now a wise and experienced combat soldier as well. One who had seen with his own eyes what the result could be if American forces were suckered in by an enemy ruse. He was concerned about the timing of Ernesto's desire. He was concerned about Ernesto's stability and commitment. It sounded too good to be true…just the sort of thing the secret police in Cuba would use to lure dissidents out into the open where they could be destroyed.

He'd have to call this one in to HQ using their encrypted and secure digital communications equipment tonight and then allow it to proceed through the proper channels. He wished he could do it this afternoon, but his orders were clear, even if time was becoming a more and more critical constraint. As he now saw it, there were two options: either take a chance on what appeared to be an almost perfect gift, or come up with another plan that would probably be equally dangerous.

Before calling in his report, he ended up sitting down with his second in command and splitting his command to pursue parallel options. He would work with three of the team members and pursue the planning necessary for utilizing the Ernesto Contrerez option. The other four team members would prepare another avenue for either capturing or neutralizing the Cuban leader before the invasion began.

Tonight he would propose to his superiors that they adopt this parallel approach as a part of the go forward plan in any case, whatever his superiors and ultimately Washington thought of using Ernesto. In this way, Hernando felt, after observing conditions here on the ground, that he could most productively and efficiently utilize his team to assure a successful mission.

April 10, 2009, 9:12 EDT
Situation Room, the White House
Washington, D.C.

The President was digitally conferenced into the meeting of his National Security team from Cincinnati. NORCOMM had made a very early morning call to the NSA, and the information from that call had quickly found its way to the President, who was on one of his American Bolstering Effort, or ABE, visits in Ohio.

Those visits had started relatively early in the war when the terrorist attacks within the United States were at their height, and when allied military prospects were being dealt one terrible blow after another in the Pacific and the Mid East. Based on his wife Linda's suggestion, the President, the Vice President, the Director of Homeland Security, and the Attorney General began to make very public appearances in the face of the danger, in order to bolster the American public's confidence and determination. The effort had succeeded beyond expectation and continued to this day, despite the continued concerns of the Secret Service in terms of protecting the President and the other leaders.

Upon getting the information from Cuba, the President, at the suggestion of his National Security Advisor and with the full agreement of the Chairman of the Joint Chiefs of Staff, had called for a meeting of the entire National Security Team to discuss the matter and arrive at a decision. The meeting was now being squeezed in before his scheduled appearance in downtown Cincinnati this morning, where he would make a speech and dedicate a new electronics packaging plant.

Addressing the assembled members of his National Security team, the President began.

"All right, every one of you has a folder containing the same information I am looking at. We have a decision to make and I believe we need to arrive at it quickly.

"Our advance Delta team in Cuba appears to have a significant opportunity that may allow for the capture of the Cuban leader. Today, in this meeting, we need to determine if it is worth the risk. General Stone, the Vice President and I have already conferred and we are of one mind. What is your take? Is this just too good to be true, or is it a viable option?"

The Chairman of the Joint Chiefs had been contemplating this very question since early this morning when the information had become available to him. His own opinion was that the military had a job to do and they all knew the risks.

"Mr. President, the team leader over there is inclined to go for it and he has formulated a good fallback plan. We have granted him permission to prepare that plan and feel that the information is worth the risk. I will have to depend on others in State or in the CIA for an analysis of the young man, Ernesto Contrerez, and his viability as a contact and concerning the possibility that his memories of our nation would lead him to this.

"I personally hope to God it is so. That would be a military, intelligence and PR bonanza all wrapped into one beautiful little package. I say we act on this and proceed."

Taking this in, the President then addressed his old friend, the Secretary of State.

"Fred, what are your thoughts?"

Fred Reissinger had his doubts. The set of circumstances was almost too good to be true. At the same time, he could see how Ernesto, despite the way the administration at the time had so roughly sent him back into the tyranny of Cuba, might well remember what he had seen and felt in Little Havana for all of those weeks back in 1999 and 2000.

"Mr. President, if this were to come off, it would be a diplomatic gold mine to use against our enemies and to influence more fence sitters. I agree with the General. I say we ask the team on the ground to use this boy and his contact and bring that old SOB here, where he can stand trial for his crimes against our nation."

Next, the President turned his attention to the Director of the CIA, Robert Ballard, and to his National Security Advisor, Bill Hendrickson, who were sitting next to one another at the far end of the conference table.

"Well, Bob and Bill, the ball is in your court. What are your thoughts and recommendations?"

The CIA Director answered first.

"Mr. President, the government official with whom we have contact has been hinting at something like this for some time. We just were not aware of the specifics. I believe it is the real thing and that we should act on it.

"While it is true that such tactics are also used to draw our operatives out in the open, we feel that if this had been the case the information would have come to us some time ago in an effort to expose our current operative. Our recommendation is to give our team the green light and let their military command issue an execute order to them."

Bill Hendrickson, the president's National Security Advisor, took Director Ballard's last statement as his cue to speak.

"I concur, Mr. President. We are being presented with an excellent opportunity here, and if the man on the ground is comfortable with it and feels he is adequately covered with an alternate plan, I believe we should let him go for it."

The President paused for a few moments as he reflected on all of this. He remembered well the international incident and furor that had been caused by Ernesto's initial rescue, his stay in America with his relatives, and then the tragedy of the ruling that sent him back to Cuba, particularly the heavy-handed way in which that ruling was carried out.

He still cringed when he thought of officers sworn to protect and to serve, spiriting a young boy off at the point of a gun and returning that child to a life of tyranny. Well, now there was a chance to right that wrong while bringing justice to the criminal who had manipulated our own weak leaders at the time, and who had committed far worse acts of war against America since.

Once again the President looked around the table through the digital video feed. After a short pause he continued.

"Any other comments on this matter?"

After a few more seconds pause during which there were no further responses, the President continued. "If not, then I am prepared to make a decision."

"General, you have permission to proceed. Have your people use this opportunity to get that Cuban SOB. If Ernesto so desires, or if it is necessary to do so to protect him, have our people bring the boy back as well. Make sure they time the capture and evacuation as we have discussed in conjunction with our press briefing and with the invasion itself.

"It's time we cleaned up the entire mess that Cuba has represented for decades, and I believe that, with their dictator in chains awaiting trial for his terrorist crimes, the entire island will quickly celebrate the end of his regime and his control.

"Like Iraq in Operation Iraqi Freedom of 2003, there will be some hard days between now and then as we clean out his staunch supporters and adherents. But, based on everything I have heard and seen, I honestly believe that we will quickly see Cuba come around and enter the family of free nations once the regime is decapitated and out of power.

"That is all."

April 10, 2009, 22:50 EDT
Presidential Suite, the White House
Washington, D.C.

Linda Weisskopf sat in the reading chair to the left of the bed and under the lamp, her copy of Jane Austen's *Pride and Prejudice* open in her lap. She was sleeping peacefully there when Norm came in and noticed her.

"How she loves Jane Austen," the President thought as he marked the place and gently closed the book.

"She must have read *Pride and Prejudice* one hundred times in our married life," he thought. "And when she finishes it, she'll read *Sense and Sensibility* again, too. Wonderful books…and a wonderful, dear woman. Thank God she has been with me all these years to help me through."

With these thoughts, the President, even though in his seventies, gently lifted her out of the chair and set her down in their bed. As he did so, her eyes fluttered open, became bright and looked into his eyes.

"Hi there, handsome," she said.

"You be careful carrying me around…you're not as spry as you used to be, even if you do keep working out and trying to fool yourself into thinking you are. How did your meeting go?"

The President sat down next to her and began to take his shoes off. As he did, he answered.

"Well, the operation will proceed in Cuba the day after tomorrow, a good 36 hours before we begin military operations. It's all set. The details are complete. The command staff is confidant all the way up the line…including me…and those young men over there are champing at the bit to get it done.

"Let's pray they can accomplish their mission successfully, and that it will have the desired impact. I know you will put in the good word with the Man upstairs to that effect, and that your communication with Him will probably have a lot more bearing than my own...but we're doing the right thing and I honestly feel the tide has turned.

"Just lots of stormy water between here and that far, peaceful shore we're trying to get to."

Linda could hear the hope and confidence in her husband's voice and she was so grateful for it. Grateful for him, for themselves, and most especially grateful that a glimmer of hope for her nation and the world was now shining.

She could also detect the weariness and fatigue in his voice.

He wasn't as spry as he once was, and the pressure was wearing and telling on him. He hid it well from most, but he could not hide it from her.

"Norm, I am so grateful and I know you are the one who can captain this ship to that far shore. I know the good Lord is blessing you to see this through. But I have a concern.

"Now, I don't want to sound like I am mothering you...but I am...just get enough rest. Listen to your body. You may be able to hide it from your advisors and those reporting to you, but you cannot hide it from me. I know how tired you are and I'm concerned.

"The Lord is using you. The nation needs you...I need you. Please don't overdo it. What none of us need is for you to be down just when we need you most. Promise me you'll be more mindful of this, okay?"

Norm knew his wife was right. Like most men, even men in their seventies, he felt if he could just stay on his feet long enough he could take on all comers. But as a man of advanced years, and as a leader who had organized and carried out countless missions, he also knew that overstretching his logistical lines, even if they were his own personal ones, could lead to disaster for the overall mission.

"She would have been as good, if not better, a commander as I any day of the week," he thought as he marveled at his wife's natural insights.

She came by so many critical insights naturally when so many others had to learn them through the school of hard knocks and the great risks that went along with those hard knocks. And in this particular issue, she was right on the money. He was tired and fatigued, and he did need to step back a bit and allow some of his capable people to shoulder more of the load.

"Sweetheart, I promise. Just keep me pointed in the right direction, and through your council I'll somehow find a way to stay on my feet."

With that, he finished putting on his pajamas, climbed into bed next to her, and asked Linda to say a short prayer for the nation as he closed his eyes and listened to her sincere pleas.

"Father, please continue to direct, and bless, our path as only You can, opening the doors that will lead us to victory over our enemies–those who would remove from man the blessings of liberty that are but a precious gift from You.

"Remind us to be humble, so that we might always seek to follow Your guidance, rather than relying on our own resources. For we know that our cause cannot succeed without Your Divine blessing and direction.

"Bless the men and women who are fighting. Bless those working here at home to support them…and, Father, bless the fathers and mothers.

"Encourage the fathers to be resolute, strong and virtuous– filled with integrity. Enable them to lead us down the path that You

would have us travel, always looking to You as their unseen, but ever-present, compass.

"Bless this mission in Cuba that Norm has spoken of. May its success lead to peace and diminished need for conflict We know that wars are a sad illustration of the fallen nature of man. But we also know that the preservation of God-given life and liberties sometimes renders them inevitable.

"Particularly now, Father, as our nation has recovered its senses regarding abortion, we pray that You would place it within the hearts of the mothers of this nation to provide their children–both those living, and those as yet unborn–with the unconditional love and nurturing that only a mother can provide…a love which is but a reflection of Thy own.

"In Jesus' name, Amen."

When she finished she heard Norm breathing evenly. She loved this man, had loved him for decades, and walked the path of life with him through thick and thin. She had faith in him and knew that his goodness, his own faith, his courage, his commitment to clear moral principle, and his determination would carry him through. After satisfying herself that he was sleeping soundly, she pulled the covers up a little more over them both, closed her eyes, and drifted off to sleep herself.

…and her prayer was repeated all over the nation that night in countless households, and all over the world in foxholes and tents. Be it through some form of spiritual contact guided by the Almighty, or by the sense of mutual sharing resulting from the bond forged in the difficult experiences they were all going through–however it came about–similar thoughts, concerns and pleadings were echoed over and over and over again, rising to Heaven as a chorus.

Maria Rodriguez in Miami held her son tightly and prayed for the safety of her husband Hernando, whom she knew would soon see more combat. Not far away, Hernando's parents offered similar prayers on behalf of their son and his young family, and thanked God for the success the nation was experiencing in the monumental conflict. They prayed for those Providential blessings to be continued, if America would just stay humble before Him and persevere.

Cindy Simmons felt it in the depths of her soul in Texas as she prepared for bed after having returned to work at the aircraft plant in Ft. Worth. Still mourning the loss of her only son, Billy, in the fighting off the coast of Australia, she now shouldered the added weight of concern for the welfare of her husband. Colonel Jess Simmons had returned to combat in the Mid East, his location and health unknown to her. But she had replenished her faith and strength at her family's ranch and as she prepared for bed in her lonely apartment. She had the same prayer in her heart that Linda Weisskopf had uttered hundreds of miles away.

In the Boston area, at her home in Nashua, New Hampshire, Elizabeth Trevor slept soundly next to her husband, Dr. Joseph Trevor. The two of them had knelt next to their bed only an hour earlier, and Elizabeth had uttered a remarkably similar prayer, seeking God's continued blessings on the nation and thanking Him for the miracle that had led to the overturn of *Roe v. Wade* and abortion practice in the United States, and asking Him for continued success in the war effort and a cessation of the conflict as soon as victory over tyranny had been achieved.

In Boise, Idaho, as Geneva Campbell was finishing the dishes and preparing for bed, she uttered a prayer in her heart for her two boys, Leon and Alan, who were both off fighting. She asked the good Lord to keep them in the protective shadow of His hand, and to use them as instruments to spread the liberty and morality that America had re-discovered by defeating the tyranny that would deny and destroy it. She asked that her husband, Jerome, would know of her love and the love of his boys up in the heavenly realm that she knew he now occupied.

…and in California, Saundra McPherson, a recently converted agnostic, in her own way offered up her thanks and the pleadings of her heart to God. Although she was not a biological mother, she had nonetheless found motherhood in the work she had recently and fiercely dedicated herself to. After decades of fetal research, using the bodies of the unborn to attempt to find her own answers to life, through the help of Dr. Trevor and his Human Reasoning Structure (HRS) methodologies…and she now recognized, through the guidance and help of God…she had discovered life itself and found her salvation in it.

Saundra prayed in the humility of her at-long-last discovered faith, that God would hasten the end of the conflict on victorious terms for the right. Maybe she could not be a biological mother at this point in life, but she was determined, with God's help, to be a mother to as many as she could of the unborn who would now live, no matter what circumstance into which they were born.

All over the nation, and throughout the free world, similar prayers, aspirations, hope and faith were being offered up by more and more men and woman who saw clearly that the path to victory and to peace was as much a path of morality and faith as it was of production and force of arms

…and those prayers were finding place, and impacting world events. But as with any large ship whose rudder can be turned to guide it through the mortal perils of the sea, the helm of history would only turn ever so slowly…and it would still lead through many deep swells, heavy squalls, and dangerous gales: Dangerous conditions that would otherwise damage or even sink the ship if the helm was not maintained with strength, commitment, dedication to right, faith, hope, and virtue.

April 12, 2009, 12:30 local time
Outside the Presidential Residence
Havana, Cuba

The motorcade was ready to leave and travel out into the countryside outside of Havana to one of the many Presidential estates that were maintained for the rest, relaxation, and recreation of the El

Presidente. Four security cars, two in front and two in back, would protect the President's vehicle which would be carrying the President, Ernesto, and Ernesto's father. Each car carried three elite and well armed security personnel.

An observation helicopter and two attack helicopters would cover the motorcade, with the attack helicopters covering the procession from several thousand feet in the air, and the observation helicopter in advance looking for any danger. Each helicopter was equipped with the latest FLIR equipment and the most advanced weapons the Cubans could obtain.

Finally, a flight of four MiG-29 aircraft, outfitted with the latest radar and air-to-air missiles, would be loitering thirty thousand feet over the vicinity of the motorcade and the Presidential group at all times. They would be controlled by one of the new Chinese AWACS aircraft the Cubans had acquired before the war started. They would be backed up by eight more MiG-29 aircraft on ready alert, four each at two airfields near Havana.

This was standard security procedure for the Cuban president, and was well known to American intelligence forces who monitored the whereabouts of the Cuban leader at all times.

In this particular case, though, thanks to Ernesto and his complicit government official, the Americans also knew the exact itinerary of the Presidential procession and they were prepared to intercept it.

"I wonder if Felix has already gotten the Americans inside the Estate?" Ernesto wondered as the car left the walled-in Presidential Residence and passed by the security station there.

Ernesto and his father were sitting behind the glassed-off driver's compartment facing the rear of the car, and directly across from the President, who was sipping on a glass of wine as they traveled.

The President sat the wine goblet down in a holder that was built into the leather armrest he was using. While he did so, he looked up and caught Ernesto's father's eye and winked. Then he addressed Ernesto.

"Ernesto, you are growing up quickly. Soon we will begin to make use of the military training you are receiving from your tutors and have you start your physical training. My young friend, you are destined to be a leader in our People's Paradise, and only the best training and equipment will be available to you.

"What do you think of that? Are you ready to actually handle the equipment that you have only played with in computer simulations to date?"

Ernesto knew by long experience not to give anything away in his eyes or facial expressions. He noticed his dad looking at him. A casual observer might have mistaken the look for pride, but Ernesto knew better. It was a look of craving...craving the power and wealth that would accrue to him if his son did well.

Ernesto answered honestly, never betraying the hidden truth in the words he now directed at the President, using the familiar nickname he had given him and which the leader loved to hear from this young man.

"Padre, the lessons have been good and I know I have done well. I defeat most of the tutors and many of the military war gamers when they go up against me on the computer.

"I am anxious now to put into practice what I have learned. I will make Cuba proud of me, and I know even you yourself will be surprised at how well I conduct field operations once I have been given the chance."

The President laughed out loud.

"Ha! See Armijo, your son has great *cajones*, as a future leader should have. He is sure of himself and unafraid. You should take some notes!

"Ernesto, I have no doubts that you will make us all proud and surprise us all with your capabilities. We will start next month, in July, and see how you handle the heat."

April 12, 2009, that same time
Presidential Estate
40 km outside of Havana, Cuba

Hernando reviewed the plan in his mind.

His team of four was already here, inside the estate. His three men were all dressed as employees of the estate, just as the governmental official had indicated and provided for. Each was well armed, having retrieved their MP5s and other weapons last night and smuggled them into the estate with the help of the official and their point of contact and his men.

Several of those men, another eight to be exact, were also inside the estate with him, posing as workers as well. All of them also carried weapons beneath their work clothes and would be tasked with handling the internal, close-in security contingent that was permanently stationed on the estate grounds, within the walls.

The government official assured them that the guards at the external security posts protecting the entries into the estate were all in on the plan and would pose no threat. They would not make any moves to assist the *gringos*, but they would also not help the government teams. Their aim would be directed high, above the heads of the Americans and the others when the firing broke out, and they would not move to assist the inner security team or those arriving with the President.

Hernando and his team were to deal with the twelve security personnel arriving with the President in the four cars. A pretty tall order, but they had the element of surprise—and they had the training and the weapons to accomplish it.

He was very concerned about those two attack helicopters and the four MIGs overhead…but he had been assured by his superiors that the Cuban air assets would be handled by the U.S. Air Force when the time came. He simply had to broadcast the execute order as soon as the motorcade arrived.

That would be in another twenty-five minutes if everything went according to plan.

"The government official, our point of contact and his men, those guards on the perimeter and Ernesto are risking everything, including every member of their families," Hernando thought as he continued to review the various aspects of the plan.

"*El Presidente* must really like this kid to respond to his request so quickly…either that or we're all being set up," he thought.

"Well, we'll know soon enough…may God guide me back to Maria safely," he concluded as he set out the serving plates as he had been instructed, preparing to join the other workers to greet the President when he arrived.

April 12, 2009, 12:55 local time
Presidential Estate
40 km outside of Havana, Cuba

Ernesto watched the security guards closely as they passed through the outer gates. He knew there were four guards at each of the three entry gates, and that their barracks nearby housed the other two shifts who were off duty. He also knew that these external guards were all a part of the plan and would not interfere.

As the motorcade entered the estate, he watched the ornate and plush grounds pass by as they drove the full kilometer up to the main buildings. The estate itself covered over twelve hundred acres and was well watered and tended. The grounds boasted acres of fruit trees, flower gardens, fountains, wooded groves, and large open spaces. There were also three stocked fish ponds and a rifle range, as well as full sized polo and soccer fields.

As they came closer, the motorcade left the asphalt main road and was now entering the circular, marble drive that led to the main building proper. The marble made for a very smooth ride for the cars in the motorcade, and Ernesto noticed that everything had gotten deathly quiet inside their car.

"It's just my nerves," he thought. "We've driven up these drives dozens and dozens of times and it's always this quiet."

The quiet was broken by the President himself.

"Look, Ernesto, they have all the servants out to greet us. Pretend you are the reviewing officer when we get out and let me know what you think. Don't go easy on them. Also, are you ready to fish right now, or do you want to eat first?" the President asked as he sat up and the motorcade began to come to a stop.

Then Ernesto saw a peculiar look pass over the President's face. He did not appreciate it, and had no way of knowing that the President had a sixth sense that had served him well over the many decades. Ever since the Cuban Revolution, the President had developed a knack of knowing when danger was present, and he paid heed to the unspoken, instinctual warnings as religiously as any pious church parishioner listened to his priest.

Leaning forward rapidly, the President rapped hard on the window and shouted, ""Manuel, pronto, get us out of here *now!*"

The driver turned and saw the look on his President's face and needed no more. He turned the wheel sharply and stepped on the gas.

Then the firing started outside of the car.

As it did, and just as the President began to sit back, a look of understanding and then unadulterated hatred passed over his features as he glanced quickly at Ernesto and his father.

April 12, 2009, that same time
Presidential Estate
40 km outside of Havana, Cuba

Hernando was just about to give the signal to attack when the Presidential limo suddenly turned its wheels sharply and accelerated. In an instant it had grazed the security car in front of it and begun to fishtail.

Disregarding the need for hand motions, Hernando first sent the execute signal to the other allied forces monitoring his communications, and then he sent a rally signal to the other four team members who were positioned outside the estate providing additional security.

He then shouted in Spanish to all of his team around him.

"Disparen!"

The eight Cubans who were working for the point of contact were positioned near each of the eight guards of the Cuban internal security detachment. They immediately drew their weapons from under their clothing and fired on their assigned targets.

Seven of those security personnel went down immediately, at which time they were dispatched by a second shot to the head. Those seven insurgents then began running from their various positions towards the main building to take up covering fire positions in support of the Delta team.

One of the security detachment, being in a position to see the Presidential limo make its sudden move, was alerted and prepared when the posing worker began to draw his weapon. He used his submachine gun and killed the rebel before his weapon could be drawn. This Cuban security guard now ran to the sound of gunfire to enter the firefight on the side of the Cuban security detachment arriving with the President.

Back at the main building, as his Cuban allies were cutting down most of the internal security detachment, Sergeant Rodriguez and his men went into action.

Two of his men dropped to the earth and immediately pulled compact Rocket Propelled Grenade (RPG) launchers from behind bushes where they had been hidden and opened fire at the leading and trailing security cars.

Both cars had already come to a complete stop, and the three personnel were trying to pile out of them when the small rockets, meant to destroy armored personnel carriers, hit the cars and detonated. The resulting explosions and infernos completely destroyed the two cars, killed four of the six personnel outright, and severely wounded the other two, who were thrown several yards away from the carnage where they lay unconscious.

At the same instant, the Presidential limo, which had clipped the security car in front of it and fishtailed halfway around, came out of the fishtail just in time to slam sideways into the wreckage of the leading security vehicle that had just been destroyed by one of the RPGs. Pushing the wreckage several feet, the limo came to a rest next to the burning vehicle where its engine stalled and would not restart.

All of the occupants of the limo were thrown violently up against that side of the car. Ernesto's father was knocked unconscious when the President was thrown into him, knocking his head hard up against the leaded glass. The President was stunned and began to disengage himself from the unconscious man, only to find himself facing Ernesto, who was fully conscious and who had pulled out the six inch switchblade knife that the President himself had given him three years earlier on his twelfth birthday, and which the President allowed him to carry wherever he went.

Meanwhile, the firefight outside the car intensified. One of the Americans with an RPG was able to fire a second round and take out the security car that had been trailing directly behind the Presidential limo. That car had stopped and its occupants had gotten out and opened fire at the team member nearest to Hernando, stitching him across the chest and in the legs, knocking him to the ground, mortally wounded.

The impact of the RPG on the car behind which those Cuban security personnel were firing from, killed all three of the Cubans, and set off another large explosion as the gas tank detonated, too.

This left the last Cuban security car and the single remaining internal security guard, all of whom had now had several seconds to take up positions away from the last car and fire on their attackers. They were trying desperately to defend the Presidential limo which was still stalled next to the wrecked and burning lead security car.

Before fire could be effectively brought to bear on them, these four men had hit and killed four of their Cuban attackers and wounded the other American Delta team member who was carrying the other RPG. But then the firepower of Hernando and his last team member and the four remaining Cubans took effect.

Caught between the remaining Americans and the insurgents, the Cuban security personnel found themselves trapped in a deadly crossfire which included yet another RPG round. With three of their numbers down, the last man raised his hands, threw down his weapon and surrendered. The entire firefight had taken less than two minutes.

As Hernando rapidly organized his remaining force to cover the stalled limo and extract its passengers, he heard the unmistakable sound of rotors approaching rapidly from the west. Looking in that direction, he saw the all too recognizable silhouette of a HIND-D helicopter coming their way, its weapons pods filled with rockets and guns.

"I thought the Air Force was supposed to take care of those guys," he commented to no one in particular, as he began issuing orders for the remaining men to take cover.

At a distance of a half mile, smoke puffs around the larger pods, and small amounts of smoke from the right side of the chin of the helicopter, announced that rockets and machine gun fire were being directed at them.

"Those idiots are going to kill their own President!" Hernando screamed in frustration as the helicopter made its first pass, explosions resounding and buffeting them on either side.

As the helicopter passed over, Hernando's men exited from their cover and fired at it from underneath, hoping to disable or destroy it. But there was no visible effect and the chopper began circling around for another pass.

Then, from well up in the clouds, a very bright light quickly fell through the ceiling and rocketed directly for the HIND. Impacting directly behind the rotor, an American AMRAMM missile literally blew off the blades of the helicopter, which then fell like a duck shot out of the air, impacting with a deafening explosion in the countryside, a little over a quarter mile on the other side of the estate wall to the east.

A cheer went up from the remaining fighters as they now surrounded the limo and demanded in Spanish for the occupants to give themselves up and exit.

There was a muffled response from inside, and two of the men rushed over and opened the left passenger door. Once it was completely opened and covered by three of the fighters, a befuddled and ruffled Cuban President exited the vehicle holding his left arm tightly; it was bleeding heavily from a deep cut wound running from just below the shoulder almost to the elbow.

Then Ernesto exited the vehicle, holding his knife to his side and smiling broadly. Guessing that he was the leader by his demeanor and the way he carried himself, Ernesto approached Sergeant Rodriguez and spoke to him.

"I present to you El Presidente. My name is Ernesto Contrerez."

Hernando could still see the younger, six year old Ernesto in this young man, remembering him from the evenings when he and his parents would stand vigil outside Ernesto's uncle's Miami house in 1999. After having two men secure the Cuban President and tend to his wound, the Sergeant turned to Ernesto.

"Ernesto, I am Sergeant Hernando Rodriguez, U.S. Army.

"An aircraft will be here very soon to take the President away. We have been asked to bring you with us, my friend, back to your relatives in Miami.

"Will you come?"

Ernesto considered this, smiling broadly. He had dreamed of this day. Then, thinking of his father, and the opportunity that true freedom might afford him, he answered the American.

"If you will get my father out of the limo…be careful…he is injured…and bring him with us, I will go with you."

Hernando did not have to think twice about it. He ordered two of the Cubans to bring Ernesto's father out of the limo, rig up a litter, and carry him the three hundred yards to where they had set up their extraction point.

As they did so, Hernando saw that his other four team members had successfully entered the estate and were approaching from the north. He also noticed through the breaks in the clouds above them, that lazy circular contrail patterns were being drawn on the canvas of the sky by circling fighter aircraft, F-15C Eagles and other aircraft of the U.S. Air Force.

"Those fly boys did take care of business," he thought.

"I just love it when a plan comes together," he said to his unwounded companion as he nodded his head upward, and pointed to the contrails above.

And then another sound came to them as they stood there near the main building on the estate. It came low over the hills and over the estate walls to the north. It was the sound of an approaching Special Forces Osprey aircraft, just like the one that had inserted Hernando and his team into Cuba on the 7th, only five days ago. Approaching rapidly, it flared overhead and then descended vertically to the ground at the designated landing zone.

Within three minutes everyone was on board, including Hernando and the rest of his able bodied team members, the now deposed Cuban leader, Ernesto and his father, the wounded Delta team member, and the body of the dead American.

After all of them were on board, the Osprey took off and within five minutes was well out over the Caribbean, escorted by no less than fifteen American fighter aircraft, flying towards the United States, where the Attorney General and Homeland Security officials were waiting to arrest and detain the Cuban President for his crimes against the people of the United States.

April 14, 2009, 8:05 EST
White House Press Room
Washington, D.C.

The room was abuzz as reporters from all of the major news services rushed to file their reports regarding the extraordinary press briefing that the President had just held. It had been a complete surprise to the news staffs because there had been no leaks to them whatsoever.

This was not too surprising because, particularly after the conclusion of the David Krenshaw affair, the Weisskopf administration had proven extremely adept at keeping stories and events very close to its chest without any leaks at all. Outside of several congressional leaks which the press suspected the administration of using to its advantage as opposed to actually having anything leaked, there were remarkably few opportunities for the press to utilize "unnamed sources within the administration" to get a leg up on any major story before it was officially announced.

What was surprising and, what had now the full attention of the press, was the subject matter of today's briefing. The headlines would almost all be phrased in similar language.

CUBAN PRESIDENT CAPTURED BY AMERICAN SPECIAL FORCES

PROOF OF CUBAN COMPLICITY IN U.S. TERROR ATTACKS LEADS TO CUBAN LEADER CAPTURE AND HOLD OVER FOR TRIAL

U.S. FORCES INVADE CUBA

The President had laid out in no uncertain terms that the United States viewed it as its right to apprehend and try anyone who was shown to be directly involved with, or behind, the types of attacks the Cuban leader had funded and helped plan on citizens of the United States. The case against the Cuban leader was ironclad in this regard. It was based on evidence gathered in 2008 through the capture of Hector Ortiz and his associates, and the breaking up of their terrorist front company, FTA Trucking. That evidence included direct testimony, taped conversations, and direct money trails back to Cuban accounts.

The military part of the operation had commenced very early that morning, long before sunrise, and was proceeding as planned. In fact, the telling thing about the military operation was the much lighter than expected resistance. There was some heavy fighting in a number of places, but it was sporadic and concentrated only in the units that were most loyal to the communist regime.

Many landings associated with the ongoing invasion, both Amphibious and Air Assault, had been completely unopposed. The heaviest fighting was occurring between Cubans themselves, in the streets, at military bases, and around the Presidential facilities.

The principle reason for the internal fighting was that pictures of the Cuban President in shackles and standing before a U.S. magistrate, the same pictures that had been shared with the press and were also being broadcast to Cubans. This was being facilitated by powerful transmitters in southern Florida, and by using television stations in Cuba which had already been captured by either American forces or by Cuban insurgents.

The pictures were encouraging many Cubans to finally rise up, certain that their dictator's power was finally broken, and that the regime would fall quickly with American forces pouring in while the remaining communist leaders were confused and clawing at one another's throats.

There were already American casualties, and it was expected that the number would mount over the next several weeks of hard fighting. But it was clear on the first day, from the outset, that the fighting would relatively quickly scale back to a mop-up operation once the centers of resistance had been crushed.

Therefore, this morning's announcement was unabashedly upbeat and extremely positive.

The President took several questions, the first of which was from JT Samson of SierraLines, who had been alerted to the news conference the day before and who was able to arrive in Washington to attend it from his home in Nevada. JT had asked specifically about the case against the Cuban President and how the international community might view the apprehension of a head of state from his own soil.

The President had responded directly.

"JT, we would never think of apprehending a citizen of another country, much less a head of state, in peacetime for non-terror or non-war related crimes.

"But this head of state, an absolute dictator I might add, has waged war on our people and has been the source for funding, and planning terror operations that have killed Americans by the thousands. By his own actions he has declared war on our nation and we are responding accordingly.

"As one of my predecessors stated, creating what has become known as the Bush Doctrine, and has been followed by this administration in the prosecution of this war...*if you are not with us, you are with the terrorists.*

"This individual has been deeply in bed *with* terrorists who have wreaked havoc on our nation and killed thousands of our citizens. There is not a rock on this earth we would allow him or his ilk to hide under. The case against him is solid and unimpeachable. it will be proven in a court of law, using our own system which is the fairest, most impartial, and freest legal system in the world.

"We apologize to no one for apprehending and bringing to justice such an individual, and will go after any others on whom we have such evidence."

This answer and the overall news of the conflict in Cuba, and the reasons for it, were being received very positively by the public. Allied nations understood and respected it. Some neutral nations protested...and enemy nations took note.

As the day wore on, the apparent success in Cuba was being attributed by many as an answer to the very prayers that they had been voicing to Heaven on behalf of the American cause, and that of her allies. As time wore on, those prayers seemed, indeed, to be answered as the operation would prove to be a resounding and quick victory and would lead to other important success in the Caribbean.

But there were yet many mighty waves and fierce winds of history that would batter against the war effort being led by the Weisskopf administration and its allies. As reasoned people of faith prayed for more help and courage, it would continue be the moral principle, faith, and courage upon which their cause rested that would hold the war plan and the ship of state it represented together as it proceeded on course and afloat.

Unknown to the press, unknown to the individuals praying for success, and unknown to the President or his administration, events of the near future would sorely test and try that faith and courage.

Those upcoming events would be guided by those other ideologies and aspirations against which the west was pitted. Ideologies and aspirations that were themselves dedicated and intent on holding their own course…a course of compulsion and force which was the brainchild of the President of the People's Republic of China, and took its form in the Three Wisdoms that the whole of the CAS and GIR had adopted and enforced upon all they vanquished. That ideology allowed for the market-based socio-fascism into which the People's Republic of China had evolved, the caste-based Republic of India, and the fundamental Islamic nations to all function under one umbrella.

Large portions of the populations in the PRC and India, and people throughout the Islamic world, had willingly embraced this ideology and social structuring set forth by their leaders. They saw that it was leading them to greater manufacturing production capability and a rising standard of living. They also saw that it was leading them to more influence in the world and their national and cultural pride was stimulated by it.

All of this was possible, even though the vast majority of the wealth and influence was going to the ruling elite within these societies, because the vast majority of the people had never been exposed to individual liberty–neither they or their ancestors–and they were culturally conditioned to follow their appointed or anointed leaders without question. They were also kept ignorant by those same leaders so they could perform the necessary labors of state and do so without question, gratefully accepting the meager increases they received as their nations acquired more wealth and territory. These people were particularly enticed by the offers of settlement on free lands in the conquered and occupied nations.

The ruling classes in these societies, either the "Party" or the religious leaders depending on the nation, had risen to their positions of prominence and authority because of their commitment to the party or the religion, and because of their loyalty to the current leaders. Most of them had been exposed to the American form of government where individual liberty and free choice within moral constraint was the basis for society in the west…and they spurned it and hated it with a passion. They believed that such freedom would lead to chaos and waste without their inspired leadership and guidance. They also understood that it would lead to their downfall and they were therefore unalterably opposed to it.

As a result of these cultural realities, the CAS and GIR had literally hundreds of millions of committed ideologues and their followers who were firmly dedicated to the death struggle with the West. It was not a case, as in Iraq in Operation Desert Storm of 1991 or Operation Iraqi Freedom in 2003, where the soldiers were more afraid of their officers and rulers than they were of American armies…at least until they saw they could be slaughtered by the technological edge the Americans possessed. Those conflicts, as masterfully as they were performed by America, were in reality surrenders waiting to happen. And they did.

No, the current fighting was more akin to the Korean War where North Koreans and Chinese, because of their cultural heritage, were willing to charge into the teeth of the American technology in an effort to push them back, despite the cost. Except this time, the side with the huge numerical advantage also possessed high technology of its own. And that numerical advantage was therefore decisive in the conflict, but only so long as the vast technological edge of the West continued to be blunted.

The PRC had masterfully used the West's wealth and technology against itself over a period of several decades to put itself in a position to achieve that very thing. Lu Pham's supercavitating creation was only one example of many. When they succeeded in maintaining near technological parity, or even an edge over the West in critical areas, the CAS and GIR surged forward, as they had done in 2006, 2007, and most of 2008.

When the West came up with a new technological innovation, as it had in late 2008 with the AGM-999/Hail Storm missile, those same nations were halted in their advance and pushed back. The technology war continued now, and had all been made possible because the West over those many years before the war had been lulled into investing heavily in terms of physical assets and capital in the very nations they were now fighting. The lure had been the promise of vast markets when China's and India's standard of living rose to the point that those people could afford to purchase the goods–accompanied by a promise of cheap labor and increased market share in the rest of the world in the mean time.

But those promises had always been hollow, particularly in the PRC where the leaders had no intention of allowing the masses to climb out of the low class labor position they occupied. Using the large numbers of people benefiting from that cheap labor (10% of 1.2 billion people is a large number), the Chinese became adept at fooling western politicians and the CEOs of western firms who saw what they wanted to see when visiting the PRC, and invested billions for the lure of the cheap labor and ultimate markets.

In the end, the two ideologies and cultures, the one fostering individual liberty and moral rectitude based on faith in God on the one hand, and the other using the compulsion of secular humanism and forced social structuring on the other, would continue in monumental conflict until one or the other was defeated and laid low for a generation or more.

It was a remorseless and bitter fight pitting the two conflicting world views against one another to the death in what was proving to be the most horrific war the world had ever seen. Many songwriters, poets, and authors had already penned a name for this time period where the lives of so many hundreds of millions were so adversely impacted, or snuffed out...they were calling it the time of the *Dragon's Fury*.

Despite the current successes in Cuba and elsewhere, quelling the *Dragon's Fury* now that it had flourished for almost three and a half years was going to require a *Long March* down the road of history. For although the tide had turned for the moment in favor of the West–in favor of America and her allies–and even though the allied powers were moving forward on several fronts, the final outcome was still very far from certain...and it would remain that way through almost four more years of bitter conflict.

Only through the conflict and turmoil of that extended period of time would it be determined whether government based on individual liberty and moral principle would survive or perish from the face of the earth.

Chapter 2

"Brave men who work while others sleep, who dare while others fly– they build a nation's pillars deep, and lift them to the sky" – Ralph Waldo Emerson

April 18, 2009, 15:48 local time
Ruling Cleric Chamber
Islamic Leadership Complex
Tehran, GIR

The meeting went on and on, as they always do. All of the Grand Ayatollahs, or Ayatollah Ol Osams, would be heard in full, along with the principle Mujtahids and a few of the Mullahs. All of the speakers had a lot on their mind, which translated into long discourses about every aspect of life in the Greater Islamic Republic, from the spiritual state of the people, to the encroachment of foreign and modern conveniences and technologies, to the state of political affairs and finally, the current military situation.

Of significant import to everyone in attendance were the briefings on the current state of the three American and western offenses now taking place in Europe south of Moscow, in the Mid East, east of Damascus, and in central Alaska. In all three areas, Western allied forces capitalizing on their victories in the late fall of 2008, were now advancing against GIR, Indian, and Chinese forces.

In addition to those briefings, however, were the myriad of other concerns that dealt with running a nation that had grown to the extent that the GIR had grown over the last four years. Numerous civil, religious, political and economic matters, indispensable to managing such a vast people and geography, were raised with this group of men and had to be resolved by them.

As he listened, and irrespective of the length of the meeting and the sometimes drawn out and boring nature of parts of it, Hasan did take it all in…every bit of it. It was his *mission*, it was his *calling*, to listen to all of it, and in the end to pass judgment and give direction...but, as he did so, he also allowed his mind to wander somewhat. In this case, it was pondering the fate of General Jabal Talabari.

"He is sorely missed," the great spiritual, military, and political leader of the Greater Islamic Republic thought to himself. "...not only as a brilliant general and strategist, but as a friend. According to Allah's will, he was taken from us...and as much as I am sorry for it, in the end Jabal reaped what he sowed.

"Allah provided him to us...and Allah allowed him to be taken from us in a like manner. Surely Allah's will and infinite wisdom are often a mystery to us...but I can see His hand in Jabal's untimely death and I accept it, knowing more avenues will be opened for our ultimate triumph in this conflict with western infidels. Then, and only then, can we ultimately turn our eyes to the east.

"But that is for another time," thought Sayeed. "Now a permanent replacement for Jabal must be put in place...a stronger, more permanent and stable leader than the interim individual we have now. Someone like Jabal, who can anticipate the enemy, particularly the Americans, and throw back this offensive they have managed to conduct around Israel, and in so doing, give strength and faith to our allies who are experiencing similar American offensive operations this spring."

In that moment, as he contemplated the matter during the overall meeting of the leaders of the great Islamic faith and Republic, the answer came to him regarding who the new overall commander of GIR forces in the Middle East and Europe should be. Allah was telling him to promote General Mahdavi Ardakani to that position.

Ardakani was a name that was already well known to all members of the leadership council...the military in particular. He was also very much respected by the political and religious leaders as well. That knowledge and respect had resulted from his daring air campaigns and his great success in the war effort. He was also known to have complete and unwavering faith in the leadership, particularly Hasan Sayeed. Such passion for the cause, ability to implement its holy objectives, and resolute loyalty to its leadership, were absolute prerequisites in the person who would fill this vital position.

The General had pulled off and successfully implemented the planning for the first major victory against American forces back in November of 2005. He had deftly planned the major air assault on their airbase at Incirlik, Turkey, and had done so in a manner that had taken the Americans by surprise, coordinating massive numbers of GIR aircraft from many different locations under the eyes of the American satellites.

That particular strategic success had been a respected achievement that many in the GIR now took for granted. Ever since the Chinese had successfully waged a satellite war against the West and fought them to a draw in that particular arena, many of these leaders had forgotten how great an advantage the Americans and the West had held. The successful Chinese satellite offensive had essentially deprived both sides of satellite surveillance, and leveled the playing field to the advantage of the GIR and the CAS and their numeric superiority.

But that more level playing field had not been in place when Ardakani had engineered his initial victory. It had been a stunning and surprising victory which had deprived the Americans of their vaunted air superiority over the skies of the so-called Kurdistan Republic. In so doing, Mahdavi Ardakani had shown his ability to overcome great odds, to mask his planning and movement from the ever-watchful eyes of the American satellites, to be willing to suffer tremendous losses in the stubborn accomplishment of his goal, and to work successfully in a combined arms atmosphere.

The perfect coordination of Ardakani's air attacks against the Americans with the GIR ground force who attacked the Kurds at the time, had made the great victory over the United States and its surrogate forces in the northern areas of the former nation of Iraq possible. That victory had in turn allowed Hasan Sayeed to personally intercede and negotiate with the Kurds to bring that territory within the fold of the GIR.

No, Sayeed knew full well that the success against Incirlik had opened the door for the complete ascendancy of the Greater Islamic Republic. It had resulted in great respect and recognition for the GIR from around the world as unexpected victors over the United States, and the instrument of their shaming. Many Islamic nations had changed their stance regarding their eventual union with the GIR as a result of that single battle…all of which had ultimately led to a major war as the United States sought to re-exert its control in the region. In attempting to contain the GIR, they had played into the greater plan orchestrated by Jien Zenim of the People's Republic of China.

"How had Zenim put it?" thought Sayeed as he contemplated those events from three and a half years ago.

"Yes, indeed, Wheels within Wheels."

In the course of the war, General Ardakani had continued to show his abilities throughout the campaign in Saudi Arabia, Africa, Turkey, and into portions of Europe where he commanded all GIR air assets in those regions during the prosecutions of Sayeed's Holy War being waged against the unfaithful and the infidels. He had been one of Jabal Talabari's closest and most trusted confidants, and Jabal had continually referred to him as a very capable and loyal general, worthy of much more of Sayeed's attention than Ardakani himself had ever sought.

But, despite their knowledge of, and respect for, Ardakani, most of the military and political leadership felt that the natural successor to Talabari should be a ground force commander. In fact the interim commander was Talabari's former executive officer, General Ishmael Abin. A career professional, Abin had risen through the ranks over many years as first a field commander, and then a ranking staff member of first Iran's, and then the GIR's, large armies. As a result, he was well positioned politically with many on the leadership council for what both he and they viewed as an almost foregone conclusion that his interim advancement would be made permanent.

But Abin would find now that he and his political supporters were all mistaken in that conclusion.

Abin was, in fact, a purely a political general, lacking the respect of the rank and file troops who served under him. And considering that he was also the source of endless intrigue and maneuvering by the command staff directly under him, an ineffective picture of political gamesmanship not well suited for the dangers and rigors of battle had taken shape in Sayeed's mind.

This picture left a bad taste in Sayeed's mouth. That type of leadership would not lead GIR forces to the victory that Hasan knew Allah expected of them. In fact, those qualities would be the very things that would keep Abin from ever being the type of innovative and direct leader that Sayeed required to contain the west's latest advance, and then ultimately push it back.

No, Abin would not be the man. Clearly, the position must go to Mahdavi Ardakani, who had both the combat leadership skills necessary and the respect of the soldiers who would be serving under his leadership. In addition, Ardakani would respect Sayeed's own considerable battlefield experience rather than being intimidated by it…and he would listen to his Mahdi's suggestions, as opposed to simply giving lip service to them.

Realizing this, Sayeed experienced another moment of certain intuitive knowledge and enlightenment regarding what one of those initial suggestions or recommendations would be: a recommendation for someone to fill a critical role on Ardakani's direct staff, the young Abduhl Selim. Selim's battlefield commission to Brigadier General had been approved a few short weeks ago by this very council.

"Twenty-two years of age and already a Brigadier General," thought Sayeed.

"It's amazing, like something you might read in an ancient history book…and his brilliant military advancement even eclipses my own. Allah be praised and bless us with many more of this young man's ilk," concluded Hasan as he reflected on the young man's unfolding legend. Abduhl would make an excellent staff officer whose ground force experience would greatly compliment Ardakani's strategic brilliance, and would do so in a manner not fettered with all of the politics, intrigue, or bias that the older general would bring to the position.

As these convictions solidified in his heart, and as Sayeed uttered a prayer of thanksgiving for the direction he felt Allah had given him, he noticed that the discussion regarding the advisability of bringing in more Chinese technicians to assist in the set-up and operation of more *ta shih* detectors throughout the GIR had reached a point requiring his input. Just now the members of the council were turning to him to seek his advice and counsel on the matter.

"My brothers, I have spoken with General Hunbaio and President Zenim himself on this issue. They are well aware of our concerns regarding the potential influence of their technicians and their lifestyle on our people.

"But the fact is, we must have these systems set up and operating throughout our territory for our own self-defense. It is vital from that standpoint that we do so, and we must have some measure of trust in our own people and their commitment to the faith, particularly at this juncture where Allah has granted us such great success in uniting all of Islam throughout the world.

"If we cannot have faith in our people to insulate themselves from the corrosive influence of these Chinese technicians…and I might add that their potential influence is much less worrisome than the influence we experienced when western technicians infested our lands…then we will tacitly admit our failure as their spiritual leaders. We will show by our own lack of faith, not only in them, but in our ability to teach them, that we ourselves have failed."

As Hasan spoke, the vast majority of the leadership council nodded their heads in agreement to the obvious wisdom of their leader's words. Once again, he cut through the political and religious bickering and positioning of so many on the council and got to the heart of the matter in such a way that the final decision was obvious to all. There would be no dissent or argument with the man almost every one of them in this council considered to be their Mahdi.

"So," he continued, "we will allow these foreigners inside our borders and the detector systems will be installed along with the newer missiles.

"For those with any lingering concerns about lasting impact, you may lay those concerns aside. I have received firm assurances from President Zenim that after the initial deployment, a training facility will be established outside of Tehran, where Chinese personnel will instruct our technicians in the full operational capabilities of the entire system, and the need for the Chinese technicians to travel about amongst our people will be phased out. They will be restricted after that date to the training facility and areas immediately around it, where we can better control this issue.

"In addition, we will begin license building of the export version of the detectors and the missiles within the year such that we can quickly become self-sufficient not only in the maintenance of the defensive systems, but in its production as well. At that point, we will be in a position to phase out any long term involvement for Chinese technicians at the training facility as well."

Having summed up the matter, Sayeed addressed his Foreign Minister and spoke to him directly.

"Minister Ujman, at the conclusion of our meetings have the appropriate diplomatic and military staff members arrange the appropriate diplomatic communiqués and paperwork to expedite treaties with the People's Republic of China to this effect.

"Now, let's turn to the next agenda item. It is one where I beg your indulgence as I am compelled to become personally involved at the outset of the discussion.

"I have received direct guidance from Allah on the matter of General Talabari's permanent replacement. General Abin will not be confirmed as the Commander in Chief of our forces in the Mid East and European areas of operation. I know this will be a disappointment to some of you who are advocating that he become the permanent Commander in Chief, but Allah's will has been made clear to me in this regard. That position will go to one of Allah's choosing, and we must set aside personal preferences and accede to his will."

Turning to his own executive assistant, he said so that all could hear, "Ashmil, send an executive communication over my personal signature to General Mahdavi Ardakani summoning him here to Tehran to meet with me personally and with the executive council."

As a number of the leadership council nodded in satisfaction and others whispered in surprise, Hasan Sayeed turned back to the assembled leadership council and concluded the matter.

"General Ardakani is to be promoted to Commander in Chief of our military operations in both the Mid Eastern and European Theaters. I expect each of you to hold this information in the strictest confidence until General Ardakani can be informed, and until the official announcement is made.

"I also expect you each to give him your full, unqualified support in the difficult task he has at hand of first containing the current American offensive, and then driving it back.

"In the meantime, General Abin will continue fulfilling his interim duties until General Ardakani determines how Abin can best serve in the new command. That is all on this matter. Let us move on to the next item on the agenda."

May 2, 2009, 10:25 local time
35 miles Northwest of Ruby, Alaska
On the northeast flank of Wolf Mountain

The *thumping* was more distant now, muted and slowly moving further and further off to the west like some freak storm that had moved across the landscape from east to west. In these climes a storm moving in that particular manner, from east to west, was a rare meteorological event. But the military operations that heralded the almost continuous thunder-like thumping in this locale over the last four days was a very much longed for and welcomed event, and it had been progressively coming closer and closer during the last three weeks as the American offensive against the Chinese had progressed in this general direction.

Stacey Urkut—or the Orka, as she was known—and her fifteen compatriots, were situated in a large cave on the northeast side of Wolf Mountain. As the war front had moved their way, they had been forced to take up this position in order to remain out of sight of the large numbers of Chinese troops retreating to the west, and to keep from being inadvertently targeted by the American forces that were pushing them in that direction.

"Particularly from being targeted by those new missiles our boys are using," thought Stacey. "Anyone targeted by those babies ends up as literal mincemeat," she thought as her nephew came back to the HQ section of the cave to provide a reconnaissance report.

"Aunt Stacey, Danny made contact with an American patrol an hour ago a couple of miles to our south, near the old Forest Service road on the shoulder of the mountain over there. Apparently they have been briefed to be on the lookout for, and to hook up with, any resistance forces in general, and members of our group in particular.

"When their lieutenant heard that Danny was a part of the Orka group, he got on the line to a captain, who called up a colonel.

That officer, a Colonel Kensington, is en route here to see you right now. They told us to watch for a Black Hawk helicopter escorted by at least two Apaches. They should be here in less than ten minutes."

Stacey's mind went into high gear as she took this in.

"Coming to see me?" she thought. The unlikelihood of this, at least in her own mind, invoked her more cautious side, which, on numerous occasions, had served them well…indeed, had been an almost pivotal factor…in their fights against the Chinese.

"Ted, now why on earth would a colonel in the U.S. Army who presently involved in a huge fight to drive the Chinese off of our sovereign soil be interested in spending time with me? And why, of all times, now?

"Are you absolutely sure of this? Are you sure this isn't some type of trick to draw us out? Did they request any specific information or intelligence?" she asked.

Ted respected his aunt's concerns. He knew her instincts to be uncannily accurate, and he understood her reluctance to immediately jump on the information he had just shared with her. It would have been completely out of character for her to have unquestioningly run out into the open to meet whomever was coming. But he had also been there himself when the word had come down from the Colonel.

"When Danny contacted me about this, I went over and met the lieutenant myself, Aunt Stace'. It's no trick. They told me that I was to inform you that the Colonel would be making an immediate visit here and that you should have your command staff ready…I guess he thinks we are a little larger than we actually are."

At that comment all of them smiled, Cheshire cat-like. The Chinese had been under the same mistaken impression for the last several months.

"Well, we do have a better knowledge of the lay of the land than our own forces, and we can just about point exactly to where the

Chinese are most apt to set up their next line of defense…but I imagine they have recon and surveillance telling them all of that.

"So, still, why me?" she asked herself and those standing with her as she made her way to the entrance of the cave.

As they stepped outside of the entrance to the cave which was sheltered by steep cliffs and heavy forest on both sides, the oncoming presence of Colonel Kensington was announced in dramatic fashion. A flight of four F-35 Joint Strike Fighters passed over at low level, two splitting to either side as they spiraled up from ground level to a loitering patrol five thousand feet overhead. At the same time, numerous contrails of higher level fighters could be seen at much higher altitude.

"Colonel Kensington must be an important spoke in this wheel to warrant all of *that* protection," Stacey commented as they witnessed the awesome display of American power unfolding before them.

Seeing this demonstration of power almost immediately took Stacey and several of those standing with her back in time almost eleven months, to when the Chinese had first attacked and then invaded America across the Bering Straits in June of last year. They would have all liked to have seen a display of such power back then to combat and halt the invasion that had cost so many American lives.

Stacey remembered the assault on Nome, Alaska, her home. She had witnessed it with her own eyes, and she had been able to report on it in real time to an astonished America using the Independent Republic website on her internet connection before it went down. Those reports had ultimately been seen by millions and had made their way quickly to the White House situation room itself.

After that internet connection had gone down, Stacey had narrowly escaped the Chinese helicopter landings and advances around Nome as she made her way into the wilderness to the east and north of the town. Her family, as well as her husband's, were native Americans and there were many of those relatives who still embraced their families' ancient historical traditions. She had always kept in close touch with them and knew of their love for the land and how they would react to this overt invasion from Asia.

Despite her fifty-seven years, she had been in excellent health and driven by a love for liberty and outrage at the attacks on her homeland. Before the Chinese were aware such movements had even been organized, she had gathered, organized, and led a band of resistance fighters against the Chinese.

It was a resistance effort that had been maintained under the harshest of conditions during the Chinese occupation, as the Chinese made every effort to hunt down and eradicate any and all who opposed them and did not accede to their rule. Stacey became known amongst her followers, and ultimately amongst the Chinese, as the Orka. Her small group, mostly acting alone, but sometimes operating with other groups, particularly remnants of the Home Guard units in the area, wreaked fair havoc on the Chinese rear areas, disrupting logistical supply efforts and killing many times their number of Chinese soldiers and officials.

The Chinese responded by systematically destroying any resistance fighters they could corner, by cruelly and publicly executing any they captured, and by conducting large reprisal massacres of citizens in an attempt to reign in the resistance. But this only served to stiffen the resolve of those brave Americans, and the resistance doubled its efforts and continued to grow.

News of the exploits of these American resistance fighters, and particularly of the Orka, made its way to the "outside" and the lower forty-eight states as America frantically first prepared, and then actually deployed, to counter the Chinese offensive and attempt to drive it back.

Unknown to Stacey, it was the result of her own initial reports, and a result the news of her continued resistance that brought the Colonel to the side of Wolf Mountain this morning. His interest in

Stacey and her group was not only a matter of current military import–it was an issue of Executive Order.

May 2, 2009, 10:34 local time
35 miles Northwest of Ruby, Alaska
500 feet above the northeast flank of Wolf Mountain

Colonel Sanfred Kensington looked down into the empty clearing below the Black Hawk helicopter he had requisitioned for this mission. In addition to the crew of the Black Hawk, which included two door gunners, he had two liaison officers and a security team of four personnel with traveling with him.

Two Longbow Apache helicopters had taken up covering positions just to the north and south of the clearing as the Black Hawk approached from the northeast. Several F-35, Joint Strike Fighters were providing mid-level CAP while six F-15C fighters were covering higher altitudes.

Turning to the pilot he pointedly asked, "Well, Captain, where are they? Are you sure this is the right clearing?"

Although the Captain didn't appreciate being questioned about whether he had piloted his aircraft and his charge to the right place, he understood that the Colonel was involved in a critical mission by order of the President, and that it was occurring during a critical phase of the offensive. In addition, it was a colonel that was asking, and not just any colonel either. Colonel Kensington was *the* point of the sword during the ongoing offensive against the Chinese, and his actions under fire had earned the respect of every man serving under his command.

"Colonel, our Apaches have members of the resistance group under observation using their thermal sensors. They are well back in the trees and now moving towards the clearing. You'll see them in just a few seconds, sir."

As the Black Hawk continued to descend towards the small clearing, which was almost two hundred yards from the entrance to the cave that the resistance fighters had been using, three members of Stacey's group did appear at the tree line and helped guide the helicopter to a safe landing.

While the security personnel fanned out in front of him, the Colonel exited the Black Hawk, stooping until he was well clear of the rotors. Coming towards him out of the trees, he saw a group of five persons, one of them clearly an older female whom he presumed was Stacy Urkut. He didn't have long to wait to verify that it was in fact the woman the President had sent him to talk to.

Approaching the group, the Colonel offered to shake Stacey's hand. "Stacey Urkut? My name is Colonel Henry Kensington."

Stacey nodded affirmatively and then gave the Colonel a surprisingly firm handshake. The Colonel continued.

"Mrs. Urkut, I am here on the express order of the President of the United States. You may not be aware of it, but your description and reporting during the opening hours of the invasion of Alaska at Nome, and your activities since that time with your resistance movement, have attracted the attention and admiration, and rekindled the hopes, of all Americans.

"The President has instructed me to offer you immediate transport to Anchorage, and from there back to Washington, D.C. He wants to meet personally with you to extend the nation's thanks for the heroic and patriotic heroism under fire that you and your compatriots have shown here."

Stacey took a step back in stunned disbelief.

The President of the United States…Norm Weisskopf, wanted to meet with her and extend *his* thanks? It was almost impossible to comprehend as she responded.

"Colonel, I don't know what to say. I owe the President and all of you thanks…we all do. We have been hoping and praying for your arrival and now here you are wanting to thank me?

"I don't know if I can accept such an offer. I have a group here that I'm working real well with and we still have a lot to do."

The Colonel had only been here for a couple of minutes, but he was already seeing how this woman had been able to accomplish what she had.

"Stacey, if I may call you by your first name, we have anticipated all of that. Two of my men here, Lieutenant Colonel Haverson and Sergeant Major Buehler, will work with your people and help organize and liaison their activities to maximum benefit for the ongoing offensive."

Stacey interrupted, "Excuse me, Colonel, for interrupting, but I'd best make something clear right now. This is not any kind of a large group. There are fifteen of us. Never have been more than twenty-five. We've operated with a number of other small groups of similar or smaller size…but this is no company or battalion of individuals you are talking about here."

Now it was the Colonel's turn to be momentarily stunned. His own intelligence had indicated that there were several hundred individuals associated with this group alone, and that information was based predominantly on intercepts of Chinese traffic regarding them and their efforts to search out and destroy the Orka and her group.

Despite the surprise, the Colonel barely missed a beat.

"That is all the more reason to acknowledge what you have accomplished…and with so few. Believe me, when word gets back to the command staff and the President, this additional information will serve to *underscore* your successes. It is also all the more reason for Lt. Colonel Haverson and Sgt. Major Buehler to learn more of your extremely efficient operations and then coordinate them, and their underlying strategies, into our own plans.

"Mrs. Urkut, I know all of this is sudden, but I've got an anxious Captain back in that Black Hawk who is eager to take off, and we have these two fine officers here, and their support, who I promise you are all very capable soldiers. What do you say?"

Ted had been listening to the exchange and, despite experiencing feelings of inadequacy in the presence of the Colonel, he interjected, "Excuse me, Colonel…but Aunt Stacey, you really ought to go with these folks. Not only do you deserve the honor of allowing the President to extend his appreciation for what you have accomplished, but every American needs to know what has happened here and understand the hope we've been able to rekindle–that *you* helped us rekindle–while we've been fighting these Chinese bastards."

The Colonel decided that his liking for Stacey Urkut's nephew was also growing by the minute…and he smiled at the comments. He wondered how many of the others in the group were "family." He marveled at their bravery and their accomplishments and was impressed with the nephew's encouragement of his aunt…and Colonel Henry Kensington was coming away with the distinct impression that what this young man had just said weighed more heavily with Stacey Urkut than all of words he himself had spoken since setting down in this clearing, or the express order of the President himself.

…and he was right.

"Alright, Ted, you're right. I'll go. I'll tell our story, but that story has very little to do with me. Also, I respect greatly both the office of the President and the man who is occupying it right now, so I guess I'd better not miss an appointment with him."

Turning to the others who had accompanied them out of the cave, and who had been listening attentively to the exchange, she addressed them, with just a hint of tears beginning to glisten in her weary eyes.

"You guys take care, and make sure you keep these Army personnel safe and in line. There's a lot of country out there and you know it better than anyone else…and it's still crawling with Chinese."

Then, her mind made up, she addressed the Colonel. "Colonel, we'd best not keep your captain waiting any longer. Let's get going."

May 5, 2009, 19:50 local time
Outside of *Mein Café*
Beijing, China

Chiang Pham was as happy as she had ever been at any time in her life. Despite the war and the hardships it was causing everyone, despite the separation from her family since she had taken the computer analyst job here in Beijing, despite her concerns for her brother who was at sea…evenings like tonight somehow made it all worth it. Particularly evenings spent with Hua Jianying, whom she considered her best friend, and her suitor.

She had been seeing Hua for well over eight months now, and every day with him was like a new journey of discovery. They had spoken seriously of marriage several times in the last six weeks and had become officially engaged the day before yesterday. Their marriage date would be in the fall, in October if their families concurred, as Chiang was sure they would.

Tonight, over dinner, they had planned a late June trip down to Tianjin to meet Chiang's parents, Lu and Song Pham, in order to officially announce their intentions to marry. Chiang had called her mother and father the night of their engagement and let them know in a more personal and informal manner between daughter and parents.

Chiang had already met Hua's parents here in Beijing and enjoyed their company immensely, particularly their warm acceptance of her despite her Vietnamese heritage. That heritage was something that Chiang found caused many people to almost immediately look down upon her, as a result of an intercultural rejection of her heritage.

This immediate personal rejection by people who knew nothing about her had come as a shock to her youthful and protected innocence when she first came to Beijing. But it was also something that she had never seen or felt a hint of with Hua or his family.

However, many of those who initially rejected her, or looked down upon her, soon found themselves reversing their stance once they found out who she was...or, more correctly, who her father was.

Her father, Lu Pham, was a People's hero and the inventor and perfector of the *Killer Whale* weapon system which had so thoroughly defeated and embarrassed the U.S. Navy. Lu Pham was a name that everyone recognized and respected. When most people found out who her father was...and she always let them find this out on their own, never being one to brandish her father's name about...their attitudes towards Chiang usually changed dramatically for the positive, whatever their initial impressions had been.

But Chiang was always sadly amused by the change of heart, and the reason for it. Although she worked with, and lived in the same general neighborhood as, some of those who had been initially negative towards her, she never forgot their initial and unwarranted condescension, and she vowed never to allow herself to trust any of those whose original opinion of her was based on other than her own personal character.

But none of that mattered when she was with Hua, her handsome suitor and a financial forecaster for the National Party Congress and himself a member of the Communist Party.

Hua's father had served in the Party Congress for over thirty years, and Hua was a rising political star himself within the party. He planned to campaign for the National People's Congress next year, and with his father's and his own party connections, he had no doubt that he would be elected. He ultimately hoped to be the youngest mayor of Beijing in the city's history...a position from which others had vaulted onto the stage of national and international prominence.

All of this fit very well into Chiang's plans for herself. She had made steady advancement in her programming analyst position for COSTIND, working on algorithms that were a secondary, backup system for the guidance of the *ta shih* anti-stealth system being employed by the People's Republic. In a little over two years she had advanced from an Analyst I position to Analyst III and had two younger programmers working under her supervision. She hoped one day to become a senior technical manager at COSTIND and to use her analytical skills to great effect on behalf of the People's Republic.

As she stared steadfastly up into Hua's eyes, standing there on the sidewalk in front of the Mein Café, she could see her dreams of their future together reflected in those beautiful dark eyes–and in the smile he shared with her as they waited for the driver that Hua's father had allowed them to use this evening. It was a future that she was excited to share in detail with her family–it was all she had ever dreamed of and hoped for. She was sure that her mother and father, and her brother, would all share in her happiness.

May 6, 2009, 08:40 local time
Staging Area, 7th Marine Division
Midway, Island

Leon was ecstatic.

"We're finally going to move off of this rock!" he thought as the commanding general prepared to address them.

The talk had been circulating for some weeks. After almost a year on the island, and a little over ten months since the tremendous battle to hold the island had been fought against the Chinese, apparently America was going to go on the offensive in this part of the world, too.

Where they were going was not known. Could it be "North, to Alaska"? Many of the soldiers surmised that it would be and they would sing out the words, in tune with the famous Johnny Horton song.

Would they be going to New Zealand to prepare for the anticipated invasion of Australia? Many of them, including Leon, longed for that prospect, figuring that the retaking of Australia would be where the bulk of the action would be occurring.

Could it be elsewhere? None of the rank and file knew.

…but Sergeant Leon Campbell was looking forward to their new orders, wherever they might lead them, and irrespective of his own preferences.

Leon was something of a legend amongst his peers. A Medal of Honor recipient from earlier in the war, his exploits and actions under fire on the island of Diego Garcia in July of 2006 in the Indian Ocean were well known to all. The fact that he had voluntarily chosen to come back into combat when everyone knew that he could have had his pick of plush recruitment jobs back in the states was something not lost on any of the soldiers here, particularly the other Marines of the 7th Division. His example and his commitment to "fight his nations battles," wherever they might be, was an encouragement and inspiration to them all.

This is not to say that Leon, as mentioned, did not have his own preferences. He was hoping that the call would come, and that the orders would send them to New Zealand so he could fight in Australia. His best friend, Billy Simmons, had been lost there when Sydney fell. Billy's body, as well as thousands of others, had never been recovered.

To his family and friends, Billy was presumed dead, killed in action, there off the coast of Australia when a LRASD, Killer Whale device had struck his amphibious assault ship. Billy's AH1Z Viper attack helicopter had been one of the last aircraft to get off the deck of the doomed ship before it was hit, and Leon had seen the pictures of that very helicopter as it had emerged from the smoke surrounding the ship…and as it cart wheeled directly into the ocean.

"No one believes anyone could have survived that crash," Leon thought. "But if anyone could have survived it and managed to get to shore and keep on fighting, Billy could...and if he didn't, then I'd just as soon be there providing direct payback to his killers as anywhere else."

As Leon was having these thoughts, the intelligence officer for the division got the attention of the officers and senior NCOs who were attending the briefing.

"Okay, men, the General has asked me to brief you on the upcoming operation before he speaks to you I can't announce at this point what our objective is. That will be announced to your Company commanders once we embark...but I can say this.

"We are going to embark and arrive on station more quickly than any other large attack operation has in the history of combat. If you will all closely watch the following short video, you will understand why."

After making this statement, which got all of their attention, the Colonel had the lights dimmed, and a digital projector near the back of the large room began displaying a video clip on the far wall.

What they all saw was astounding. It was something new and, as combat veterans and as Marines, they all recognized the import of it immediately.

The video lasted a good five minutes. There was absolute quiet in the room as these combat veterans watched the display of America's latest technological innovations as they would be applied to their fight. When it was over, the intelligence officer continued.

"What you have just seen is classified as top secret and cannot leave this room. It has been shown here to help you prepare your individual units for our next operation, entitled Operation Lightning Bolt, which will begin in five days, during which time you will be training hard to make use of what you have just seen.

"I'll now turn the time over to General Atkins who will complete the briefing."

General Atkins approached the small podium. He could feel an almost palpable electric charge in the air. These Marines were ready to go on the offensive. They had taken the worst the enemy could deliver here on Midway months ago and they all sensed that now was the time for America to strike back.

And the general knew that America and her allies were striking back. Operations in Alaska and around Israel, though still very hard fought, were going better than expected...and ahead of schedule. Now, here in the Pacific, the first arm of a two-armed offensive against the Coalition of Asian States in the Pacific would begin...and the troops of the 7th Marine Division and supporting commands were going to be the ones to kick it off.

"Gentlemen, I know you are all tired of waiting, so I am going to make this fairly brief. The time has come...we are going to strike when and where the enemy least expects it, and we are going to do so with devastating effect!"

Immediate cheers filled the room, but they quieted rapidly as the general held up his hands and motioned for silence.

"Each of your company commanders has a package indicating what your orders are as regards deployment in Operation Lightning Bolt, which preparation will begin tomorrow as we prepare for the arrival of the transportation you have just been privileged to review. That arrival will occur five days from today.

"Each of you should be prepared, as should the personnel over whom you hold command, for this historic and critical mission. We will be supported in this by the U.S. Air Force and the U.S. Navy as they escort us to the objective and then provide air cover and support while we secure that objective. The Navy is using a new and unique method of pre-positioning materiel in theater which will augment and support our activities once we've attained our objective.

"Although that final objective is not mentioned in the orders being distributed to your company commanders, the nature of your role and the equipment you will require is spelled out in some detail.

"Final mission planning and prep will occur en route, including secure video conferencing between separate units as we travel towards the objective. This will include a live feed from our Commander in Chief, President Weisskopf.

"That is all."

May 12, 2009, 07:40 local time
The White House Situation Room
Washington, D.C.

Norm Weisskopf considered the import of Operation Lightning Bolt as he watched the real time display on the screen at the far end of the room. He had given the final execute orders less than twelve hours ago, after the troops had all embarked and staged off to the west of Midway Island.

This operation was much different than the large offensive operations currently being conducted in Alaska and the Mid East…and different from the operation about to kick off in Europe to the south and east of Moscow.

In fact, this operation was meant to dovetail with the European Operation which was sure to attract significant attention from both the GIR and CAS high commands.

"And that is exactly what we want," thought the President.

"We're going to deliver a little Sun Tsu of our own."

But those operations were traditional offensive operations involving hundreds and hundreds of thousands of troops and their materiel, and the long lead time staging required to make those large operations possible. At least those types of lead times had always been traditionally required. Operation Lightning Bolt was aimed not only at the CAS, it was aimed at breaking that mold and allowing large numbers of allied troops to very swiftly appear in the most unexpected places with all of their equipment and support.

This revolutionary operation and its import were readily apparent with but a glance at the real time images being displayed on the far wall of the situation room...and those remarkable images had everyone's rapt attention. Displayed on that wall were eight flights of four aircraft flying in formation about 50 feet above the wave tops in the Western Pacific Ocean. They were simply the largest aircraft ever seen in any military operation.

Oh, several of those in the room had seen these aircraft as they were developed, manufactured, and tested...but seeing so many of them now in an actual operation was awe inspiring and simply dumbfounding . Propelled by four very large and very advanced turboprop engines on each wing, the transport aircraft were over three hundred feet long, and had a wing span that was in excess of five hundred feet! Each aircraft's body was easily fifty feet in diameter, flattened on the bottom side to allow for water operations, both takeoffs and landings. They could also land on unimproved landing fields like a C-17, as long as there was sufficient clearance for their tremendous size.

As they watched, the picture zoomed out and revealed several escort aircraft flying along with these behemoths. It was then that the true size of the aircraft became apparent. A flight of four F-22 Raptor aircraft appeared as little more than a group of flies when compared to the monstrous transports they were escorting. To the left of the entire flight, and flying somewhat above them, a flight of four tanker aircraft could be seen coming into view. Despite the large size of the KC-10 tankers, the large C-90A transport aircraft easily dwarfed them, too, making them seem small and almost insignificant in comparison.

The President marveled at the coordination...it had every appearance and trapping of a very large and complicated naval transport operation, except it was flying in the air and doing so at well over 350 knots.

"And though the tankers look small and insignificant when compared to these super-transports," thought the President, "In fact they are the life blood of the entire operation, just like a group of UNREP ships is to a naval operation."

The pictures they were watching were being taken from well over one thousand feet above the aircraft, which continued flying less than one hundred feet above the surface of the ocean. What the pictures didn't show, but what something everyone in the room was well aware of, were the over two hundred other supporting aircraft that were escorting and supporting the entire operation: the largest single grouping of F-22 fighters in history and an equal number of F-15C and F-15E aircraft.

The President knew that the entire flight would be joined in a few moments, as they neared their destination, by Naval aircraft off of the USS Shanksville, which had been able to clandestinely position itself two hundred miles from the objective of Operation Lightning Bolt. The Shanksville was being escorted by the largest group of SUB CIWS equipped vessels yet assembled, and was also itself equipped with the Anti-Killer Whale being deployed by the U.S. Navy.

In addition, five of the recently launched Alaska Class SSTN nuclear transport submarines, which were carrying the remainder of the Task Forces supplies, were stationed offshore from the objective as well. They were being escorted by the U.S.S. Jimmy Carter and the U.S.S. Connecticut, which were both still impervious to Killer Whale detection.

Although the SSTNs were capable of self-defense and equally quiet, the two Sea Wolf class, with their larger weapons load-out, their proven track record regarding the LRASD devices and their remarkable speed, would provide the most capable defense possible for these new underwater behemoths in America's growing arsenal, being dutifully stockpiled in the defense of liberty.

The design of the exterior lines of the Alaska class had been based on the Sea Wolf's proven qualities in order to achieve the same results when confronting the Chinese LRASD devices. This first combat deployment of the class involved every ship of that class that had been built to date. Still undetected and now just off the objective, the design had achieved the intended level of stealth and quiet despite their mammoth underwater displacement of over 40,000 tons!

This awesome show of force amazed the President, despite his involvement in its planning and production over the last three years. The development of these two systems, one airborne, the other a subsurface naval system, had been two of America's most closely guarded secrets as the war progressed, and in face of the almost constant barrage of bad news.

The entire concept of "Rapid Deployment" had been studied for years at the Pentagon and within the prestigious U.S. military war colleges. Things had come a long way from the very traditional methods of World War II and the Korean War. Beginning in the Vietnam War, large numbers of men were moved by jet airliner aircraft, allowing them to arrive quickly in theater. But the problem remained of having them meet up expeditiously with their heavy equipment. Faster transport vessels were designed and built which doubled the speed and capacity of older ships. Still, time requirements were viewed as just too great for the literal mountains of heavy materiel required for a large, modern army.

Pre-deployment and staging philosophies were developed and instituted in the 1980s, which significantly improved the situation. Mountains of materiel were strategically placed around the globe by the U.S. Military at defensible bases calculated to be near any conceivable major trouble spots. But the strategic positioning still did not reduce the time requirements to anything approaching the "rapid" deployment desired and envisioned. In 1991, in Operation Desert Storm, an operation which the President himself had led and with which he had therefore been intimately familiar, it had still required six months to build the force to the necessary size and state of logistical support to allow for the defeat of the Iraqi armies that had invaded Kuwait, and were positioned in southern Iraq.

Twelve years later, in 2003, when the United States again fought Iraq in Operation Iraqi Freedom, logistics, technology, and operations had improved to the point where a smaller force could be more rapidly deployed to accomplish the larger mission of invading all of Iraq, and occupying it while supporting the Iraqi people in the election of a regime that everyone had hoped would prove friendly to the West. Despite the improvements, that buildup had required over four months.

Many of those newer pre-deployment methodologies had been dealt devastating blows at the beginning of World War III in 2005 and 2006 by resourceful and committed GIR and CAS forces who overran many of the pre-positioned staging areas, and who developed weaponry that had countered the critical advantages of nuclear powered aircraft carriers and submarines upon which the ability to execute those rapid deployment philosophies had rested.

So the war colleges had gone back to the drawing board, and within two years had perfected concepts that had already been under consideration when hostilities broke out. Those concepts had coalesced into operational plans and equipment had been developed or modified to support them. In 2008, America's new production lines began to address the issue in top secret factories built in remote areas of the intermountain west and the desert southwest. The culmination of these efforts was what was being witnessed for the first time with Operation Lightning Bolt.

Thirty-two massive C-90A transports were carrying the entire task force very rapidly towards their objective. Five massive Alaska class SSTNs were already onsite and represented a pre-positioned staging area themselves. This massive movement of men and materiel would not be accomplished in a time frame measured in months…it would be accomplished in a matter of hours and days.

Now, as the large aircraft approached the U.S.S. Shanksville rendezvous point, the President tuned into the latest verbiage of the ongoing briefing. This portion of the briefing was being given in preparation for the President's own address to the entire task force in just a few minutes at the conclusion of remarks by the National

Security Advisor, Bill Hendrickson, and the Chairman of the Joint Chiefs of Staff, General Jeremy Stone.

"Each aircraft can carry a combination of over two million pounds of men and materiel. That equates to sixteen main battle tanks, or twenty infantry fighting vehicles, or close to two thousand troops and their personnel equipment. They can also carry F-35C Joint Strike Fighters or AH1Z Viper attack helicopters in a special stowed configuration. Up to eight of either of those aircraft will fit into one of those transports along with the people and equipment to support them. Those aircraft can then be unloaded and made operational within twenty minutes.

"The United States Marine Corps now has forty-eight of these aircraft in its inventory and many more in the pipeline. Operation Lightning Bolt will be employing forty of them. As you can see on the monitor, thirty-two of those are involved in the initial effort to move the entire 7th Marine Division and its supporting commands, augmented by sixteen F-35Cs and sixteen AH1Zs, onto the objective. They will be on that objective within the next hour.

"Elements of the escorting aircraft, both U.S. Air Force and U.S. Navy off of the U.S.S. Shanksville, will begin a massive attack in the next ten minutes to prepare the objective for landing and to suppress any and all enemy air or missiles defense.

"We believe the surprise will be total, and the shock overwhelming, to the 100,000 personnel that are deployed by the enemy in and around this objective.

"Let me remind you that what we are witnessing is an unprecedented event in the history of warfare. In the next hour, over thirty thousand troops and their equipment will be landing far in the enemy's rear, near the pivotal city of Magadan on the Sea of Okhotsk. This city is the logistical control point for all of the enemy forces in far eastern Asia and Alaska. In essence we will set up a large pincer operation against an enemy force of over one million Chinese and their equipment, positioned between our advance in Alaska and their rear at Magadan."

At this point, Bill Hendrickson turned to General Jeremy Stone, the Chairman of the Joint Chiefs of Staff.

"General Stone will now give a short briefing of the overall military ramifications of this operation. General?"

General Stone wasted no time and jumped right in. He knew the President was scheduled to go on the air in just a few minutes and he wasn't about to delay this particular Presidential address.

"Thanks, Bill. Folks, as the National Security Advisor has indicated, this operation is historic, both in its execution and its implications.

"In short, we have planned for our forces to engage the enemy first in Alaska and then on the Asia mainland near Magadan. While the attack around Magadan is proceeding up the enemy's logistical supply line, we expect our Alaskan offensive to push the Chinese across the Bering Strait back into Asia.

"When this happens, we anticipate a complete victory in eastern Asia in a relatively short time frame as those forces are cut off from all hope of outside support or intervention. Their only recourse will be to either surrender, or face total destruction in place.

"And this is where things get exciting. Along with that victory will come the development of a staging area for ultimate attacks on Japan, Korea and mainland China from the North. This will represent a situation which the enemy will not be able to ignore and one that will allow for the exertion of equal pressure by our forces advancing out of New Zealand next month.

"We expect the buildup in eastern Asia that will make all of this possible to occur very quickly. Another eight C-90A aircraft are four hours behind this initial wave. Over the next twenty-four hours, as we set up the rotation, eight aircraft will be arriving every four hours until our force is brought up to the planned level of two hundred and fifty thousand and their equipment...within five more days.

"That's a brief description of where we are headed with this."

When General Stone turned the time back over to Bill Hendrickson, the National Security Advisor listened briefly to his ear phone and then turned to the President.

"Mr. President, they are indicating to me that we are two minutes away from your address. The time is yours."

As the cameras focused on the opposite end of the table, where the President was sitting flanked by a United States flag on one side and the Seal of the Presidency on the other, President Norm Weisskopf prepared to speak.

May 13, 2009, that same time
Flight 4A, C-90A
350 Miles Southeast of Magadan

With the presentation by the President about to begin, Leon Campbell, like tens of thousands of other American service personnel, prepared to listen attentively. They all had the utmost respect for the "old man," both because of his own service record, and more importantly, because of the way he had led them and the nation since the outbreak of hostilities over three and a half years earlier. As Leon thought about this, he also looked with anticipation to the upcoming operation and what it would mean for him.

He had put in his transfer request some time ago and his company commander had informed him just yesterday that the transfer had been approved. After Magadan had been taken and secured, and as follow-on forces pushed north, Sergeant Leon Campbell would be traveling far to the south to New Zealand. Of necessity, his path in getting there would be a circuitous route, one that would take a good week or more for him to make. Magadan was well behind what was currently perceived as the Chinese front lines…but that was what this operation was really all about, to show the Chinese that traditional front line advantage no longer applied when it came to fighting the United States.

"Well," he thought. "That will take care of itself in due course. My road to New Zealand and the South Pacific Theater of Operation lies through Magadan. Better listen up to the President now, though. Here he comes."

In the White House situation room, at command facilities from the Pentagon, to Hawaii, to Alaska and in the air to the southeast of Magadan, the image of the President of the United States appeared on countless monitors and screens.

"My fellow compatriots and defenders of American liberty. Today we embark on a new phase of this war. No more will we allow ourselves to be manipulated at the discretion of a merciless and tyrannical group of nations and their leaders who have pushed us to the very brink of extinction.

"We showed last fall, and are showing again this spring, what we can do against these enemies when we apply the new and unparalleled edge we have developed in traditional warfare methodologies. That edge includes our moral underpinnings, our level of training, the innovation that individual liberty allows our equipment to benefit from and our absolute commitment to that liberty. As a result of this, we are now steadily pushing the enemy back on several fronts.

"But the road is long and the path difficult. The enemy is numerous and well entrenched. The traditional route, while achievable, will take us far too long and will cost far too many lives, both the lives of our own people as well as those of the many innocent civilians throughout the world who have come under the rule of these diabolical monsters.

"Today, each of you represents the cutting edge of new methodologies and new practices. You represent America's asymmetrical response to the enemy's asymmetrical warfare of terror, hate, lies, deception, and genocide.

"Because of the bravery, commitment, virtue, and liberty you represent, we are going to hit the enemy behind their lines…we are going to show them that old rules no longer apply, that we can bring unimaginable and irresistible force to bear on them whenever, and wherever we chose. For the Chinese, that demonstration begins today with you warriors. For our other enemies, similar demonstrations will come in due course.

"Know that we, your leaders, support you and are with you in this. We have all faced grave danger and violence in this affair. It has been unjustly and viciously unleashed on us…both our forces abroad and our people here at home. This White House from which I speak had to be rebuilt as a result of that very type of destruction, and the blood of patriots who died bravely for their country stains this ground as well.

"As General Patton said in World War II…*it is not your job to die for your country; it is your job to make sure that those other SOBs are dying for their country*. We intend to demonstrate today that the enemy can expect to do exactly that, and that they can expect to do it in unimaginable numbers.

"We will force them to *die in unimaginable numbers* until there is not so much as one of them left who will be willing to so much raise their hand in support of the ideologies and national purpose that their sick and perverted leaders have directed them towards…let alone continue to die for them."

When the President made this statement, his inflection rose and no one listening could miss the steel or determination in his voice. Spontaneous cheers arose in several places around the globe, including the situation room and within those transports that were carrying the personnel who intended to put the President's statement into bold and immediate action.

Raising his voice over the din, but in no way trying to dissuade the emotion, the President concluded.

"Godspeed to each and every one of you. The thoughts and prayers of your countrymen go with you in this struggle…particularly today as you firmly plant the banner of liberty on the continent of Asia, the home ground of our enemies."

May 13, 2009, that same time
CIC, U.S.S. Shanksville
125 Miles south of Magadan, Sea of Okhotsk

Admiral Darcy watched the display in the Combat Information Center as the initial waves of aircraft from the Shanksville and from Task Force Lightning Bolt began hitting their targets.

By all accounts, resistance in the air was light and there had been very few launches of anti-aircraft missiles in response. Surprise seemed to be complete and initial concerns about high attrition rates now seemed as if they would not materialize.

"Thank God," the Admiral thought as he considered this.

"No doubt we will lose several aviators today, but those losses could have been much, much worse. It appears that our intelligence and psy-ops efforts have paid off."

Those efforts that the Admiral contemplated as he continued to watch the threat boards had indeed paid off for the United States. In a reversal of what the Chinese had applied last year over and around the Bering Strait, the Americans had intentionally underplayed their hand regarding Magadan and their access to it.

For months, the chain of Kuril Islands, which protected entry into the Sea of Okhotsk from the Pacific Ocean, had been harassed by American forces. Both U.S. Navy surface and subsurface forces had sporadically fired Tomahawk cruise missiles at various radar and monitoring stations along those islands. No point of the chain was focused on, just a general harassment from both U.S. Navy vessels and from Navy and Air Force aircraft.

Whenever the Chinese made a foray with their forces against these attacks, the Americans beat a hasty retreat, never committing anywhere near enough forces to consider waging a pitched battle against the Chinese. Follow-up reconnaissance missions by hyper velocity HR-7 and the larger SR-77 aircraft had shown a definite trend on the part of the Chinese over those months to consider the attacks less and less seriously.

The enemy's cavalier attitude had all paid off perfectly yesterday as the Shanksville battle group transited a narrow strait into the Sea of Okhotsk south of the Island of Lopatka. That transit had occurred within a few hours of one of the harassing attacks which had taken out the radar and monitoring equipment in that area and also sunk two Chinese patrol boats well to the west. U.S. intelligence had determined that those two ships were tasked with patrolling that strait and its approaches over the next two days.

"Now months of effort and planning are coming together with this assault...but it hasn't been without cost," thought the Admiral.

One Los Angeles class attack submarine lost, one Arleigh Burke class Aegis destroyer severally damaged, six B1-B bombers, and five HR-7 aircraft and their crews lost in the exchange.

"God rest their souls...God grant that their sacrifices will have been worth it," concluded the Admiral as he returned his full attention to the displays his personnel were resolutely monitoring and updating so they could communicate most effectively with the forces that were now engaging the enemy.

In addition to the attacks on Magadan, three smaller air strikes and one SAG force were prosecuting strikes at sea against Chinese shipping. Several container ships and a full convoy of transports escorted by Chinese guided missiles destroyers were finding themselves under attack at the moment.

More ships, aircraft and their personnel were going directly into harm's way in order to ensure the success of Operation Lightning Bolt.

As at Magadan proper, with these attacks it appeared that surprise had been complete. Radio traffic monitored between those forces and their headquarters and support forces indicated that the Chinese were shocked at the level of force being applied here, so far from the front lines.

Those Chinese command and control groups had now clearly determined that this was no mere harassment or diversionary attack…this was the real thing.

May 13, 2009, one hour later
Magadan, Siberia

The U.S. Air Force and U.S. Navy attack aircraft continued to pound positions, but they were now on the peripheral of the target zones as the huge C-90A transports approached. Air superiority had been quickly achieved as only eight Chinese SU-33 aircraft had been in the air patrolling the skies over Magadan when they had been assaulted by over forty F-22, F-15 and U.S. Navy F-18F fighter aircraft. The resulting dogfight had been brief but bitterly contested. All eight Chinese aircraft were downed at the cost of three American F-15 fighters and one F-18.

With their more modern avionics, better stealth and newer electronics, no F-22s were destroyed. The remaining thirty-six U.S. aircraft took up rotating patrols as American troops assaulted the airfields that would soon be home to those very fighters patrolling overhead.

To accomplish the ground assault, Operation Lightning Bolt had more than twenty C-17 Globe Master aircraft accompanying the C-90A transports. These aircraft were raining down over five thousand paratroops to the two airfields located at Magadan.

Only twenty minutes after the initial alarms went out, and while eighteen U.S. aircraft had drawn off the Chinese CAP and twelve more ensured that no more enemy aircraft were able to take off from the airfields, parachutes had filled the sky and U.S. soldiers had begun to land. Along with the air strikes, soon heavy mortar and machine gun fire had quickly been directed at whatever Chinese troops were trying to assemble.

With their headquarters facilities, prepared positions and barracks already thoroughly decimated by close air support, the Chinese defenders on the ground were extremely hampered in organizing any large scale defense. Just the same, a few fierce pockets of resistance did develop, mainly centered around the few surviving armored personnel carriers, and light tanks–and in particular around two ZU-23 units that survived the air assault.

Normally used to interdict medium to low level attack aircraft, the commander of Chinese air defense in that particular sector had wisely ordered the radar units in those vehicles turned off in order to save them. He then had them concealed in a nondescript warehouse and offered them to the young Captain who had taken charge of the ground defense for the base.

The Chinese captain employed those units very effectively. Establishing a defensive perimeter near the warehouse, he had the two ZU-23s and two accompanying infantry fighting vehicles remain concealed in the building while his ground troops retreated hastily in front of the American advance in that sector. This movement served to draw the American forces forward and then, just as American forces began passing the warehouse, the captain ordered the concealed ZU-23's and IFVs to attack. The ambush worked as they caught the two most forward American platoons by surprise and completely decimated both of them, killing twenty-three and severely wounding another seven soldiers.

Ultimately, one of the ZU-23s was destroyed by a LAW anti-armor unit attached to the Company that had lost those platoons. The second ZU-23 was destroyed by an F-15E Strike Eagle that was called in for close air support by the mortally wounded commander of the second ill-fated platoon.

Despite inflicting these losses, the Chinese defense of the airfield was futile. Outside of the ZU-23 and a couple of other pockets of resistance, the American troops rolled over both the military and civilian airfields and were prepared to secure them for American aircraft landings within the hour, well ahead of schedule.

As the drama of the doomed Chinese defense of the military airfield played itself out, the C-90A transports began to arrive on the sea shore outside of Magadan. Close air support aircraft and a battalion of American paratroopers (who themselves had landed a half hour earlier for just this purpose) secured the two major landing zones on adjacent beaches and ensured that no SAM or heavy caliber weapons were in a position to threaten the arriving transports.

Those huge transports arrived at the two landing zones in two waves of eight aircraft each. The first wave at each landing zone comprised four aircraft with infantry load outs carrying almost eight thousand men each. Those four aircraft were accompanied by two aircraft carrying armor, a total of thirty-two M1A1 Abrams tanks…and by two aircraft carrying mechanized infantry, a total of forty light armored vehicles (LAVs).

As each aircraft touched down in the water and powered up to a sliding halt on the undefended beaches, its nose swung upward like a C-5A Galaxy, and revealed two separate levels for the disembarking of troops and equipment. Those soldiers in the aircraft carrying infantry poured out from both levels, down ramps that extended onto the shore. Those aircraft carrying armor vehicles disgorged that armor and their crews from the lower level, while maintenance and support troops used the ramps from the upper level.

Outside of a few cases of small arms fire and one case of light machine gun fire which were quickly suppressed, there was no opposition. Within thirty minutes, following the pattern and training that had been drilled into them over the five-day period while they awaited the arrival of the aircraft on Midway Island, all of the troops and their immediate equipment were on shore and utilizing their staging areas to move further inland.

Twenty minutes later the second wave of aircraft arrived at each landing zone and approached the positions for the disembarking of their troops and equipment. This wave had been prepared to loiter well offshore if resistance to the first wave warranted it. As it turned out, it did not. Resistance remained light.

In this wave, there would only be eight of the huge transports– two infantry loaded aircraft for each landing zone, with four more carrying armor and mechanized vehicles. The remaining two aircraft at each zone carried the invasion force's attack helicopters-AH1Z Vipers, and its F-35C VTOL fighter bomber attack aircraft.

The tragedy of the day occurred while these aircraft were just touching down onto the water and powering up to the beach. Forty kilometers to the north of Magadan, a battery of Chinese short range ballistic missiles had just set up to provide direct fire onto the American beach areas. Four other such batteries had already been discovered and destroyed by American aircraft before they could fire. But this battery of sixteen missiles avoided detection and launched its missiles before American aircraft could respond.

The ballistic tracks were almost immediately noted by American AWACS aircraft that accompanied the task force, and seconds later by Aegis cruisers and destroyers in the Shanksville carrier battle group that were closer in to shore. Immediately the interception of the Chinese missiles was handed off to, and engaged by, the Theater Ballistic Missile defense missiles on the appropriate Aegis escorts.

But, although those escorts were much closer to Magadan than the Shanksville herself, they were still several miles off shore and the amount of time was just too short to successfully engage and defeat all sixteen missiles. If a Patriot missile battery had already been set up at either of the two captured airfields, then perhaps the tragedy could have been avoided. As it was, four of the missiles made it through the Aegis TBM defense and impacted at the eastern most landing zone.

There were several very anxious seconds as General Atkins and Admiral Darcy waited to see if the detonations were nuclear, biological, or chemical—or if they were standard high explosives. But there were no weapons of mass destruction employed by the Chinese on this day. They remained committed to their own high command policy decision made earlier in the war to not make unilateral use of their nuclear, biological or chemical weapons, and therefore not play to the American and Russian strength in this area. But the high explosive detonations were severe enough.

Three of the missiles exploded in or near the staging areas of the first wave of transports that had already landed, and where thousands of personnel were busily dispatching more and more men and materiel inland. Over four hundred personnel and several light armored vehicles were destroyed in those blasts. More tragically, in a freak coincidence of timing, one of the missiles landed just offshore as the second wave of transports was approaching. That missile hit the right wing of one of the C-90A transports carrying F-35C aircraft for that landing zone.

The impact severed the wing, causing the aircraft to skew and dip into the water. As it did so, its own weight and momentum sheared the tail entirely off of the aircraft. The forward section, which still contained a full wing and the sheared-off half of another, spun hard in the water as it dipped further, ripping off three of the four engines on the intact left wing.

The catastrophic opening of so many hydraulic, electric, and fuel lines while the aircraft's equipment was still operating resulted in a fire on the intact wing that rapidly spread towards the main body of the aircraft. It came to a halt in about twenty feet of water and began to settle to the bottom, as it burned. Personnel were pouring out of emergency access doors along both sides of the aircraft and out of the rent in the back of it.

Three large explosions occurred in the body of the aircraft as the fire reached fuel, ordnance, and other combustible materiel stored on board for the F-35Cs. These explosions resulted in a massive fireball within the body of the aircraft that moved quickly, trapping and burning many men before they could get out.

On the lower deck, a large number of personnel were forced to make the horrific choice of either facing the intense fire, or staying where they were and succumbing to the rising water on that deck. Scores of personnel drowned as the rapidly rising water in that portion of the aircraft made their decision for them.

In the end, of the almost twelve hundred personnel on board that aircraft, only three hundred and eighty-two survived. All eight of the F-35C aircraft were completely destroyed. The wreck of that C-90A would remain there just offshore for over a year as feverish logistical operations and enemy counter attacks made it impossible to conduct any large scale salvage effort.

That wreckage, and more that would be added to it, would serve as a mute but stark message to American servicemen who fought in and around, or were processed through, Magadan over the next twelve long months. It would do the same for those who would see it through digital imagery. It was a message regarding the reality of the continued terrible sacrifice necessary to preserve freedom and overcome the commitment and doggedness of a dedicated and ruthless enemy who wanted to destroy it.

Those enemies were far from defeated and would prove, over and over again, that they were still capable of inflicting, and more than willing to wreak, death and destruction on American forces and those of her allies wherever they could be engaged in furtherance of their own aims and designs.

Later, as historians looked back upon it, it would be apparent that the American invasion of Magadan served to markedly increase the bloody tempo of the intense combat for the entire war. A veritable firestorm would ensue in and around Magadan as the Chinese contested America's foothold. And that firestorm would escalate around the globe through the remainder of the war.

The new and bloodier tenor of this war would be most evident on foreign shores like the one at Magadan, but it would also make itself felt in more periodic intense attacks on American soil directly, as future events would soon show.

May 13, 2009, 09:45 local time
Executive Council Chambers
Politburo, Beijing, China

Jien Zenim was extremely unhappy. The incessant ringing of his personal phone at a very early hour this morning was the certain tip-off to news and events that would place him and the entire executive committee of the Communist Party of the People's Republic of China on edge.

Jien couldn't stand unexpected disappointment, failure, or reversals to plans long laid.

The news today from the far east on the Sea of Okhotsk represented just that type of occurrence…and the entire leadership council knew it. Continuing to address them all, now that the initial briefing and information had been communicated to them, Jien's displeasure was evident in the berating of his subordinates who should have prevented such a disaster from occurring. As the President of the People's Republic of China and the leader of the largest, most militaristic and populous alliance the world had ever witnessed…and as the architect who had planned it all…Jien felt he was well within his rights to chastise those on whom he depended.

"By our own estimate, upwards of thirty thousand Americans materialize out of nowhere and attack, and then take the most strategic and the most critical logistics point for all of our forces operating in Alaska, and none of you can tell where the breakdown has occurred?

"The dodging and political posturing I am hearing here this morning has NO PLACE in our discussions. We must know what the real conditions are in Magadan and we must know how they came about.

"I am beginning to believe that the breakdown exists right in this room…and if I cannot be persuaded that this is not the case, I will solve the problem myself, very quickly and, I assure you, very permanently."

Turning to the large screen projection on the far wall, where he knew several others who were joining the conference by secure video conferencing, President Zenim picked one of those participants, one he felt he could trust completely and who was among the most competent military minds in all of China, and addressed him.

"General Hunbaio, what do our research and development scientists tell us about the new method the Americans have utilized in this landing of theirs?"

The President hesitated for just a few seconds as he asked this question, long enough so he could look around the table and glare at several of those sitting with him in the conference room in Beijing. Then he concluded, "Please share something definitive with us…as opposed to the hand wringing and excuses I have been witness to so far this morning."

General Hunbaio, the military commander and senior scientist at COSTIND, the Chinese defense industry research and development conglomerate, considered his feelings about this attack.

He was surprised by it…by the Americans' ability to produce so much new technologically advanced equipment so quickly, given the circumstances they had been subjected to. Three and a half years ago virtually all of their major, heavy manufacturing had been cut off cold.

"All of that outsourcing, all of those factories...gone," thought the General as he tried to conceive of how he and his own nation would have reacted in similar circumstances.

Their energy dependency had also taken a tragic toll on their ability to fight back, as many of their energy sources had become unavailable to them at that same time. Many other segments of their economy, including most of their high tech, had also been outsourced to Far Eastern nations, China most predominant among them, and to the subcontinent in India. The war had cut them off with swiftness as well.

"And we thought, with finality," reflected the General before beginning his response to President Jien Zenim's request.

Yet, here and now, less than four years later, somehow the Americans were able to produce an operation of this magnitude and technological advancement right here in Asia, far too close to the People's Republic.

It was amazing...but not altogether surprising to him. He had determined long ago not to take for granted or underestimate the will of the American people and their leaders...irrespective of the hype, and irrespective of the significant gains the PRC had made under certain American administrations. Not taking them for granted or believing the hype had allowed him to secure Lu Pham out of Vietnam so many years ago to develop the LRASD weaponry that had been so effective against the Americans to date. He determined in his own heart and mind that that same trait would serve him and his nation now as he sought for and found a way to counter this new development.

"Mr. President. The technology the Americans have employed is not new. You may remember that in the 1930s, the rich American, Howard Hughes, produced and flew a similar type aircraft. It was called the Spruce Goose, and it employed exactly the same principles of a large aircraft using the surface wave accompanying the passage of the aircraft to produce additional lift on the underside of the aircraft.

"The Americans have studied this issue for a long time in a quest for a true rapid deployment force of large size and magnitude.

"With their operation in Magadan, they are announcing to us that they have deployed just such a force. I am sure they expect us to understand their message…that they could send a similar force towards Tianjin or any of our other ports, or those of our allied and pacified nations tomorrow.

"Given the one grainy picture I have been able to look at this morning, I would say that the design of the large, super transports the Americans have employed is a larger, newer version of a design one of their major aircraft companies came up with about eight or nine years ago.

"That design was a little smaller and had only two engines on each wing. But it was huge nonetheless and looked very similar to this aircraft. I believe the company called it the Pelican, but it was never chosen for military procurement or production and it has apparently remained on the drawing board…until now.

"My own opinion is that the Americans are presenting us with a wonderful opportunity in this. After the shock wears off, and after we develop effective strategies to deal with it, those large, relatively slow moving aircraft will prove to be coffins for many more American personnel. They are much easier to destroy than a ship protected by aircraft, submarines and escort vessels.

"Clearly the key will be to determine where they are apt to strike, and then make sure our defenses are prepared accordingly…perhaps we can prepare a rapid deployment counter force of our own for this…I am not sure yet, but we already have the best minds at COSTIND working on it.

"Now, Mr. President, if I may, we are also working on a plan and operation to interdict and destroy this current force off of

Magadan. Admiral Lu Pham has some ideas in that regard using the LRASD devices and I believe we should move forward with a counter attack based on those plans as early as possible. Everyone here knows the success we have experienced as a result of the LRASD weaponry. The latest innovation which allows those weapons to be programmed with criteria so they can broach the service and become a missile has already proved successful. The Admiral is suggesting that we put on a major demonstration of this capability off of Magadan to match the Americans' demonstration.

"I will brief you all later in the day, and more fully tomorrow evening, on those plans. That is all I have at this time, Mr. President."

Jien Zenim knew that he could count on General Hunbaio and Admiral Lu Pham. They had not let him down in this entire affair…perhaps it was time to do something on the Executive Committee that would serve as a warning to several of the others.

In addition, the President knew it was time to take the counteroffensive to the Americans, and not only at Magadan.

"Excellent, General. Proceed with your planning as rapidly as possible. Please invite Admiral Lu to accompany you tomorrow for your briefing. I would like to meet with him and you personally before the briefing of the full executive committee."

Turning to the entire assembled committee, the President then continued. "In addition to this counterattack on the American forces at Magadan, I believe it is time that we issue the final execute order for our culminating operation in the United States. We cannot afford to allow conditions to continue, where the American morale is building as a result of their recent string of successes."

Addressing himself directly to the Chief of the People's Republic Intelligence Agency, the President continued. "General Zham, please ensure that the final approval and execute order for the operation next month is communicated to our operatives there in the United States. Keep us informed as to the progress and as to any complications. Communicate our express wishes to the commander on the scene that the operation must be conducted at all hazards, where there is any significant chance for success. Successful completion of his mission is vital to our overall strategy. Make sure that you emphasize that fact to the entire chain of command."

Chapter 3

"I regret that I have but one life to give for my country." – Nathan Hale

May 17, 2009, 09:48
Offshore
Magadan, Siberia

Landing and logistical operations at Magadan continued unabated. Every few hours, eight or more C-90A aircraft landed, disgorging more and more men, materiel, weapons, and equipment.

The 7th Marine Division and follow-on units which were now comprising what was being called the 12th Army, had pushed well inland along the superhighway and rail system the Chinese had built for their own massive buildup a year earlier. There were simply no major Chinese units to stop them. The head of the Chinese snake was over 1,500 miles away, locked in mortal combat with allied troops around Nome, Alaska.

They dared not turn their back on those allied forces…and yet, they dared not allow the Americans in their rear to continue the buildup and advance out of Magadan. They were caught in a classic pincer, like the North Koreans of the 1950s when General Douglas McArthur had pulled off what had been thought to be an impossible American landing at Inchon, trapping the North Korean army far to the south as they advanced on Pusan.

Now the Americans had repeated the feat, using their new super-transport technology and their advanced rapid-deployment methodologies.

But the Chinese were about to respond.

Flying north over the Sea of Okhotsk, a Chinese air armada equal in size to that of the American one used to affect the landing, the largest single Chinese air attack in their history, was now approaching and about to engage the Americans.

400 SU-35 and SU-37 aircraft, 200 enhanced TU-22M+ bombers, 200 of the new J-10E fighters, 150 attack aircraft of several varieties and over 200 support aircraft were involved. By 9:48, over 100 of the leading aircraft in this vast air armada were approaching the American picket ships and the extents of American AEW and AWACS coverage at the edge of the American defense of Magadan.

What ensued was what American fighter pilots called a giant "fur ball," a dogfight of massive proportions between American aircraft on patrol out of Magadan and from the U.S.S. Shanksville, and the Chinese fighters in the vanguard of their attack.

The fighting was ferocious as the Chinese, using their own high technology aircraft and benefiting from several years of combat experience, faced off against American fighters that, outside of the one squadron of F-22 Raptor fighters now based at Magadan, held little technological edge over their Chinese adversaries. In the training arena as well, after the years of combat the Chinese had experienced, what was once a clear American advantage had now nearly been negated.

At first, during the initial engagements, the dogfight went to the favor of the Chinese, with their vastly superior numbers coming to bear near the edge of the battle space, out near the U.S. picket ships and the edge of American AEW and AWACS coverage. That advantage allowed the as yet unmolested Chinese bomber aircraft to launch large numbers of LRASD weapons at those picket ships which began to take them out, one by one. By 10:15 AM, that line of picket destroyers and frigates had been reduced to a shambles and the Chinese continued to press on.

Now, as the moving dogfight approached closer to Magadan, the Chinese had to contend with more and more American aircraft and naval vessels in more defensible formations. And the American aircraft and ships fought ferociously to defend a contingent of ten C-90A aircraft that were still in the water, frantically unloading their supplies in an effort to finish and take off before the attack wave could arrive off of Magadan.

Soon, the Chinese fighter advantage and advance began to wane, particularly as the F-22 Raptor aircraft and Aegis vessels took their toll, fighting at a three or four to one ratio against the best the Chinese had, the J-10E and SU-37 aircraft.

By 10:45 AM, twenty miles out from Magadan, the Chinese offensive stalled and a dogfight of rough parity began to play out. Both sides lost more and more aircraft, the continued Chinese superior numbers now being offset by the capabilities of the F-22s. Both sides were many hours away from having any reinforcement aircraft arrive, but both sides had plenty of tanker aircraft in the air, and so the fight continued as first one side, and then the other, would make assaults on one another's tanker and command aircraft.

The Chinese attack aircraft tried again and again to break through the American air barricade to the beaches and to the newly installed American installations at the airfields and along the major highway. But they were foiled in the attempt by the few reserve aircraft the Americans held back to defend inland points against breakthroughs.

In the end, this scenario played to the Chinese advantage in attacking the C-90A aircraft and allied shipping near Magadan. The C-90s, with the fighting now so close, were unable to take off and they remained close in to shore, waiting for the ultimate American victory that would allow them to depart.

But now, the remainder of the TU-22M+ aircraft came into play. As a result of the Americans having their hands full turning back the attack aircraft and employing the balance of their fighters against the Chinese fighters, these bombers were able to approach right up to the perimeter of the Chinese air advance and launch their LRASD weapons. A contingent of twenty-five aircraft, which carried the latest programming for the LRASD, defined the main thrust.

The Chinese knew in advance that the C-90s would be in the water, and that had accounted for the particular timing of the attack. Coast watchers that they had deployed all along the Kuril Islands had turned the tables on the Americans for this battle. As the Americans had used those islands to lull the Chinese into a false sense of security so the Shanksville battle group could transit them, the Chinese coast watchers had, over the last five days, held their peace until the appointed hour to reveal the exact timing and duration of C-90 flights.

As two groups of twenty Tu-22M+ aircraft approached on each flank of the American position, the twenty-five aircraft carrying the latest version of the Killer Whales made a supersonic dash up the middle, low to the water.

The American AEW aircraft vectored all the resource that they had towards the first two groups of twenty TU-22M+ aircraft. All but ten of those Chinese aircraft were ultimately shot down, but not before eighteen launched LRASD weapons. While those weapons were streaking toward various American escort ships in the harbor, and as four of them detected and attacked two of the large SSTN transport submarines, the third group of twenty-five TU-22s arrived.

All of these aircraft were able to launch their Killer Whale devices which were programmed to place the highest priority on the parameters that the Chinese had calculated would detect and prosecute C-90 aircraft sitting in the water…and use the special attack profile that had been developed for them. The Chinese programming proved to be very accurate.

Only six of the LRASD weapons were intercepted by American defenses as they approached the big transport planes. All American personnel on shore and at sea could do was watch in horror as all ten C-90A aircraft were utterly destroyed by the large LRASD weapons which used a pop-up attack profile to come out of the water, rise completely above the aircraft and then crash down upon those aircraft from above as they sat motionless offshore, unloading their troops, equipment and cargo.

By 11 AM it was over...there was now much more debris in the waters around Magadan for those transiting the staging area to look upon.

Luckily for the Americans, they had unloaded most of the men and materiel from the transports before the attack. But the loss of almost one-quarter of their total inventory of C-90A transports in one confrontation was a tremendous blow...not only to the total inventory of equipment, but in real terms to the rate of buildup that could be sustained at Magadan. That buildup would now be slowed by over 30% of what it had been.

In addition, the U.S. Navy had been hit hard, losing three Aegis destroyers, an Aegis cruiser, three frigates and one of the new SSTN transport subs. Those two transport subs had used their SUB CIWS systems and had fought well. But one of them had been attacked simultaneously by three LRASD weapons that had overwhelmed its defenses. It along with all of its supplies which had yet to be unloaded, were a complete loss, lying broken and ruined on the floor of the Sea of Okhotsk.

One hundred and thirty-one U.S. aircraft were destroyed, including forty-two F-16s, twenty-eight F-15s, twenty-three F-18Fs, twelve F-14Ds, eleven F-22 Raptors, all ten of the C-90s, two EA-6Cs, two E-2C Hawkeyes, and one E-3 Sentry.

The loss of the SSTN, the C-90 transports, and of so many F-22s at one time would come as a shock to the American system, and once again demonstrate that in the face of overwhelming numbers, even the highest technology becomes vulnerable. That shock would reverberate throughout American think tanks and war colleges for months to come.

But the fight had also been very costly for the Chinese. Of the over 1,100 aircraft attacking the Americans, over five hundred would not be coming home. Only seventy of the enhanced TU-22M+

bombers came away from the fight. Almost all of the SU-35s, half of the SU-37s and most importantly, a full 75% of the J-10 fighters were also shot down, along with several tankers, three AWACS and almost one hundred of the attack aircraft.

Chinese production would be hard pressed—as would American production, to keep up with the losses that resulted from the second battle of Magadan—and it would not be the last. Over the next several months, a hot and expensive contest to see which side had the will, the fortitude and the resource to outlast the other in the battle over Magadan would continue.

May 21, 2009, 03:27 local time
Approaching the Trans-Syrian Pipeline
85 Miles Northeast of Damascus
Syria, GIR

Colonel Jess Simmons was very worried. In all the flying he had done and all of the combat he had seen, he had never been placed in a position where he was not in control of his aircraft.

Oh, he had taken fire, and even some damage, but his skills had been such, and the damage had been light enough, that he had never felt the slightest doubt about his ability to get his aircraft and his electronics and weapons officer back to base...until today.

The GIR was conducting a massive counterattack all up and down the line in this sector north and east of Damascus. Allied forces that had pushed well beyond Damascus and were approaching the Trans-Syrian pipeline were now experiencing a fierce enemy counterattack that had started yesterday, late in the day.

That attack had come precisely after the reserve AIM-999 Hail Storm missiles had been used to achieve the latest allied advances, and so there were no others available for use against the counteroffensive that the GIR was mounting at this time, and it would be at least another 24-48 hours before any could be spared from either the Syrian desert to the east, or Egypt to the south and west.

Realizing this, the allied command staff had recommended and approved the use of layered conventional forces, to absorb and then roll back the GIR counterattack, preparatory to AIM-999 strikes the day after tomorrow. Colonel Simmons and his flight of Comanche aircraft were an important part of that layered defense.

His command of those stealthy reconnaissance and attack helicopters was very adept at penetrating enemy lines, and determining the locations and the disposition of enemy forces on the ground, and then delivering critical attacks to those enemy forces to soften them up and prepare them for heavier attacks by either Apache helicopters, Multiple Launch Rocket Systems or aircraft of the U.S. Air Force. That air support could range anywhere from fast-moving attack aircraft providing close support, to more strategic attacks from B-2 Stealth bombers or even AIM-999 missiles…

…and softening up the enemy advance columns for that type of support is exactly what Colonel Simmons had been doing early this morning.

But the GIR had responded uncharacteristically quickly and in great strength with several squadrons of the new, GIR export version of the Chinese J-10 aircraft. Those light, very nimble, and highly advanced fighters were fighting the U.S. JSF and F-15 CAP to a standstill, and even penetrating the American CAP in several areas of the front in support of the advancing GIR armor and mechanized infantry.

It was just such a penetration that had caught Colonel Simmons' flight of four aircraft after a squadron GIR aircraft had disposed of, or driven off, the American fighters that were protecting them. On the first pass, these Chinese fighters severely mauled the American helicopters, shooting down two RAH-66s outright and severely damaging the Colonel's aircraft. That damage was severe enough that Jess knew he was not going to make it back to base…he was not even going to make it back to his own lines.

As the reality of the hopelessness of his position finally sank in with the failure of more and more systems, Colonel Simmons keyed his radio and reported to both his weapons officer and to the controlling command aircraft.

"Marty, get ready. We're going down.

"Night Watch Three, this is Dingo flight leader issuing an urgent Mayday. I say, Mayday, Mayday, Mayday…We are going down. Coordinates are…"

But the transmission was cut off in mid-sentence when total electrical power to the aircraft failed, and the Comanche went into an unstable flat spin. The Colonel tried to autorotate the aircraft to a semblance of a "soft" landing, but further control surface and circuitry failures made it impossible for him to regain control of his aircraft.

As the crew of the last healthy helicopter in Dingo flight looked on, Colonel Simmons' aircraft landed hard, bounced once, and then rolled over on its side before slamming to earth again, its rotor shattering and the aircraft rolling over several times before coming to a smoldering stop against a rock outcropping.

The surviving helicopter had time to make one low level pass over the now heavily smoking wreckage and communicate its location before jinking hard to the left to avoid an enemy missile, and then desperately evading continued attacks as it made its way back toward friendly lines.

May 20, 2009, 19:27, that same time
JSF Production Facility
Ft. Worth, Texas

Cindy Simmons shuddered for just an instant as a cold tremor passed over her like the frigid wind from a Texas blue norther. It was something entirely unexpected, and something physically impossible to explain here in the large building housing the F-35C Joint Strike Fighter assembly line in north central Texas where Cindy found herself in the late Spring of 2009.

"Jess," she immediately thought.

She didn't understand it, but deep in her heart and soul she felt that something must have happened to Jess.

She was only an hour and a half into her shift. For just a moment she stopped work and just sat there...thinking...worrying. Finally, out of necessity, as the pressure of doing her part in producing these important tools for the defense of America and liberty bore down on her, she put the thought out of her mind and went back to work.

She did so with a prayer that the tremor had been just a physical thing, brought on by something in the air around her rather than some sort of ominous, instinctual premonition. She was all too familiar with the aching void that would forever exist within her since the loss of her son, Billy. And she hoped that she was now simply projecting that ache onto her longing to see Jess safely home. The thought of living the rest of her life with two such voids was unimaginable.

Somehow, deep inside, she knew that something was desperately wrong...and, no matter what she did, she could not entirely shake that gnawing instinctual knowledge. But she would just have to place it in God's hands. His will would be done, no matter her fears, wishes, or premonitions. So she slowly and deliberately closed her eyes, and shook her head, as if to deny such unpleasant thoughts any residence there, and continued–although absentminded and preoccupied–with her work.

Despite her strong faith and unyielding optimism, those unpleasant thoughts continued to plague her, no matter how hard she tried to banish them. Later that night–deep into the night–she would sob quietly into her pillow, praying that her husband, her best friend and love, would be brought home safely to her. But somehow a stubbornly intuitive part of her already knew that the Lord would not be answering this prayer in the way that she hoped He would.

May 21, 2009, 03:29 local time
Back on the Ground
85 Miles Northeast of Damascus
Syria, GIR

Chief Warrant Officer Marty Walker regained consciousness with a start. As he oriented himself and tried to gain his bearings, he realized that his head was pounding with a terrible, blinding headache, and he was lying on his side. The memory of how he came to be in this awkward and unnatural position in his Comanche helicopter came flooding back to him. Thick black smoke was entering his compartment rapidly and he realized he had to get out...now.

Normal operation of the canopy in this position, with the helicopter on its side, was impossible so Marty quickly kicked out the side window, which was now surreally situated over his head. As he reached with both hands to pull himself out of the smoking wreck, white hot pain shot up his left forearm, and he was unable to grasp anything with that hand. Looking at that arm and seeing the sharp warp between his wrist and elbow, he realized that his left arm was broken, and so he concentrated his efforts on pulling himself out of the wreckage using his right hand only.

After several very painful seconds and a tremendous exertion, Marty was able to free himself and slide down the side of the aircraft to the ground.

As soon as he was shakily standing on his own two feet, he quickly made his way to the front of the aircraft and the other crew station to check on his pilot, Colonel Jess Simmons.

It was worse than he had feared. The forward compartment was partially crushed and full of smoke, and the Colonel was clearly unconscious and hurt badly with blood running down his forehead. Pulling off the emergency access panel, the Chief Warrant Officer rapidly disengaged and then released that canopy section behind which the Colonel was trapped. He then began to unhook the Colonel's harness and began to pull his limp body out of the aircraft.

Walker knew he would have to exert pressure on his broken arm and use it to help pull if there was any chance of getting the Colonel out. Steeling himself for the pain, the Chief Warrant Officer began to pull, trying his best to ignore the blinding pain as he tried to save his commanding officer and friend.

As he pulled, sparks began igniting within the compartment and a fire started that spread rapidly. Painfully trying to pull the Colonel out of the wreckage, Marty encountered resistance, and quickly found that the Colonel's left leg was badly mangled in the wreckage and he was unable to pull it free. The fire was beginning to reach that appendage and the sickly smell of burning flesh mixed with the fuel, electrical fire, ordnance, and other smells associated with the wreck of the aircraft.

Marty became desperate and knew that time was running out. He could not safely stay and work with the Colonel for more than a few seconds. Feverishly trying to disengage the Colonel's leg from the wreckage, he finally was able to use his good hand to bend a control panel back off of the leg and free it.

Using the good hand to pull at the leg, Marty discovered unnervingly, that the Colonel's damaged leg was almost completely severed half-way between the knee and hip. The bone had been cleanly broken by the impact with the control panel and only a large hunk of flesh behind the bone held the leg to his body. The same fire that had now severely singed Marty's good hand, had cauterized the Colonel's leg so the bleeding was not as severe as it otherwise would be. But Marty could tell that the Colonel's life now hung in the balance of what happened in the next few seconds.

Using all of his strength, and somehow ignoring what would otherwise be unbearable pain, Marty pulled Jess Simmons free of the aircraft and down to the ground, where Marty rolled them both away from the wreckage as quickly and as far away as possible. Before they had rolled over three times, there was a tremendous explosion that lifted them several in the air, throwing them perhaps fifteen feet from the now fiercely burning hulk of their aircraft.

Marty Walker pulled his unconscious commanding officer into the rocks and made his way, slowly, painfully, to a depression near the top of the rock outcropping. From that vantage point he had a good view of the forward area of the battle where the enemy was advancing. It also allowed him to activate his emergency radio beacon and make contact with the SAR units already airborne and looking for Colonel Simmons' wreckage.

May 21, 2009, 03:42 local time
Forward Command Post, U.S. Forces
80 Miles Northeast of Damascus
Syria, GIR

"Sir, we are in contact with Colonel Simmons' rear seater, Chief Warrant Officer Walker. He indicates that the Colonel is severely wounded but alive, and that there are a minimum of eight enemy armored personnel carriers or tanks approaching his position.

"He waved off the first SAR unit, which was going to have to abort anyway because we don't have anything close to air superiority in the area. He's requesting immediate close air support."

Colonel Kevin Martin, who had listened intently to the Lieutenant's update, scratched the two day stubble on his chin as he took the facts in and tried to visualize that sector of the battlefield and the available assets at his disposal.

American forces had slowed the enemy advance this morning, but they had not stopped it. Colonel Simmons' own flight of Comanche helicopters had represented the point of the sword in that regard, and a MLRS strike that they had called in moments before going down had severely mauled the forward elements of the enemy advance in this section of the battlefield.

"In fact, their calling in that strike probably saved them from capture or death to this moment," Colonel Martin thought. "If that strike had not occurred, the enemy would already have pushed well past Simmons' and Walker's location."

But that spot was now exactly where the enemy was focusing, and the efforts to rescue the two aviators were now serving to sharpen the enemy's focus.

Due to the instability of the air situation, the sector's JSTAR battlefield control aircraft, with its synthetic aperture radar and combat control capabilities, was well off to the southwest and was not in position to cover the downed aircrew, or the forward headquarters from which Colonel Martin operated for that matter…and these facts deeply concerned the Colonel.

"Okay, get on the line to HQ and request a priority air support package to assist in the extraction of these guys. Ask 'em to bring up the JSTAR aircraft to cover this entire section of the battlefield and request whatever CAP they have for the job.

"We need a heavy duty CAP to drive off the enemy aircraft and keep them off…and we need to sanitize the ground area of enemy armor and mechanized units. Have Walker operate as our on-the-ground forward air controller (FAC) to coordinate the support he needs to keep from being captured or overrun, and to prepare the area for extraction."

May 21, 2009, 03:59 local time
Forward Headquarters, GIR 7th Army
95 Miles Northeast of Damascus
Syria, GIR

General Abduhl Selim considered the information coming in from the front. The Americans were focusing efforts on a non-critical portion of the forward portion of the battlefield, and that mystified him. That position was neither strategic nor very defensible. Why would they be focusing their efforts there?

"Go over it one more time, Captain. I want to know the details of how this pitched battle developed."

The captain, a man ten years older than the general himself, but one who had come to respect the general's experience and his leadership just the same, reviewed for General Selim what they knew.

"General, we were ahead of schedule at 0230 hours when the Americans began interdicting our forward elements with attack helicopters protected by a strong CAP.

"Your order of 0245, committing the reserve air units, served to blunt this American effort, but did not fully contain it. Our forward progress was severely curtailed by a massive American missile strike at 0320. That strike was not an attack by their new missiles. It was an attack by short range ballistic missiles that we analyzed and determined to be from forward deployed American MLRS units off to our southwest.

"In fact, we were able to backtrack the missiles' trajectory and utilize a combination of SU-35 and SU-25 aircraft to locate and destroy two batteries of American MLRS units involved in that attack.

"Very soon after that attack, our fighter aircraft in that sector broke through the American air cover and savaged several flights of American attack helicopters, some of which had served as forward air control for the missile strike we had experienced only a few moments before.

"The pitched battle began to mount shortly thereafter as our forward units began advancing into the area where the American helicopters were downed. The force on force structure has escalated ever since, focusing around a minor outcropping of rock…"

The Captain leaned over the map, checked his figures and then pointed to an otherwise nondescript portion of the map that had numerous green unit markers on it representing GIR forces, confronted by a smaller number of red markers representing American forces.

"…here. This is where the air and armor forces are converging on both sides."

Clearly, someone, or something, of great import to the Americans had gone down there. Something they felt was worth concentrating all of this firepower to protect or save.

"How can I use that against them?" the General asked himself.

"If I can but hold the Americans in place in this exposed position for enough time, perhaps…"

Looking at the map and the lay of the land, as well as the advancing units in that particular sector, the young general quickly saw a set of conditions he felt he could capitalize on.

"Captain, contact the commanders of these four armored battalions from the 73rd and the 27th mechanized infantry division here, that are now approaching the battle. I have new orders for them.

"In the meantime, contact General Abin and inform him of my intention to draw from our air force's assets towards the coast. I want another wing of J-10s and two wings of SU-35 aircraft directed here immediately."

May 21, 2009, 04:17 local time
Rock Outcropping
85 Miles Northeast of Damascus
Syria, GIR

Marty Walker surveyed the terrain and the conditions around him. Thus far he had been able to call in significant air and fire support on advancing GIR formations and avoid capture or death.

Those GIR units that had initially tried to capture him" and the colonel had all been destroyed or dispersed by the support he had received, but the overall GIR advance had continued and had partially enveloped his position to either side. A few moments ago several American Bradley Fighting Vehicles had gotten to within two hundred yards in an attempt to rescue them, but they had then had to withdraw under intense enemy fire that had destroyed three of the units and sent the others back to the west.

During the fighting there had been three SAR wave-offs, and one SAR helicopter had been shot down by enemy fire. From the fireball that had resulted off to his south and west, he knew there were no survivors. But he knew that the situation had gone beyond saving him or Colonel Simmons…although keeping Colonel Simmons out of enemy hands was something he had been directed to ensure at all costs, and something to which his command was willing to dedicate tremendous resource as well.

Now there was a pitched battle going on all around him. The enemy was pouring more and more men, materiel, and aircraft into this area of the battlefield, matching and trying to outdo American efforts. Based on what he was hearing over the radio, over twenty enemy aircraft had broken off from one of their large formations and attacked the U.S. JSTAR aircraft that was covering the area well off to the south.

Although all twenty of those enemy aircraft had been shot down, five of them had gotten close enough to the JSTAR to launch medium ranged radar-guided missiles at the large American aircraft and it had been hit and brought down, lost with all of its crew. It was a tremendous loss to allied forces–and it would prove to be a costly one.

Marty was amazed that he and the colonel were still alive. There had been a few very close calls involving tank fire, enemy air attacks and enemy missile attacks. Twice, enemy infantry, despite the supporting attacks by American aircraft, had very nearly overrun his position, and he had been forced on one of those occasions to use his service pistol to shoot and kill the last two attackers.

The colonel remained unconscious, but his condition had stabilized as a result of instructions Marty had received over his radio and the crude application of a tourniquet to his mangled leg. Every so often Marty loosened that tourniquet a little for a few moments in the hopes that some circulation would get down into the lower leg. But from the looks of the horrible wound, and the extent of the severed flesh, Marty doubted much blood was getting there or that the leg could be saved unless they got Colonel Simmons out of here very soon.

Now, a final attempt to reach their position and extract him and the colonel was about to be made by an entire company of M1-A1 Abrams tanks and a battalion of mechanized infantry. It was to be accompanied by the largest surge of American aircraft yet that would try to gain at least temporary air superiority over this section of the battlefield. If they did, a helicopter extraction would be attempted under the covering fire of the armor and the mechanized units. If not, then those units themselves would extract the two men from that outcropping of rock that was now serving as their fragile fortress.

May 21, 2009, 04:32 local time
Forward Headquarters, GIR 7th Army
95 Miles Northeast of Damascus
Syria, GIR

The Americans were committing their strength just as Abduhl Selim had hoped. When it came to rescuing one of their own, they were very predictable. What he considered the foolish American resolve to rescue their own at all costs was something Selim had seen used against them on a smaller scale several times. He now intended to use it against them on an even larger scale.

Their major thrust was now underway, pointed towards that insignificant outcropping of rock…and that seemingly insignificant rock formation had their full attention. He had committed just enough forces there…actually large numbers of men and equipment…to hold their attention and convince them that they would have to themselves make an equal or larger commitment if they were to accomplish their objective.

It had been a quick-witted and dicey decision. Too little force, and the Americans would accomplish their task too quickly and pull back away from the trap Selim planned for them. Too much force, and the Americans would realize they could not accomplish their objective and would withdraw from the trap as well. Abduhl believed he had timed and proportioned it just right.

Now, though, it looked like the American rescue effort, if indeed that was what it was, would be at least temporarily successful. It would only appear that way because the GIR forces in the area were using that initial degree of success as a lure. The GIR forces in that immediate area would intentionally appear not strong enough to stop them.

And that was just fine. As Selim hoped, it would serve to pull the Americans further in. For that very purpose the general had spent the last half hour rerouting and redirecting significant forward forces to the west of the outcropping to serve as his main thrust. With the destruction of the American battlefield control aircraft, despite the significant losses in achieving it, Abduhl was now confident he could pull off his overall plan successfully.

Turning to his chief of staff, the general issued the necessary orders.

"Have the 73rd and the 27th begin their advance now. Make sure they understand that our air forces and other committed units will be holding the enemy in place to their east, and that their main task is to completely envelope the partial envelopment we have already accomplished at the focal point…and to do it in strength.

"We will allow the 17th, the 3rd and the 51st divisions, which are advancing as a part of our 2nd echelon, to completely destroy any remaining resistance the Americans caught in our trap might care to offer."

May 21, 2009, 04:45 local time
Rock Outcropping
85 Miles Northeast of Damascus
Syria, GIR

For just a brief moment, Jess Simmons came to. He was very groggy and his pain was intense, but he realized he was being carried by several men and he could hear the sounds of a Black Hawk helicopter increasing the speed of its rotor as it prepared to take off. Above that noise, the sound of a pitched battle could be heard. The heavy *crack* of tank fire interspersing the sound of explosions, and automatic weapon fire seemed to be coming from all around…most of it very nearby.

Jess slowly opened his eyes and saw Marty's shoulder above him to the left. He realized that Marty was one of four soldiers that were carrying him on a stretcher…and his memory began to return.

The crash…they were down. But for how long? He saw Marty glance down at him, notice his open eyes, and smile at him.

"Hang in there, Colonel Simmons. We have some welcome visitors here and we're about to get you on board this beautiful Black Hawk and get you the hell away from here. Just hang on!"

Marty stopped talking and turned away as they approached the waiting helicopter and passed the end of the stretcher he was carrying to a corpsman reaching out of the helicopter. As this was happening, Jess Simmons sighed and closed his eyes.

"So we survived the crash," he thought…but then an intense pain on right side of his head, coupled with a terrible spasm in the thigh of his injured leg caused him to black out and lose consciousness once again.

As Marty and one of the other medics climbed into the aircraft, and as the door gunner fired a long burst of machine gun fire at a target somewhere to their right, the helicopter's rotor rapidly gathered speed, and the sound of the jet engines pitched to a scream. Then, the Black Hawk tilted slightly forward and took off into the earliest bare shade of gray of the morning.

May 21, 2009, that same time
Forward Command Post, U.S. Forces
80 Miles Northeast of Damascus
Syria, GIR

"They've got him! Sir, they've just taken off and are under a secure CAP making their way back to the rear. They indicate that Colonel Simmons' condition is critical, but stabilized for the moment.

"Ground units are beginning to pull back, but report heavy fire coming from all sides and that their corridor for escape is rapidly shrinking and closing…

As the Lieutenant said these words, Colonel Martin urgently held up his hand.

"Hold on a minute, Lieutenant. Everybody be quiet."

As a few whispered comments circulated amongst the command staff, the colonel became more insistent.

"I said, BE QUIET!

"Can you hear that… to our rear? Sounds like heavy engines and tracks."

Then, from fewer than five hundred yards to their rear, as soon as the first GIR main battle tank in the column cleared the hill above the headquarters encampment, the unmistakably loud *CRACK* of that first GIR tank's main gun was heard, followed by the almost instantaneous explosion of one of the fuel trucks situated a mere 100 feet from the command tent.

As the Colonel shouted, "Everybody out of the tent! We are under attack!" an entire barrage of fifteen 120mm main guns sounded from the advancing company of GIR T-90 tanks. They were targeting the three M3 Bradley Fighting Vehicles and the four TOW missile-armed HMMVs tasked with providing security for the camp. They also were targeting the command and control vehicle version of the M3 and the tent it was parked next to…the command tent itself.

The resulting explosions destroyed two of the M3 IFVs and all four HMMVs outright. They severely damaged the command and control Bradley and also completely destroyed the command tent where Colonel Martin had just been listening to the briefing regarding the successful extraction of Simmons and Walker. Every person inside the command tent, including Colonel Martin, was killed before they had time to escape.

The troops caught in the American forward headquarters returned brave, but largely ineffective fire. Similarly, the surviving Bradley put up a heroic fight. But sixteen enemy T-90 tanks rolled into the camp and crushed every bit of that resistance, losing two of their number to the Bradley and having another tank disabled by ground fire from the troops.

The American headquarters facility was completely and utterly destroyed. With that destruction, the envelopment of over eight thousand forward American troops and their equipment was completed, and another rung in the rising ladder that was General Abduhl Selim's list of accomplishments was achieved. Around the Middle East, amongst GIR enlisted soldiers and officers alike…and spreading to the high command, Selim was now being referred to more and more often by his new nickname…as the Mahdi's Young Lion.

May 28, 2009, 09:35
Near the Lincoln Memorial
Washington, D.C.

Johnny Chen knew he had to be particularly careful. His Chinese features were not overly apparent, but it was obvious that he was of Far Eastern descent and these days in America, that almost always garnered additional attention from both the authorities and from normal citizens who might otherwise be considered simple passersby. Given Johnny's current task, any attention was bad.

He simply did not want to be remembered by anyone who might see him around the national monuments today. It was too close to the date of the operation, but it was also a final reconnoiter that Johnny alone had to make.

In an effort to try to deflect any unwarranted or undesired attention, Johnny always had an "America – Love it or Leave it" sticker on his small Toyota pickup truck, which was now parked not far away. Also, he always went out of his way to find clothes that were made in America, and was always willing to talk about his loyalty to American-made products to anyone who would listen.

During his drive across America for this operation, he had had numerous conversations with individuals about the state of affairs in the world, particularly with those who mentioned his Far Eastern features. He always made it a point to leave them with the firm knowledge that Johnny Chen was a loyal American, who had been here many years, who had come from the Republic of China–from Free China–and who detested with a passion the Communist rulers of the mainland. By the time he and whomever he talked with parted company, he usually had them believing that here was one Chinaman who was willing to lay down his life for his country.

…and he was.

The only problem, of course, was that his country was in fact the People's Republic of China, and everything about the facts of his history was a lie…with the exception of his being here in America for many years.

Those many years ago, Johnny's route into the United States had taken him over the southern border as what the Americans termed an "OTM illegal alien," OTM standing for "other than Mexican." This was as opposed to the use of the many COSCO container ships visiting American ports back in those years that had delivered other Chinese émigrés directly to American harbors.

If he had been caught while crossing he would have simply been lumped into the early statistics of the Immigration and

Naturalization Service's (INS) OTM statistics and returned to Taiwan where his meager paperwork indicated he was from.

But Johnny had not been caught, and it had turned out that getting into the United States across her southern border had been ridiculously easy…and up until the actual outbreak of major hostilities in 2005 and 2006, it had remained so.

That was why Johnny still had the "sleeper" contacts and the resources to work with in operation he was about to unfold. Those types of contacts and resources had already served him well once before in the conflict with America. It had been Johnny who had infiltrated Vandenberg Air Force Base in California over a year and a half ago in September of 2007 and shot down a Titan IV B booster that was carrying a critical new American KH-12 satellite into orbit.

Due to his good fieldcraft and training, and due to his patience, Johnny had completely escaped the dragnet put out by American authorities on that occasion and had returned to his job at a local Lompoc, California, dry cleaning business. His cover had been that he was on vacation, and he had the receipts and the testimony of hotel clerks to prove it, had he ever required an alibi. But the need had never arisen and the U.S. authorities were still trying to solve who had shot down that Titan rocket now, over 18 months later.

But that was then, and this was now. Johnny had already been in the Washington, D.C. area for ten days and had met with his team three times. They had reviewed their part, reviewed each of the assignments and the positioning over and over. All of them had been to the area around the memorial for a personal look, and now Johnny was here today for one last look at the terrain where he and his team would play out their part in the operations three days from now, on Saturday, May 31st, during the big festivities.

Johnny knew that at least two other teams, maybe more, would be involved and that those teams were from at least one other nationality. He was relatively certain that long hidden and very important operatives like him from one or more of the Islamic nations would be involved, but he was totally compartmentalized in his own plans and had no contact with the other team or teams, and had no awareness of what their specific plans would be.

"Probably several different attempts will be made, ensuring that at least one of them will be completely successful," he thought as he strolled past the monument and onto the circular drive that surrounded the Lincoln Memorial and provided access to it.

Johnny knew that the Americans could not be allowed to savor their victories of last fall. The festivities on Saturday meant to accomplish just that. For the Americans, the day was intended to honor those victories, particularly the one in Alaska. To tell their people that they were back in charge and had the enemy backpedaling. For Johnny, Saturday would be directed at showing the Americans that no one was safe, that their victories were meaningless for their people here at home…that not even their heroes were secure. No not even here in their very capital.

He contemplated the impact on American morale that a successful mission would have as he walked down the sidewalk along the intersecting road that led to where Independence Avenue and Ohio Drive came together just south of the Memorial. At this point, across Ohio Drive, along the Potomac River, would be where he and his team would be set up. There was a food vendor there…a friend, set well away from the immediate security zone of the festivities that would be occurring in front of the Lincoln Memorial. The food stand was on the sidewalk there that paralleled the street, leading to parking areas that served the Memorial and West Potomac Park.

Walking on the other side of the street past that food stand, he checked the fields of vision and fire one more time. Everything continued to look good and he was more certain than ever that if events on Saturday caused the action to flow his way as anticipated, he and his team would be in the perfect position to successfully fulfill their mission.

May 29, 2009, 16:23
Outside of the Oval Office
The White House
Washington, DC.

Sitting just outside of the door to the Oval Office in the White House, Stacey Urkut marveled at the fact that she was actually here, about to talk personally to the President of the United States in his office, the Oval Office.

From the battlefield encounter with Colonel Kensington, she had been flown to Anchorage on May 2nd and had been allowed a generous two days to get herself oriented to living back in civilization...and to get cleaned up, for which she had been extremely grateful. Then, she had spent almost an entire week working with intelligence officers and members of the command staff for the entire Alaskan theater, sharing with them what she knew and what she had experienced. It may not have seemed like a formal debriefing to her, but the military command in Alaska was very anxious...and very grateful...for the opportunity to in fact debrief her.

On May 11th she was flown to Seattle, Washington, where an event in her honor was held and where she met the Governor of the State of Washington and the Vice President of the United States, John Bowers. From there, she and the Vice President had made their way across the United States where Stacey had the opportunity to speak at several rallies in cities from Los Angeles to Salt Lake City to Denver to Dallas to Atlanta, Chicago, Philadelphia and Baltimore.

For security reasons, the Vice President had traveled with her only so far as Dallas. Thereafter she was in the company of the Secretary of Defense, George Crowler, who had been as gracious an escort as the Vice President had been.

She had arrived in Washington, D.C., only yesterday for her long awaited meeting with President Weisskopf. She was sitting outside his office now waiting for that meeting which she had been told would begin momentarily.

A young man, her escorting Secret Service agent, was sitting just across the hall from her. His name was Burt Stevens and he was the head of the President's Secret Service detail.

He had been very nice, and had engaged her about her experiences in Alaska as they had made their way from the entry area here to the Oval Office, and as they had sat here for the last three or four minutes. Coming from a military background himself, the agent had appreciated what Stacey had been through and had been very understanding, complementing her on a job well done.

The door to the office opened and the President's Chief of Staff came out, noticed Stacey and offered his hand to her.

"Mrs. Urkut, welcome to Washington, D.C. Welcome to the White House.

"The President is very anxious to meet you. Please, follow me. He is available now."

After shaking the Chief of Staff's hand warmly, Stacey followed him into the room.

And there it was. Just as you would see on TV, or in the history books. The large desk, the pictures, the windows with the views outside...and the President getting up from the desk and stepping across the room to greet her.

"Mrs. Urkut, it such a pleasure, and I must say, an honor to finally meet you."

The President met her halfway across the room between his desk and a grouping of couches and chairs where four other gentlemen were already seated. He shook her hand graciously and then offered to have her sit in that grouping of chairs.

"Mrs. Urkut, allow me to introduce these four gentlemen to you. I believe you already know George Crowler, the Secretary of Defense. This is Fred Reissinger, our Secretary of State and this is General Jeremy Stone, the Chairman of the Joint Chiefs of Staff."

Turning to the fourth man, the President continued.

"And this is JT Sampson. You may be aware of his internet news site, SierraLines. Although it is somewhat out of the ordinary, because of his relationship to this administration, he is here today to listen to and report on this meeting to the American people. He will also, if you are willing, conduct an exclusive interview with you after the meeting…to get the more personal side of your story out to the American people.

"That interview is entirely up to you, Mrs. Urkut. Do not feel shy about refusing any interview with the press."

Everyone in the room, including JT Sampson, chuckled at this.

"But I will personally vouch for JT. He has been the most honest, most thorough, and most understanding editor or news executive I have ever met…and he is a loyal American to boot."

As the President introduced each of the gentlemen, they each stood and shook hands with Stacey, briefly expressing their gratitude to her and their thanks at meeting her.

Stacey recognized George Crowler immediately from her time on the road coming to Washington, D.C. She also recognized Secretary Reissinger from so many news reports over the last several years as the international scene became more and more unstable and strained. But she was not as well acquainted with the General, who preferred to stay in the background, working with the various chairmen of the military branches, executing the orders and policies of their commander in chief and his Secretary of Defense.

She was very familiar with JT Sampson. She had tracked the growth of his site on the internet from its early days, when he had personally run almost all of it with his wife, and when so many of his writers and editors had been just ordinary Americans trying to be involved. She was proud of JT, from his personal early involvement in issues, like the Klamath Basin Water Crisis of 2001, all the way through his tremendous rise as a news powerhouse during the election of President Weisskopf in 2004.

"Thank you, Mr. President, and all of you gentlemen. It is I who feel honored and awed to be here in your presence. Thank you for inviting me…it is something I never expected, and certainly never sought.

"JT, I will be happy to give you that interview. I have admired you for several years as I lurked on the Independent Republic web site and heard so much about SierraLines. We were all riveted by your reporting and by reporting from members of the Independent Republic regarding the Klamath Basin Crisis in 2001.

"Thank you for that involvement and example."

JT knew that his opportunity to engage Stacey Urkut in later conversation was now a certainty. He was grateful for the President's direct invitation to this meeting and the potential opportunity to have such an interview.

But he did not want to go into that in detail now. This was the President's show, so he responded to Stacey simply.

"Mrs. Urkut, your example rises far above all of that and I know that. That is precisely why the President has us all sitting here today in the Oval Office."

Thankful for the cue from JT, the President took the opportunity to get to the heart of the meeting.

"Now, Mrs. Urkut…"

Stacey respectfully interrupted the President. "Mr. President, please feel free to call me Stacey."

The President was grateful for the interruption giving him permission to address her in such a manner.

"Thank you, Stacey, I was going to ask if that would be okay. As you can see we are all overjoyed to have you here with us today. I want you to know exactly why.

"For months we have prayed that this meeting would be able to take place…that both our own efforts from this office and our military and civic personnel, as well as those of you and so many other brave Americans there in Alaska would make it possible.

"And now those efforts and the help and direction of Almighty God have opened the door and here we are.

"As you know, we are presenting you with the Medal of Freedom the day after tomorrow. It is the highest non-military award we can bestow upon a citizen of this nation. Like the Medal of Honor, it is reserved for a very select few who rise above and beyond their call as citizens of our great Republic.

"And that call as a citizen is already a high calling. Higher in my estimation than in any other country because of the blessings of liberty we enjoy in this nation. That liberty places upon each of us great responsibility to be involved…to make sure that our voices are heard such that all of our liberty can be benefited thereby…and prolonged.

"Such liberty requires high moral caliber and fiber…and this is another great responsibility of our citizens. Without that moral fiber, we cannot remain free for very long.

"So, the calling as a citizen of the United States of America is already a high one…and Stacey, you have shown all of us the epitome of not only answering that call…but rising far above it.

"Your reports from Nome, aired on the internet by you on the morning of June 23rd of last year, caught the imagination and the attention of all Americans and riveted us to our chairs, or on our feet, or wherever else we happened to be at the time.

"The invasion of America by foreign enemies, and the on-scene reporting of it in the face of grave danger will be remembered throughout our history like the ride of Paul Revere...because that is exactly what it became.

"We had already been at war for several years...and we had already been attacked brutally on our own soil...but now the enemy had come to claim that soil. It was something far too many thought could never happen.

"So despite our heightened awareness as a result of the war and so much carnage from continuing terror attacks...and despite the great lengths to which so many Americans had already gone to support the war effort...there was still a certain level of complacency. Your vivid images of that invasion and your messages that accompanied with them amounted to a clarion call that brought home the final reality and brutality of our enemies to everyone.

"As the President, and on behalf of the people, I can only humbly thank you for your willingness to do so, and for your bravery in so doing."

Stacey wanted to speak, and the President could tell that she would like to downplay what she was hearing, but the President pressed on.

"Please, Stacey, let me continue, because you are deserving of every word of praise I have uttered and more.

"After getting the message about the invasion of America out on the Independent Republic website, and after that message had been picked up by every major news service in this nation and in the free world, you continued to broadcast right up to the moment that you either had to leave or face capture or worse from our enemies.

"For most, that would have been far more than enough...but not for Stacey Urkut.

"From there you went on, as 57 year old woman behind enemy lines, to form an effective resistance movement against the Chinese invasion. You accomplished this at continual mortal danger to yourself and your brave compatriots…and you took the battle to the enemy.

"I will tell you, Stacey, your story and that of your compatriots, which you have so articulately and straight forwardly shared as you traveled here to Washington, will go down in our history as being pivotal to the cause of liberty and freedom. As in the crossing of the Delaware River, as in the battle of Gettysburg, as in our victory on Guadalcanal in World War II…your efforts kept the enemy occupied and off balance so that our military had the time to prepare for the great victories that followed last fall.

"We all thought…and I must admit, as a former military man myself, I thought…that there must have been hundreds of you in your group alone. We read the intelligence reports. We marveled at the amounts of resource the enemy was committing…and like the enemy, we underestimated you and the will of your comrades in arms.

"I cannot tell you how stunned we were to hear that you had accomplished what you did with so few.

"May God bless you, Stacey…you are probably the most deserving person in the history of our nation to receive this award. If I could legally do so, I would recommend you for the Medal of Honor."

As the President finished, the other gentlemen in the room all nodded their heads in agreement…they were simply awed at what had happened in Alaska…what had set the stage and prepared the way for the successful defense of Anchorage, and the pushing back of the Chinese there in November of 2008, only six month ago.

There were tears in Stacey's eyes. She could tell that this was no political posturing. The President was speaking from his heart. She knew that he and others in this room had experienced the losses and the horrors that war could bring.

"Mr. President, I do not know what to say. I only did what I felt compelled to do in the face of such aggression against our country and against my friends and neighbors.

"So many have died. So many have been hurt…have lost everything.

"I simply cannot accept, for myself only, the honors you bestow …"

As Stacey paused, everyone in the room felt the slightest stirrings of unease in the pit of their stomach. America needed her heroes…now more than ever…and Stacey Urkut was a hero to the nation. One the nation needed, just as they had needed Leon Campbell and others up to this point in the conflict. What would they do if Stacey Urkut simply would not accept?

As the President prepared to interject, Stacey relieved all of their anxiety.

"But I will accept it on behalf of all of those who fought with me. They are the true heroes…from young men barely 16 years of age, to old Native American council leaders in their sixties. Their stories are the ones that really need to be told…not a middle-aged woman's like mine. I will also accept it on behalf of all of those who suffered so much through the Chinese occupation.

"I just pray for all Americans that our forces are victorious…very soon…and for all free people everywhere thereafter. We are trusting you, Mr. President, and these capable men and women around you…and our brave personnel in the field all over the world, to make sure that happens.

"I know now, from my travels, from seeing firsthand all across this nation how people have come together to face our enemies…that it also depends on each and every one of us. I am thankful for the opportunity to do my part whenever and wherever I can."

May 30, 2009, 22:50
Room 2312, Hyatt Hotel
Washington, D.C.

Sitting in their room watching an old John Wayne/Jimmy Stewart movie, Joe and Elizabeth Trevor basked in one another's presence.

So much had happened over the last several years and it had all served to draw them together. Their difficulties in having children…Joe's dedication to his work and Elizabeth's struggles to come to terms with that dedication during that time period: the events leading up to Joe's first Nobel Award with the Human Reasoning Structures, or HRS as they were now well known; the war and Elizabeth's close call with death at the hand of terrorists outside of the Raythone facility in Salem, New Hampshire; the excruciating events and feeling associated with working with Saundra McPherson, and what they had both viewed as her underhandedness in dealing with Joe's methodologies and her use of it in furtherance of her quasi-legal fetal tissue studies; the unmitigated joy at how that very work had led to the discovery of the HRS in fetal tissue, and how it led to the overturn of abortion practice in the United States with the pivotal Supreme Court decision last year; and how that had led to a Noble Prize for Saundra McPherson, who had experienced a dramatic change of heart, and who was now their close friend–and who was in fact just down the hall from them now.

Through all of those experiences, Joe and Elizabeth's relationship had grown until now they could both say, without reservation, that they were of one heart and one mind. And they had been of one heart and mind in the decision to travel down here to Washington, D.C. to watch the presentation of the Medal of Freedom to Stacey Urkut for her phenomenal activities during the Chinese invasion of Alaska.

Reflecting on all of this and on the dramatic turn of events in the war effort, Elizabeth sat up from watching the movie and took her husband's hand in her own.

"Hon, isn't it phenomenal what is happening?" Elizabeth asked with excitement. "I mean, look at our own lives and the events we have been blessed to be a part of.

"It just seems like there is such a tremendous outpouring now and it's affecting so many people all over the world. Like we've turned a corner or passed through a critical juncture in all of this, and are actually making up ground.

"As the President said in his Christmas speech, the Hand of Providence, our Father in Heaven, is lending us His support now . While I have no doubts that there's still a lot of pain and anguish we are all going to experience…"

Speaking of pain and anguish immediately brought thoughts and feelings of her close friend, Cindy Simmons, and reminded her that not everything was rosy or would be considered a *tremendous outpouring* by those adversely affected.

Cindy Simmons had been planning to join them here for the presentation. It was going to be one of the biggest public events and celebrations in American history, certainly the largest since the beginning of the war. But Cindy had called a few days before they were scheduled to leave and informed them of Jess's critical injuries in the fighting in Syria and his serious condition.

"…Cindy's pain is just a little too close to us for us not to recognize that…but still, we have to honor people like Mrs. Urkut in what she accomplished and our armed forces who achieved the victory in Alaska.

"Things like that need to be an example to us all, and help us through things like what Cindy is experiencing. I'm even more anxious to get down to Texas and help her prepare for Jess' homecoming as a result of this."

Joe listened to what his wife had said. She was always close to the true spirit of things while he plodded along pragmatically and analytically in her wake. As a result, over the years, after they had been able to overcome some of the natural friction that such differing approaches created, they had discovered that they could compliment one another extremely well. Once they made the mental decision to focus on the complimentary nature of their differences instead of the potential friction…their relationship had matured naturally, allowing them to face trials together that otherwise might have torn them apart.

"Honey, I am excited about all of this too…and I look forward to the events of tomorrow and getting back down to Texas for a few weeks to help Cindy. I hope we can be there when Jess gets home …I can't wait to see his smiling face…and you know that guy will be smiling no matter what else.

"Who knows, we might just, as they say in Texas, stay a while, and help him get back in shape on his ranch. We can certainly afford it, and I can get the time off at work if necessary.

"In the meantime, scoot over a little and sit back so I can see John Wayne, would ya?"

May 31, 2009, 11:53
Presentation Stand
In front of the Lincoln Memorial
Washington, D.C.

The presentations and festivities had been under way for over an hour. Dignitaries from all around the country were speaking and extending their congratulations and thanks to the President, the armed forces, and to the guest of honor, Stacey Urkut. Other honored guests from all over the free world had made their way here…to honor and commemorate the victories of late last year and the offensive operations they had generated that were continuing that very day.

Over one million people were literally filling up the Constitutional Gardens that ran from the Lincoln Memorial to the Washington Monument, and The Mall that ran from there back to the

Capitol building. An excellent sound system was strung up all along the way, all around the Reflecting Pool back beyond the Washington Monument, so that everyone could hear.

People were assembled at the Vietnam Memorial and around it, in the trees in between and as far away as the Jefferson Memorial where a special gathering area had been set up for overflow visitors. Video displays were set up for live feeds of the proceedings at all of these places, and throughout the wooded areas in between so everyone who was not in a direct line of sight...or was too far away...could watch the events.

People were picnicking with their families. The temperature was warm, but not oppressive for a late spring day in the nation's capitol. The press was broadcasting live to an excited and hungry nation. The good news was contagious and the viewing and listening audience for the event was expected to be one of the largest ever in the free world.

Security was tight.

The Secret Service was, of course, out in force surrounding the President close in to the presentation platform, and surveying all of the ground and air approaches thereto. The Park Service Police, augmented by the Capital police, were spread liberally throughout the crowd–almost six hundred officers present watching for any suspicious activity or movement in the crowd. There were over fifteen hundred National Guardsmen manning blockades, checkpoints and observation points in, and particularly around, the huge crowd. Over two thousand Marines were on alert.

Around the entire perimeter police and National Guard helicopters were patrolling from the air. Higher overhead, a combat air patrol of no fewer that sixteen F-22 Raptor aircraft surveilled the entire region. The ground-based Aegis Ballistic Defense missile batteries around the capitol were on their highest degree of alert and, along the Potomac, no fewer that three Aegis vessels, one cruiser, and two destroyers augmented the ground-based missile defense.

The presentation to Stacey Urkut of the Medal of Freedom was supposed to occur promptly at noon. It was one of the principle highlights of the day. The President was about to approach the podium and make his own speech prior to presenting the award, after which time Stacey Urkut would speak to the entire nation, and the free world, herself.

Joe and Elizabeth Trevor and Saundra McPherson were seated fifteen rows back in front of the presentation stand in an area reserved for VIPs and special guests. That section extended over fifty rows back and seated over two thousand foreign dignitaries, high ranking government officials, and other guests of note like the Trevors.

Saundra McPherson, sitting next to her friend Elizabeth Trevor, was proud to be here.

"Yes," she thought, "Proud."

It amazed her. Where a little over a year ago she had been totally cynical of her government in general, and particularly belligerent towards the Weisskopf administration, now she sat in rapt attention at the presentation of an award by this administration for efforts in a war that a year ago she would have called unnecessary at best, and self-inflicted at worst. But now all of that had changed.

The unexpected discovery of the Human Reasoning Structures in early fetal tissue from Europe that she was digitally modeling had literally changed her world and the world around her. It had altered her worldview, and opened up the opportunity for the patriotic fervor that she felt today…something she had never really felt before.

Once she knew, beyond doubt, that the fetus was a living, reasoning human, like most of America she had stepped back in revulsion from what she had been doing. She was just surprised and ashamed that she had not realized it earlier, that it had taken an unmistakable and unarguable scientific proof to draw a conclusion that her own common sense should have told her long ago. She had already determined that she would spend the rest of her life making up for her previous, misguided beliefs.

Now, here she was, with her good friends the Trevors, and the President was beginning to address them as he prepared to present Stacey Urkut, a woman about Saundra's own age, a medal for heroism and citizen involvement that went above and beyond her normal duty as a citizen.

"My fellow Americans, as other speakers before me have already indicated, we are gathered here today…"

May 31, 2009, that same time
3 Miles Away in Quincy Park
Arlington, Virginia

The equipment had been unloaded and set up now for several minutes, partially obscured by the three pickup trucks in which it had all arrived. There, at the northeast corner of Quincy Park, those three pickup trucks were now parked in a triangular shape, right on the grass of the park as two of the drivers prepared to open up the end of the triangle and allow the *packages* to depart.

As they did, three ultralight aircraft throttled up their engines and began rolling along the grass to the southwest.

All three aircraft were outfitted with very powerful engines that developed much more horsepower than normal ultralight engines required. All three of the frames of these particular ultralights were made of very light, very strong, and very expensive composite material that allowed the aircraft to carry up to five times their normal weight. And each of them was carrying that full weight today.

One small-framed pilot was on a no return mission in each aircraft, strapped to 500 pounds of heavy explosives encased in shrapnel of all types.

As all three small aircraft cleared the pickup trucks and gathered speed in the open park, the leader of the team, who was known in America as Sam Hennison, but whose birth name was actually Sami al-Hinnasi, stood in the middle of the vacant ground between the trucks and silently bid them farewell.

"Go with God, Allah Ahkbar!"

May 31, 2009, that same time
Driving North on Quincy
Approaching Washington Blvd.
Arlington, Virginia

Nate Thomlason caught movement out of the corner of his eye as he approached the intersection of Quincy Avenue and Washington Boulevard.

He had seen the three late model pickup trucks in his peripheral vision sitting in the park and figured they were just some local people enjoying the late spring weather by picnicking in the park. But the movement from between the trucks attracted his attention.

Slowing down and turning his head for a better look, he saw the three ultralight airplanes lumber out from between the trucks that he realized now were further apart than he had thought. But it was those three ultralight aircraft that caught his attention.

"Those aren't supposed to be here," he said to himself.

"What in the world do those people think they're doing?"

Thomlason was an off-duty member of the local Home Guard Unit here in this part of Arlington. Having been an active member of the Home Guard for over two years now, he made it his business to know the Homeland Security rules for the area. There was a flight restriction for all light aircraft this close to the D.C. area, and all ultralights had to fly at least six miles further out.

"They're less than three miles from the Potomac River here," he thought.

And then, as realization flooded into his mind, he voiced his thoughts out loud.

"My God, the big presentation over at the Lincoln Memorial!"

Nate always carried his communications gear with him in his vehicle, as well as his M-14 rifle. It was something that would have been unheard of four years ago, but it was a fact of life now.

As he came to a quick stop while pulling up to the curb, Nate called in his report of the three ultralight aircraft, which were now lifting off from the grass and becoming airborne, and asked for backup. He then grabbed his rifle and exited his vehicle.

May 31, 2009, three minutes later
Private Garage on F street near 21st
Washington, D.C.

At the appointed time, the large garage door opened and very quickly, three heavy-duty, armored, panel vans, labeled with official-looking Brinks Security logos drove out of the garage and separated. Two turned right onto F Street and headed for 21st, while one turned left and headed for 23rd.

All three had additional armor on their sides and the latest armored glass on their windshields. It was the specially engineered glass armor that allowed those inside to shoot out through the windows, but would stop high velocity bullets from penetrating it. All three were loaded with over four tons of high explosives.

The first two vans turned south on 21st and crossed Virginia Avenue, in full view of a platoon of National Guard soldiers who had a blockade set up across C street, on the far side of 21st.

The first van picked up speed and drove directly for the concrete roadblock that was designed to keep trucks from driving through the blockade and penetrating further into their perimeter. But this van had no intention of trying to get past the blockade. Its sole purpose was to destroy it.

The soldiers, who for an instant had been fooled by the official looking nature of the security van, now began shouting for the van to stop. As it crossed C Street towards them, they opened fire and people in the vicinity began to scream and scatter.

The fire was ineffective in stopping the heavily armored van, which ran headlong into the concrete barrier and then detonated with a deafening explosion that engulfed the entire squad of troops, several of the concrete barriers and a number of bystanders. The shock wave and blast severely damaged the structures along C Street and set off fires, while tossing around the people within its reach–and breaking them–like so many twigs.

The driver of the second van had held back to watch the effects of the explosion. He closed his eyes immediately before the blast and said a silent prayer to Allah. The blast passed over and shook the van terribly, but it did not destroy it. As the dust was hanging heavily in the air, the driver started forward to make use of the path that had just been blown in the security perimeter surrounding the presentation at the Lincoln Memorial that had just been so loudly and brutally interrupted.

May 31, 2009, 11:58
Presentation Stand
In front of the Lincoln Memorial
Washington, D.C.

The explosion had been several hundred yards away from the ceremonies and no one in the immediate vicinity of the President or the crowd there had been injured…yet.

The President was just about to wrap up his remarks and present the Medal of Freedom to Stacey Urkut when he had caught just the slightest out of place motion out along the diagonal road that led from the Memorial circular drive over to the intersection of 21st and Constitution Avenue, where C Street could also just barely be seen beyond. When he turned his head in that direction to get a better view, the large truck bomb had gone off.

As the smoke and dust cloud was angrily billowing up, and as the President watched the rapid advance of the shockwave along the diagonal road, bedlam broke loose around the presentation stand.

Panic took hold of most of the people in the dignitary area and then in the large crowd behind it, a pandemonium that spread like wildfire and had people rushing madly to get away from the detonation. That mad rush, and others like it in the next fifteen minutes, would be the most lethal part of the attack.

Two Secret Service agents, one the head of the detail, Burt Stevens, rushed over to grab the President so they could protect him and guide him towards his armored limo which was parked a good hundred feet away from the presentation stand. Just as they reached for him, the shockwave from the bomb arrived and knocked them all to the ground. As his protectors got up off of him–they had covered him with their own bodies–the President quickly regained his feet and looked for his wife.

There she was, not fifteen feet away and just beginning to get up off the ground herself, her own Secret Service agent detail already standing protectively around her.

"Burt, you've got to get me, the First Lady, the Secretary of Defense, and Mrs. Urkut to the limo and away from here," the President ordered as the agents quickly combined them all into one group. "What are you hearing?"

As the agents surrounded and protected them, and began to guide them all behind the presentation stand towards the limo and the rest of the security detail vehicles parked on the circular drive, the head of detail quickly responded to the President.

"Nothing yet, Mr. President, just lots of unanswered questions. We'll know more momentarily, I am sure. Let's just get you and the First Lady out of here."

Before getting to the limo, the head of the President's Secret Service detail received a concrete report through his ear phone which caused him to immediately begin scanning the skies around them.

"Aircraft approaching…three of them."

May 31, 2009, that same time
Secret Service Sniper and Stinger Team Position
Atop the Washington Monument
Washington, D.C.

There were two expert marksmen operating as counter-snipers and a two-man team manning a Stinger missile launcher atop the Washington Monument. By the time the explosion at C and 21st Streets occurred, that Secret Service detail had already received the call about the potential threat of ultralight aircraft. That initial report, as it filtered to them there atop the monument before the explosions, was simply of ultralight activity near Arlington, Virginia, in violation of airspace restrictions.

With the initial report, they had all hoped that the situation just represented errant citizens in violation of the flying regulations around the Capitol.

But with the tremendous explosion to the north and east of the Lincoln Memorial, and with the more detailed report now that there were in fact three ultralight aircraft approaching, all hopes of those types of simple explanations vanished. An assault was being made on the President of the United States, the man they were charged with protecting at all costs.

"There, at two o'clock, just coming over the Tidal Basin in front of the Jefferson Memorial!" one of the snipers exclaimed.

As the other sniper called in the location, and as the Stinger missile team prepared to target the aircraft, one of the members of that team noticed movement in his peripheral vision, and turned his head back towards Constitution Avenue and the White House.

"We've got another one, just crossing Constitution Avenue behind us!"

Both small aircraft were flying no more than a hundred feet off the ground and jinking wildly as they approached the Washington Monument. Both were flying at approximately 50 miles per hour.

The leader of the detail instructed the Stinger missile team to take the closer threat, the one behind them, which was now ascending and clearly making an attack on their position.

As this was occurring, a U.S. Army National Guard Black Hawk helicopter swooped in directly behind that aircraft and began pursuing it, firing an M-60 machine gun at the dodging target.

The agent holding the Stinger launcher was frustrated at the sudden appearance of the National Guard helicopter…and so was his equipment.

"I can't get a lock…I'm oscillating between the ultralight and the chopper, but it wants to target the chopper…can't you call that guy off?"

Flinching momentarily as another tremendous explosion resounded from the direction of the Lincoln Memorial, the leader of the detail had only a split second to make his decision, and it was a fateful one.

"The Guard will bring that guy down, switch to the second target. He's going to be tough to bring down with a bullet until he gets closer.

"See if you can take him before he gets across the Tidal Pool."

The Stinger team did as they were ordered, and quickly moved across the room, pivoted, got a clean lock on the approaching aircraft just as it crossed back over land…and over thousands of panicking citizens…and fired.

The stinger rocketed from the top of the Monument with a *WHOOSH*, leaving heavy smoke in its wake and momentarily blinding the agents on that side of the Monument. The missile quickly approached the ultralight, whose pilot saw it coming and immediately dove towards the crowd. Just before the missile impacted, some of the ill-fated members of the crowd below heard him yell, "Allah Ahkbar!" At that instant he detonated the package of explosives behind him and disappeared in a blinding flash, into which the Stinger missile dove, and also exploded.

Over 4,500 shards of metal, ball bearings, and other shrapnel were blasted at high velocity out of the explosion and into the crowd of people below, all of whom were now madly running from the intersection of Independence Avenue and Constitution. Scores were killed by the explosions. More still were killed by the crush and stampede of the crowd; hundreds more were injured.

At the same moment, another violent explosion occurred over towards the Lincoln Memorial as the third armored truck ignited. The pilot of the National Guard Black Hawk helicopter had no time to consider or worry about that third large explosion. His aircraft had already taken the other ultralight under fire and had wounded the pilot in his left thigh, causing the aircraft to begin to fly unstably as its pilot tried to maintain control of the aircraft. It became impossible for him to continue jinking to avoid the attacker behind him and he knew his fate was sealed.

The Black Hawk was now closing in for the kill from behind the ultralight aircraft which was only a hundred yards from the Washington Monument. Just as the gunner was preparing to take the final shots, the second terrorist pilot, finally realizing that he would never make it to his target, which had been the sniper team atop the Washington Monument all along, chose to detonate the explosives on his aircraft. In so doing at that particular instant, he unwittingly achieved his original purpose.

The explosion of the improvised destructive device threw shrapnel in all directions. Blown forward by the blast, hundreds of pieces impacted against the sides of the Washington Monument, a number of them finding their way into the observation post where the Secret Service agents were stationed. One of the agents was killed outright and another injured while below, the sky was raining shards of metal.

As the leader of the detail quickly checked for any sign of life from the dead agent, a crackling, wrenching noise in the air outside of his position drew his attention.

"My God," was all he had time to whisper to himself.

The blast from the second ultralight also expanded to the rear, and threw shrapnel behind it…right into the path of the oncoming National Guard helicopter. As the pilot madly adjusted his collective and cyclic controls to avoid the blast by climbing over and around it, the shock wave struck the helicopter and jammed both his cyclic and stabilator control systems into position. It also severely damaged the tail rotor. At the same instant, shrapnel blasted through the compartment, killing the pilot and severely wounding the copilot.

With the aircraft locked into its current attitude, the tail rotor tearing itself apart, and the helicopter beginning to spin wildly, the Black Hawk impacted the side of the Washington Monument, five feet below the doomed Secret Service detail leader and the remainder of his team, who were mercifully, quickly incinerated by the fire and blast that raced through their observation deck.

…and there was still a third ultralight.

May 31, 2009, that same time
Near the Presentation Stand
The Lincoln Memorial
Washington, D.C.

After the initial explosion, when the head of the President's Secret Service detail received word of the approaching ultralight aircraft, another warning was quickly communicated.

Another truck was seen racing east on C Street towards the site of the initial explosion. This was followed almost immediately by yet another warning, a third armored security truck was approaching along 21st Street.

Burt Stevens informed the President, "Mr. President, we have to turn around and get out of here right now…more threats are appearing all around. Two more truck bombs are coming this way and will be here before we can make the limo.

"Follow me," he urged as he led them away from the Memorial, to the south and west.

As he did so, two agents, who had retrieved a LAWS (Light Armor Weapon System) out of one of the armored Suburbans parked in the circular drive on the south side of the monument, ran to the northeast corner of the Lincoln Memorial and took up a firing position there.

Just as they got set up, there was a mad crackling of small arms fire and then another resounding explosion to their northeast, where another of the armored trucks set itself off against the last concrete blockade manned by National Guard troops, this one on Constitution Avenue.

The agents with the LAWS moved back behind the wall on the interior of the Memorial to avoid the worst of the shock wave, which blasted across the area, again knocking everyone in its path to the ground. When they returned to their position, they were greeted by the sight of an armored security van speeding madly out of the dust and debris, right down the diagonal road toward the Lincoln Memorial and the President's retreating party.

There was no time to wonder; there was no time to waste; there was only time to react in defense of their President.

"Target acquired. FIRE!" shouted the agent manning the weapon as his partner prepared another round.

But a second missile would neither be necessary, nor possible. Just feet from the circular drive, the missile impacted the onrushing truck and there was a third violent explosion. The shock wave from this explosion was not contained by trees or buildings. The two agents at the northeast corner of the Lincoln Memorial were killed immediately by the overpressure. The individuals in the President's party, now almost two hundred and fifty feet away and moving to the southwest down a slight incline away from the monument, were thrown down for a third time, this time much more violently.

As Burt Stevens got the President, who was now nursing a painfully dislocated shoulder, up–and as his comrades began carrying the First Lady, who had broken her leg, they were all briefly mesmerized by the final events at the Washington Monument, where the ultralight aircraft blew itself up in front of the pursuing National Guard helicopter, which then crashed into the Washington Monument itself.

"Dear God," the President uttered to himself. "It's like the 3-15 attack, 9-11 all over again."

May 31, 2009, that same time
Near the edge of the reflecting pool
In front of and below the Lincoln Memorial
Washington, D.C.

Between the time of the initial explosion and the helicopter crashing into the Washington Monument, no more than three minutes had passed. But, to those caught in the terror attack, those three minutes seemed like an eternity…and it wasn't over yet.

Joe Trevor had thrown his wife to the ground while urging Saundra McPherson to get down herself….and he and Elizabeth had wisely stayed there, avoiding the deadly pandemonium of the large crowd. As Joe now lifted himself up off his wife, he saw that Saundra was nowhere to be seen.

Hundreds of people were laying scattered about on the concrete and asphalt areas above them immediately in front of the presentation stand and the Lincoln Memorial. None of them were moving.

Others had been violently thrown down the steps by the last truck bomb's shock wave, towards where Joe and his wife had taken refuge against the ground. Luckily for Joe and Elizabeth, because they had gotten low to the ground there at the bottom of the steps near the end of the Reflecting Pool, and because they had stayed that way, they had been spared the worst of that last shock wave as its strength passed well above them in the air.

"Honey, we've got to get up and get out of here now," Joe said to his wife who was just coming to her senses.

As Elizabeth kneeled there next to his side, her hands clinging to his arm, Joe surveyed the situation.

To the east, thousands of people who had fled in the direction of the Washington Monument were now scattering into the trees of West Potomac Park and the Constitution Gardens. To the west, there was carnage all around the Lincoln Memorial and Joe felt that they could probably expect more attacks in that area.

To the north, from where the initial explosions had advanced, Joe could find no sane reason to try to escape in that direction.

He looked to the south and west. About one hundred yards away he saw a group of individuals picking themselves up off the ground. Several of them were obviously armed and must be Secret Service agents or plain-clothed policemen. Then he recognized the President.

"Elizabeth, look! There's the President's team."

For a moment he was tempted to get up and run to them, seeking their help and the help of the agents. In fact, his wife, Elizabeth, was already standing and starting to find her voice so she could yell to them.

Wisely, Joe pulled her back down to the ground next to him.

"Honey, get down here! No way can we approach those agents and the President now. They'll shoot anyone they don't know who comes near him.

"We have to stay down and get under more cover and move away from here. Let's move into those trees there on the other side of that sidewalk, and then move back towards the Washington Monument."

Looking in that direction, Joe started for a moment when he saw soldiers approaching from the direction of the Washington Monument. Then he recognized them as National Guard and saw that they were stopping and rendering aid to other citizens.

"Look, there's a group of National Guardsmen coming this way. Let's see if we can reach them and point them towards the President's party...maybe they can help."

May 31, 2009, that same time
Coming out of the trees
Along the Reflecting Pool
Washington, D.C.

Saundra McPherson had never been so shocked and so frightened in her life. And understandably so.

Nothing she had ever experienced had prepared her for what was happening that morning in front of the Lincoln Memorial.

Despite Joe calling to her to stay down, she had fled blindly away from the explosions as group fear took hold of her and the crowd rushed away in a panic. She had narrowly avoided being trampled herself, and had seen many bodies being run over by the feet of tens of thousands as she rushed into the trees.

Now, several minutes, and several explosions later, she was a little more calm and she started wondering where Joe and Liz were, and what had become of them.

She also reflected on the horrific events she had just witnessed and survived.

Oh, she knew they were at war…and of late she had come to appreciate the importance, the utter necessity, of her nation prosecuting that war to the fullest extent. She also knew, as did every American, about the many attacks that had been conducted against her fellow citizens and against the infrastructure of her nation–but it had never happened close to her. And until last year and her own change of heart and attitude, deep inside she somehow believed that maybe America deserved what it was getting because, in her worldview, somehow America was too rich, too well off, and therefore must be exploiting other nations.

That's what had been taught to her in her public education on countless occasions–that's what had been taught directly to her in the universities. She had come to accept it…to believe it…until she had discovered firsthand the lie of abortion. And when that lie came tumbling down within her, the others were not far behind.

Still, having a change of heart in an ideological sense is something altogether different than having the cruel, harsh, bloody reality of it staring you straight in the face…or trying to kill you. She now understood for herself, beyond a theoretical, laboratory sense, what her enemies were all about…and that was about destroying her and as many of her countrymen as possible.

After the final detonations near the Lincoln Memorial and the fighting over by the Washington Monument, Saundra stepped out into the open near the reflecting pool, about halfway between the Lincoln Memorial and the Washington Monument, on the Constitutional Garden, or north side of the pool. She saw some National Guard troops coming her way and was just raising her hand to wave to them.

That's when she noticed a loud buzzing noise coming through the tops of the trees. She looked up–and saw another ultralight aircraft bank over the tree line in front of her, and begin following the reflecting pool towards the Lincoln Memorial…on a path that would take it right over her. Transfixed, she could only stare as the small aircraft got closer and closer.

May 31, 2009, that same time
Flying low, Above the Reflecting Pool
Washington, D.C.

Mohammed al-Hinnasi, the pilot of the third, and as yet unaccounted for, ultralight aircraft, guided his plane towards the Lincoln Memorial, looking for the President of the United States and his party…hunting them.

His brothers in the faith had accomplished their mission just exactly the way his father had told them.

At 19 years of age, Mohammed was ready to sacrifice his life for Allah. He had been raised to prepare for this sacrifice. His father, since the time he was a boy here in America, had taught him to bide his time, to be patient, to be quiet and to observe…but never to forget who the Great Satan was…the great enabler of the persecutors of his people and the center for everything lewd and corrupt in the world. And he had internalized the message…learning, waiting…and now his time had come.

He had flown literally at tree-top level, his small landing wheels actually touching the highest leaves and branches at times.

Twice he had dipped into small clearings or openings in the trees to avoid police helicopters…and he had swung back to the west when his brothers attacked the Washington Monument and were spotted by that National Guard helicopter.

Now, he was certain that the other attacks he had heard and seen must have either killed the President, or flushed him from his cover.

And he was right.

As a number of National Guard troops took note of him from below, and began to raise their rifles to their shoulders to shoot at him, he observed that over beyond the tree line to his front and left was a group of individuals, several of them in dark suits carrying what had to be the distinctive submachine guns of the American Secret Service.

"Yes, there they are," he thought as he jinked his aircraft first left, and then right to avoid fire from the National Guard troops. And then he began to put pressure on the stick to steer his flying bomb in the direction of the President.

"Praise Allah!" he muttered to himself. "Accept me into the next life and shower upon me my reward of eternal bliss with my many virgins."

And in that instant, his wish to be taken into the next life was granted…though not to the reward he desired.

A brilliant bright light and thunderous explosion ended all conscious thought for Mohammed al-Hinnasi as he and his small aircraft were hit by an AIM-9X missile fired by a F-22 Raptor that had moments before picked him up out of the ground clutter, tracked him, and then fired upon him as soon as a solid infrared lock-on was achieved.

Almost immediately after the explosion created by the air-to-air missile, an even larger one occurred as the explosives Mohammed was carrying also detonated and showered the entire area with shrapnel, pieces of the aircraft…and what remained of Mohammed.

Once again, hundreds of citizens were maimed and several dozen more were killed…including, tragically, Nobel Prize winner Sandra McPherson, who was still standing there transfixed, almost immediately below Mohammed's aircraft when it was hit by the missile and exploded.

**May 31, 2009, 12:01
The Food Vendor Stand
Ohio Drive and Independence Avenue
Washington, D.C.**

Johnny and his people had watched the panicked crowd pass by after the explosions. At first a mad rush of thousands and thousands of uninjured people and the entire team had stood in the lee of the stand, fearing that the stand may topple over on them and they all be trampled...then the torrent became a rush, and that became a steady flow with more and more of the passing people having been injured. Finally, after that last explosion over the reflecting pool, the flow had diminished to a trickle.

At the first sound of the attack, his entire team had all quickly knelt down and assembled their weapons, which had been hidden inside the food containers of the food stand and which were all made of synthetic materials to avoid detection. As they did so, they also clothed themselves in their official U.S. Park Police hats and light jackets which purposely matched the trousers that each of them wore.

In that first panic, no one questioned them as they prepared to do battle. In fact, once they saw the official-looking Park Police uniforms, many looked to them for direction and Johnny and his team very coolly and professionally directed them away from the carnage towards safety further to the south and west along the Potomac and along Ohio Drive.

Then, as the crowd thinned, the team fanned out around the stand, taking up their pre-planned cover positions behind individual trees, waiting.

It had been Lin Worthington who saw them first.

"There, about two hundred yards out, just crossed Independence and moving into the Park on the other side of the diagonal."

Johnny looked that way and…there they were. It was not exactly where they had expected the President's entourage to emerge…but it would do.

There looked to be five or six agents, the President, who was holding his arm close to his body, a woman being carried by two of the agents, another man, and another woman.

"I see them. Let them move as close as they will come, and then on my command, Lin, you and I will concentrate our fire on the President. He's the tall older man in the suit holding his arm close to his body."

Turning to the three other team members, Johnny then continued.

"You three concentrate your fire on the standing agents first, and then on the two holding the other woman."

Taking their positions, they all waited on Johnny's command. As the President's group approached rapidly, but at an angle, they came nearer and nearer to what would be their closest approach to the Chinese team.

"Wait…wait…any second now."

"Uh oh, they've seen us. Open fire!"

May 31, 2009, that same time
West Potomac Park
Washington, D.C.

There hadn't been any other attacks for several seconds. Not since the U.S. Air Force had taken out the ultralight over the reflecting pond.

Stacey Urkut took stock of the situation around her.

The head of the President's Secret Service detail was talking seriously and with animation into his mouthpiece and listening to replies through his earpiece. Stevens was arranging a pickup of the entire group by Marine One in a clearing only fifty yards in front of them. The Marine helicopter with an entire squad of Marines would be there in less than three minutes.

Stacey had been shocked by the attack and the violence right here in Washington, D.C. It had taken her several minutes to get her bearings, but when she did, she was not a middle-aged woman in the pretty pantsuit anymore. She had quickly reverted back to the Orka...she had been injected into the same type of environment here in Washington that she had lived through for the past several months in Alaska.

Looking to her right, she made out several men standing in the trees over closer to the river, who appeared to be dressed in official uniforms of some type or another. Coming up next to Burt Stevens, she touched his arm and pointed them out.

"Those look like Park Police," Stevens said as he glanced that way.

"Maybe they can..." ...but then he, too, noticed their posture...their stance...and he turned his head back quickly for a better look.

Stacey began to voice what they had both already realized, the tone of her voice now catching the President's attention along with one of the other agents.

"If those are our guys, why are they shielding themselves from us with those trees?"

"And why are they..."

Before Stacey could finish, Burt Stevens suddenly ran towards the President, shouting.

"Everybody down! We're coming under attack!"

Almost immediately several things happened at once.

The supersonic snaps of bullets began sounding all around the President and the group of people with him, followed instantly by the report of small arms fire from the Chinese.

Burt Stevens went down just as he reached his President in a brave, but vain effort to get to him before he could be harmed.

The President took a bullet to his shoulder which spun him around violently and he began to fall. Before he hit the ground, another one passed cleanly through his side.

A squad of National Guard troops came out of the trees to the northwest, saw what was happening and began to pour fire at the group that was attacking the President, catching the President's party in an inadvertent crossfire which severely wounded the Secretary of Defense before he could find sufficient cover.

The two agents holding the First Lady dropped her and rushed towards the President, firing at their assailants as they came.

Another of the agents, lying in a prone position, began to provide accurate covering fire for those agents trying to reach the President.

Stacey Urkut and the last agent, who were closest to the President, also began running towards him–Stacey running to pick up the submachine gun dropped by Burt Stevens, and the other agent trying to reach his President and drag him to safety. As they did so, the sound of the approaching Marine One helicopter began to be heard over the sound of gunfire.

As the American fire began to take effect, first one, then a second of the Chinese attackers went down.

Johnny and Lin ignored the agents and National Guard soldiers who were firing at them and their other team members. They concentrated on peppering the ground around the fallen President, wanting to ensure that they fatally wounded him.

One of the Secret Service agents now dove in front of the President and took up a prone position in front of him firing back at Johnny and Lin. Johnny heard the hollow thud of a bullet impacting Lin but did not have the time to look over that way and see how badly he was hit.

He saw the impact of first one, and then another round from his weapon hit the agent lying on the ground, silencing that agent's return fire. Johnny now tried to quickly make his way several yards to the east to try to obtain a better angle of attack on the motionless President.

He did not notice Stacey Urkut, who had picked up the weapon lying on the ground from where Burt Stevens had dropped it, and who was now charging Johnny's position, firing as she came. He also did not notice that he was the last member of his team firing.

As he quickly found the position he was looking for, he took note of the Marine helicopter that was just settling to the ground to the east of the President, Marines pouring out of it as it did so. Pausing briefly to notice this also caused him to finally noticing the individual charging him from his left side.

Quickly turning, he came face to face with a wild woman, screaming at the top of her lungs as she charged within ten feet of him. Before he could raise his own weapon, Stacey Urkut, the Orka, fired a three round burst directly into his face…and Johnny Chen dropped stone dead to the earth.

May 31, 2009, 12:07
West Potomac Park
Near Marine One
Washington, D.C.

Stacey wandered back over to the area where Marine One had landed. As she came closer she saw a Navy corpsman working diligently and quickly on the President. Another one had just looked to the First Lady, and seeing that her injuries, though painful, were not fatal, he quickly moved on to the Secretary of Defense.

Another Corpsman was feverishly working on Burt Stevens.

The Marines and the remaining Secret Service agents had set up an inner perimeter around the President and Marine One and the National Guard was busily establishing an outer security zone.

At her express and insisted request, two of the Marines had carried the First Lady gently over to her husband, who was lying flat on his back and continuing to bleed severely…though the Corpsman had successfully stemmed the flow from the shoulder wound.

But the wound to his side was bleeding profusely and proving impossible to stop…and there were two other bullet wounds. One was a deep flesh wound to the calf, the other was a frothy, bubbling chest wound, which had penetrated the President's left lung.

As Stacey stepped up, she watched as Linda Weisskopf held her husband's hand, and though suffering terribly herself from her broken leg which had yet to be set…she said a soft prayer.

"Dear God, please preserve Norm's life…please help him hang on until they can get him to the good facilities here nearby.

"If it be Thy will dear God, help him recover and lead this nation to victory over these monstrous and abominable foes."

…at this point Linda's voice broke, as she continued, exerting her own simple faith into the equation.

"…and if not, dear God, make us strong to carry on in his absence and receive this good man unto Yourself."

…and more quietly, in almost a whisper.

"…and help me to carry on somehow without him."

As Linda sobbed once and then somehow gained control, President Norm Weisskopf's eyes fluttered open and he lifted his head slightly, catching his wife's attention.

Speaking weakly, but in a steady voice, he comforted her while he gazed intently into her eyes.

"Sweetheart, it's going to be all right. This nation is going to prevail...and so will you. Don't worry for a minute about that."

Surprisingly, despite his severe condition, the President continued on now, reflectively.

"You know, the dark cloud that has enveloped our nation for so many years has been broken...it's dispelling, just as George Washington foresaw.

"...and the bright light that has broken it into pieces has been the humbling we've experienced through adversity and the light of truth that has burned through that adversity, breaking through the darkness that had clouded so many hearts.

"I have seen it. There may be a hard road ahead, but I now know that this nation will persevere because it has the will to persevere, it has its rediscovered moral compass for guidance and it has the Hand of Providence for support.

"Sweetheart, I have not been an overtly religious man...but I have known the truth in my heart and done my best to live according to it despite my failings.

"So, don't worry over me, darling, I have done my part."

Stopping, and looking more weary by the moment, the President closed his eyes as his wife's tears ran down her cheek and dripped onto his ashen face.

The corpsman continued his work, but he, too, was captured by the emotion of the moment...the passing of a great man...and his own eyes glistened brightly.

Finally, President Norm Weisskopf, a hero to all Americans in the course of the war, and for many, many years before it...and a hero to freedom-loving people all over the world, summoned the will and strength to open his eyes and speak once more.

"God bless America, Linda…and thank God that I have seen its salvation. It's enough."

Looking up at his dear wife of so many years, the President continued…more weakly now.

"You know, for so many years I wondered why that quote from the young Nathan Hale has always been one of my favorites.

"It wasn't until this very moment that I understood why."

Looking up at his wife more passionately now…almost desperately, he reached out with his good hand and held as tightly as his fading strength would allow onto her collar.

"Oh Linda!…I'll miss you so…but we'll see each another again and we'll be reunited in peace and true liberty…everlasting liberty."

Finally, with a tear rolling down his own cheek, his weak voice concluded.

" …always, always remember that…always…"

And with those words the President's head fell back against the ground and he closed his eyes.

As several Marines quickly carried him and Mrs. Weisskopf onboard Marine One and the big helicopter quickly took off, the President's lungs failed and he stopped breathing.

The brave and dedicated Naval Corpsman worked feverishly over him, trying to revive him. First, he used mouth-to-mouth resuscitation, and then, when the President's heart also failed, he resorted to CPR. But all of the efforts by the Corpsman proved futile and the President of the United States died of his wounds before the helicopter ever Bethesda Naval Hospital.

Chapter 4

"An enemy hath done this" – Ezra Taft Benson

June 1, 2009, throughout the day
Worldwide

The news of the death of President Weisskopf spread like wildfire across the entire planet. Everyone, both friend and enemy alike, recognized that a bulwark of the defense of the free world had been brought down, and they all wondered exactly what impact his death, particularly at the hands of the enemy, would have on the overall conflict and their own future.

Friends and allies mourned and prepared for the worst. Enemies rejoiced and planned to follow up on what they perceived as a great advantage with more of the same, believing America must surely succumb now. But, despite their momentary success, they would once again misjudge and underestimate the character and firm resolve of the American people and their allies in this overall affair.

In the United States:

Vice President John Bowers, along with over 190 million other Americans, had been immediately aware of the attack as a result of seeing it graphically displayed on the TV they was watching. The Vice President saw the President's attention drawn to the site of the impending first explosion and then watched his, and the crowd's, reaction to that explosion. The video had been wild and disjointed from that point on as cameramen were knocked to the earth–or worse–by blast and shock waves, and the pictures kept changing to whatever view the networks could make available at the time.

All of America saw the graphic display of the crash of the Black Hawk helicopter into the Washington Monument obelisk. It became the video footage that epitomized the entire attack, being played over and over again, much like the footage of the airliners plunging into the World Trade Center on 9/11/01. But unlike the Twin Towers, the Washington Memorial did not fall.

The final firefight that took the President's life, other than as caught on some very vague pictures and video footage from a great distance, was not captured live on tape, so most of the nation learned of the President's death some time after it occurred. After numerous rumors regarding the President's fate had begun to circulate, an official announcement had been made late yesterday afternoon by an emotional Presidential Chief of Staff from the White House Briefing Room.

But John Bower had benefited from the numerous secure communications he had with the Secret Service, the Military, and the Department of Homeland Security. He and his staff had followed the movements of the President as they retreated away from their assailants throughout the attack, even if they couldn't see the President's movements on TV. Ultimately those movements had brought the President right into the line of fire from Johnny Chin and his assailants, and John Bowers officially learned of the President's death within minutes of his last breath…

…and he literally felt the mantle pass to him upon realizing that the President, his good friend and mentor, was dead. He, John Bowers, was now the 45th President of the United States. An office…and a calling…he had never sought. One he had only seriously contemplated from an almost war gaming standpoint throughout the course of the war, after President Weisskopf had requested, and he had accepted, his nomination to become the Vice President.

"Which vacancy was caused by these same animals, when they killed Alan Reeves," thought Bowers has he continued to contemplate all that had occurred in such a short period of time.

Despite the analytical nature of the planning, *just in case*, he, along with everyone else, had thought that Norm Weisskopf would not be taken from them.

But now, President Weisskopf had been killed…and in a traumatic and brutally quick fashion. Now, all of wise preparations that had been made at the insistence of the President himself, and with the assent of Congress, had come into play.

After the President, the White House" and the Congress itself had been attacked at the outset of the war, in March of 2006, killing the Vice President and many members of Congress, the Continuation of Powers Acts had been proposed and enacted in Congress. Since that time, the Vice President's entourage always included the necessary personnel and legal authority to quickly swear him in as President in the event of a successful attempt on the President's life.

In fact, the entire line of succession to the Presidency, to the sixth person, who was the Secretary of Defense, traveled with just such an entourage at all times. No more than three of the people in the line of succession were permitted by law to be at any one event simultaneously. And all six of them were required to be situated in at least three different localities, separated by no less than three hundred miles each, at any time.

In this case, John Bowers was sworn in as the 45th President within five minutes of the official confirmation of the President's death. In a clear voice, he recited the Presidential Oath to a U.S. District Judge, one of the special group of six who now traveled with the first six successors at all times.

"I, John Bowers, do solemnly swear that I will faithfully execute the Office of President of the United States, and will to the best of my Ability, preserve, protect and defend the Constitution of the United States, so help me God."

As it turned out, and as had been the case on March 15th, 2006, one-third of the line of succession to the Presidency had been killed. In March of 2006, it had been the Vice President and the

Secretary of Defense. In May of 2009, it was the President himself and, once again, the Secretary of Defense, for George Crowler had died from his wounds early on the morning of June 1st.

Americans in general were reacting with shock and outrage to the attack, and particularly to the death of their beloved President. Since the times of George Washington, there had not been a President who was more widely accepted and revered by virtually all of the citizenry than Norm Weisskopf. In both cases, their leadership during military conflict and the perception that their unique capabilities contributed monumentally to the salvation of a people was what engendered their universal acceptance and respect. In George Washington's case, his providential leadership was called into play during the nation's traumatic "birth." In Norm Weisskopf's case, such leadership was needed in a battle for the preservation of the nation's founding principles and in defense of its people's very lives and freedoms. For both men, there had been no viable contender…against Norm Weisskopf, the principle contender had failed to garner even one electoral vote.

From opinions expressed in editorials, on call-in talk shows, over the internet, and in barbershops across the land, the outrage and anger were palatable. But after well over three years of war, the anger was not a blustering, or a passion-of-the-moment kind of anger. To those watching closely, it was more of a determined set to the jaw, a more deeply engrained resolve kind of an anger, one that grits its teeth and is determined to persevere, no matter the cost, no matter the length of time required.

And it was a mindset that was shared by the vast majority of the people and was now being reflected in the vast majority of the media outlets, who, through the course of the war and as a result of their own losses and betrayals, had adopted a much more American and liberty-oriented viewpoint…more similar in nature to the news media of World War II. JT Sampson's example and leadership in this area had proven indispensable to the change in nature, and this was particularly evident in his response to the President's death.

The result was becoming clear: America was coming even closer together, becoming more united, more resolute and more determined as a result of the killing of their President. And in this way, the plans of America's enemies had not panned out, even if they didn't know it yet.

Despite the immediate loss, despite the slight hesitancies and mistakes that necessarily accompany such an abrupt transfer of power, it was the additional unity, determination, and resolve that would figure most heavily into the course of future events as far as the United States was concerned–qualities that would be very much needed for the free world to persevere.

In China:

When Jien Zenim received verification that the final phase of operation Hung-Lu-Dung had proven successful, and that President Weisskopf was dead, he was elated. As a part of his long-term planning, he had initially calculated that the successor to George W. Bush, who had been a strong foreign policy President for the Americans, and who had represented a major obstacle in Zenim's plan for Asian hegemony for the People's Republic, would either be the wife of the President before Bush, or someone closely associated with that former administration. He had done all in his power to engineer it that way.

In much the same way as the American presidential administration of the 1990s had been one of the most enabling features of Zenim's plan, that next administration would have enabled him to usher in the final phases of his, and the leadership in China's long-held beliefs and goals for China. The 1990s American administration was something that had been financed, cajoled, blackmailed, subverted, and used to the benefit of the PRC for all of its eight years. The resulting bonanzas that had accrued to China in technology, manufacturing, currency, and economy had ensured the furtherance of the final phases of Zenim's planning. He had engineered things that that way, too.

But he had miscalculated. The successor to Bush had been a shock and surprise. Weisskopf had proven even more resolute against the PRC than Bush. Norm Weisskopf had become the greatest impediment Jien Zenim had ever encountered in American leadership, and his election to the presidency had necessitated the addition of all phases of operational plan Hung-Lu-Dung as a follow-on to Operation Breath of Fire, the plan that had ambushed the Americans so completely off of Japan in March of 2006, and had attacked their homeland so devastatingly and savagely at the same time.

Initially, Breath of Fire was supposed to have so disabled and so discouraged the Americans that the new Chinese-engineered administration and media in America would have quickly sued for an end to hostilities. The war would have ended rapidly, with an understanding between the PRC and the new American administration that a new world order had been established, giving rise to China's prominence in Asia and a new order in the Mid East. With their almost complete and foolish acceptance of the straw man argument that a service economy was better than an economy that actually produced something, the Americans would have hardly recognized that a declining America and a disjointed Europe would never truly be able to compete. But with Weisskopf and his administration in control in Washington, bolstering American resolve and spirit, Zenim's well-laid plan had been prevented from complete success.

Zenim hoped now, with the Weisskopf problem addressed and resolved once and for all, that China and the entire Coalition of Asian States, along with their powerful ally, the GIR, could find their way back to the original path that would lead to a quick resolution of hostilities and the new understanding and order he still planned to implement.

Celebrations in Beijing, Shanghai, Hong Kong, and elsewhere throughout China and Chinese-held territory over the death of President Weisskopf were joyful, reminiscent of the celebrations in parts of the Arab world after the 9-11-01 attacks. The Chinese people believed that the Americans would lose heart and soon accept a new reality: that with their great and resolute leader now gone, and with clear indications that they faced a determined enemy capable of striking them within their homeland to this day, even after their success of the last few months, hostilities must cease.

But like their leaders, they would soon learn that this was not to be the case. Once again, they would underestimate the historical uniqueness of American resolve.

In India:

President KP Narayannen had breathed a sigh of relief when he heard of President Weisskopf's death. He had not sought conflict with the Americans, had hoped it would not be necessary. Even during those initial attacks in March 2006, when his allies, and fellow members of the then-new CAS, the Chinese, had attacked America, he had held back, not confronting the Americans directly. Instead, India had concentrated on Sri Lanka, areas along the Himalayas, Bangladesh, and parts of Burma…and with great success.

But he had known that conflict with the Americans at some point was inevitable. His nation was rising out of its Third World status, and not just for particular members of the old caste system. The material wealth being accrued by a larger and larger segment of the vast Indian population through its success in the Siberian Economic Development Pact, and through its own expansion, meant that the people needed even more room to expand. India, along with China and Indonesia, had set their collective eyes on conquering Australia…and to do that would mean removing the American influence from the Indian Ocean.

And that task had fallen to India and President Narayannen, who was under great internal pressure from his Foreign Minister, Rahmish Patel, whom the President by then had recognized as a mere lackey for the Chinese…but a powerful political lackey who had to be taken into account. He had ultimately approved of a plan to attack the Americans, and he had turned it over to his capable scientists and military planners. With America weakened already in the Pacific and

Mid East, under full scale assault in both of those areas at the time, the Indians had struck, and struck hard.

In early July of 2006, the Indians had attacked the American 5th Fleet and U.S.S. Enterprise Carrier Battle Group in the Indian Ocean. It had been a multi-pronged effort and a vicious fight …and it had cost the Indians dearly. But thanks to the innovations of Indian technology coupled with the Chinese LRASD weapons, and the resulting airborne version of the LRASD, the Americans had been defeated on the sea and the U.S.S. Enterprise had been sunk along with most of its escorts.

That Indian victory had led to the attack on, and ultimate occupation of, the American base on the island of Diego Garcia after another vicious and costly fight. With that victory, American influence in the Indian Ocean had ended and American presence was no longer felt or seen there. And, with the exception of occasional submarine attacks and a few forays by some of their naval surface action groups and long range aircraft, the Americans had not returned.

But those victories had also produced a very real and direct warning from the American President, Norm Weisskopf.

Weisskopf's Secretary of State, using back channels communication sources, had contacted the Indian President with a personal message from Weisskopf that was worded very straightforwardly. President Narayannen could remember the short, terse wording to this day:

"President Narayannen, you shall be held directly and personally responsible for the attack on the U.S.S. Enterprise and the deaths of so many Americans. You and your administration's rejection and betrayal of republican principles, and your alliance with abject tyranny, will ultimately be recognized as the war crimes and crimes against humanity that they are, so help me God."

Again, President KP Narayannen breathed a sigh of relief. Weisskopf was dead; perhaps his personal vendetta had died with him. *Surely the new American President, this Bowers, will be someone we can negotiate with, should it ever come to that.* Given current circumstances, Narayannen was hoping that the negotiations would not be about his own well being, but about America's.

In the Greater Islamic Republic:

Hassan Sayeed had mixed emotions about the operation that had resulted in the killing of the American President.

Oh, he had gone along with it and looked forward to it, assigning two of his best teams…precious resources that had been reserved in America against just such contingencies. And they had succeeded.

But the advances that the young General, Abduhl Selim, had made in Syria, which had ultimately carried him right up to the foot of the Golan Heights and almost resulted in a major breakthrough into Israel itself, had now been reversed.

Employing those damnable and deadly new Hail Storm missiles of theirs, and using them in increasing abundance, the U.S. and Israeli forces had reversed those gains and pushed GIR forces back beyond Damascus once again, this time completely overrunning the Trans-Syrian pipeline and pushing as far north as the petroleum processing facilities in Homs.

If they were not contained soon, the Americans would be approaching the more critical facilities in Baniyas on the coast…

…and this is what gave rise to Sayeed's mixed emotions. He had urged that the GIR/CAS alliance focus the attacks within America on the more practical, more immediate military impact of attacking the plants that were assembling these Hail Storm missiles.

In the last two months, GIR and Chinese intelligence had identified the three major Hail Storm missile production plants within the United States. They were operating under tight and heavy security in California, in Texas, and in Ohio…but all three locations could be vulnerable to the major type of operation like the one that had been executed in Washington, D.C.

Sayeed understood, and had ultimately gone along with Jien Zenim because Zenim had correctly pointed out that mounting three major operations at once would be much more difficult and would require significantly more time to plan and organize.

Zenim felt that their alliance needed a major success now, and could not afford the time or risk that waiting to mount three operations would take...

This concern was principally founded in the realization that American Homeland Security and Home Guard efforts had been increasingly successful in thwarting and eliminating both Islamic and Chinese cells within America. The GIR/CAS alliance would have to pull out all the stops, using its most closely held and critical assets to mount the single major operation in Washington, DC, against the President.

And they had.

"What was it Zenim had said that had ultimately caused me to see Allah's wisdom in the attack on Weisskopf?" the great Imam thought.

Something along the lines of, "Perception is reality, particularly among the Americans. If they see us successfully conduct this operation, despite how badly it drains our reserves within America, they will presume we can do more...and this new presumption will occur on top of the major loss of morale and inspiration that will come about through the death of their leader."

And so Hassan Sayeed had gone along with the plan and used his own most valuable assets...and he had rejoiced with the success.

But with the very real reversals GIR forces were experiencing, he still wished there were fewer Hail Storm missiles available to the Americans and their allies...much fewer. And he couldn't help but think that anything they might have done to preemptively blunt America's new technological and battlefield advantage would have ultimately proved valuable. But Hassan Sayeed knew well that regrets represent the foundation of nothing constructive, so he banished any 'if only we had…' thoughts from his mind.

In Europe:

The European nations, who were deeply embroiled in the conflict on two fronts, were also grief-stricken and demoralized by the loss of Norm Weisskopf…particularly France and Germany, who were Europe's two production and military powerhouses.

It was an interesting dichotomy for those two nations at a time when such dichotomies were not being considered.

The French and Germans, before the war, and during its initial stages, when America and the United Kingdom were going it alone, had distanced themselves from the war in general and from America in particular. With shades of the same arguments that had been made during America's Operation Iraqi Freedom in 2003, those European powers had implied, at the start of military confrontations in the fall of 2005 in Iraq, that many of the issues leading up to the war had been America's fault to begin with. They also argued that America's motives were not really motivated towards the freedom of the Iraqi or other Islamic peoples, but more towards oil interests and establishing a geopolitical balance in the region.

Both of those arguments were stances that both Germany and France would later have to reverse, just had they had ultimately had to do in 2003, when conditions and the passage of time revealed to all the error of their position.

The English, and ultimately many of the Eastern European democracies, had stood resolutely with America. By early 2006, both Spain and Italy had done likewise. But France and Germany in particular had been reluctant, and even counterproductive to allied efforts to contain the GIR and China.

When the invasion of Turkey, a NATO ally, had ensued after Syria announced its union with the GIR and then combined the Syrian army with the GIR and crossed the frontier into Turkey, Germany had finally responded, fulfilling its NATO obligations admirably, and fighting hard alongside American, Turkish and other allied forces. But the Germans had made it clear at that point that its commitment was not in any kind of a global context, and France had taken no action, either militarily or diplomatically.

As conditions had deteriorated over the next eighteen months, and as terror attacks began to hit home on European soil in both Germany and France, attitudes changed. With the invasion of Europe by GIR forces after the Greeks had allied with the GIR to complete the defeat of Turkey, Europe had finally become fully aware of the imminent danger it faced. When GIR forces pushed deeply into Romania and other Balkan nations, Europe had finally gone into full mobilization to try to repel the attack.

Russia had not taken part in the conflict at all during this period. From the very beginning, they viewed themselves in an optimum situation to benefit from both sides' struggles. On one hand, they entered into the Siberian Economic Development Treaty with China and India, opening that vast territory of Siberia up to exclusive exploitation by those nations in exchange for significant sums of hard capital. Ultimately that arrangement had been extended to all CAS member nations and to the GIR.

On the other hand, Russia had continued to receive and respond to allied requests and commitments for infrastructure development and economic stimulus packages meant to ensure that the Russians did not enter into a military compact with the CAS and GIR. While extending these offers, Europe and America, who wanted above all to keep either CAS or GIR forces from threatening Europe from the east, had also warned of sanctions, boycotts and tariffs, should Russia continue to develop its economic relationships with the enemies of the west.

The Russian President, Vladimyr Puten, had handled all of these diplomatic maneuverings deftly and with obvious negotiating skill. He used his Foreign and Economic Ministers to great advantage in playing both sides to Russia's benefit.

And the game had worked for a time…that is, until March 18th of 2008, when Siberia had declared its independence from the Russian Federation and had moved immediately to solidify a strong alliance with both the CAS and GIR.

That move had led to war, as the Chinese knew it must, and as they and their allies had planned. They were thus well prepared to conduct immediate warfare operations against the Russians.

Being quickly routed from the whole of Siberia, Russian forces soon found themselves facing masses of Chinese and Indian soldiers on their own borders. Those large armies then rolled over the Russian border into the motherland itself. Russia's attempt to stop these forces with nuclear weapons had been negated by the very capable and advanced mobile Ballistic Missile Defenses the Chinese had developed and deployed with their forces.

The Russian President, very late in the day, was reduced to seeking help for his nation's salvation from both America and Europe, the very nations he had scoffed at and taken advantage of. It had been a bitter pill for him to swallow, and one he was not entirely sure the allies were willing to extend to him.

But they had, and Vladimyr Puten had been particularly impressed with Weisskopf's and America's treatment of him and his nation in their hour of need, despite issues of the past.

Before Russia was attacked, Weisskopf had been very direct in his warnings regarding Russia's ties with China. Puten had scoffed and taken lightly warnings of any potential Chinese Operation Barbarosa, referring back to World War II days when Russia had aligned itself with Nazi Germany and then had been betrayed by Nazi Germany in June of 1941.

Despite the scoffs, that is exactly what had occurred and America's financial and military assistance, along with that of Europe, had ultimately helped turn the tide of war against the Chinese, Indian and Islamic invaders, right at the very gates of Moscow.

Yes, Vladimyr Puten and all of the European leaders would miss Norm Weisskopf. Puten considered him the best sort of friend and ally one could have, who, despite having had his advice and counsel turned away, stood willing to assist Mother Russia in her hour of need.

All of these leaders wondered what sort of President this John Bowers, who was an unknown quantity to most of them, would be and whether he could pick up the reins and continue to move the prosecution of the war forward, while maintaining the strength of the alliance of nations involved against the combined might of the CAS and GIR.

In South America:

At the time the President of the United States was killed, the war in South America had evolved into a continual scene of bloody stalemate. In Panama, Colombia and Venezuela in the north, and along the Argentine and Brazilian borders in the south, the ebb of battle flowed back and forth, although some progress was being made in the approaches to the Canal Zone in Panama and in some areas in Argentina where Brazilian forces had penetrated.

Brazil and Colombia were the major allied combatants in South America, assisted by American and English forces who were fighting in special forces operations in Colombia, and in larger numbers in Central America, working their way south through Panama. Against this, the nations of Panama, Venezuela, and Argentina had formed the Coalition of South American States and allied themselves with the CAS and GIR. China had several hundred thousand troops fighting with the forces from these nations in Panama and in Colombia.

Although in the past six months troops from Ecuador, Paraguay, and Chile had joined in the fighting against the CAS and GIR and their allies, the real driving force behind allied fighting in South America was Brazil. The other, smaller South American nations and their forces would have been otherwise too weak to stand against the combined weight of the Panamanian, Venezuelan, and Argentine forces, supported by the large numbers of Chinese.

The President of Brazil, Henrietta Maldenado, who had assumed the office of the Presidency after their beloved President Alfonzo Hermosa had been killed by a Chinese decapitation strike in June of last year, had considered herself a close friend of the American President.

Within a day of her taking the oath of office, President Weisskopf had called her himself and had spent over two hours on the phone with her, talking as one respected leader to another, taking her immediately into his nation's confidence, committing America's unwavering support to winning the war, and ensuring the freedom and liberty of Brazil and all of South America.

Over the last year, she had developed a kinship with this older man. She was the president of the largest democratic republic in South America. He was the president of the largest democratic republic in North America, and the strongest one on earth.

In all of their conversations, in all of their meetings, he had never treated her as anything but an equal and her respect for, and trust in, him had grown accordingly...she had begun to look to him almost as a child would look to a father.

She had wept openly when news of his death had arrived, even as the leaders of the nations she was embroiled in combat with had rejoiced.

"He will be sorely missed," she thought as she contemplated the road ahead and prepared to address a special meeting of her own security and military advisors the day after Weisskopf's death.

"Ladies and gentlemen, as you all know, this earth has been deprived of a true defender of liberty, a true patriot, and a wonderfully good man.

"We know something of such loss as these same enemies deprived us of our own Panther of Brazil when they killed President Alfonzo Hermosa last year. On a personal note, even as President Weisskopf and his wonderful wife, Linda, sent their condolences and offered up their prayers on our behalf last year, we should now pray that Linda will be comforted and strengthened through this crisis, and that all Americans take heart in their hour of loss, and know that we here in Brazil will stand by them, just as they have stood by us.

"We cannot…we shall not be deterred. If Zenim and Sayeed and their allies think for a moment we shall be cowed or moved to entreat with them as a result of this heinous act…they have terribly miscalculated. And this error on judgment will represent another in a long series of miscalculations.

"Just as they miscalculated when they shot down the International Space Station and its wreckage crashed in Rio and killed so many of our countrymen, they are miscalculating now. They thought that because our country had taken a more social government path, that they could convince us to blame that horrible tragedy on America, whom they were fighting. They thought that we would blame the Americans and be more disposed to their motives and objectives…that we could be manipulated by them through the deaths of so many of our people.

"But they were wrong.

"They miscalculated then and our nation saw through their manipulations to those who were truly responsible…to them, and we declared war on them instead.

"And now they have miscalculated again.

"In this fight for liberty and for peace, we can never afford to lose sight of these facts in prosecuting this war. We can never afford to allow our people to lose sight of these facts either, though I have complete faith in them and their ability to see the truth of these matters.

"We will not rest, we will not be deterred, we will not stop until those leaders and those nations who caused that great destruction to our nation, and who continue to cause it today, are utterly defeated and every visage of their power and government is removed from any position of influence and destroyed."

June 4, 2009, 09:48
Capitol Rotunda
Washington, D.C.

The new Bowers administration announced on Monday, June 2nd, that the President would lie in state in the Capitol Rotunda from 9 AM on June 4th through 9 PM on June 9th, twenty-four hours a day. The former First Lady had agreed late in the day of June 1st, while she was still in the hospital. The President would then be buried in Arlington National Cemetery in a nationally televised event on June 10th, with Linda Weisskopf in attendance in a wheelchair.

Now, a little over forty-five minutes after the taped-off path around the casket had been opened to the public, over two hundred thousand people were lined up to pay their final respects to the departed president. The line stretched out of the Capitol Building, across the street and down the mall, all the way to the damaged Washington Monument and looped around it halfway down the other side back towards the Capitol.

That number of two hundred thousand waiting in line to see Norm Weisskopf would remain constant, give or take fifteen to twenty thousand, for the entire five and one half day period, except on Saturday, June 6th. That Saturday was when the presentation of the

Medal of Freedom to Stacey Urkut had been rescheduled to take place...in front of the Lincoln Memorial, the presentation to be made by President John Bowers.

In all, well over three million people would come and pay their last respects to the President as he lay in state. They came in spite of the danger...many came as an act of defiance to the potential for danger and to show solidarity in the face of it. Husbands, wives, children, young men and women, wheelchair bound, grandparents, the feeble–every creed and color who loved and were loyal to the United States of America–they all came, and would have kept coming had the opportunity to do so lasted longer.

June 6, 2009, 11:58
Presentation Stand
In front of the Lincoln Memorial
Washington, D.C.

The time corresponding to the attacks of the prior week came and went without incident. The presentations had proceeded as planned and there had been no further attacks as John Bowers began his speech regarding the presentation of the Medal of Freedom to Stacey Urkut to a crowd that was estimated to be in excess of one and a half million people.

President Bowers marveled at the monumental display of fortitude. His faith bolstered almost to the point of tears, the President began.

"My fellow Americans, we are gathered here this morning and afternoon to honor one of our own. Last week's ceremony was meant to honor the heroic sacrifice, actions and bravery of an individual who stood against our enemies, against all odds...and fought back.

"Today we will continue with and complete the ceremony that was so brutally interrupted just last week. America will recognize and honor her heroes–Stacey Urkut deserves to be recognized–our nation deserves the honor of recognizing her heroism. We will not be intimidated as a people. We will stand firmly, and in so doing, we will also honor the many more who have now sacrificed their all for our nation.

"Nine hundred and fifty three names were added to that hallowed list as a result of last week's attack. Over two thousand eight hundred more were injured.

"Our own president sacrificed his life…and it was a long and distinguished life of sacrifice and service. God rest his soul. God bless his dear wife and family.

"Linda Weisskopf has given me permission to share something very important with all of you…as a voice of comfort and strength to our citizens and our allies, as a word of warning to our enemies.

"In his final moments, the President had a number of things to say to his wife and those attending him. Much of it was personal, but these words that he spoke were intended to reach the ears of every American. He said the following, only moments before losing consciousness prior to his death.

"There may be a hard road ahead, but I now know that this nation will persevere because it has the will to persevere; it has its rediscovered moral compass for guidance and it has the Hand of Providence for support."

"My fellow citizens, let this be our expression of faith…our rallying cry…WE SHALL PERSEVERE!

"We shall persevere because of the faith, the morality, the dedication, the liberty, the ingenuity born of that liberty and the resilience of this people. And we shall persevere because a just God rules in the heavens and will support the cause of liberty, as He has done in the past.

"We will persevere because there are literally millions of Stacey Urkuts out there, who, when faced with monumental challenges and abject threats to their life and liberty, rise above those challenges and threats and somehow come off the winner...or contribute monumentally to the ultimate victory."

Turning to Stacey, who stood with him on the stand, and as more than a million people cheered both her and the words of their new President, John Bowers continued.

"Stacey Urkut, on behalf of a grateful nation, and for gallantry and dedication and citizenship beyond the call of duty while fighting the Chinese invasion force in Alaska...and in confronting that same evil here last week when you personally confronted and killed the assailant who had shot the President, we present you with the Medal of Freedom.

"May you wear and display it proudly, and may your actions, your sacrifice, your bravery, your dedication and your faith, be a role model for all Americans, young and old, military or civilian, from the local government officials up to and including all of us who have been elected to represent the people on the national level."

As Stacey Urkut accepted the award and approached the microphone to say a few words, over one hundred and eighty million Americans all over the world watched her, as well as uncounted tens of millions all across the free world.

June 6, 2009, that same time
Various locations
America and the Free World
Off the coast of Liberia

Alan Campbell listened via radio transmission to the President's address and now as Stacey Urkut began her acceptance speech. He tried to contemplate how this middle-aged woman could have accomplished all that had been attributed to her. Upon reading about it last week before the initial ceremony, he had commented to his gunny, "You know, Sarge, I would have been hard pressed to do what this lady did. Can you imagine?"

The Sergeant, a veteran of over twenty years, had seen enough in his career to not discount anything.

"Campbell, the human spirit is capable of things we can't even imagine. Given the circumstance and her upbringing...despite her age and physical conditioning...I can imagine it. I have seen some pretty unlikely people do some amazing things."

Now, as Stacey spoke, and as he and his comrades waited off the African coast, in the latest U.S. Navy San Antonio class amphibious ship, Alan felt that he could hear those qualities in the woman's voice. Somehow, he knew that this woman had done all that had been attributed to her and probably a lot more. This in turn bolstered his own faith and confidence.

He was a U.S. Marine!, and he was about to go into combat for the first time in support of the allied buildup that would soon strike at the underbelly of the GIR defenses in Africa.

Those same defenses had mauled earlier Brazilian and English attempts to break through and gain access from across Africa to the upper Nile River in an attempt to position themselves to either advance on Egypt or cross the Red Sea onto the Arabian peninsula.

But now over two hundred thousand American troops were going to reinforce well over one million African, Brazilian and other allied troops who were forming up in Liberia to make the transit into the interior–a massive offensive that would try to surround GIR forces resisting the Israeli, British and American advance to the south out of Israel.

Alan was proud to be a part of this force. Proud to be assisting the downtrodden in Africa...yet, as most sane people are, he was also concerned about his first combat. How would he do? Would he support his brothers in arms? Would he survive? Would he be wounded like his own brother Leon?

"Momma, I just hope you are prayin' for me back home," he thought. "Technology has provided us the advantage more often than not, but prayers are our most powerful weapon."

Outside of Montague, Texas

Cindy Simmons, in the comfort of her ranch home outside of Montague, Texas, listened as Stacy Urkut continued her address. She was joined there by her good friend, Elizabeth Trevor, and her husband, Joe. The Trevors had arrived only a day earlier after completing their Washington debriefings, at the hands of the Park Service Police and the Secret Service, and after attending a memorial service for their friend, Saundra McPherson, who had been killed last week in the attacks.

Cindy had tried to convince her friend that she and Joe need not come, even though she had been looking forward to Liz's visit. But Elizabeth and her husband would have nothing to do with Cindy's arguments against their coming.

"It's times like these when friends have to rely on each other, Cindy," Liz had told her over the phone.

"You need us there…and now we need you as well."

Cindy had been concerned that their place was at their own home, or the home of their daughter, Patricia. But Liz had come up with the idea of having Patricia take some time off from her schooling in Chicago and visit them all in Texas. Patricia was eager to spend some time with her parents after hearing of their traumatic experience.

"Pat would love to come home to Texas for a couple of weeks anyway, Cindy. She's in between semesters and has the time, and there are a lot of people she knows down there from the years we spent in the DFW area."

So the Trevors had arrived and they had all spent the evening talking, reminiscing, comforting one another and planning for the future.

Jess would soon be coming home, too.

Cindy had gotten the word just a few days ago. With the combat operations continuing, and intensifying, the days when relatives could fly over to the major hospitals in Europe and see their loved ones were over. He would be flown to the United States in two weeks and would be in a position to come to the Veterans Hospital in Dallas, so he could come directly home.

Cindy would meet him at the Joint Services Base in Ft. Worth, and the Trevors had decided that they would stay on with the Simmons through June and celebrate the 4th of July with them before they returned home to the Boston area.

All of this had been communicated and planned last evening, and Cindy was grateful for her friends' willingness to support her and Jess during this time of need. She was also happy that she could be of comfort to them after their traumatic experience and the loss of their new-found friend.

Last night they had talked for some time about Saundra, and Cindy had marveled at the change that had taken place in the life of that woman...of her dedication to the unborn after discovering the truth and proof of their humanity. She would never forget the optimism and joy that Elizabeth had expressed, despite the grief at Saundra's recent demise, as a part of her faith in the life hereafter.

"I believe that Saundra has been given the opportunity to administer to and take care of those spirits...the young children who were aborted," she had said.

"She's with them now and I believe that the comforting and ministering is mutual, perhaps even more so for what those spirits can do for Saundra, and that God in His wisdom has brought them together."

That discussion had been of great comfort to Cindy, even though Elizabeth had not necessarily intended it that way. It helped Cindy as she continued to cope with the loss of her son. Oh, she believed she would see him again in the hereafter…and she looked forward to it and wanted to be able to express joy at that anticipated reunion, just as the Trevors expressed their joy for Saundra's…she just wasn't quite there yet. She still had a little more grief to work through. She prayed she would be able to get through it soon…soon enough for it not to be any additional burden to Jess.

Just as this thought and prayer passed through her mind, she was brought back to Stacey Urkut's remarks and the comments she was making at that particular moment.

"So, Mr. President, I accept this award on behalf of all of those with whom I fought…on behalf of so many who were lost, who gave their lives in defense of our liberty and way of life. I include in that number our former President and Secretary of Defense, whom I had met and who had been so gracious to me, and who were such stalwart leaders and defenders of our nation.

"There are so many who have been lost…but they are really not lost to us. Our enemies underestimate our faith and its impact in our lives if they believe they are lost, and that the loss will demoralize us to the point of defeat.

"On the contrary, we shall be even more dedicated, even more committed to defeating our enemies, whatever the price. The memory of our departed friends demands it. Their spirit lives on to comfort us with their dedication, their commitment and their love.

"In addition, in my faith, their very essence–their own individual spirits–live on in the hereafter, a hereafter we all must face some day. I look forward to facing it with head held high in God's own time…it is not for me to choose that time. God's timing is His own. But He promises us a joy-filled reunion with those good people who went before. And that is the promise to which we all must hold fast.

"Truth be known, this promise was the only thing that really enabled me to do what I did in Alaska. I attribute it to my Maker and His will concerning me, and the life He has taught me to live...a life where I need not fear...where I know all things are in His hands and it is but for me to accept and follow His will to the best of my ability.

"Sometimes His will is difficult for us to comprehend, let alone accept...especially when we see the lives of good people being lost at the hand of those with evil intentions. But if we hold fast to the knowledge that He is in control, and that we need but look to Him for guidance, wisdom and strength, we cannot help but prevail.

"Therefore, I accept, and I dedicate this Medal of Freedom to Him and to all of my comrades in Alaska and elsewhere who have sacrificed so much in defense of liberty...for liberty is a gift from Him that no man has the right to take from us. Not now...not ever.

"Thank you...and God bless our nation...and God bless you, Mr. President, and those you work with."

As Stacey Urkut moved to take her seat and the President turned the podium back over to the master of ceremonies...and as millions around the world cheered the words of integrity and commitment that had swelled their hearts...Cindy Simmons found tears flowing softly and silently down her cheeks.

With the fall of each teardrop...and as they gradually fell faster, and then just as gradually abated...her grief over the loss of her son abated, as if in answer to prayer. Somehow, Stacey Urkut's message had touched and healed her heart and allowed her to let go. Billy would always occupy a precious corner of her heart, but that corner was no longer cloaked in a heavy black veil. Cheeks glistening with moisture, Cindy Simmons looked heavenward and thanked God for the wonderful cleansing that Stacey Urkut's words had brought. She found herself quietly whispering the familiar words, "The Lord works in wonderful and mysterious ways..."

Elizabeth and Joe held her, and one another, all of them touched by the poignancy of the moment, all of them feeling the miracle of what was happening.

In Havana, Cuba

In Cuba, the telecast of the ceremony had been carried live on the local television broadcasting equipment that had survived the fighting. In addition, the U.S. occupation forces had set up monitors in many public buildings and in public parks wherever possible.

The turnout by the citizens of Cuba had been amazing.

It seemed to Sergeant Hernando Rodriguez that these people literally thirsted for liberty, despite the decades of communist rule which had held them in bondage. To the amazement of many Americans, but not coming as a surprise to the Cuban American community, the citizens of the island nation had been quick to throw off their communist leaders…from the highest offices, to the local commissars, and party leaders.

Oh, the hard line adherents to the ideology and the party structure had fought, and they had fought hard. But, as was the case in Operation Iraqi Freedom over six years earlier, without the general support of the people, who were glad to see the old regime go, the party's adherents' prospects were hopeless.

By the first of May, major combat maneuvering by U.S. forces was complete and the large Cuban military units in their Army and Air Force had either been defeated, or, for the most part, had surrendered.

By the end of May, when the President was attacked and killed, most of the hard line, hold-out units had been rooted out and destroyed. With shades of the Iraqi operation in 2003, a Cuban "deck of cards" had been established and, by the end of May, thirty-seven of the fifty-two depicted on those cards had been captured or killed.

The attack on the President had resulted in some more heated firefights over the last week as the few remaining communist leaders tried to use that event to bolster their waning support and create a more general uprising against the Americans.

But their efforts failed.

Firstly, using the event to show themselves and try to fight was a military disaster of tremendous proportions. American firepower and logistics were so overpowering that these fights, though fierce, were always brief and lopsided in their outcome. The hold-outs played into American hands by engaging them directly.

Secondly, the Cuban people, outside of a miniscule minority who had profited from the old system…and most of those had also seen the handwriting on the wall and were unwilling to show any active or public support…were wholly unwilling to support any resistance to American occupation and rebuilding.

The Cuban people *wanted* Cuba be rebuilt.

As far as Hernando could see, the communication efforts by the Cuban American community in Florida over the years had been more successful than any of them could have dreamed. The Cuban people held out a bright hope for liberty…and, when the opportunity was presented, they were grabbing it with both hands and with gusto.

"I should have sensed it, after what happened with Ernesto," thought Hernando. "What happened in the heart and mind of that fifteen year old boy was a microcosm and a precursor to what had happened to the entire country. We just didn't see it."

Now, after listening with satisfaction to Stacey Urkut's words, and as he saw that the Cuban people had listened to those words with as much, if not more, genuine comprehension, Hernando began to eagerly contemplate his return home to his family for an extended leave next month…to his wife, his child, and his parents.

His son, Felipe, was almost two years old! How amazing! He could not wait to see him again. This time he would have some real time to spend with him, to play with him and get to know him.

Maria, in their last phone call, had informed him that she was pregnant with their second child! He had wanted to cry for joy and shout out loud all at once...in fact, back in the barracks amongst his comrades, that was exactly what he had done.

He loved her so and was so grateful for her love, for her outlook on life and her innocence and purity. He would do all within his power to protect that gift...to protect their life together...to protect the liberty and opportunity for their growing family.

And his parents. What could he say? They were so proud of him...he could sense it in their letters and in the brief calls he had the opportunity to make. He sensed his Dad's pride when the two of them talked about their mutual experiences.

Hernando's dad had joined the local Home Guard Unit and pulled sentry duty four times a week. Nothing too exciting had happened, but he had called in several suspicious activities, and Hernando knew that whatever facilities his dad watched were being watched by a loyal and completely dedicated American. He was just as proud of his dad as he was of him...and he was proud of both of his parents for how they had raised him and taught him to appreciate the freedoms and great opportunities he had in America.

Now, after seeing his original homeland liberated, he was certain that the people there would embrace those same liberties and opportunities. The anticipation filled him with joy and pride. He would have so much to share with all of his family.

In Boise, Idaho

Geneva Campbell turned off the TV set.

"Such a contrast between this week and last week," she thought.

Last week she had been anticipating the types of feelings that she had experienced this week, only to have those expectations dashed by the violent attack on the President and the crowd.

Those attacks had punctuated the angst she felt about the war in general. She was not against the war. Far from it. She knew it had to be fought and she knew it had to be won at all costs…it was just that the potential cost to her was so great.

With two sons in the fight…her only two sons…she was constantly concerned for their safety and welfare.

Leon had already been severely wounded, and he had gone right back out as soon as he was fully recovered, turning down all attempts to offer him a plush and safe stateside job in recruiting.

Alan had followed in his brother's footsteps and joined the U.S. Marines as soon as he could, and was now on his way to who knows where to fight the enemy.

Both of them were full-blooded U.S. Marines and she was so proud of them. She knew she could petition for non-hazardous assignments for at least one of them since they were her only sons and since they both were destined for hot combat zones.

But she would not…she *could not* do that to them. Each of them was so dedicated to the country they had learned to love and the liberty and opportunity it afforded.

"And they know what that opportunity is all about," she reflected as she continued to bask in the warm after effects of the rousing speeches and patriotic ceremonies she had just witnessed.

"Leon got himself an education, pulled himself up by the bootstraps and brought us with him out of the ghettos in Chicago.

"I don't care what any of those race-baiting politicians or their lackeys say …what Leon accomplished could only happen in America. And that same opportunity is available to anyone who wants to break out of the dead end, destructive habits that otherwise would keep him down…and, in spite of the naysayers, carve out his own success, just like Leon did."

For that reason, Geneva Campbell and both of her boys had been ardent supporters of President Weisskopf and his policies. He did not play to the stereotypes or the special interests. His interest, clearly and unambiguously, had been in America, her people and her constitution.

"And it looks as though this new President, this John Bowers is cut from the same type of cloth," she thought.

From everything she could see, from everything she had heard, he was an individual who was committed to America and her people, with little or no political ambitions outside of simply being dedicated to doing the job his oath required of him, just as Norm Weisskopf had been.

If this proved to be the case, Geneva was certain of one thing: she and both of her boys would be equally ardent in their support of President Bowers. And she was certain that the vast majority of Americans would be strong in their support as well.

The nation was at war. It had been attacked and seriously hurt. There was no time or room for political posturing and all of the maneuvering and games that went along with it. And the people knew it.

"Perhaps we will finally realize that there never was any room for it," she thought.

"Allowing such nonsense is what produced all of the problems and conditions that brought us to this point…to the possible defeat and destruction of our country and all we hold dear."

And America had indeed come frighteningly close to being defeated as the enemy had advanced on all fronts. Now, though things seemed to have turned in favor of her country, Geneva knew that the outcome was far from certain.

"Just like Norm Weisskopf said," she remembered. "There's a long road ahead."

That knowledge, that a long and arduous road still lay between the current set of circumstances and victory…between war and peace–a peace that would see her sons safely back home–led her to think once again of Alan and Leon and to turn her thoughts, her aspirations and the desires of her heart upward to heaven in a prayer to God that they both would be kept safe.

At the U.S. Marine Staging Area in New Zealand

As his mother was having these thoughts, Leon Campbell was walking away from the area where he and his unit had gathered with so many others to listen to the live audio of the presentation ceremony back in Washington, D.C.

"What an inspiring presentation," he concluded as he contemplated the speeches and the events that had led up to them.

"If Stacey Urkut is any indication at all of what our people back home are becoming…then the enemy has already lost and just doesn't realize it yet."

Thinking about such things always caused him to look forward to the day when the war would end and when the world would be back at peace and he could get on with his life. But he wouldn't allow himself to dwell on such daydreams too long…there was just too much land sitting between now and then, and he knew that winning back that land was not a foregone conclusion. The price in blood, in lives, and in sacrifice and hardship would be great.

He had finally arrived in New Zealand on June 2nd after navigating a circuitous route that led him to this staging area for the offensive back into Australia. That route had ultimately taken him all the way back to Midway Island by air, and then he endured an interminable wait as the Chinese counter-offensive against Magadan had everything in an uproar, causing delays as aircraft and ships were marshaled to evacuate the severely wounded and to beef up defenses in anticipation of more such attacks.

From Midway he had ultimately made his way to American Samoa, and had seen the Republic of China (Taiwan) and the Japanese governments in exile and the military forces they had been able to salvage from their defeats in 2006. Those forces had been augmented by American and other allied advisors, personnel and equipment and now represented a formidable force of their own.

And they needed that force. The enemy had advanced as far as New Caledonia, the New Hebrides Islands, and the Loyalty Islands to the west. The front lines of combat on the sea were drawn even closer to the west, between those islands and Fiji, extending up through the Tasman Sea and the Coral Sea to the east of the Loyalty Islands, up to the east of Tarawa, the Marshall Islands and Wake Island, all of which were in enemy hands.

Fiji was under constant attack, and there was just not sufficient allied force in the region to adequately protect it and the staging areas in American Samoa and the even larger areas on New Zealand where Leon would spend significant amounts of time. Allied planners would not allow the CAS to take Fiji, and would resist at almost all costs any obvious invasion attempt, but they could not afford to defend its airspace on a full-time or massive basis. So the attacks and the destruction there continued. And there were frequent air raid warnings and actual attacks in Samoa as well.

During the six days that Leon was on American Samoa, three air raid warnings, and one actual attack had occurred. That attack had consisted of fifteen Chinese bombers escorted by forty fighters. They had broken through allied air defenses to the west, over Western Samoa and attacked the capital of Apia, causing significant damage.

Allied defenses around Pago Pago were stronger and more layered, so the strikes on American Samoa had been thwarted . But the damage and destruction in Apia were real, and just too close for comfort. Luckily, there was no significant impact in Pago Pago, where the major Republic of China, Japanese, and other united Pacific Island governments in exile were staging their forces.

Ultimately those forces would serve as one of the major thrusts into enemy territory, slated to work their way up the island chains from New Caledonia and the Loyalty Islands, through the New Hebrides, the Solomons, and the Admiralty Islands towards an eventual liberation of their homes as they converged with the other prongs of what was envisioned to be the great Pacific offensive.

But the attacks out of New Caledonia and the New Hebrides were still too close and too frequent and they served as a constant reminder, to the people and the military forces gathering in the Samoan Islands, of the capability and proximity of the enemy.

Upon arriving in New Zealand, Leon had found that in New Zealand the attacks were even more frequent than they were in Samoa. The attacks were also much larger as the Chinese, Indian, and GIR forces recognized that the greatest threat to their gains was located here, and they took measures to address it. As a result, the enemy committed larger air and naval forces to attacking allied forces gathering in New Zealand in the hopes of causing significant damage to those forces.

Those forces, comprised of American, British, Brazilian, and free Australian personnel, were clearly gathering for the attack on Australia. Already over three million allied men at arms had gathered on the two Islands of New Zealand, with the majority of them staging near Wellington on the northern island and around Christchurch on the southern island.

The supporting forces also represented the largest concentration of allied naval power in the world, including both of the United Kingdom's new large deck carriers and five American nuclear carriers, all of which were now outfitted with the SUB CIWS, protecting the islands. The United States also had eight of its Sea Control Carriers in the area, four of them the older Tarawa or Wasp class amphibious assault ships that were operating in a dual mode, and four of them the new Hampton Roads Class Sea ships which had been designed and built from the keel up for the sea control mission. The Canadians had both of their newer HMCS White Horse Class ships in attendance as well. All in all, seven large deck carriers and ten Sea Control carriers were operating off the coast of New Zealand with all of their escorts and the vast number of other ammunition, replenishment, oilers, and troop carriers that were gathering for the great invasion.

Once they were all assembled, those naval vessels, and the forces they would carry or protect, would make up the largest invasion force in the history of warfare.

An equally large and impressive air armada was gathered in New Zealand. And it had to be massive because the CAS production lines throughout mainland China, India, and the former Asian Tigers were producing aircraft, weaponry, and ships at a phenomenal rate to throw into the maw of a battle anticipated to the south and east of their Australian conquest. It was all the massive allied air force could do to counter the increasing enemy numbers.

Finally, Leon had noticed the abundance of missile defense systems, and he was glad to see them…not just the standard SAM sights with Hawk, AMRAAM, and Patriot batteries, but also many of the new land-based AEGIS cells that held theater anti-ballistic missiles.

"You gotta know that the Chinese and Indians are tempted to use their nuclear capability against what we are doing here," he thought.

"But with this many anti-ballistic missiles around, they dare not open that Pandora's box...at least I pray they won't."

Aboard the U.S.S Jimmy Carter off of Magadan

The captain and crew of the U.S.S. Jimmy Carter had not been able to listen live to the broadcast of the presentation ceremony where President John Bowers awarded the Medal of Freedom to Stacey Urkut. Nor had they been able to hear Stacey's inspirational comments in reply. They had been beneath the waves involved in sea denial operations to any Chinese vessels, surface or sub surface, that tried to approach areas of Magadan and the continuing operations there.

And so far they had been completely successful.

When the Chinese had attacked the anchorage and the staging areas with their aircraft, and when they had unleashed the LRASD weapons, it had been the Jimmy Carter, and her sister boat, the U.S.S. Connecticut, which had killed four of six LRASD devices that were successfully intercepted in the attack on the C-90s. But that had not been anything close to enough. All ten C-90's and one of the four SSTNs had been destroyed and American operations had been seriously retarded.

But only for a short time.

America's rotation of C-90 aircraft that were replenishing and supplying new troops to the operations out of Magadan was adjusted to account for the losses. But there procedures and operations were also modified to combat the attack profile the Chinese had developed. They would not be caught by surprise like that again.

In addition, in order to make up for the loss of the C-90s, the three surviving SSTNs, which carried as much materiel as a large amphibious assault ship and had been scheduled to depart the area of operations, had made two extra trips back and forth to Midway Island to pick up men and materiel that had been originally slated for later C-90 flights.

In this way, though the buildup ramped up more slowly, America was still able to maintain its overall schedule at Magadan. A large number of troops and mountains of materiel just arrived a little later, but simultaneously, whenever the SSTNs came in.

Now, as the SSTNs prepared to depart the area of operation for good, under escort from the U.S.S. Connecticut, Captain Simon Thompson prepared his boat for its next assignment.

That assignment would once again involve a mission using his embarked SEAL team under the command of Commander Barry Sheffield. Once again they would be secreted behind enemy lines for a critical intelligence gathering mission.

The Jimmy Carter was no stranger to such a mission behind enemy lines. Through the course of the war, it was the boats of the Sea Wolf class that had somehow not been factored into the Chinese recognition profiles, so they had thus far escaped the deadly targeting of the LRASD weapons.

To date, no one could explain the Chinese lapse, but the Captain was understandably thankful for it, whatever the reason. The LA class boats and the newer (but smaller and less heavily armed) Virginia Class boats were all subject to the deadly algorithms of the Chinese Killer Whales. Somehow, in the Chinese intelligence bonanzas and victories of the 1990s when so much damaging information had been gathered by them–or given to them–the Sea Wolf class specifications and information had eluded them.

"They probably wrote it off as just three boats," the Captain thought. "Figured that, in the overall scheme of what was coming, they would deal with us later. Well, it's later and they still haven't tagged a Sea Wolf–and we've certainly given a good account of ourselves."

Two of the boats, the Connecticut and his boat, the Jimmy Carter, operated in the Pacific Theater of Operations, with one of them operating sometimes in the Indian Ocean. The third boat, the namesake of the class, the Sea Wolf, operated in the Atlantic and Mediterranean.

They were principally tasked with interdicting high value naval targets or disrupting the flow of oil by destroying as many large super tankers as they could find and target, as they made their way along the major sea lanes to India, China, Japan and Australia.

The Chinese knew of their mistake...they had surmised early on that the attacks occurring where no enemy combatant was accounted for had to be the work of the Sea Wolfs. They were applying as much of their technical and scientific resource as possible to solving the problem, and there was continuous intense pressure on the CAS and GIR military to find and sink the Sea Wolfs.

But they hadn't been able to do that yet...despite some very close calls.

Simon Thompson could not count on two hands the number of times that God-awful sound of approaching LRASD weapons had enveloped his boat...and then passed on as the weapons failed to acquire the Jimmy Carter.

He was certain that, on at least two occasions, those weapons had passed not more than two hundred feet from his vessel.

Now they would be going into the very mouth of the dragon again. Pitting American ingenuity, training and will against the technological advances, the training and the steel-hard will of their enemies.

And the Captain knew that sooner or later the Chinese or one of their allies would figure out the Sea Wolf riddle. And when they did, that knowledge was likely to be announced in the disappearance of one or more of the three vessels.

Thompson was thankful that the Jimmy Carter and both of the other boats had been rotated into dry dock and retrofitted with the SUB CIWS. He was also grateful that the new programming for the Mk-50 Barracuda torpedo was proving successful in intercepting oncoming Killer Whales. But he was under no illusion that such successes would last indefinitely. Once their enemies knew that they had a Sea Wolf sub on the run, they would launch everything they had at her and use all of their resources to track her down, overwhelm her defense and kill her.

It was against that eventual day that Captain Thompson prepared and trained his crew. They could never afford to become complacent. In combat, and against a resourceful enemy, complacency kills. When the time came, they would all have to be top notch and perform at 110% in order to survive. And their survival would not happen at the drop of a dime, or by accident. To survive against this foe, they had to continually sharpen their skills and procedures.

Speaking of now…the Captain had just been informed that they had just received the transmission of the audio portion of the Medal of Freedom award ceremony that included the President's speech and Stacey Urkut's acceptance. The Captain was anxious for the crew to hear it, and he was anxious to hear it himself. They had all been deeply saddened by the death of President Weisskopf. For folks like him, in addition to his Commander in Chief and the ultimate command authority, the President had assumed almost a father-like role and had represented a paternal influence in his life…for much of his crew, the President's role had been more reminiscent of that of a grandfather.

The President had not only embodied good leadership, as an individual deserving of great respect. He had also become someone they would all die for, or for whom they would go to the ends of the earth. This crew had done just that, by unquestioningly obeying his orders because of the trust and faith they all had in him. Somehow, for them and for most personnel in America's armed services, during the course of the war their loyalty to the President had gone beyond just the constitutional prerogative to obey his orders. It was something much more personal than that. It involved a personal loyalty to a man deserving of such.

But he was gone and now they had a new President. Every one of them looked forward to hearing directly from him as their new Commander in Chief. Every one of them, either consciously or in their sub-conscious, was waiting to see if John Bowers would prove worthy of wearing his predecessor's mantle. Somehow, deep inside, they all knew that they needed such a leader for the rough road ahead.

As Commander Sheffield stood next to him there in the control room, Captain Thompson took the handset, clicked the transmit lever, and spoke to the crew.

"All hands, this is the Captain.

"Listen up. We have just received the audio from the event back in Washington that concluded three hours ago. It is of our new CINC, President John Bowers, and his presentation speech at that Medal of Freedom ceremony. It is also the acceptance speech of Stacey Urkut.

"We're going to play it now. It will last about ten minutes and I ask everyone whose duties will allow it to listen carefully, and consider the message and words of our new President.

"Those whose duties prevent them from listening now, and other crew members who would like to listen to the message again later, can listen to the recording at any time from the ship's files. Just see the XO or your section chief to arrange it.

"After the conclusion of the presentation, I will make a few comments about what was said and then talk about the orders we have just received for our next mission.

"Here's the President of the United States…"

Over the ship's intercom system, the President's words began.

"My fellow Americans, we are gathered here this morning and afternoon to honor one of our own. Last week…"

June 14, 2009, 05:23
High Mountain Meadow off of Deep Creek
Near Ibapah, Utah

Ever so slowly, the surreal light was giving way to shades of gray, that would in turn give way in the east to more golden colors preceding the dawn.

Slim loved this time of morning as he watched the horses up here in the high meadow on the upper reaches of Elk Creek (pronounced Elk "Crick" in these parts), surrounded by granite sentinels. They called the place he was camped in Sentinel Bowl, and it was one of his favorite places to tend horses in the late spring and early summer on the far western border of Utah, only a few miles from the Nevada line.

It was remote country, the closest town being the small town of Ibapah about fifteen miles to his north and west, population less than one hundred. To stumble upon any real civilization, you had to go five divides over and one hundred and fifty miles to the northeast, to the suburbs of Salt Lake City.

"And I reckon that's just about far enough…maybe not even far enough," thought Slim as he considered a place, the Salt Lake Valley, where something on the order of a million people lived.

Slim seldom, if ever, approached any such place. He'd been a cowboy for all of his life. He knew nothing different. He wanted nothing different. He pretty much enjoyed just being left alone to tend the animals and to associate…occasionally…with his other cowboy friends in a good game of poker, or a good meal of steak and potatoes.

There was those around him who said that life had passed him by…that he ought to get a little more into the modern era. But he had freely chosen the life he lived…the one he loved, and he did not regret it one iota. His wife was long since dead. His two kids visited him on occasion and he even got to hold the grandkids when they came by. But leave the life he loved? Not a chance.

Besides, he was still good at it...always had been. If you needed some horses tended or broken, or cattle herded...if you needed fences mended or built, or if you needed a corral, Slim was your man. When it came to livestock, he could tend 'em, and he could mend 'em. All over western Utah and eastern Nevada, from Elko and Ely down to Cedar City, Slim was known as a hardworking, totally reliable hand who liked nothing more than to work outdoors and keep to himself.

At sixty-eight, though his face was weathered, he had the physique, the lung capacity and the stamina of most "modern" men who hadn't cracked fifty yet, so he figured that he was doing okay.

This morning he was tending McCalvery's horses, and would be watching them all summer. He loved the Sentinel Bowl because it was high and it was remote...the air was clear, and here in the late spring the wind still blew cold and invigorating...and you had a view that was sketched by God's own hand.

Down below, the Deep Creek valley seemed to be swimming in the surreal light of a full moon that itself had not yet set. Hundreds of cattle were being tended down there by younger cowboys and, throughout the night, Slim would hear the night-herd song being sung by them as they lulled the cattle and kept them from getting restless. Slim loved that sound carried up here to him on the wind. It took him back to his own younger days and the times he'd spent with other young cowboys those many years ago.

Slim didn't think too much about world events, but he and the other cowboys could not help but be impacted somewhat by them. Most of the really young cowboys, those younger than thirty, were off fighting. You couldn't help but miss them.

Several of the others were enlisted in the local Home Guard Unit and took time off to stand another kind of watch...watching over the conveniences and infrastructure and necessities of modern man. As cowboys who had spent their lives watching over things, they were good at it.

In addition, there were large areas of Nevada, off further to the west, that were restricted ground for military training and testing. That was something that had been the case for many, many years and the installations there would normally produce occasional sounds that would drift over the ranges and reach them here. But now, with the world at war, those sounds were much more frequent and originated from areas now much closer to them.

Slim figured that those unsettling sounds were something to get used to, because all of that land was now constantly in use in the training of the large forces America was employing in this war, and in the testing of more and more systems to counter their enemies.

The way Slim figured it, if those sorry Chinese Communists, radical Islamics, or those Aztlan whackos, or whatever they were calling themselves these days, ever got through to him here in the mountains…he'd give them what for. He was still a crack shot with his Model 94, and he knew how to survive and move around in the wilderness.

Considering this, he did allow himself to contemplate one of the few modern events he had taken the time to witness in the last several years. That had been the Medal of Freedom ceremony after the killing of President Weisskopf.

He had held a deep respect for the former President, and had cast his ballot for him. Slim always voted, and he always voted for the man whom he felt could best do the job. He read the papers and he listened to the talk and he always made his mind up well in advance of any election. He might not be into a lot of the modern conveniences, but he didn't view voting as either modern or convenient…he figured it was a necessary part of being able to enjoy the free life of a cowboy.

Anyhow, he'd wanted to not only hear the new President, John Bowers…and he'd liked every bit of what he had heard…he wanted to hear Stacey Urkut speak. He felt an odd kinship to that woman whom he had never met. He figured, honestly and sincerely without any fanfare, that the way she had reacted to those Chinese bastards in Alaska was exactly the type of thing he would do here.

…and he'd liked everything she had said, too.

While he was contemplating all of this, and as the hour approached 5:30 AM, the pulsing, rumbling noises began.

It was way off in the west, but it was deep and it was getting louder. The very earth beneath his feet began to tremble ever so slightly in unison with the strange rumblings. As it got closer, the animals began to get disturbed and Slim got up to quiet them down.

Then the first rumbling was joined by another, and then another, until finally there were four distinct and separate pulses that were all somehow combining into one huge sound that was coming closer and closer.

…and as it came, the very sky began to lighten with much more than the dawn. And the tremendous strobe light effect was coming from the west, not the east. This was no dawn light. This was a light of obvious unnatural origins.

The horses were rearing now and Slim could tell that down in the valley a regular stampede was in the making. Luckily, the ropes Slim had set out for this high meadow corral last evening were holding and all of the horses he was watching were contained.

But the great rumbling continued to grow and the pulsating lights approaching from the west grew brighter.

Then, looking westward above the valley and across the Goshute Range, Slim saw the first…then the second, and third and fourth pulsing lights approaching…they were too bright to look at directly and Slim had to turn his head as they approached.

As the horses continued to rear behind him, Slim could do little more than stand there in transfixed awe and obliquely watch the spectacle as it approached and passed overhead.

"My God!" Slim thought. "We're launching something big into space…four of them at once."

All four lights were climbing very high, getting further away in the heavens even as they passed overhead. When Slim was once again able to look at them, he saw them all pass well above the feathery reach of some very high cirrus clouds as they continued onward…and upward.

He began to comprehend something of the distances and the speeds involved, and he realized that, although the four space craft and their payloads appeared relatively close together, they must be a significant distance apart.

As they got higher and higher into the atmosphere, their pulsating seemed to make them appear to be a slow, very bright twinkling, as if though they were surreally winking at him as they continued on. Slim watched in awe, not knowing that each of those pulses that were creating the deep rumblings were in fact miniature nuclear detonations against a specially designed shield which translated the force of the explosion into the nuclear pulse thrust that was taking the vessels into orbit.

Slowly the rumbling subsided and, as the horses began to settle down, the rapidly departing lights became little more than very bright strobing dots moving further and further off to the northeast in the heavens, as if to greet the dawn.

"Well," he said to himself, "you sure learn something new every day.

"I knew we had a lot of military exercises and training going on in Nevada, but I had no idea we were launching space ships from over there."

...and outside of a very select few... which this morning had been added to by hundreds of other ranchers, cowboys, tourists and people otherwise out in the mountains and deserts of western Utah and eastern Nevada, neither did anyone else.

Oh, to be sure, on the western outskirts of Salt Lake City a number of early morning risers had seen the strobe light effect in the sky and felt the, by then much diminished, rumblings. But those who did see it wrote it off as distant storms or lightning over the mountains, and most just slept peacefully through it all.

Which was precisely the way the United States military high command and civilian command authority hoped it would turn out and remain for as long as possible. The new President himself had only learned of, and given final approval to, the plan the day after the Medal of Freedom ceremony in Washington, D.C.

But the launching into space of the four large spacecraft on June 14, 2009, using the latest American technology, a single stage to orbit (SSTO) technology soon to be officially dubbed the Orion nuclear pulse boosters, was a date that would later be marked by historians as a turning point in the war.

It would also be recorded as a date that marked a turning point in the history of mankind.

Chapter 5

"I shall always remain confident of the American people's ability to rise to any challenge." - Norman Schwarzkopf autobiography, 1992

June 22, 2009, 18:49
Executive Council Chambers
Politburo, Beijing, China

Slim and the other cowboys and ranchers in Utah and Nevada were not the only ones to take note of the spectacular American launches into space. In addition to the American authorities monitoring the flights, Chinese personnel who had been scouting the perimeter of the various Nevada test facilities, but who had been unable to penetrate those facilities as of yet, also took note of what they saw and passed it on.

In addition, Chinese space monitoring stations in Mongolia and elsewhere within the occupied borders of Chinese territory, including the rebuilt facilities on the Island of Tarawa that the Chinese had again retaken from the Americans in 2007, all took notice of the objects entering earth orbit from trajectories originating out of the continental United States, and they recommended that something be done about them immediately.

That was why this meeting was being held. General Hunbaio was completing his briefing regarding what they knew of the launches and the objects being monitored in space.

"In summary, these launches represent unprecedented advancements for the Americans in heavy lift and in power. The four lift vehicles that they utilized were much larger than anything the Americans have used before for satellite insertions, and they are clearly powered by nuclear pulse detonations, using small, specially designed nuclear explosions to provide thrust into space.

This is not a new avenue of research. In the late 1940's and early 1950's the Americans studied this type of SSTO technology extensively. If they have perfected it...and based upon this insertion into space we must assume they have...their lift capacity will greatly exceed the size and lift capability of the largest Russian craft, or any other...and the resulting technological advantage is cause for great concern.

"As a result, the Americans have successfully inserted these large payloads into geo-synchronous orbit above the United States, and they did so with a minimum amount of exposure over our territories. They are busily constructing a station of some type there as we speak."

One of the executive committee members, Minister Win Chu, the Minister of Transportation and an individual who commanded significant internal security and regulatory forces of his own, interjected at this point. His frustration at hearing that the Americans were maintaining any significant presence in space, even for a week, was obvious. It defined an intolerable situation.

"Then use every anti-satellite weapon at our disposal and either destroy these craft and their payloads where they stand, or bring them down."

The General respectfully waited for the Minister, who was a long time ally and trusted confidant of President Zenim, to finish.

"Minister Win, our initial attempts to intercept these craft with those very weapons as the they went into orbit above us proved unsuccessful.

"Our failed attacks strongly suggest that the Americans have perfected and armed these spacecraft with significant laser defenses. Our current analysis indicates that there must be nuclear reactors of considerable power generating capability on board each spacecraft.

"This explains their abilities both in terms of positioning the large payloads, and in warding off our kinetic energy interception efforts.

"Right now, all four of the craft have unloaded their payloads. And assembled them into a facility of some type…a large facility at this position."

Using his pointer, the general leaned over the table and identified a position in space above the United States on the table top display apparatus that was projected onto the screen being used in the presentation to the executive committee.

"From this position, it is difficult for our mainland or Pacific Island facilities to get a clear picture, either visually or electronically, of all that the Americans are doing. The *ta shih* devices do not have the range to determine whether or not the Americans are using novel stealth material and technology in this venture …so we are unsure of the exact magnitude or disposition of these American forces in space.

"But, at this position they are still vulnerable to our attack.

"President, Minister Win, and other members of the Executive Committee, we have a proposal prepared that will describe how we can go about attacking the Americans at this location.

"I will now turn the time over to our newest member of the Committee and ask him to present that proposal to you. The operation is his brainchild. He is a People's Hero and the perfector of the singular weapons that have allowed us to push the Americans out of Asia and the Western Pacific Ocean and keep them out.

"The People's Republic had made many technological advances during this conflict and in the years leading up to it, but Lu Pham's creation must be recognized as the advancement, above all others, that has reaped the most rewards.

"Admiral Lu, please brief the rest of the committee on the attack plans."

**June 22, 2009, that same time
Executive Council Chambers
Politburo, Beijing, China**

Approaching the front of the council chambers, Lu Pham found it difficult to believe that he would be making such a presentation. He had been a member of the executive committee for less than a month, and he had thought he would sit in relative silence in such conferences for many years before counseling these others on matters of policy or state security.

The call for Lu Pham to serve in this capacity had come from Chin Zhongbaio, the Chairman of the Chinese Ocean-going Shipping Company (COSCO) and a member of the Executive Committee himself. That he, Lu Pham, would be tapped to be a Committee member had come as a complete shock to Lu, particularly after it was described to him that President Jien Zenim himself had made the request. He did not know the President personally and, though he had attended a few meetings that had also included the president, Lu had never imagined that Jien Zenim had taken personal note of him at all.

But as shocking as the offer to become a member of the Executive Committee of the Chinese Politburo was, it was one he readily accepted...and due to the President's overwhelming influence on the committee as a whole, it was one that was approved without dissent, open or otherwise.

Chairman Zhongbaio, General Hunbaio had done so much for Lu and his family over the last seventeen years. Their guidance and affirmation had finally allowed him to realize decades-old dreams and to keep promises that were just as old...promises to his long-deceased parents.

Lu had recognized for some time that all of those efforts in his behalf had been a part of the larger plans engineered by Jien Zenim himself, plans that included the Three Wisdoms, whose principles ruled China and all of the CAS...and extended to the GIR as well.

Well over sixty percent of the earth's population now lived under governmental systems that operated with those principles in mind.

They were principles Lu himself had ideologically and sincerely adopted, and that his family had also adopted. They had not only adopted them, but they genuinely believed in them. The principles were straightforward and simple, and challenged their enemy's notion of individual sovereignty and self-promotion with what Lu considered the ultimate statement about how the welfare of the many was the ultimate goal.

1. "All men and women are equal."

2. "All share equally in the bounty of a working and industrious society."

3. "One goal, one thought, one people for World peace."

Lu knew that he owed most of his success, and the elevated and comfortable position of his family over the last twenty years to Jien Zenim. So a call to serve which originated from the President himself...to serve with him...was a request which Lu Pham immediately and gratefully accepted.

These musings all flashed through Lu's mind in but a few seconds as he approached the front of the room and the position just vacated by General Hunbaio. Taking the pointer from the table, and advancing the computerized presentation to the slides he had prepared for this briefing, he addressed the entire committee.

"Mr. President and members of the Executive Committee, I am humbled and grateful to be standing here before you today.

"We have been presented a great technical and military challenge by the Americans. What they have accomplished is significant and there are many, many ways their accomplishment can be used to harm us, our allies, and our peoples if such advances are allowed continued success.

"We must not, and will not, allow that to be."

As Lu continued talking, President Jien Zenim and several of his closest confidants were pleased beyond measure at Lu Pham's opening remarks and with his positive attitude and demeanor.

It was a demeanor and an attitude he had earned, and it was one that was much needed on this committee as a whole. As the president watched, he could see that Lu's enthusiasm was contagious.

"...and well it should be," thought Zenim. "Lu has been successful in almost everything he has been involved in. From the Killer Whales to the recent efforts that are upsetting and slowing the American plans at Magadan.

"We will make good use of Lu Pham's can-do, positive attitude on this council...we must embrace such optimism if we are to prevail. Putting Lu Pham in this position will infuse these older ministers with his spirit...and Lu himself will become another valuable and life-long ally in the process."

Lu Pham continued.

"The Americans have presented us with monumental challenges in the past...and we have overcome them. Everyone thought that their vaunted AEGIS system, the one protecting their aircraft carriers, was unassailable...and yet we challenged and defeated it.

"We did so by exploiting the greatest weakness in that system and then saturating it with weapons of great speed and with sufficient numbers to overwhelm what defense they could muster.

"We have consistently kept up with and overcome their efforts to modify and upgrade their defenses and we have maintained our advantage. We know this is true by the reality of the facts we see around us.

"When was the last time an American aircraft carrier sailed with impunity within 500 miles or more of the Sea of Japan, the China Sea or anywhere near the Philippines?

""It has been years now.

"Let me give you two other examples.

"For years the Americans had their way in the skies over most nations who would dare oppose them. They used their stealth technology to fly with impunity through the sovereign airspace of those nations. They even did so at the beginning of this conflict.

"They do so no more.

"At the outset of this conflict, the Americans also used their satellite and GPS technology to great advantage against us and our allies. We won battles and lands from them only at great cost in numbers when facing this technology.

"They do not enjoy that advantage anymore either.

"In fact, it is their effort to reassert this type of dominance in space that we are facing, and, as with the other examples, we shall prevail here as well. And we will prevail by employing the same tactical philosophy with which we defeated their carrier battle groups, by using speed and overwhelming numbers.

"The Americans speak of defense in depth…layered defenses…as a means to help ensure the capability of defending their high value targets. It is a good philosophy that has served them for many years. In the case of their carriers, it was a flawed defense, and in this case, it does not serve them at all.

"In space, they do not yet have true layered defenses. They have a single defense that they have just implemented. As with AEGIS, we are going to cut through that defense and we are going to do it with speed and with numbers against which they cannot successfully defend.

"I trust that upon hearing the details of the plans that I am about to share with you, the entire council will be as swift and decisive in approving it as I expect our forces shall be in implementing it."

June 25, 2009, 02:54
Presidential Bedroom
The White House, Washington, D.C.

The incessant buzzing in his ear awakened President John Bowers immediately. It was not the first time he had heard it, and it certainly wouldn't be the last...but at 2:50 in the morning?

"Well, it must not be too earth-shattering," the President thought, "Otherwise they would be here in the room carrying Jane and me out of here."

Rising quickly and taking as much care as possible not to awaken his sleeping wife, the President whispered an acknowledgement into the telephone handset by his bed and then rapidly dressed and exited the bedroom into the hall.

There he found the head of the graveyard detail of his Secret Service team accompanied by Bill Hendrickson, his National Security Advisor.

As they immediately made their way to the elevator that would take them deep below the White House to the situation room, Bill Hendrickson spoke to the President.

"Mr. President, it's started. The Chinese are making an all-out effort to destroy Point Conception."

June 25, 2009, that same time
Point Conception Station
Geosynchronous Orbit above North America

Captain Bart Wynn surveyed the condition of his command, United States Space Station Point Conception. He quickly assessed its defenses against the developing Chinese attack from his commander's console in the CIC. The Chinese were clearly making an all-out effort to bring Conception down…and, if he had any say in the matter, they would fail in that effort.

Captain Wynn had ridden up to orbit aboard one of the four new spacecraft America had developed for this mission. They were all true single stage to orbit vessels that utilized a large supply of miniature nuclear explosive devices to boost them into space. Two of the vessels, the United States Space Ship (USSS) Orion and the USSS Nebulae, designated as LSC-D (Laser-armed Space Corvette – Defense) 001 and LSC-D 002, were specifically designed for the mission of creating and controlling this space station at Point Conception. The other two, the USSS Gaspra and the USSS Ida, designated LSF-RX (Laser-armed Space Frigate – Recon and Exploration) 001 and LSF-RX 002, were larger, more heavily armed vessels, capable of larger payloads and had been designed for deep space assignments. All of them were reusable, shuttle-like craft that were capable of powered landings on the earth once they reentered Earth's atmosphere.

They were also quite capable of defending themselves in space, and the payloads that the two corvettes had carried into space were even more capable in that regard, as the Chinese would discover shortly.

The two corvettes assigned to the station formed the command and communication modules of the USSS Conception, while the payloads they carried formed the primary defense and living modules. The corvettes were a semi-permanent part of the station and were not scheduled to return to earth for over two years, when they would be replaced by the next class of craft, which would be more capable and would take up permanent residence at the station.

The crews would be in place for their entire tour of space duty, scheduled to last here on the station from twelve to eighteen months. The way Captain Wynn looked at it, this was war and they had a mission to perform here in geosynchronous orbit above America, and they would fulfill that mission at all costs.

The two frigates, the Gaspra and the Ida, after shedding a deceptive external skin and leaving portions of their payloads here to assist in the creation of Conception Station, had proceeded further out into space. They did this by first using conventional fuel and rockets to achieve a desired thrust that carried them approximately twenty thousand miles distant from Conception Station, where they then deployed a light sail devices to first achieve, and then maintain the velocity that would allow them to reach their objective within the time constraints imposed by their mission planning, just short of nine months later.

They would indeed be traveling much further out into space.

As a result, The crews' on the Gaspra and Ida had tours of duty that would last somewhat longer than the personnel working here at Conception Station, but they would rendezvous here on their way back to earth eighteen months from now, after what would hopefully prove to be a successful and monumental mission.

Their departure using conventional propulsion had been shielded by the positioning of the station and by their stealthy design characteristics which would keep prying Chinese or other enemy radar and thermal sensors from detecting them. Their exotic exterior material was of such a nature that radar and thermal energy signatures were either deflected or completely eliminated. Except when traveling by nuclear pulse thrust, which could be used at any time to augment their other propulsion capabilities, they would be invisible to their enemies.

It had been hoped that their departure and continued voyage had been kept a complete secret from their enemies…and they had been completely successful to date in realizing that hope.

But all of that was not material to the next few minutes, when the fate of the USSS Conception and its personnel, and the credibility of the engineers and designers who had developed it, would hang in the balance. The future of America's presence in space during the war, and, as would later be recognized, the ultimate outcome of the war itself would also hang in the balance.

Captain Wynn absorbed the information coming into the CIC. He had long since understood the reason that experienced naval officers had been chosen to command the growing number of United States Space Command (USSC) vessels.

The environment in which he was now operating was much less a flight deck, and more like the Combat Information Center of a major naval combatant. In fact, the CIC had been designed using the principles learned in modern naval war fighting In this case, the vessel was in space, but he was being tasked with, and exercising, all of his naval command and leadership experience.

Each of the two corvettes carried two banks of new laser cannons called Laser Weapons Systems (LWS) that got their energy from the nuclear reactors that powered the craft and the station. Those reactors were the latest, most proficient, and most miniaturized designs that America had ever produced and they were specifically designed to work in conjunction with the environmental systems, the laser weaponry, the research systems and the communication and sensory systems that the corvettes carried

In addition, each of the craft carried two kinetic energy weapons called Kinetic Energy Defense Systems (KEDS), which fired depleted uranium projectiles at hyper-velocity speeds. They used a derivative of the Hail Storm missile's solid state electronic fire controllers to propel those projectiles at a variable rate, depending on the engagement.

But those defenses were only a part of the station's defense capabilities. The defense module had included the provisions and equipment necessary to deploy the station's two primary defenses.

One of these was a bank of sixty-four Block Vs Standard missiles and the latest AEGIS radar and software modules to control them, specifically modified for space engagements. The entire system was known as SPAEGIS. The system, like its naval and land-based cousins, was designed to control all of the station's defenses, including those on the two craft that were now a part of the system.

Each of those Block Vs missiles had a small tactical nuclear warhead and a range of over 250 miles. They were intended for use against just the sort of attack the Chinese were staging: massed missiles and kinetic projectiles.

"They think they can attack and take down this station like they did the International Space Station three years ago," the Captain thought. "Well .... let 'em try it."

Captain Wynn's thoughts on the destruction of the International Space Station by the Chinese came from eyewitness experience. He had been the commander on the Space Station at the time of the Chinese attack, and if it weren't for the fact that the shuttle Discovery was docked with the Space Station at the time, and the crew evacuated by means of the shuttle just moments before the attack, he and everyone else on board would have been killed.

As it was, the hulk of the Space Station had fallen out of orbit and to earth, impacting in Brazil, killing many thousands in Rio de Janeiro. That tragedy had resulted in Brazil joining in the war against the Chinese as allies of America.

Captain Wynn was confidant that his defenses would prevent any repeat of that terrible episode. The nuclear warheads on the Block Vs Standard missiles would literally blow holes in the "shotgun" pattern of projectiles meant to take out Station Conception. They would also be targeted on any large groupings of missiles approaching the station.

Then, once any targets, or "vampires" in colloquial naval jargon, had gotten past the missiles, that's when the lasers and kinetic energy weapons on the two corvettes would target any "leakers" as they approached closer to the station. The Captain was quite confident in their capabilities as well. They had performed admirably against just such attacks as they made their way in orbit to this point.

Any Chinese weapons that were able to get through those two layers of defense would then run hard up against the last defense measure, which had also been carried aloft in the payload of the defense module.

This final defensive layer was a reactive mesh of fine but tremendously strong poly-carbon, called Poly-Carbon Reactive Mesh (PCRM), that was arrayed around the station in a harness. The harness holding it in place was flexible and had fifty remote controlled thrusters which could control the location and shape of the mesh depending on the attack profile. That mesh was also engineered to allow either missiles or projectiles to be fired out through it, but would use its carbon strength and explosive reaction to destroy or deflect any object attempting to penetrate it from the outside.

Finally, Captain Wynn knew that the structure of the station itself, like naval ship construction, had been designed for battle. Airtight, strengthened bulkheads, and thick dogged hatches. A skeleton structure made of the hardest metals and composites available, and an all steel exterior skin with Kevlar armor covering critical spaces.

"These babies were not cheap, and they are not "light", but neither are aircraft carriers," thought the Captain.

"We aren't going to be caught in a defenseless position again, like we were on the ISS three years ago."

The time for the initial engagement of the Chinese attack had come. Their first wave of missiles and projectiles were coming into range.

"You may commence firing," the Captain ordered as weapons officers and their personnel began launching Block Vs missiles and preparing the lasers and kinetic weapons for engagement.

But while the Chinese were unaware of the exact nature of the specific weapons the Captain would employ against them, their planners had made allowances for many of the principles upon which those specific weapons operated.

June 25, 2009, that same time
275 miles away
Approaching Point Conception Station

Two hundred Chinese anti-satellite missiles were approaching Point Conception. Each was loaded with high explosive warheads and each was traveling at orbital speed. They were coming at the American space station in five waves of forty missiles each. Each wave approaching simultaneously from slightly different angles of attack along the same threat axis, as much as orbital mechanics would allow.

Interspaced between the simultaneous waves of missiles, were clouds of thousands of heavy metal projectiles which had been released by other missiles after they had been inserted into orbit...over five thousand projectiles in each wave, and there were five waves of these also targeting the station.

The Chinese had held very little back, just enough to counter any single satellite launches the Americans or their allies might attempt under cover of this battle. It was their intent, with the massive attack, to completely overwhelm whatever defenses the Americans had, and to obliterate the American presence in space.

June 25, 2009, less than a minute later
240 miles away
Approaching Point Conception Station

Station Conception targeted five Block Vs missiles on each wave of Chinese missiles. They were programmed to detonate in a line immediately in front of each wave. The station targeted two missiles on each "cloud" of projectiles.

The first engagement against the missiles was successful for the Americans, but not completely so. Three waves of Chinese missiles suffered over 90% attrition and only two missiles from each of those groups continued inbound towards Conception. The other two attacks on Chinese missiles were less effective, allowing seven missiles from one group and five from the other to proceed on towards the station-and each of these missiles was relatively widely dispersed from the others in its group.

The engagement against the kinetic projectiles was more effective in percentages, knocking off course or vaporizing over 95% of the projectiles in each wave. But this still left five waves of several hundred projectiles still approaching the station in patterns that would intercept the station and either destroy it or do it great harm.

At this point, a weakness in the American system became evident. The Chinese attack, due to its approach from the opposite rotational direction of the space station, was approaching at two times the orbital speed. In gyro-synchronous orbit, this amounted to something over 2,000 miles per hour. This meant that, in less than two minutes, the attack would come too close to the station for continued Block Vs missile engagements.

The American system had to analyze the effectiveness of the first attack before launching a second one. Captain Wynn had elected not to activate the SPAEGIS provision for launching a second wave based on projected effectiveness of the first engagement. He determined that, with only one bank of sixty-four missiles, the risk of using precious missiles on potentially incorrect projections was just too great. He was confident that he would get in two waves of the Block Vs missiles, and that his secondary and final defenses would then suffice.

He was right…but only in part.

Precious seconds ticked off until solid information about the nature of the remaining Chinese threat was available and the system engaged the remaining vampires. The system had used thirty missiles for the first engagement; it now fired another twenty-six missiles, leaving only eight missiles in reserve.

This engagement individually targeted each of the remaining Chinese missiles and targeted the remaining dispersed clouds of projectiles with two missiles each.

June 25, 2009, three minutes later
140 miles away
Approaching Point Conception Station

More small nuclear explosions lit up space, this time much closer to the station.

Captain Wynn was concerned, as were his subordinates, but that concern was buried underneath the professionalism and effectiveness of their training. They performed their duties and tasks without pause and without waver. Their very lives depended on them not breaking their routine or wasting precious seconds.

SPAEGIS quickly informed the controllers in the CIC that two Chinese missiles somehow made their way through the nuclear fireballs set in their paths. The engagements of these missiles was immediately assigned to, and slaved to the lasers and kinetic projectiles on the two American corvettes attached to the station.

At this point, when Captain Wynn saw that only two missiles had gotten through his Block Vs missile defense, he issued some direct orders that modified the SPAEGIS defense parameters.

"Have the system target the leaker missiles with one of the LWS systems from both the Nebulae and the Orion!

"Use the KEDS and other LWS from those corvettes to knock down the leaker projectiles.

"Do it NOW!"

The duty officers and operators quickly programmed the system to do as the Captain instructed.

There were only twenty seconds left until missiles and projectiles would begin impacting Conception Station.

June 25, 2009, three minutes later
Within twenty miles
Point Conception Station

The lasers from the two corvettes performed effectively and quickly, destroying both of the remaining Chinese missiles.

But the remaining Chinese kinetic projectiles from all five waves were now approaching the station. They were greatly dispersed as a result of the two Block Vs nuclear missile attacks and each had to be targeted individually, based on the threat that it posed. They still numbered over three hundred separate projectiles.

These were now coalescing into a single, widely dispersed cloud of projectiles. The lasers and kinetic weapons aboard the two corvettes performed well against these objects, but there were just too many individual projectiles to destroy or deflect in such a short amount of time. One hundred and sixty-five of the projectiles made their way through the station's point defenses and now approached the PCRM defense.

That device had deployed some eight miles out from the station and had made a final adjustment after the final engagement of Block Vs missiles. There wasn't time to adjust to the effectiveness of the point defenses. One hundred and fifteen of the small projectiles were destroyed or deflected by their collision with the PCRM. Another twenty-six missed the PCRM altogether, having been sufficiently deflected by prior action to cause them to miss the station in any case.

But twenty-four projectiles succeeded in making their way all the way through every layer of the American defenses. They either passed through holes left by projectiles that had impacted the mesh just prior to them, or they passed through small areas of coverage that the mesh had missed in its deployment.

Fourteen of these projectiles shredded the primary communications antennae on the communications module, destroying the high speed digital interface at the same time. Ten of the projectiles impacted the station along a line that stretched between the living and defense modules, penetrating those modules in seven places, and creating havoc in the secondary, alternate command center for the SPAEGIS system. Six personnel in that area were killed and another four were injured before they could be evacuated to air-tight, secure areas of the station. Another three personnel who were on sick leave were killed in their bunks in the living module.

Backup communications with the Station were somewhat slower and more cumbersome, but Captain Wynn informed his superiors on earth that the station had survived and was still capable of putting up a fight and performing its mission.

It would be eight hours, requiring a four hour EVA by three personnel, before something approaching normal communications between the USSS Conception and its control facilities in Nevada, or the alternate facilities in California or Florida could be re-established. It would be two days before repairs were sufficiently far along in the alternate SPAEGIS command center that it could be manned without the need for space suit protection against the vacuum of space. Two cabins in the living module were beyond repair and were evacuated until more serious repair equipment and the necessary material could be launched into space.

That launch and re-supply would occur much sooner than originally planned, and it would be repeated many more times than had been planned as well. As was the case with American forces off Magadan, the USSS Conception was in a position most threatening to the Chinese and their allies, and they intended to use every means at their disposal in the effort to dislodge it.

June 25, 2009, early morning
News Stations throughout North America

Radio and TV news outlets all over the country carried the dramatic footage of the engagement in space. The hundreds of bright flashes could not be missed by anyone who was awake at that hour and chanced to look outside. The brilliant flashes from small nuclear explosions lit up the sky across much of North America, much like a thunderstorm lights up the sky with its lightning flashes.

But these flashes were much, much further away, and there was no resounding *BOOM* or roll of thunder accompanying them.

Numerous calls to emergency 911 numbers in cities, counties, and states were vaguely answered as the operators and dispatchers themselves knew nothing of the event. Calls by state agencies to federal agencies for the most part suffered from the same lack of information and ignorance.

The Department of Homeland Security and the Defense Department both released official statements at noon Eastern time regarding the matter. They were worded exactly the same and represented the official government statement regarding the engagement. All of the major radio and TV networks picked it up, as well as the major internet news sites.

"The numerous flashes in the skies over the United States this morning are nothing to be concerned about. There is no danger to the continental U.S.

"Our forces have established a defensive station in space over North America that our enemies are trying to destroy or dislodge in space. That is all than can be shared at this point.

"The enemy has been unsuccessful in their attempts. We are confident that they will continue to be unsuccessful, although they will most certainly try again and the public may witness more displays similar to this morning's.

"Pray for our service personnel, wherever they may be engaged. Thank you "

This announcement did much to allay the public's immediate fears and quelled some of the more frantic and hysterical speculation that was beginning to be spread across the nation by noon on that day. But the statement and the event itself were also recognized by the vast majority of the people as representing a significant change in the nature of the warfare.

It was a change, despite its potential serious consequences, that most Americans welcomed.

America was taking the initiative in ways the enemy had not expected and that enemy was now being forced to react to American moves as opposed to the other way around, which had remained the case through much of the war.

It was indeed a change welcomed by America and her allies.

June 26, 2009, late in the day
2500 miles west of the Japanese Coast
Control Room, USS Nevada, SSGN Trident Submarine

The trajectories had been back-tracked from all of the launches of the Chinese anti-satellite weapons and their launch locations had been identified. Now America was going to respond. All of those launch coordinates were entered and the missiles were ready to launch.

It would be the first launch of these specially modified Trident missiles in anger. Sixteen of her twenty-four missiles would be launched. Each had ten independently guided warheads, MIRVs as they were known. One hundred and sixty devices were about to rain from the sky on launch sites throughout northeastern China and Mongolia.

Captain Lanier had arrived on site at the launch coordinates twenty minutes earlier, and had used the sophisticated detection equipment on his boat to thoroughly check the surrounding waters for any sign of the enemy.

Outside of his two Virginia Class SSN escorts, there were no other vessels or aircraft in the area, and he was a hole in the water. Or at least he would be until he made these missile launches. Then he would have to "shoot and scoot" the heck out of here.

He was confident that the Chinese were very capable of tracking the trajectories of his own missiles back to this spot, and he wanted to be long gone before any of their aircraft or ships equipped with Killer Whales arrived.

"You may launch the missiles when ready," the Captain ordered and the final countdown followed.

At the appropriate moment, first one missile was launched and then that one was followed in quick succession by fifteen others. They all broke the surface of the sea, through the tops and bottoms of swells, with tremendous geysers of water marking their exit points. They quickly rose up through the low ceiling with increasing speed.

Soon, the missiles had risen high enough in the atmosphere for the CAS radar coverage out of Japan to take note of their passage and relay alarm throughout the Chinese military and political hierarchy. Before the final trajectories were calculated, Jien Zenim and every member of the politburo, wherever they were located, were being whisked by security personnel into hardened bunkers in their specific locations, or to airfields for hurried takeoffs, where time permitted.

Once it was clear that the targets were military launch sites in Mongolia and northeast China, tensions lessened somewhat, but it would not be until impact verified that the payloads were non-nuclear that a Chinese nuclear retaliatory attack against mainland America would be stood down.

Before that happened, the Chinese KS-3 anti-ballistic missile defense system came into play. Having proven their success at intercepting Russian ballistic nuclear missiles over Russia in the previous year, the Chinese hierarchy had deployed these systems profusely around the Chinese capital and around all critical war industry sites and military bases. They had full confidence that they would perform equally well against the Americans.

They were disappointed in that expectation.

American miniaturization technology had developed to the point that each MIRV warhead employed no less than ten very realistic and very accurate decoys. These decoys did not remain with the actual warhead itself as did their Russian counterparts. The American technology allowed the decoys themselves to independently target what otherwise would be considered legitimate locations. To the surprise of the Chinese defenders, instead of a maximum of one hundred and sixty expected targets from sixteen Trident tracks, they were faced with over one thousand.

This fact would reverberate throughout the Chinese defense and political leadership, particularly in COSTIND where General Hunbaio would be sorely pressed to respond, and to explain why this capability was not known beforehand.

The large numbers of re-entry vehicle warheads, even though only 10% were actual, made the Chinese solution infinitely more difficult. Several critical minutes were lost in analysis of the attack patterns and the Chinese system almost became so involved with the analysis that no decision was made before impact.

Finally, with only a few seconds remaining before initial impact, when it became clear that virtually all of the anti-satellite launch sites were targeted by one group of threats, and that two other groups were exclusively targeting critical military manufacturing sites and critical economic infrastructure sites, the Chinese elected to focus on these four hundred threats.

Commands were issued, priorities were set and the Chinese began launching KS-3 anti-ballistic missiles.

The KS-3 missiles performed well given the time constraints, but they were wholly ineffective in preventing the almost complete destruction of China's anti-satellite launch facilities. Only thirty-five of the one hundred forty actual warheads were destroyed. Another two hundred and fifty KS-3 missiles were wasted in intercepting harmless decoys.

The massive follow-on attack against the USSS Conception that was planned for the afternoon of June 26th, would not occur. All the Chinese could muster was a relatively weak attack that day, one that the remaining missiles on the Conception, coupled with the lasers and kinetic energy weapons on the two corvettes, was able to handle without further damage or loss of life.

June 27, 2009, 23:11
National Security Agency
Washington, D.C.

After the attack on the USSS Conception Space Station, Bill Hendrickson had spent over sixteen hours in continuous discussion and debate with his most talented analysts, and with those from the Defense Department as well. Ultimately it was determined what the extent of damage actually was on the Conception and what was needed to repair it. They also spent considerable time analyzing what it would take to ensure the continued ability for the Conception to defend herself in the face of the Chinese attack profiles, as well as how the Chinese might modify that profile to be more effective. With only eight Block Vs missiles remaining, the entire command chain knew that the Station could not fend off another attack like the one she had just repelled, much less any improvements the Chinese were certain to factor in.

As if to emphasize this, six of those eight remaining missiles were used to defend the Conception against the much smaller attack the Chinese mounted against the station on the afternoon of June 26th.

Several anxious minutes were spent by the President and his senior military advisors as that attack played itself out. Those moments were even more anxious than the attack of the 25th because everyone knew how vulnerable the station was, and how much depended on keeping Point Conception controlled and protected until the other American space mission returned.

Although the numbers of personnel involved were small, only forty-six on the Station and fifteen each on the outbound Space Frigates, the strategic import was immense.

"And the Chinese recognize it as much as we do.

"Thank God the Nevada's attack was successful," the National Security Advisor said to himself as he wearily lifted his briefcase for a brief trip home.

"If they had pulled off another massive attack yesterday, we would have lost the Conception and everyone on board.

"Well, now we've done all we can to protect her and we have the process in place to keep it that way for as long as it takes."

This had been accomplished with four more launches out of Nevada that very morning, the morning of June 27th...the last four corvettes in America's new spacecraft inventory, all of them designed to re-supply the Space Station and for self-defense. Once again that morning American space vehicles were observed climbing high into the heavens over eastern Nevada and western Utah.

All four had run the gauntlet of what was now only minor Chinese anti-satellite attacks and all four had rendezvoused with the Conception late in the day of June 27th. They carried the repair material and the equipment necessary to allow the crew of the

Conception to repair the major of damage she had suffered, or similar damage that she might suffer in the future.

In addition, they delivered another complete defense module loaded with another 64 Block Vs missiles. This module was the last one available to the United States until more could be manufactured, and since these were working prototypes, it would be at least two months before that manufacturing line was finished with the first production units.

"But if we want to keep Conception up in space, these units are necessary," Hendrickson thought as he approached the guard station and prepared to exit the building.

With that additional module and with enough missiles to replenish the almost empty SPAEGIS cell already in place on the Conception and with the 128 spare missiles that were also delivered, Captain Wynn would have an inventory of 256 Block Vs missiles for defending his vessel. As a policy decision, based on the magnitude of the attacks the Chinese were willing to conduct, the United States determined to not allow the stock of spare missiles in place at Conception Station to fall below 64 missiles at any time.

Depending on the frequency and nature of the attacks, and depending on their effectiveness, that policy decision would require the United States to replenish the Space Station much more often than had been initially contemplated. It would mean America's production facilities, like the Skunk Works and other very sensitive and secret installations, were going to have to ramp up significantly to produce the missiles, the vessels and the material necessary.

"We're just going to have to, as they say out west, cowboy up," he said to himself as the guard at the security station checked his identification.

"What's that you said, Mr. Hendrickson?" the guard asked.

"Oh, it was nothing, Jim," Hendrickson replied as the guard retuned his identification and unlocked the gate.

"I was just talking to myself.

"We'll see you tomorrow," he said as he walked through the turnstile and reached for the door that led out into the secured parking garage facility.

"Okay. Good night, Mr. Hendrickson," the guard replied.

"Have a safe drive home."

June 30, 2009, 19:00
Secure CAS-GIR Conference line
Executive Conference Room, the Politburo
Beijing, China

"Then we are agreed," said Jien Zenim to the other two leaders on the line with him.

"We will make the offer to the Americans and their allies July 2nd and give them four days to respond, offering a mutual cease fire across the board while they consider the offer."

Jien Zenim waited for the reply from Hasan Sayeed of the GIR and KP Narayannen of India. They had been on the line for almost three hours, discussing and going over Jien's dramatic peace plan initiative.

Basically it called for first an armistice, which would last no more than six months, and then a complete peace treaty which would lock in borders that would be recognized and respected by all nations signing the accord...and those nations would be every major combatant currently involved in the conflict.

Jien was convinced, and now both Sayeed and Narayannen reflected that same conviction, that the three of them could easily bring all GIR and CAS countries into agreement with this. They were all also convinced that if the United States, the United Kingdom, Brazil, Israel, and Russia signed on to the agreement, then they would bring all other nations who had been fighting for the allied cause into the fold as well.

And the terms, given the current position of military forces, were very conciliatory and generous from the CAS and GIR perspectives. It had taken Jien the better part of the three hours to convince particularly Sayeed that China and the GIR should give up some of its current hard-won gains.

The world map would reflect these changes and would depict the new world order that Jien felt was necessary if the CAS and the GIR were to maintain their predominance in Asia and the Mid East and parity with the United States and Europe.

In order to accomplish that, Jien was willing to lay all of the following on the table.

- Complete, orderly withdrawal of Chinese forces from Alaska, Panama, and South America.

- Complete withdrawal of Chinese, Indian and GIR forces from New Caledonia, Tarawa, the New Hebrides, the Loyalty, the Solomon and the Admiralty Islands in the Pacific.

- The sectioning of the Continent of Australia into four new nations, one Islamic, one Hindu, one Chinese and the entire southeastern corner of the Continent to be returned to the exiled government of Australia.

- Recognition of Israeli borders that extend from the Golan Heights westward to the Mediterranean Sea on the north, from the Sea of Galilee down the Jordan River to the Dead Sea and from there to the Red Sea on the west, and including the entire Sinai Peninsula on the South, bordered by the Suez Canal.

- Withdrawal of all GIR forces from the Continent of Europe, granting the former European holdings of Turkey on the European continent to Greece.

- Withdrawal of all GIR and CAS forces from Russia, back to the Siberian border, recognizing the new nation of Siberia as an independent nation.

- The complete demilitarization of space.

- All other borders within occupied, defeated or allied nations would remain as they are, meaning that the GIR would encompass all of North Africa and all of the Middle East, including Turkey, except for the nation of Israel.

It would mean that Chinese and CAS influence would remain in effect, governing all of Korea, Japan, the Philippines, the new Chinese Province of Formosa, all of the China Sea, with the former nations of Thailand, Burma, Singapore, Malaysia, Bangladesh, Nepal, and Sri Lanka simply ceasing to exist, becoming a part of China, India or other CAS states.

The sea lanes from the Mid East, through the Indian Ocean and into the Pacific Region through the China Sea, would be surrounded and completely dominated by GIR and CAS nations.

All in all, these conditions represented the necessary strategic positioning for China, India, and the GIR to control commerce and regulate it in favor of the CAS and GIR alliance into the foreseeable future…and to establish them both as individually equal to either the United States or the European Union. Working together as an economic block, it would assure their ascendancy over both of those rivals.

But Sayeed and Narayannen had to go along in order for it to work, and Zenim believed they would.

It was Sayeed who spoke first.

"You are proposing much, President Jien," the Grand Ayatollah and Imam said.

"The footholds we have in Europe are very strong, as is the position where our forces control all of the Australian continent.

"Recognition of the Zionist state of Israel has always been a very sore point for us, particularly now that they control all of the Holy City of Jerusalem. I can hardly imagine the ruling Mullahs and other Ayatollahs of my faith agreeing to this last point in particular."

Zenim had expected the most resistance from Sayeed. Sayeed was a man of sincere and absolutely committed faith. But he was also a man who considered himself God's mouthpiece to his people...in fact, if truth be known, to all of them and one day that could be a problem.

"Hasan, take this to Allah...he will see the wisdom in this and communicate it to you. Islam occupies all of its truly holy sites and for once, they exist under a united and faithful Islam. No western influence and no corruption.

"Israel's and America's growth and influence will have been contained. The infidels will have been taught a lesson and all of Islam, from the Pacific Ocean, through the Mid East and across Africa is united.

"If you received direction from above and communicated it to your ruling counsels, I am sure they would not only understand, but would accept it.

"It is not for me to say...but I would ask that you consider it and then take it to the one you receive direction from."

"Could it be true? Was Sayeed hearing an acknowledgement of Allah's existence and guidance from Zenim?" Sayeed asked himself when the Chinese President was finished talking.

As he considered the words, Hasan Sayeed was sure, now that he thought about it, that he had heard a bit of a patronizing tone in the Chinese leader's voice...and he did not like that at all. A discomfort bordering on disgust immediately registered on Sayeed's face and Jien Zenim thought for a moment that he had pushed too hard.

But then Sayeed continued to reflect. Although his immediate, instinctual emotional reaction to the perceived patronizing tone was evident, Sayeed did not let it rule his thought process or his ultimate reaction. He was too disciplined by the years, by experience, and by his own faith for that. The GIR leader knew that Zenim had worked with him to make all of the things the Chinese leader had just spoken of a reality.

"Have we accomplished enough of the task for now?" he asked himself…and his God.

After a few more seconds, he came to his determination.

"I will think and pray over this. Perhaps it is enough. Perhaps we have made the gains that Allah would have us make at this time."

Knowing full well that the gains he spoke of were only meant for this current time. Never for an instant would Hasan Sayeed concede his overriding and preeminent calling. And that was the unification of all of Islam…meaning, according to the Holy Koran, the unification of not just all of the current Islamic nations, which he had already accomplished, but the unification of the entire world under that holy banner.

July 2, 2009, 21:15
Situation Room, The White House
Washington, D.C.

By the morning of July 1st, the GIR and CAS leaders had come to their conclusion. Hasan Sayeed had agreed in principle with the proposal, but wanted to present it to his ruling clerics, mullahs, and other Ayatollahs before the plan was actually implemented.

The Indian president had gone along with the plan immediately. He saw it as an opportunity to extend an olive branch to the West and, more importantly, to reduce the wartime influence that Minister Patel was increasingly exerting.

With an armistice, followed by an eventual peace, KP Narayannen knew that his administration would be hailed as one of the strongest, most successful and most popular Indian administrations in the history of their nation.

So, with provision that the offer was preliminary, and would require fine tuning if the West accepted it in principle, the proposal for an armistice and the steps to a permanent peace were communicated to the United States.

President Bowers and a surprised Security Council were now reviewing that proposal. Bill Hendrickson, the National Security Advisor, was leading the discussion regarding the proposal itself and what the National Security Agency, Pentagon, and State Department analysts had been able to make of it.

"Mr. President, this first slide is an illustration of current conditions with respect to actual physical control throughout the Pacific and Asia."

He pressed a button on the remote control, and the display on the screen brought up an image of the Pacific Ocean and Asia, from Alaska and the Hawaiian Islands, across all of Asia, the sub-continent and across the Middle East.

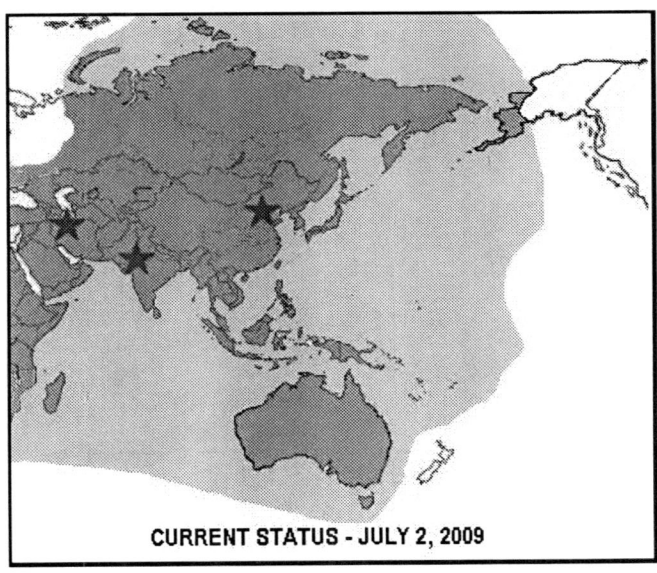

"As you can clearly see, from the western end of Alaska across the Pacific to New Zealand, and basically all points westward, the enemy is in control. We have made a very slight incursion at Magadan which is being fiercely contested.

"All of Asia and Australia are in enemy hands, as well as all major Islands stretching between them.

"Outside of Israel and areas to the north and east of Damascus and to the south towards Egypt, the entire Mid East is currently controlled by the enemy.

"Large areas of Europe, despite progress around Moscow, still lie in enemy hands, as does all of North Africa and all of East Africa.

"This next slide will show what the CAS and GIR have proposed as an armistice and ultimate peace plan for these same areas:

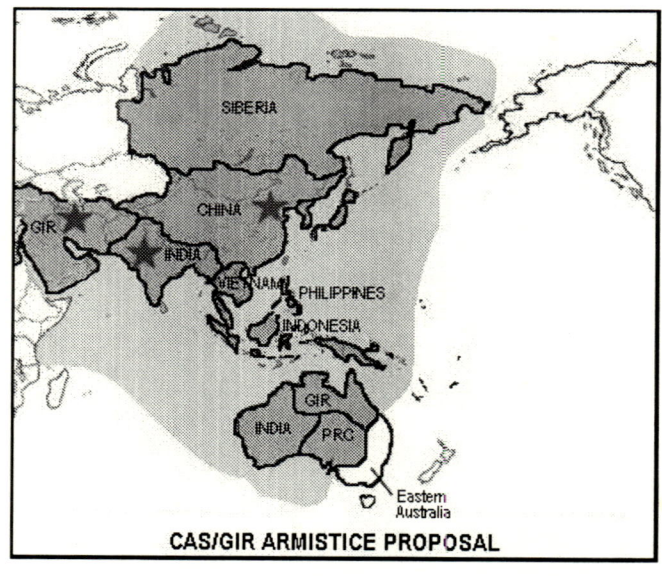

"In this slide, we see to what extent the enemy is willing to go at this point in the conflict to stop the fighting.

"They propose a complete withdrawal from Alaska and from many southwest Pacific Islands. They also propose a free Australian state on the southeast coast…the most fertile and rich part of the continent.

"They are also proposing a withdrawal from all countries in Africa that are not GIR signatory states, withdrawing from all of Europe back to the Siberian and Turkish borders. Those are significant amounts of territory that would be returned without a fight.

"In exchange, as an overview, they are calling for our withdrawal from the Magadan area, for Greek annexation the European portions of Turkey, and for our acceptance of all other acquisitions by the CAS and GIR armed forces."

The new President, who had been in office only a month, but who had been involved in the war from the outset, wanted to hear from his closest advisors. Although the Vice President and Secretary of Defense offices had not been filled yet, those nominations were expected to be approved by Congress within the week. Both of those men were sitting in the room now with the President and already occupied very important roles within the government. So the President respectfully turned to Secretary of State, Fred Reissinger, and Chairman of the Joint Chiefs of Staff, General Jeremy Stone, for their input and comments.

"Fred, what are your thoughts on this proposal? I have to admit that I am quite surprised," the President asked as he turned to Secretary Reissinger.

"I never expected this bunch to make anything that might be remotely viewed as a concession."

The Secretary of State, who had been one of the closest advisors and friends of President Weisskopf, and who had come to trust and respect John Bowers since Norm Weisskopf had appointed him National Security Advisor in 2004, and later as Vice president after the death of Alan Reeves in 2005, was also surprised by the proposal. He knew that there were several of their allies, particularly in Europe, who would be positively disposed towards an armistice.

But he just couldn't countenance it himself.

"Mr. President, although some of the nations who make up our coalition will probably feel inclined to negotiate with our enemies over such a proposal, and although I am also personally quite surprised that such a proposal has been made…still, I am personally opposed to it.

"Despite their ceding lands that they now control back to us…what they are left with, diplomatically speaking, and I believe economically speaking as well, represents nothing short of an almost complete victory for them…and we would be giving that victory credibility and acceding to it by seriously considering any such proposal of theirs."

As the Secretary of State paused for a moment to gather more thoughts, the President interjected.

"Fred, I am also personally dead set against any negotiation with these people.

"But, from an overall diplomatic standpoint, once they have had time to consider it…and it has gone to all of them, just like it has come to us…the question is, who will continue to stand with us against the CAS and GIR, and who will vacillate?

"Today in this meeting, we must answer that question to our own satisfaction from a diplomatic and international standpoint."

The Secretary of State replied. "Exactly, Mr. President…that is exactly the issue. I believe that our most staunch allies, and those from whom we receive the vast majority of our worldwide materiel and personnel support will solidly stand with us against this proposal.

"The United Kingdom, Israel, Canada, Spain, Brazil, Italy, certainly Russia…and all of the governments in exile…Australia, Japan, the Republic of China, Turkey, etc. They will all unite behind us and oppose anything short of an unconditional surrender on the part of the CAS and GIR.

"Having said that, we can probably expect France and perhaps Germany, some of the Scandinavian countries and perhaps some of the African countries to want to give this type of proposal some traction…to negotiate some kind of an end to the war on the most favorable terms. Basically many of the countries who have opposed our foreign policies in the past and who have been relatively untouched by the fighting to date within their own borders."

The President considered this. What would happen to their coalition if France and Germany in particular, who were providing significant men and materiel to the fight in Europe, blanched and either made a separate peace or tried to reinvigorate the United Nations' influence? To date, the UN had been proven wholly ineffective in dealing with the global conflict because so many of its adherents were unwilling to either defy or face down the blatant actions of China and the GIR in particular.

This was because so many had showed themselves for what they were: actual allies in the effort to undermine and destroy true liberty in the world. They had used the wealth of the west in general, and of America in particular, to means and ends that were harmful and destructive to American ideals and the traditional American way of life…culminating in this very conflict.

John Bowers had come to the conclusion, just as President Weisskopf before him had done, that he was unalterably opposed to any re-invigoration of the UN in its former form to mediate or become officially involved in the resolution of the crisis. Its mostly empty corridors and meeting chambers could remain that way in perpetuity as far as he was concerned

"Do you believe, Fred, that any of the nations who would be inclined to negotiate about this, would seek a separate peace?"

Fred Reissinger had already considered this, trying to gauge the strength and intentions of the leaders of those nations.

"Mr. President, while I believe there will be pressure from within their political apparatus to do so-and that may manifest itself in some pretty large demonstrations…I don't think so.

"Doing so would place them in a quandary…a significant quandary. They would have Russia as a fully mobilized force on their eastern borders and they would have our coalition, also fully mobilized, on their western and southern borders.

"They might get a respite from our enemies for a season, but I believe that with the examples from Korea, Japan, Australia, Turkey, and Russia, that their leaders know in their hearts that any arrangement made with these nations, will ultimately turn to the destruction of those very countries trying to come to some accommodation with them.

"So, in answer to your question…no, I do not think that they will do any more than talk about negotiating as a means to try to gain some political leverage over us. When we show what I presume will be our categorical rejection of this notion of turning over half the world to theses despotic nations, they will come into line and hope to use their "show" to their own benefit later, if things don't go as we hope they will."

The President knew this would be the case…and he was sickened by it.

"Will they never learn?" he thought to himself.

With that distaste in his mind and with the disgust apparent on his face, he turned to Jeremy Stone.

"Well, Jeremy, what are your thoughts?

"Specifically, are we capable of winning this fight unconditionally…with or without some of the nations Secretary Reissinger just mentioned?"

The old general was a fighter…always had been. He was also a very effective leader as evidenced by the long line of successively responsible positions he had held within the military.

He had been reluctant to accept the President's request to be appointed Secretary of Defense. He viewed it as a political position- and he hated politics. But he appreciated and respected men like Norm Weisskopf and John Bowers who could operate in that arena and who could do so keeping their loyalty and oath to the Constitution intact…all the time, 24/7.

After sharing these thoughts very openly and frankly with John Bowers, he would never forget the words this relatively young man had spoken to him.

"General, that is precisely why I want you in this position. Like Admiral Crowler before you. You are a military man who exhibits exactly what you say you respect in Norm Weisskopf and myself. If I didn't think that, I would never have considered you."

That had iced the deal and General Stone had answered the call. He would be the Secretary of Defense, and like his good friend, the late Admiral Crowler, he would do a damn fine job of it for his country and according to his duty.

"Mr. President, I am convinced that if it were just the United Kingdom, Canada and Brazil who were allied with us, we would defeat these enemies. When you add to that a fully mobilized Russia and the grit, determination, and fighting spirit of Israel, the ultimate result is foregone. In those nations combined, we have the will, the technical capability, and the forces to get the job done.

"That job would be significantly more difficult if we had to rule out direct or unopposed access through the continents of Europe and Africa, but we would still accomplish the mission.

"Mr. President, we *must* get this job done. Now is the time to slay and dismember this dragon. If we allow the CAS and GIR to consolidate their gains and manufacturing capabilities in the vast areas that they have conquered-and would still hold after such a proposal-then we will face an even more difficult task in ten years, perhaps one where the ultimate outcome will be in serious doubt.

"Those are my thoughts, Mr. President."

For another two hours, the President, offering only limited observations himself, continued to listen to everyone on the team. In the end, they were of one mind: the proposal that China had tendered on behalf of all of the CAS and GIR, could not be accepted-it had to be flatly and totally refused.

The President summed up everyone's mindset in unambiguous terms.

"Thank you all for your input.

"I believe that we must flatly and utterly reject the proposal, in the strongest terms possible…unilaterally if necessary. We can never accept a peace that enslaves our conquered allies and friends and that leaves these monstrosities in place to plague the world at a later date. Band-Aid diplomacy never succeeds when the force with which you are reckoning is intent on eventually enslaving you. It merely postpones the gruesome inevitable. The cancer must be eradicated, not treated with temporary salves.

"Let me tell you what I think this proposal really means-it means we have these animals on the run. They are afraid. They are looking to retain as many of their gains as they possibly can now, before we ultimately take them back from them. I believe their own analysts are telling them that this is exactly what is going to occur, if this war is allowed to continue.

"They have been unable to dislodge us from either Magadan or Point Conception, despite their best efforts-and they are not going to dislodge us from those places.

"Magadan will ultimately result in one of the largest defeats or surrenders in the history of the world. As you all know, all told we have estimated that there are four to six million personnel stretched out between our forward positions to the north and east of Magadan and our forces in Alaska. Those CAS forces are cut off and their fate is sealed as long as we do not falter or waver.

"Point Conception and the deep space mission it has produced and is supporting, will be the most strategic issue in this entire conflict within another eighteen to twenty months. The enemy suspects this, but is wholly unaware of the details and the ultimate impact it will have…but again, success will only occur if we do not falter or waver.

"We are absolutely not going to falter or waver…not on this administration's watch.

"Aside from this consideration, elsewhere the enemy is losing personnel and materiel in tremendous proportions, wholly disproportionate to our own losses. I do not mean to discount our own losses because they have been costly…-severe both abroad and here at home. But theirs are much more severe, even when you factor in the vast populations they have to pull from.

"Fred, make your contacts and explain our unambiguous position on this proposal. Between now and tomorrow night, I want scheduled discussions with Prime Minister Thatch, President Puten, President Maldenado, Prime Minister Schwarz, Prime Minister Suárez, Prime Minister Malroney, and Prime Minister Nitanyahu. Beyond that, I will make myself personally available to any of the other allied leaders who want to speak with me.

"Schedule it…and, oh, by the way, if the French President wants in on that schedule, please make sure to extend the offer and then arrange it.

"Beyond that, I want a direct response from all involved parties to be jointly made on July 4th, in the afternoon. As many of those leaders who can meet with me…let's say in Iceland if possible...should be prepared to stand with me as I read a joint statement. Others who cannot be there, I would like to see video conferenced in so all of the free world-and you can bet our enemies as well-will see our complete solidarity in the face of this callous and arrogant proposal.

"We want to demonstrate so they all can see this attempt by our enemies to end the conflict to their great advantage. They must all know, directly, unambiguously and forcefully that at this point nothing short of the unconditional surrender and the utter destruction as governing and ruling bodies of our enemies will suffice for us and our allies."

July 4, 2009, 13:30 Central Time
The Simmons' Lazy H Ranch
Outside of Montague, Texas

Colonel Jess Simmons was finally home. He had been stateside for almost two weeks, and he was thankful to God in Heaven for it.

He had been convalescing, and it looked like he would continue to do so for many, many months to come, alternating his time between here at home and the Veteran's Administration Hospital in Dallas.

The doctors, miraculously, had been able to save his leg-but not its full functionality. He had little feeling in his knee joint, and even less in his ankle and his toes. Apparently the nerve damage had been severe enough that his ankle function would be severely constrained for life...very stiff. He would walk with a definite limp, not only from the stiff ankle, but also because that leg was now almost two inches shorter than the other. Too much bone and tissue had been damaged, and had been removed in the surgeries and the fight to save the leg.

At some point, the doctors indicated that the lost tissue and bone structure could be reconstructed with artificial material, but only by conducting several more serious operations and prolonged periods of therapy after each. Jess Simmons was determined to go through all of it. He wanted to be as physically whole as possible…for his wife…for the ranch…for his country.

Thinking of his family caused his heart to immediately well up with so many profound and conflicting emotions. His love for his wife, Cindy, and his pride in how she had handled everything from his departure, to her involvement in the war effort and, most importantly, through the loss of their son. That love and pride washed over him…and it washed over the void he had after the loss of that only son, Billy.

He was thankful beyond measure that both he and his wife had been able to come to terms with that void…that their love for their son and their faith that they would see him again one day, had won out over their feelings of sorrow and grief and the desire to crawl into a cocoon made of that grief and be completely consumed by it.

They had shared with one another their stories of how the good Lord had touched each of their hearts and healed them over the loss of their son. How the destructive pain associated with that loss had been replaced with a natural sorrow at his absences, but also with the assurance of their eventual reunion.

Those stories, and their impact on the heart and soul, had united the Simmons and drawn them even closer as a couple in a natural and spiritual way, strengthening their love and bridging the long months of separation that the war had made necessary.

Those same stories would be shared over and over, in quiet moments, with one another, with their church family and with all of their good friends, for the rest of their lives.

Contemplating all of this as they finished their July 4th dinner, Jess Simmons looked up, down the table at those who were there with them, and felt inclined to say something.

"Cindy…honey," he began, catching her attention and that of the others at the table.

"Mom, Dad and Joe, Liz and Pat…I just want to thank each of you from the bottom of my heart.

"I want to thank you for being here…for taking time out of your own lives…and, Joe and Liz, for taking time during difficult personal trials of your own, to make time for us here.

"You are all an example and inspiration to me of Christ-like service and living. I could never thank you enough for that…or for your support during the long months…and years of my absence fighting in this war.

"It is especially meaningful on this date, when we celebrate the freedom we enjoy in this nation…the freedom whose preservation this war is all about.

"You are all true friends…and Cindy, you are my best friend…my eternal friend…thank you from the bottom of my heart…I am so proud of you…so thankful to you."

With that, Jess had to stop…he was on the verge of tears.

Jess's dad, Bud Simmons, who had always been a man of few words, replied simply.

"Son, I think I can speak for everyone here at this table when I say, thanks back to you. You are the epitome of everything you have just thanked us for…and we all know it."

Almost embarrassed by his own feelings and emotions, Bud Simons hastened to add.

"Now, someone turn on that TV over there and let's listen to the President over dessert."

July 4th, 2006, that same time
Outside the U.S. Embassy
Reykjavik, Iceland

JT Sampson had flown with the press pool to Iceland. It had been a surprised and rushed trip brought on by a call from the administration's press secretary. That call had finally established for JT that his good association with the administration had survived the loss of President Weisskopf, whom JT had looked upon as a mentor, and from whose loss JT doubted he would ever fully recover.

Now, he and his associates, who were made up of two SierraLines employees who had traveled with him and four technicians who had been hired here in Iceland, were set up to make a live internet broadcast of the allied response to the CAS and GIR proposal for an armistice.

That broadcast was going to be picked up by several of the major cable networks and carried live on cable television as well. It was in fact the contacted broadcast of the announcement that the Simmons and Trevors were watching back in Texas.

It was a momentous occasion. Rumors were flying wildly about a potential cessation of hostilities. JT had developed an instinct about public opinion, through his years of faithful news reporting, and he believed that, although most Americans would welcome a cessation of hostilities, any such cessation now would leave a hollowness in the hearts of most...as if an important job had been left unfinished.

JT was excited about being here to personally report on the response. Despite his success, despite his major news media executive status, JT still loved to personally do the on-scene reporting.

There were some who felt that this personal quirk of JT's was stymieing the full growth potential of SierraLines...but JT felt otherwise and was determined to run the leading Internet News organization as he saw fit...besides, the vast majority of shares were still in his and his wife's names.

So, until and unless someone acquired enough shares to challenge him, he would continue with his "quirk" and seek out the news stories that he felt best qualified to cover, while ensuring that his other reporters got an equal opportunity to do the same.

"This is JT Sampson with SierraLines here in Reykjavik, Iceland, reporting at the scene of the imminent announcement of the allied response to the unprecedented armistice proposal by the Coalition of Asian States and the Greater Islamic Republic.

"For security reasons, the location of the allied response to that proposal was not announced until the live feeds were set-up and the broadcast began just minutes ago.

"That proposal has been made public now for over twenty-four hours and has generated a tremendous amount of speculation and unofficial announcements. To this moment, it is unknown how many of the allied leaders will either go along with, or participate in, the announcement…or what will be the exact nature of the response.

"The President of the United States is now approaching the podium. Ladies and Gentleman, the President of the United States."

John Bowers held in his hands the official response of the allied nations of the world to the CAS and GIR armistice proposal. The winds were causing the papers to rustle somewhat, but the clipboard to which they were attached held them down adequately.

A line of distinguished leaders from various nations flanked the President to either side, and several smaller video windows with other leaders appeared on the screen as he began to speak.

"Today I will respond on behalf of the free nations of the world directly to the armistice proposal by the Coalition of Asian States and the Greater Islamic Republic. The leaders of many of those responding nations have joined me here in Reykjavik, or by video conference from their capitals.

"You can see them each either standing here next to me on my right and left, or in the smaller video windows which should have appeared on your screens wherever you are watching.

"As such, I not only speak for the citizens of the United States of America, whom I personally represent, but I speak for all citizens of the free world who are embroiled in this conflict and whose leaders have agreed to this response.

"To be specific, those sovereign and free nations who have joined with us in this response include all of the following:

United States	Canada	Brazil	Spain	Italy
United Kingdom	Israel	Germany	Denmark	Poland
Russia	Romania	Hungary	Austria	Norway
Czech Republic	Ecuador	Columbia	Honduras	Latvia
Netherlands	Ukraine	Lithuania	Liberia	Nigeria
South Africa	Iceland	Ivory Coast	Costa Rica	Peru

"In addition, the following official governments in exile, whom we have been able to contact and arrange to have present here, and whose nations have been brutally conquered and occupied, have also joined us in this response:

Republic of China	Turkey	Oman	Malaysia
South Korea	Mongolia	Singapore	Thailand
Australia	Nepal	Kuwait	Laos

"There are others, either conquered or coerced into making accommodations with their brutal antagonists, whom I am sure would also join with us if we could contact them.

"As it is, this overwhelming number of free nations has joined us in solidarity in our unequivocal, unflinching, and unwavering response to the Coalition of Asian States and the Greater Islamic Republic.

"…and this is our official response:

"To you, Jien Zenim, Hasan Sayeed and KP Narayannen, and to all of those who have allied themselves with you, and have joined together to make this vain, inglorious and infamous proposal, we say the following…

"NUTS!

"If you have any doubt as to our meaning, read up on your history of World War II, and pay special attention to the Battle of the Bulge.

"The answer is no!

"The only acceptable end to this conflict will occur upon your complete and unconditional surrender to allied forces.

"Until that time, there will be no negotiations, there will be no turning back, there will be no armistice, there will be no cessation of hostilities and there will be no accommodation with your murderous regimes.

"I trust we have made ourselves clear.

"In closing, to our occupied allies, to our personnel and citizens trapped behind enemy lines…and to the impoverished and trodden down people of these horrible regimes, we say the following, quoting the man, Norman Weisskopf, who will certainly go down in history as one of the greatest leaders in American history and one of the greatest friends to peace-loving and freedom-loving peoples in the history of the free world…

"*Fight on.*

"*Do not despair. As surely as the sun rises in the east, we are coming. The time will arrive when like at Normandy on June 6th, 1944, you will look out and see the sea and the sky filled with the innumerable host of your comrades come to liberate the captive and put down the tyrant.*"

"Let me add a few other words to that which I believe are relevant to our current situation. They are the words of the great American patriot, Patrick Henry,

"We shall not fight our battles alone. There is a just God who presides over the destinies of Nations, and who will raise up friends to fight our battles for us. The battle, Sir, is not to the strong alone. It is to the vigilant, the active, the brave. Besides, Sir, we have no choice. If we were base enough to desire it, it is now too late to retire from the contest. There is no retreat but in submission and slavery!"

"All American citizens and our allies should remember these sentiments and feelings as we move forward in this struggle. We should lean on and rely on one another…and we should lean on and rely on our faith in a just and merciful God.

"A wise individual once shared with me the following…

"Work like everything depends on you, but pray and live like everything depends on God, because in the end, it does.

"Thank you, and may that just God bless our cause and our efforts. May He bless each of our free nations. And may we continue to look to Him for guidance, strength and wisdom in the days and weeks and months that lie ahead.

"Good day."

July 6th, 2006, 10:25 Eastern Time
Meet the Nation
WNN Broadcast Studios
New York, New York

The host of the weekly talk show was carefully guiding the interview with Bill Hendrickson, the National Security Advisor, towards its conclusion.

"Mr. Hendrickson, the coalition that the President enumerated in his Reykjavik speech is, as you have stated, very impressive. It is a continued reminder of the former President's capabilities in foreign relations, and a testament to the widespread support of the effort against the CAS and GIR.

"In spite of this, there were some very notable nations that were not listed by the President as agreeing with the response to the peace proposal from Coalition of Asian states and the greater Islamic Republic.

"France, Sweden, Mexico, Yugoslavia, Egypt, Chile…none of those names were included on the list of nations that responded so negatively to this peace proposition.

"How does the administration explain this?

"I'll tell you, there is talk of a developing rift in the allied coalition against the CAS and GIR.

"For example, what impact would there be if France ceased her efforts in the fight…if Mexico became neutral or hostile?"

Bill Hendrickson always found it difficult to believe that people like this host still existed, even in the midst of this fight for the nation's survival-for this very host's survival-a fact that apparently had not yet occurred to him.

"Some people just are incapable of getting it," Hendrickson thought, "Even if they have been hit directly between the eyes by it, as everyone in this nation most certainly has been.

"There are always quibblers. There are always apologists. There are always those who are willing-almost eager-to fault America, no matter her noble aims, or the ignoble aims of her enemies," he reflected, sadly.

Someone who made his living by trying to tear down the efforts of those who valued and defended the freedom of the country…who did all in his power to create a divisive stir during actual combat…had always been an enigma to Bill Hendrickson.

Individuals like that represented something he could not muster an ounce of respect for.

Yet, he was fiercely and completely dedicated to this man's freedom to do so. He knew as well that this show reached many millions of households. Because of that, he was anxious to represent the facts and truth of the situation to those millions.

"Let me answer your question in a couple of ways.

"First, the proposal by the CAS and GIR was not a peace proposal in the least. It was a barely veiled attempt on their part to consolidate the gains and conquered territory that they have already amassed, and to avoid our growing capability to defeat them on the field of battle."

The host interrupted, "Well, Mr. Hendrickson, it sure looked to me like they were willing to give up a lot of already conquered territory. I mean, look at the map. Vast stretches of the Pacific, their continued stubborn hold on western Alaska, the richest part of Australia, all of their advances in Europe, and all of Russia back to the Siberian frontier.

"I would hardly call that a veiled effort to consolidate everything they had gained. I would call it a serious peace proposal."

The National Security Advisor let the host talk himself out. He was not about to be drawn into an argument where neither side listened to the other…or contribute to an atmosphere in which neither side could get its views across to the listening audience.

"Well, that is perhaps what they wanted us to think, but when you look at what they were willing to, as you say, give up, and compare that to what they were going to be keeping, the picture becomes very clear.

"From a strategic standpoint, from an economic standpoint, and from a military standpoint, they would have placed themselves in a very strong, almost unassailable position for decades to come.

"They were also asking us to accede to the conquest, occupation and assimilation of hundreds of millions of free people, who are our friends and allies.

"If we were willing to allow that, we would be tacitly admitting defeat and would live with that legacy hanging over us all from now on. We could not, ethically, morally, or ideologically accede to such conditions and still call ourselves Americans.

"Now, here's the second way in which I shall respond to your question.

"It is clear to all of us who are analyzing these things that the CAS and GIR planners understand that the tide of battle has turned as a result of the victories we experienced late last fall and early this year-and the progress we have been making since. Our own production capabilities have been regenerated, despite their military and terrorist efforts to the contrary.

"Our dependencies on energy, agriculture and many other critical areas have been completely eliminated and we are once again a totally self-sufficient nation. Our enemies know this…those few nations who did not join us in the official response know this as well.

"This very proposal by the CAS and GIR, as the President has stated, is the clearest indication of their own knowledge of this. Our enemies are on the run, and we intend to keep them on the run until they wave the white flag…meaning, until they surrender unconditionally."

With only a few seconds of broadcast time left, the host took the opportunity to end the interview and his weekly show.

"Thank you, Mr. Hendrickson.

"Ladies and gentlemen, you have been listening to Bill Hendrickson, the National Security Advisor to the President of the United States, discussing this week's allied rejection of the armistice proposal by the Coalition of Asian States and the Greater Islamic Republic.

"It was a momentous decision in response to a proposal many have been calling the last serious chance for peace for another three to four years.

"Please join us next week, here at the same time, when our guest will be…."

July 6th 2006, 20:52
Presidential Offices
Beijing, China

Jien Zenim finished reading the entire transcript of the response the allied nations had officially sent back to him and the other leaders of the CAS and GIR. It was a very short document.

Oh, he had seen the video of the affair…of the new American President and his lackeys all lined up to refuse the offer Zenim and his compatriots had made. But he always waited to read the actual print of any diplomatic negotiations before he reached his final conclusions.

You never knew what might show up in the actual verbiage of the official printed documents.

In this case, his patience was in vain. The official document was in fact an exact transcript of what the President had said.

…and in this case, Zenim's final reaction was exactly the same as his initial one when he had seen John Bowers read it…

He cursed horribly…and long.

Chapter 6

"Where love is, God is." - Leo Tolstoy

August 23, 2009, 19:07 local time
West of Kavacha
On the Kamchatka Peninsula

Corporal Alan Campbell crouched lower in the ditch that he had taken shelter in with most of the rest of his platoon, hugging the ground as machine gun fire stitched back and forth along the top of the ditch...fire that was methodically seeking out the exposed portion of any Marine's body revealing itself above the crest of that small rise less than a foot above Alan's head.

The fighting was fierce and had been hotly contested from the moment of their landing six days ago near the town of Kavacha on the northern Kamchatka Peninsula. In those six days, Alan's Marine battalion, along with the rest of the allied landing force, had been able to advance only twelve miles to the west and had only penetrated eight miles inland.

While it was true that the beachhead itself was now relatively secure, that certainly had not been the case for the first three days when enemy fire had destroyed two of the large transports and had shot down several American aircraft.

Seeking to open up another front against the Chinese forces retreating from Alaska and ensure their defeat and capture en masse exploiting the advance of allied forces out of Magadan, the allies had landed over one hundred thousand troops here in the northern half of the Kamchatka Peninsula. The invasion force had been formed by combining several American, Canadian, and Central American commands. New North American recruits, battle hardened forces from Central America, where Panama City had fallen and the Canal

Zone was once more in American hands, and combat experienced forces in Africa where the offensive into central Africa had gone better than expected, all made up the new allied Asian invasion force.

Alan's entire division had been transferred from central Chad after a large battle in which they, along with a supporting crack Brazilian division, had routed five GIR divisions to the north and east of Lake Chad.

After that victory, and as American, Brazilian, African and other allied forces continued deeper into Chad to threaten GIR forces in Libya and Sudan, Alan had been transported with the other Marines in his division back to Nigeria to Lagos, the capital. There he and his comrades had quickly been loaded aboard several T-90A transports and transported away from the continent of Africa.

Using more new T-90A transports, all of the necessary forces had quickly been staged in the Aleutian Islands and then transported across the Bering Sea to the Kamchatka Peninsula. It was hoped that in so doing, and then in building that initial force to over one half million men, several things would be accomplished.

1) Any retreat to the south down the peninsula by the large enemy forces under relentless Allied assault in Alaska could be prevented;

2) The enemy security forces and large naval base at Petropavlovsk could be cut off and isolated;

3) The allied forces on the Kamchatka Peninsula would proceed to the north and combine with the even larger allied force now moving well to the north of Magadan, and present an invincible anvil upon which the Chinese Alaska invasion force would be hammered and destroyed.

"But it sure isn't workin' out that way yet," thought Alan as an enemy missile barrage screamed overhead.

Dense cloud cover had blanketed the area for two weeks prior to the invasion and American intelligence had failed to penetrate it to the south of Kavacha. Had intelligence been able to pierce those clouds, they would have witnessed the staging of large Chinese reserves to reinforce beleaguered Chinese troops in Alaska.

Without that knowledge, the American landing had come on shore just as three divisions of Chinese troops were passing through the area on their way north to reinforce their comrades fighting in Alaska. The collision of the American landing effort and these Chinese reserve forces was creating a nightmare for American and allied planners as the invasion force was bogged down from the beginning by unexpectedly heavy, and mission threatening resistance.

Now, the long drainage ditch in which Alan found himself had filled up with hundreds and hundreds of Marines from several companies. As one of those companies provided suppressing fire from a multi-lane bridge over the ditch to their east, and as American AZ-1H Viper attack helicopters and F-35C Joint Strike Fighters circled down from above to give support, Alan and the rest of the men in the ditch were ordered to rise up and charge the enemy positions that had them penned down.

The word was passed down that Alan's particular company had been ordered to lead the way.

At the given moment, Alan's company commander shouted, "All right men, here we go!"

"Up and over the top! Follow me!" he urged as he personally rose up to lead the attack…

…and was immediately thrown into the bottom of the ditch by the impact of several bullets that tore a bloody line across the upper half of his body.

Instantaneously energized by the graphic death of their commanding officer, the Marines spilled out of their makeshift bunker with an angry, deafening roar and charged across the two hundred yards of open ground towards the grouping of buildings nestled against the foothills to their north. Other companies to their left and right joined in the assault as machine gun fire raked them, and mortar fire rained down upon them.

Alan was shocked at his calm.

The last six days represented the first really fierce combat he had been involved in. It was nothing like the rout they had caused with the GIR forces in Chad.

Men were falling dead and wounded all around him–right next to him as he charged into the face of determined enemy resistance. He knew he should be frightened, but his long months of training and his determination to eliminate this pocket of enemy who were killing and maiming his friends, coupled with adrenaline pumping into his veins, took full control of his actions. Just as they were supposed to do.

Explosions riddled the building complex as the Viper helicopters rippled off volley after volley from their rocket pods. Larger bombs and missiles from the attack aircraft obscured the view, literally collapsing entire buildings and creating tremendous amounts of smoke and dust as the Marines approached.

The pall of smoke created by the damage of the air assault acted as a smoke screen for the Marines, severely inhibiting the enemy's ability to direct fire on the advance. Fewer and fewer Marines were falling as the wave of attackers ran into the smoke drifting to the immediate south of the building.

At this point, American air support moved their attacks further to the west of the buildings, targeting groups of enemy soldiers either firing in support of their forces in the buildings, or trying to organize counter attacks to the wave of marines now breaking on the complex of buildings itself.

The XO in Alan's company noticed a building thirty yards to the west of where Alan's platoon had just taken cover behind a cinderblock wall.

"Campbell!" he shouted, getting Alan's attention and that of several of the Marines with him.

"You are in charge of the 2nd platoon now. Both Lieutenant Brandt and Sergeant Fern are down. Take the 2nd platoon and clear out that building there to your west. Contact me when you have done so.

"Do it now!"

August 23, 2009, 22:45 local time
West of Kavacha
On the Kamchatka Peninsula

Darkness had descended on the Kamchatka Peninsula and the sounds of heavy fighting had moved well to the west and north as American forces took advantage of the breech they had made in enemy defenses late that afternoon. As those forces did so, Alan and his comrades were getting a much needed rest, taking shelter in the very buildings from which they had finally driven the Chinese less than ninety minutes earlier.

There had already been a short staff meeting where plans for the evening and the next day had been sketched out and initial orders had been issued. Another meeting, slated for 03:30, would provide more detail. In the meantime, they had been ordered to secure their perimeter for the night and get some rest.

It looked as though, for the near term, Alan would be the de facto platoon leader. The lieutenant had died before he could be evacuated back to the landing zone and the sergeant, who had been severely wounded in the right hip and the groin, would be heading home. Until replacements could be brought up, Alan was now in charge of fourteen other Marines.

After issuing the necessary orders and performing a communications check with headquarters, Alan studied maps of the surrounding terrain and their initial objectives and orders. Then, before retiring for some rest, he pulled out the letter he had received from his brother, Leon, last week to read it once again. He got such comfort and strength reading about the experiences of his older brother, despite the many edits that appeared from the military censors who went through the mail.

Alan could understand that—the removal of any tidbit of information that might help the enemy here in the combat zone was something he would gladly put up with. After seeing so many of his own ruthlessly killed—no, butchered would be a more fitting term—Alan appreciated and respected the absolute need for operational security.

The way he figured it, he would gladly suffer through the rigors out here in the field so his mother, friends, neighbors, and countrymen could retain those basic freedoms back home. That was a big part of what this was all about.

So, though the communications took many weeks—even months—to pass between them, and although there were sometimes significant portions of the wording blotted out…Alan was always listening to mail call to see if he had received anything from either Leon or his mother.

"I wonder what my bro will think of me being put in this position?" he thought.

"Whatever it is…it'll include some good advice, and I sure look forward to it."

The XO and one of the senior sergeants had already talked to him and he had welcomed and appreciated their input. He was surprised to learn that as a result of other injuries and death, all of the staff sergeants were already assigned to other platoons and could not be spared for his. Both the XO and Sergeant Myerwood had explained to him that his prior leadership and composure under fire had convinced them that he was the best Corporal in the company and therefore the one to fill the void.

While he was grateful for their confidence in him–and he eagerly took and applied their advice and counsel–there would be nothing like getting some personal advice from his older brother. Leon had always been a hero to Alan, long before the action on the Island of Diego Garcia that had led to Leon's Medal of Honor. Throughout their lives Leon had provided leadership, kindness and friendship that Alan recognized was rare for older brothers in the best of circumstances…much less in the gang-infested projects where they had been raised by a God-fearing mother.

Tonight, before he finally nodded off to sleep, he wanted to review his brother's letter one more time before writing him and letting him know about his current circumstances and then asking what Leon thought…what his advice would be.

Alan had thought that his own combat experiences were fierce and harried. But Leon's letter had shown him know that it could be much worse. That "much worse" was exactly what his brother, Leon, was now experiencing.

Alan's mind kept going back to two parts of two separate letters from Leon, written a week apart, to which he now turned and began reviewing again.

"We've been at sea for —CENSORED— days. By the time you get this…I am sure we will be ashore, or will have died or been defeated trying.

"Apparently, and they either don't know and can't go into it…or if they do know and for security reasons they will not go into it…but apparently the battle at sea over here has been tougher than expected, not that anyone expected a cakewalk. The enemy still has too many of those Killer Whale weapons and no one is taking those suckers for granted I can tell you…particularly when you are out here on a transport ship.

"Regardless of how fast these new —CENSORED— ship designs are…regardless of how well protected by our own defenses

on board and by the escorts traveling with us…I can tell you I will not be satisfied or happy until I have dry ground back under my feet.

"Just the same, I wish I could tell you, particularly after some of my experiences earlier in the war…how great it was to see so many American and allied ships off of CENSORED , CENSORED and CENSORED of ships Alan…it was unbelievable. The living embodiment of President Weisskopf's…God rest his soul…famous speech back in 2006 after the March 15th attacks.

"And so there we went…off to kick the Chicoms and the radical ragheads out of CENSORED , and win it back for freedom A big bunch of ships and escorts went with us towards our goal…another big bunch of ships and escorts towards other objectives. Several groups of carriers and their escorts out in front of us all to sweep the seas clean of the Chinese and Indian navies.

"And seeing all of those new ships…all of those new carriers, large and small alike and their escorts…there was not one of us who doubted that the time for complete payback on the high seas had arrived. Got lots of ships and sailors to make up for…to make things right for.

"Well, we were supposed to make the transit in CENSORED days…but now it's been much longer. By the time you get this…or by the time I can even send it, things will have resolved themselves.

"Isn't that the way life is?

"Anyhow, they aren't resolved as I write this and each of us is anxious to get a crack at CENSORED and taking it back. We are worried sick over our comrades at sea…and worried about our own safety out here…images of those Chinese super torpedoes haunting our every mile forward.

"But forward we MUST go, little brother (snicker, snicker, snicker…and only snickering because I haven't had a 'little' brother for a long time…now you're a younger brother I know). There is no *going back and as you know, there is no giving in or surrendering to these devils. They are committed to their cause–destroying us. I know you have seen enough by now to understand that. Never forget it.*

"I'm glad President Bowers rejected the enemy's proposal for an armistice. He saw right through them. Nice to see him spit in their eye. He said exactly what any of us out here fighting these animals already know. Nothing short of unconditional surrender is acceptable after what they have done.

"Oh well, I am dragging now...getting too philosophical. I'll write more when I can."

Reading those words the first time had given Alan cause for worry over his brother's safety. Along with everyone else, he knew that a man's life in a combat zone was always in peril...especially considering his own experiences as a Marine. That firsthand knowledge only heightened the concern, particularly for one's own kinfolk.

Reading the letter again, after his latest combat experiences and battlefield appointment to platoon leader carried additional poignancy for Alan. He longed to be able to sit with his brother...to speak of the pain, the butchery of warfare that he had witnessed and knew must continue until this enemy had been vanquished. He wanted to talk about the loss of good friends and how you cope with it, both in the short term and over the long haul.

Sergeant Meyrwood had been almost like an older brother to him...perhaps even a father figure. Now he was severely wounded and could die. The lieutenant was dead...a man Alan had looked up to and trusted with his own life. A man who had done so much for Alan ever since he had been assigned to this outfit after training. Now he was gone.

Alan knew that Leon had experienced all of this...which made the next part of his letter even more apropos to Alan's current feelings.

"Well, Alan, it's —CENSORED— days later now.

"Sorry I didn't get this mailed sooner...but soon after I had finished the last portion of this letter...our task force moved into the waters off of —CENSORED— and we conducted a massive landing near there.

"How can I tell you what I am feeling?

"I am here on —CENSORED— soil now and we are in the fight for our lives. I mean literally.

"It's worse and more intense than anything that I have experienced to date...and that's saying a lot.

"Before our —CENSORED— ships went in, a fleet of —CENSORED— of the new large —CENSORED— transports went in —CENSORED— miles to our —CENSORED—. The diversion worked...we were able to land...but just barely. I'll get to that in a moment.

"All of those aircraft, each with almost —CENSORED— personnel on board were lost. Destroyed...gone. None of them made it to shore. All of those folks are gone. It was a total disaster!

"My God...it's hard to take it in even now, six days later. Hard to comprehend.

"Apparently the Chinese believed our major plans included massive invasion using —CENSORED—. They had shore launched versions of their Killer Whales positioned at each major landing area...in numbers. Supposedly a special configuration for —CENSORED—. It was a slaughter...and I can't talk about it any more. I knew and trained on NZ with a lot of those people.

"Here, we came in conventionally and a lot of those weapons went —CENSORED— trying to —CENSORED— . I saw —CENSORED— of them rise —CENSORED— less than a —CENSORED— from us, but our point defenses, both the —CENSORED— and the —CENSORED— took them down.

" ~~CENSORED~~ - don't have that luxury.

"We still lost, ~~CENSORED~~, Alan. I saw them get hit by these monsters and go down…and they went down so fast! My God, bro…I can't describe it to you.

"Our ability to land here a little further to the ~~CENSORED~~ - was purchased at great cost…in pools of our brothers' and sisters' blood.

"But we went on in…into the fight of our lives. For ~~CENSORED~~ days our ~~CENSORED~~ waves were penned down on the shore. I came in right behind that ~~CENSORED~~ wave, but then we couldn't land any of the additional personnel behind us because ~~CENSORED~~ couldn't get off the beaches.

"We couldn't achieve air superiority so the fighters had to duke it out right over us…the battle swaying first one way…and then another. When the enemy was in control, we were being bombed and strafed on the beach.

"All the while missiles were flying both ways. Some over our heads towards the ships at sea. Some right at us. Others, of our own, flying right back at the enemy.

"If you have ever read about D-Day and the experiences on Omaha Beach…that is how it must have been…except here it was even bigger and more prolonged. We weren't off the beach late in the day…or the next…or the next.

"So many of the people I have come to know and trust with my life are gone…but we continue.

"I know momma was praying for me Alan…I can't explain it, but I could feel it. God kept me and the others alive on that beach until we finally fought and clawed our way off of it.

"That was ~~CENSORED~~ days ago and now we are fighting our way through ~~CENSORED~~…most of which are still destroyed *and ruined from the initial fighting when the Chinese came through here pushing our forces out.*

"I can imagine how Billy Simmons must have felt. There are so many refugees...except that now, after almost a year and a half of Chinese rule in this part of ~~CENSORED~~ *...and well over two years in other parts...well, the original* ~~CENSORED~~ *citizens are shockingly small in number, and in a pathetic state.*

"Now, in the act of liberating a place where these monsters have been in power, what we already knew to be true, we now see - a horror show that would make Steven King want to turn away in fear.

"We are not just fighting the CAS and GIR soldiers here...we are also fighting the hundreds and hundreds of thousands of their civilians they have relocated here to take ~~CENSORED~~ *lands as their own.*

"They are being distributed weapons and fighting as militias against us. Fodder to keep us penned down as their regular forces try to maneuver...and they don't mind at all using whatever original ~~CENSORED~~ *citizens who are unlucky enough to be in their path as shields and pawns.*

"I can understand why the ~~CENSORED~~ *resistance groups we hear about in the mountains have been branded by the Chinese as such terrorists. There is no mercy or pity being shown on either side. It has been a literal battle for survival and until we landed, the* ~~CENSORED~~ *left here were losing it.*

"Again my younger bro...I cannot begin to describe the scene of horrible images I am witness to. All you can do is push it down, grit your teeth and keep on fighting.

"There aren't many prisoners being taken on either side as we have entered the fight either. Some of the Indians will give up...but the Chinese and the Muslims that have been moved in here are fighting to the death...like the stories you used to hear from World War II. Somehow, human life, to these people, is much more

expendable, seems much less valuable, than it is to us. And, when you are fighting an enemy like that, they can sure use that kind of philosophy and culture to their advantage.

"Well, I'll write a little more later about word I have received from mom at home and to ask how things are with you. I hope to get this finally mailed off to you tomorrow.

"Right now, our short reprieve back at what you might call an R&R area is over and it's back to the front and the ~~CENSORED~~ *mountain range.*

"Forward, into the interior!"

Alan felt the same thrill he had experienced the during the first reading of this part of the letter when he discovered that his brother had survived the landings on Australia.

All of them already knew about the disaster near New Castle on the Australian coast and until he had received and read through this letter…he had not known whether Leon had been one of those thousands who had died there.

But Leon's words about their mother's prayers rang true with Alan…because he had felt it too. At the time, he had not recognized it…but now, after reading and thinking on Leon's words again, he knew that his mother's faith had been with him too here in Asia on the Kamchatka Peninsula.

It also helped to read about Leon's determination in the face of much more appalling conditions, to continue to give his all…being further bolstered and strengthened in his resolve by the very hardship and difficulty he was experiencing.

If Leon could do that there in Australia…Alan knew he could do it here on the Kamchatka Peninsula.

…and he would.

September 2, 2009, 01:17 local time
Task Force Commander's Conference Room
U.S.S. Shanksville
650 Nautical Miles East of Brisbane

Admiral Ben Ryan was relieved after hearing the latest intelligence assessment of the enemy location and disposition. After the last engagement the remnant of the large PLAN fleet had withdrawn north, deep into the Coral Sea to lick their wounds and to resupply themselves.

As the Commander in Chief of U.S. naval forces in the Pacific, or CINCPAC, Ryan would be spending the next four days reviewing ongoing plans for CTF 77, the large combined task force whose assignment was the protection of the allied forces that were conducting the continuing invasion of Australia. Admiral Styles, the commander of CTF 77 was working with his commander, Ben Ryan, to further refine those plans based on the current situation.

And out here on the tip of the sword, as is often the case in warfare, those plans had changed somewhat as a result of the large engagement with the Chinese over the last forty-eight hours.

"And after that last missile and Killer Whale attack, saying that this is the tip of the sword as far as naval action is concerned is almost an understatement," the Admiral thought.

Now, here in the task force commander's conference room, surrounded by his staff and the other battle group commanders, along with two other members of Admiral Ryan's staff, Admiral Styles continued the discussion, picking up after the intelligence report.

"We can't allow the Chinese to regroup and resupply up there in the Coral Sea if we can help it.

"They hurt us yesterday…as each of you know…but we hurt them more and they have withdrawn. We need to follow up on this victory and do everything in our power to harass them and force them into a position where we can destroy them. This is no time to rest on our laurels. That kind of passivity often turns victory into defeat.

"And we still have more than enough assets to accomplish that mission and ensure that the areas around the invasion anchorages remain secure."

The admiral said this because Combined Task Force (CTF) 77 consisted of several individual carrier battle groups and surface action groups. All of them had been in almost continuous fierce engagements with the Chinese for the last three weeks.

It had taken every bit of power that the CTF possessed to force the issue and push the Chinese north out of the waters of the Tasman Sea surrounding Sydney and southern Australia. Yesterday they had succeeded in pushing them completely into the Coral Sea, far to the north and east of Brisbane, against which the American carriers could now conduct air attacks.

At the start of the Australian invasion operations, CTF 77 had included six augmented American CBGs, a British Task force consisting of both of the United Kingdom's new full size carriers and a Canadian task force centered around their new White Horse sea control carrier. Each of the American carrier battle groups included a nuclear powered super carrier, one American sea control carrier, and all of the escorts necessary to defend them. Those escorts included one Ticonderoga class Aegis cruiser, two Arleigh Burke class Aegis destroyers, one Spruance class destroyer, one of the newer class DDX destroyer and two nuclear attack submarines...a mixture of advanced LA class boats and Virginia class boats.

To most effectively organize all of this...and to defend it...Admiral Styles had organized three American carrier task forces that included two of the augmented CBGs each, and a joint UK/Canadian task force which included all four of their carriers. The resulting powerful American forces included four carriers, two Aegis cruisers, four Aegis destroyers, and four other destroyers in each task force. All in all, the allies had sixteen carriers in the New Zealand area when the Australian offensive began.

Finally, the combined task force also included three SAGs centered around Aegis destroyers that had Spruance and DDX destroyers accompanying them.

Altogether CBT 77 represented the most formidable and monumental allied naval force at sea. Its defenses included a massive array of the most advanced missile, radar, sonar, CIWS, SUB CIWS and high performance aircraft technology on the planet.

Yet all of that had barely been enough to counter the massive air and naval forces the Chinese and other CAS and GIR nations were throwing against them.

In the last three weeks the Chinese had sunk one American super carrier, four U.S. sea control carriers, one of the full-deck British carriers, severely damaged another American super carrier, and sunk several escort vessels from various allied nations. Two of the sea control carriers that had been sunk had gone down in the last forty-eight hours. Of the sixteen carriers CBT 77 had started the Australian operation with, six had been lost, one was damaged, and nine were still in the fight.

But the Chinese had fared worse. They had thrown twelve of their Beijing class carriers and three of their full-deck Mao class carriers into the same fray…and had now withdrawn into the Coral Sea with only five Beijing class carriers left. A loss of ten carriers over that three week period.

And that did not begin to account for all of their losses.

Fifteen Chinese major surface combatant ships had also been sunk. Literally hundreds of land and carrier based aircraft had been shot down as they attempted to penetrate through to the American capital ships.

"No," Admiral Ryan thought as Admiral Styles continued, "we may be hurting…but they have been decimated."

"Jerry is right. If we can lure them into another major engagement…we just may break the back of their naval power here off of Australia."

And Admiral Styles was now formulating a plan to harass and push the Chinese into just such an engagement. Turning to CINCPAC, he started to lay it out.

"Admiral Ryan, by using the U.S.S. Connecticut and augmenting her with five of our attack submarines from CTF 77, that submarine force can make a rapid transit up to the south of New Guinea. Once there, I believe we can 'herd' the Chinese into a trap somewhere in the Coral Sea to the south of the Solomon Islands.

"Here's how I propose we do it," he said as he turned his attention to the entire group.

"…and I want a full discussion of the possible enemy response before we finalize the general plan and then send you off to develop the details to successfully pull this off."

Referring to a large display of the Australian Theater of Operations, the Commander of CTF 77 continued his discussion by pointing to that display.

"Now, we'll keep the Kitty Hawk and its entire group right here, to the northeast of Newcastle to continue covering the principle invasion anchorage, but close enough to ferry additional aircraft to this operation if necessary.

"The combined UK and Canadian task force will continue to protect the southern approaches to Sydney in the Tasman Sea off of Cape Howe."

Turning to the United Kingdom and Canadian task force commanders, Admiral Styles couldn't help but recognize and congratulate them on their part in the offensive to date…and to give them some commander's instructions regarding the upcoming operation.

"Admiral Weatherly, you and Admiral Tomlinson have done an outstanding job down there and we commend you for it. You will be tasked with covering our backs in this operation.

"Don't be surprised if the enemy tries to probe your position in strength to see if there is something they can exploit while we are up north. We are confidant that the two of you will show them the error of their ways should they try.

"Just make sure you don't get sucked into any premature major action down near Melbourne. We are not in a tactical position to secure Bass Strait and Tasmania at this time."

Addressing the rest of the group as a whole, the Admiral then continued. "Okay, as you can see, all of that will leave us with the Shanksville, the George Bush, and the Ronald Reagan and their battle groups, which include the Hampton Roads and the Essex, to act as the anvil against which our fast attack subs will drive the Chinese. I expect we can set that up here, in this area well to the south and west of Rennell Island.

"If we do this right, we can create a turkey shoot in the air against the Chinese…and then deal with their surface combatants at our leisure, creating a pincer between our subs to the west, and our large combined task force here to the east.

"That's a 10,000 foot view of the plan…now let's get down to some particulars."

THE BATTLE OF THE CORAL SEA: 9/4-9/5/2009

September 4, 2009, 04:07 local time
Combat Information Center
PLAN Carrier Zenim
300 kilometers northeast of the Santa Cruz Islands

Admiral Xi'n analyzed the developing situation reports with a critical and experienced eye.

From the reports he was receiving of submarine attacks to the west and air and missile attacks to the south, it was clear that the Americans were executing a masterful pincer movement. They were on the verge of sucking the remnant of the large PLAN fleet that had been protecting the eastern approach to Australia into a deadly trap…and Xi'n was going to have to allow it to happen, to a point.

It was a risk…both to the five Beijing class carriers and all of their escorts in that force to the south…as well as to his own force here north of the Santa Cruz Islands as he made flank speed towards the developing battle.

The Admiral's powerful task force consisted of the fully repaired and refurbished Zenim and her sister ship, the Xia, accompanied by four of the new naval "strike-at-sea" upgrades to the PLAN Tactical Attack Ships, four of the Chinese latest phased array air defense destroyers, four of the anti-submarine and surface strike cousins of the air defense vessels, and three of China's latest nuclear attack submarines.

Although the Admiral was not entirely certain of the exact location of the Americans, he had a wave of twenty-four of the improved recon LRASD weapons moving towards their expected location and hoped he would soon be able to pinpoint it with more exactness.

Turning to the Captain of the Zenim, who had accompanied the Admiral from the bridge to the combat information center and who was standing with him monitoring his duty officers at their various stations, the Admiral inquired.

"Captain, what is the latest update on operations to locate the American fleet."

After a brief animated conversation with one of the duty officers, who handed the Captain a printout of the latest sensor readings, the Captain responded.

"Admiral, we just received the latest information from the recon LRASD units and we believe that they have now penetrated the outer ring of picket ships in an American formation.

"Just minutes ago an American Spruance class destroyer and a Los Angeles class attack submarine were detected and engaged by our recon LRASD units. From acoustic signatures relayed from the scene of the engagement, it is clear that the LA class submarine was sunk and the destroyer was damaged and limped away off further to the west where we can engage it separately at our leisure.

"Based on their programming, the other LRASD units continued on, inbound towards the south and east, towards where we believe they will locate the American formation. I am prepared to order our strike package to launch towards that location now…here, to the south and west of Rennell Island.

"It would be at the maximum range of our aircraft…but with refueling aircraft meeting the strike package on their way back, they will have plenty of margin…and we can communicate with them as to the exact location of the American force while they are en route.

The Admiral considered this carefully. A large strike at this range was a gamble, but every passing minute increased the risk of his task force being discovered by the Americans. With that engagement that just resulted in the sinking of the American submarine and the damaging of the destroyer, the American Admiral down there would now know that a potent threat of some sort was off to his north somewhere…and he would be anxious to investigate.

"Order the strike package launched as you have outlined, Captain, and then maintain a heavy CAP over this task force and position a strong barrier CAP off to the south and west per operation plan Sea Tiger.

"In addition, by the supplementary provisions of that same plan, contact the reserve maritime strike squadrons on New Caledonia and Santa Isabel Islands and have them launch their aircraft in a second wave of attack after our strike package engages the enemy.

"As soon as the American force is positively identified and located, I expect to see that first wave of seventy-two TAS launches of the new ballistic LRASD units. They should arrive either just prior to, or in conjunction with, our strike package.

"I'll be up on the command observation deck monitoring those launches if you should need me. Carry on."

The Admiral was certain that the Americans must still be unaware of the presence and exact location of his task force. They simply had not had the time to determine it, since the engagement with their picket vessels. He wanted to get his strike package launched, his CAP in place and have those ballistic-assisted LRASD weapons launched before that particular circumstance changed.

The Admiral was correct in his assumption that the Americans had not had time to pinpoint the location of his task force in the time that had passed since the LA class submarine had been sunk and the Spruance class destroyer damaged. They didn't need to.

Admiral Styles of CTF 77 had been made aware of the location of the Chinese task force approaching from his north ten minutes prior to the engagement with the picket vessels and was already taking measures to address it.

September 4, 2009, 04:29 local time
Bridge, U.S.S. Hampton Roads
200 miles south of Rennell Island

The U.S.S. Hampton Roads, designated as CVE 24, was the namesake of the Hampton Roads class of Sea Control Carriers that the United States was now producing in large numbers. She was the first dedicated sea control carrier built by America, as opposed to the conversion of large amphibious assault ships to that role prior to her launch. She was outfitted with the latest American technology for both air support, strike at sea, and defense.

She carried twenty-four Joint Strike Fighters, three E-22B, Osprey AEW aircraft, and three CV-22 Osprey patrol aircraft for long range, high endurance anti-submarine or anti-surface warfare. She also carried four Sea Hawk helicopters for shorter range anti-submarine duties. She also was outfitted with both phased array and conventional radars and included her own Aegis system that could interface with all of her escort ships.

For self defense, she carried an Mk41 vertical launch group of forty cells which held thirty-two Standard missiles and thirty-two ADCAP Sea AMRAAM (called SAMRAAM) missiles. She also mounted two RAM launchers holding sixteen missiles each and four Phalanx CIWS. For sub surface defense, she was outfitted with four SUB-CIWS to defend against LRASD Killer Whales.

In addition to all of this, the Hampton Roads class was capable of carrying out the duties of a mid-sized amphibious assault ship, supporting over eight hundred Marines and their equipment. In the course of this war, with the new T-90A transports and the new SSTN transport submarines, it would be rare that the sea control carriers would be used in that role.

Fitted for the sea control role, with all of the air superiority and strike aircraft, she was capable of acting as either the center of a sea control task force of her own, or supplementing a larger nuclear carrier in an augmented CBG.

In this case, the Hampton Roads was operating in the capacity of the center of a sea control task force positioned to the north of the principle American naval force engaged in this large battle. The two large American carrier task forces further to the south and west were in the process of squeezing the remaining vessels of the Chinese task force that had been defending Australia between them and the submarines task force to the west. This was exactly according to Admiral Styles' overall plan. The Hampton Roads and its escorts were acting as a buffer force between the major American forces and anything the Chinese might throw at them from the north.

In addition to the picket destroyer and attack submarine that had been placed well out on the threat axis towards what was perceived as the most likely threat, the Hampton Road's group had a new air-defense variant of the DDX destroyer, a batch IIA Arleigh Burke Aegis destroyer and a Ticonderoga class Aegis cruiser as escorts. A very potent force indeed.

It was the pickets of the Hampton Roads buffer force that the Chinese recon LRASD units had attacked, and it was this task force that those same Chinese units were now in the process of discovering, twenty minutes later.

"Captain, our outer-ring Ospreys are picking up multiple enemy Killer Whale signatures approaching from the northeast…the count is up to twelve, from the same general bearing where the O'Brien and La Jolla were engaged.

"Closest range is now twenty-two miles."

Based on the earlier report from Admiral Styles of a large Chinese carrier task force off to their northeast, and based on the engagement twenty minutes ago with his outermost pickets, Captain Terrance Thurmond, who was in command of the Hampton Roads and the entire group, TF 77.3, had expected this report.

As the task force commander he knew his role was to interdict attacks aimed at the major U.S. forces from this quarter, and to soak up any such attacks. His forces were about to do just that.

"Okay, these are probably an initial wave of their whales from that Chinese task force Admiral Styles warned us about.

"Have the entire group tighten up to a condition two subsurface defense formation anticipating attack by the whales…but warn everyone to expect both aircraft and missile follow-on attacks.

"I want the barrier CAP pushed out another fifty miles in the direction of those Chinese carriers and launch the ready alert birds to beef up our inner ring CAP."

As the Captain turned to speak with his chief of staff, the duty officer overseeing the specialists who were monitoring the approach of the Chinese LRASD devices shouted.

"We've got an activation! Now another!"

"Enemy devices are going active across the board and are now approaching at very high rates of speed."

Captain Thurmond responded crisply and with efficiency born of long practice. Every American and allied sailor expected at one time or another to be under Killer Whale attack. The Hampton Roads had been under this threat since her initial shakedown cruise and had been under attack on several occasions since coming to the waters of the southwest Pacific, first off of New Zealand as the invasion of Australia was staged…and now in the waters off of Australia itself.

But in those other attacks the Hampton Roads had been a secondary target traveling in the company of one or more much larger full-size, nuclear carriers. Today she would be the primary target and Captain Thurmond knew it.

"Place all SUB CIWS systems in the inner ring on full automatic and slave them into the task force defense system here on board the Hampton Roads.

"Continue monitoring airborne threats in high priority mode…we can't fixate on any single threat."

September 4, 2009, that same time
Combat Information Center, U.S.S. Shanksville
450 miles southwest of Rennell Island

The pace of combat was becoming frantic. Admiral Styles was in the process of directing two separate strike at sea packages and two missile engagements against a Chinese task force to his west and now another to his northeast.

"In subjecting these bastards to a pincer movement we have been caught in one of their own making," he thought as contemplated the progress of the package already making its way towards the remnants of the task force with which the Chinese had been protecting their Australian conquest.

That package was the largest of the two…it had been the principle objective of the operation…and was directed against the five Beijing class carriers. It was approaching the Chinese vessels in conjunction with a large cruise missile attack that had been launched by several of the escort vessels in the Admiral's main group.

"Give me a status on Cobra," the Admiral commanded as he now saw enemy missile designators on the main display, rising to intercept his own cruise missiles.

The Admiral's chief of staff, a Lieutenant Commander who was right on top of the latest intelligence, answered. "Sir, the enemy is fully aware of our attack and, as you can see, is firing missiles at our wave of attacking cruise missiles. We have over eighty missiles in that attack.

"In addition, Commander Hennigar, the strike leader, is indicating that enemy aircraft from a sizable enemy CAP are being vectored against his aircraft as we speak. He believes his escort is strong enough to allow the attack aircraft to get through and he has gone to full power to press the issue.

Pausing for just a moment, the Lieutenant Commander listened briefly but intently to the latest communication coming through the headset he was wearing.

"Okay, we're getting reports of a massive missile launch form the Chinese task force…

"Looks like in addition to anti-air missiles there is also a large counter strike being launched from the Chinese as our aircraft are approaching."

The Admiral considered this report. He had over one hundred aircraft approaching that western Chinese task force and they would be in the thick of their attack in the next few minutes…right on the heels of the cruise missiles which were attacking now.

He knew that all of the ships in CTF 77 would be preparing to receive the missile attack that his chief of staff had just referenced. Barrier CAP would be moving into place, ships would be positioning themselves and the AEGIS system would be fully engaged. He knew that his task force was as prepared as it could be for just such an attack…particularly if the Chinese were not able to support that attack with aircraft…and he believed he'd caught them before they could launch from that quarter.

So, Admiral Styles was relatively certain that he had caught the primary target of his operation perfectly within his pincer…exactly according to plan. But he was very concerned about the Hampton Roads group. She was hanging out there between him and that second large Chinese task force to the northeast and he was positive that the Chinese were going to launch their largest attack from that quarter.

He felt like he had been maneuvered into throwing his strongest attack at those Beijing class carriers, only to learn that two of the larger Mao class carriers with a very large escort group were driving hard for his flank.

Luckily, with the Hampton Roads group positioned to the northeast for just such a contingency, that flank was not exposed. Captain Thurmond was a very capable naval officer and he would have his entire group alerted by now and preparing to receive whatever the Chinese could throw at him.

Nevertheless, Admiral Styles had a feeling that Thurmond was going to need help. Although he'd had to wait while his major attack finished launching, fueling and clearing the area, the Admiral had ordered a second strike package to be prepared to launch immediately after the first. He hoped he could hit that new Chinese task force before they could hit him.

"How about preparations for Python…where are we?"

Again, the Lieutenant Commander responded.

"Admiral, the tankers, AEW and EW aircraft are already airborne. The fighters are launching now and will be followed by the Super Hornets and the JSF attack aircraft.

"We expect the package to be completely fueled, formed up, and on its way in the next fifteen minutes."

"Fifteen minutes?" thought the Admiral. That would seem like an eternity. Who knows what the Chinese from that new group will be doing in that time. Fifteen minutes is almost 200 miles for a strike group…or even further for supersonic missiles.

"Well, inform the captains of the Shanksville, the Bush and the Reagan to pull out all of the stops and have their air operations sped up if at all possible for Python.

"I believe we are going to have to…"

At that moment, Admiral Ben Ryan stepped into the CIC and motioned for Admiral Styles to step over to him for a confidential conversation.

"Look, Jerry, I know your hands are full. But I just got flash traffic from Pearl and decided you needed to hear this immediately. Later we'll brief the staffs.

"Intelligence is indicating that there is a high likelihood of the CAS using their tactical nukes against us here and against the invasion beachhead in the near future. They indicate that if we continue to press inland and if we are particularly successful in decisively defeating the PLAN in this battle, enemy local high command has been given the green light to plan and then execute an attack on us.

"Apparently, a highly placed informant got the word out, and the President wants us to take the threat seriously.

"He is working through State and through the CIA to deliver a back channel message to the Chinese, Indians, and the GIR that he hopes will lessen the threat. That message is apparently very straightforward and represents a new NCA strategy.

"Where President Weisskopf depended on our TBM to forestall and defeat any theater level engagements and would only launch in retaliation for a successful hit on our forces, or an attack against CONUS, President Bowers is taking a different stance.

"This is the text of his message:

Any nuclear attack launched against any American or allied forces will result in a full scale nuclear attack in response.

"He's not beating around the bush, Jerry. That is exact text of the message going to the Chinese and their allies. We need to plan and prepare accordingly.

"Hopefully the President's message will have the desired effect. My guess is that the successful insertion of the new space station and its ability to defend itself and the continental United States has figured heavily into this new strategy. I'm told that within ninety days we are going to launch another station into geosynchronous orbit above us here in the southwest Pacific.

Admiral Styles was uneasy about the new nuclear policy…and not because he disagreed with it or thought it wrong. He did not let his unease show and he would faithfully follow the orders and directives of his commander in chief. He was certain, should things go well here in Australia and elsewhere for the western allies, that the Chinese and their allies would be more and more likely to turn to their WMDs. He understood exactly what the President was doing and he agreed with it.

"We have the advantage and we need to push it and play to our own strengths," he thought to himself.

Just the same, he did not relish being on the receiving end of a nuclear attack. That is what caused the unease. No one, not even the most courageous and resolute of military leaders, could face that possibility without a shudder.

"Ben, this means we're going to have to reconfigure the positioning of the ships in the task force for a possible nuclear attack. Because of the greater separation between them, that will make us much more vulnerable to the conventional attacks we already know are coming. It's a real catch 22."

As Admiral Styles paused for a few seconds while he thought it out, Ben Ryan empathized with him. He had gone through this same thought process after receiving the message and while coming down to the CIC to discuss it with Styles. He was anxious to see if Jerry came to similar conclusions as he had in considering the trade-offs necessary for security of the task force in the current dual-threat circumstances. He was pleased when he heard what Admiral Styles came up with.

"Ben, here's what I intend to do. I am going to place the TBM Aegis ships out further on the threat axis for those nuclear threats in a full nuclear defense posture. The inner ring will go to a sixty-five percent separation. Far enough to provide time for further separation in the event of a nuclear strike warning, but close enough to provide a reasonable conventional defense umbrella.

"I'll have my chief of staff get to work immediately on this and we'll implement it as soon as a workable plan is drawn up.

"It's going to be tough to implement right in the middle of our ongoing strike at sea and defensive operations…but that's why we get paid the big bucks I guess," Admiral Styles finished jokingly.

It wasn't the exact solution Ben Ryan had come up with, but it was more than adequate and in some respects it was even better than what he would have proposed.

"Take some consolation that you will soon have that station up over you, Jerry. I can't tell you how gratified I was to hear that it would be going up over the Australian Theater of Operations. A lot of lobbying went into that decision.

"The Israelis, the Russians and our own people in Alaska lobbied equally hard and long, particularly since it'll be six more months before the next one goes up.

"But the next six months here in Australia are going to be pivotal and will set the stage for the future course of the war."

Jerry Styles considered his superior's words as he wrote out a message to his chief of staff and had an orderly take it to him.

"Well, I have to tell you, Ben, once that station is in place I will feel significantly better about our chances to stop any full-scale nuclear ballistic missile attack without taking some major hits.

"…with the proven effectiveness of the Chinese TBM …they may be tempted to try it anyway if they begin losing a lot of ground.

The Admiral paused just a moment…

"I'll tell you something else, Ben. I like President Bowers. I like him a lot. A lot of people were concerned about the size and fit of the shoes he had to fill, but I think he's going to fit into them just fine.

"In fact, he may need to buy a larger pair of those shoes at the rate he's going before all is said and done."

**September 4, 2009, 05:15 local time
Forward VLS Control Station
PLAN Amphibious Assault Ship Chongqing
250 kilometers northeast of the Santa Cruz Islands**

The launch of the new tactical ballistic missiles, those with the Killer Whale acting as the terminal guidance and warhead, had gone off without a problem. All thirty-six missiles had been launched from the Chongqing and the teams responsible for the operation had completed the reloading process for the second wave of missiles whenever the commanders ordered it.

…and that order was not long in coming as a second wave was launched against the American task force to the southwest.

Kao Pham was particularly proud of these launches. They were the latest innovation of his father's LRASD weapons…a new wrinkle for the Americans and their allies to have to contend with.

These LRASD weapons only carried the rocket fuel and rocket engines to be used for final guidance underwater. The huge ballistic missiles, which the Chongqing carried along with three of her sister ships, would provide the long-range delivery that the LRASDs normally depended upon for their own conventional fuel and propulsion. Not having to include the dual propulsion or the fuel for it had significantly reduced the size of the weapons and allowed them to be fitted as a final stage onto the large ballistic missiles.

"My father's legend just grows and grows," thought Kao.

"Designer and implementer of the weapons that pushed America's aircraft carriers out of the western Pacific and which have been used to keep them at bay all across the world, Hero of the People's Republic and now a member of the Politburo itself.

"Now, as the Americans counter that technology, my father manages to stay one step ahead of them it seems."

Kao's entire family had made the transition to Chinese life, and Chinese loyalties many years ago. His father, Lu, had realized a life-long ambition to develop technology and systems to counter the Americans. His mother, Song, had realized her dream of raising her children in a nice home, without the fear of want, where Lu's fierce resentment and dislike for the Americans was appreciated and not apt to bring disfavor on the entire family. His sister, Chiang, had been able to pursue her chosen field of study and work and had done very well.

"In fact," Kao thought, "she too has contributed to the capabilities of the Chongqing."

Her work was directly related to the algorithms the *ta shih* detectors used to engage the stealth aircraft the Americans employ. A fact for which Kao and every sailor on the Chongqing was grateful.

"I wonder if she's actually going to marry that politician?" Koa asked himself as he thought about Chiang in far-away Beijing.

"When I met him on leave after they had announced their intentions, he seemed likable enough…and he seemed truly interested in Chiang," he thought.

Koa had wondered if the interest was real…if perhaps his feelings were more a function of the influence that their father's prominence might garner…particularly since he had become a member of the Politburo and the executive council. But now that he had met them, and spent several days with them, he was convinced that the attraction was genuine…and that it was clearly mutual.

"And then there's me. I'm out here having the time of my life sailing around the world and learning about electronics myself…despite the dangers.

"Who knows…maybe I'll go career when this is all over."

Kao had been promoted to a section chief on the Chongqing. He oversaw all maintenance functions by enlisted personnel for an entire battery of VLS anti-air missiles located near the bow of the vessel. That included the missile reloading, the missile hatch functions, the readiness of the missiles and the maintenance and integrity of the launch tubes. Much of this was automated, but the equipment that the automated system operated had to be maintained and kept in perfect working order for potential combat.

This meant that Koa, as section chief, not only had to have extensive knowledge of the machinery and its operation, he also had to understand and be able to assist in troubleshooting the software and electronic systems that drove it. He and his people had to understand how to repair the equipment or its controls…or to be able to operate portions of the system manually, if necessary, during combat operations.

It was more than achieving high marks on the readiness and maintenance charts, and it was more than competing for the highest sustainability rankings. It was a matter of life and death during combat and Koa understood it and was able to convey it to his team..

"While consistently hitting those high marks on the charts I might add," he thought to himself as his communications light winked on brightly and the incessant chime of a call came through.

He spoke into the microphone. "Chief Pham."

The duty officer over anti-air engagements in the combat information center responded immediately.

"Chief, this is Lieutenant Wu. Your systems all look nominal, what is your estimation of their status for prolonged operations?"

"Uh-oh," thought Koa. "Don't like the sounds of that. The Americans must have located us."

He did a final check on his own monitors and assessed the status and the operation of the equipment…equipment that he had become intimately familiar with over the last three and a half years.

"Lieutenant, everything is not only nominal, it's in excellent shape.

"I don't expect any down time on our account…even if we have to run through all of the missiles in the hold."

Koa, in his mind's eye, could see the smile spread across the Lieutenant's features.

"Great, Koa. Prepare for imminent action. Our own attack force reported a large enemy strike about three hundred kilometers out and approaching.

"You'll get the official order soon, but you might as well get your people ready now.

"Wu out."

September 4, 2009, 05:24 local time
Combat Information Center, U.S.S. Hampton Roads
190 miles south of Rennell Island

Captain Thurmond counted the impact and losses from the initial LRASD attack as he prepared for the onslaught his sensors and barrier CAP now told him was approaching.

The reconnaissance version of the Chinese Killer Whales were not as sophisticated in their attack profile or capabilities as other variants…and the Captain was grateful for that. Against Spruance destroyers or other combatant and non-combatant vessels not equipped with the SUB CIWS defense, the normal, straight-on attack profile of the huge supercavitating weapons was still horrifically effective. And that was the exact profile that these long-range surveillance weapons used.

But against vessels equipped with the SUB CIWS, unless the enemy was able to overwhelm those defenses by sheer numbers, the straight-on attack mode could be effectively defeated. Each ship in Thurmond's task force was equipped with the SUB CIWS and those systems provided the edge in defending the task force against the sixteen Chinese devices that had located them.

Still, it had been a harrowing experience for the Hampton Roads and two of her escorts, and it had turned deadly for the third escort. The DDX air defense destroyer, the U.S.S. Townsend, had been severely damaged when one of the three Killer Whales attacking her had been destroyed only one hundred feet from her starboard side, near her fantail and rudder on that side.

The detonation had warped several bulkheads and jammed that rudder into a twenty-four degree cant, while buckling the screw shaft on that side as well. Twelve personnel had been killed and another eight injured in the resulting explosion, flooding and fight to keep the ship afloat and maneuverable.

"Well, that crew had worked wonders in the last half hour and the Townsend was afloat, mildly maneuverable and still in the fight," the Captain said to himself.

"But how long will she or the rest of us be able to hold out?"

That answer would not be long in coming.

The Chinese had a wave of SU-37 and SU-34 aircraft that had battled their way through the Hampton Road's barrier CAP over one hundred miles to the north. Over thirty Chinese aircraft had broken through and were now approaching as the inner ring CAP of eight aircraft was vectored towards them. Thurmond knew that those eight aircraft would not be able to hold them all back.

As this stark realization began to coalesce, his air defense duty officer called out.

"Vampire! Vampire! Vampire!

"Multiple ballistic tracks now approaching…count is twenty and rising…now thirty…now forty!"

Ultimately the count went to seventy-one missiles as the Aegis system on all of the ships went into action, both against the incoming ballistic missile tracks and the approaching aircraft. Seventy-one rapidly approaching missiles coming up behind the thirty-two aircraft that were closer, but approaching more slowly.

As it was, the ballistic tracks were going to arrive just before the aircraft and the four vertical launch cells of the three escort vessels and the Hampton Roads itself began emptying at those approaching missiles. Then they would also be taking aim at the aircraft as they came into range and as the system rated threat levels, the value of the vessels targeted and the time and space requirements available for each intercept.

The Theater Ballistic defense capability of the Ticonderoga and Arleigh Burke Aegis vessels came into play first. While the incoming missiles were far out of range of the normal standard missiles, the two ships quickly launched all twenty-four of the combined TBM inventory and downed twenty of the ballistic missiles before any of the surviving Chinese weapons were even in range of the remaining American missiles.

With fifty ballistic missiles still inbound on very rapid ballistic tracks, Aegis set high priority in these targets as they flashed towards the American task force. But these missiles were coming faster than what the extended and medium range standard missiles, or the newer ADCAP SAMRAAM missiles were designed to intercept.

They were simply coming too fast for any type of assured intercepts.

But Captain Thurmond, his personnel and their equipment all tried just the same.

Between the Hampton Roads, the damaged Townsend and the Arleigh Burke and Ticonderoga vessels, which contained a total of three hundred and ninety-four missiles in their vertical launch tubes, over two hundred and fifty missiles were launched at the Chinese ballistic missiles…but only twenty-three of the remaining missiles were destroyed.

In that same time period, another one hundred missiles were launched at the approaching Chinese aircraft. Twenty-one of the thirty-two aircraft were destroyed, but seven of the destroyed aircraft launched their missiles before their destruction and all remaining eight attack aircraft were able to launch their cruise missiles as well…each aircraft launching two missiles each.

A total of thirty super-sonic cruise missiles were now also approaching the task force and except for the close in weapons system like the Phalanx CIWS and the RAM missiles, there were no Aegis missiles left to defend the task force.

As the cruise missiles rapidly approached, a strange thing happened that all of the defense officers on all of the American vessels noticed at the same moment. The ballistic missiles had some type of separation that dropped away from the oncoming ballistic tracks.

"Rapid change of aspect on ballistic vampires!" cried out the air defense duty officer on the Hampton Roads.

"We have a separation of some sort. The ballistic tracks have continue inbound.

"Those tracks are now going to pass over the task force at an altitude of three to five thousand feet!"

Captain Thurmond was immediately concerned about the potential for nuclear detonations over the task force, but he didn't have any weapons that could prevent it…and he didn't have time to worry either. The cruise missiles launched by the aircraft were now approaching…and they were coming in on courses that would impact his ships.

The close-in defenses performed relatively well against the cruise missiles. Of the thirty approaching cruise missiles, twenty-one were shot down.

But nine missiles impacted the American vessels. One on the Townsend, two on the Arleigh Burke destroyer, and three each on the Ticonderoga cruiser and the Hampton Roads.

Given its already reduced state, the damage to the Townsend, was significant. It continued to make headway, but was trailing thick black smoke from a hole in its superstructure just above the waterline. The Arleigh Burke escort was moderately damaged, particularly to its rear VLS cells, which, fortunately, were all empty at the time of impact, minimizing the damage. It continued to make full headway and was capable of continuing the fight. The Ticonderoga cruiser was severely damaged with hits in its engineering spaces, the helicopter hangar spaces and to the forward gun mount and VLS cell. Its rear VLS cell still contained ten missiles and both of its Phalanx CIWS were still operational as the big Aegis cruiser lost headway and was in the process of going dead in the water.

The Hampton Roads lost the operation of one of its two elevators, took a hit just below the bridge that destroyed the ability to pilot the ship from those spaces, and had its flight deck holed toward the aft portion of the ship, also starting a fierce fire in the hangar spaces below. She continued on unabated, but smoke was pouring from the hits she took and her effectiveness was impacted, as was that of the entire task force...at just a time when she would be needing everything she and her escorts had.

Just before the first of the cruise missiles impacted his ship, Captain Thurmond distinctly heard his sub surface defense officer make a surprising announcement.

"I've got multiple incoming supercavitating weapons!

"Five...ten...no, now over twenty devices. All on a bearing consistent with where those ballistic tracks separated. Now approaching at..."

KA-BLAM!

The cruise missile explosion stunned Captain Thurmond momentarily and knocked him off his feet. As he was helped back to his feet by his aide and others near him, the other two cruise missiles struck the Hampton Roads.

BLAM...BLAM!

The next two hits were not as close to the CIC, but rumbled heavily through the entire ship just the same, causing everyone in the CIC to grab on to something sturdy to keep themselves from falling again. But, aside from some minor cuts and bruises, everyone in the CIC was okay. As he prepared to issue orders to determine the extent of the damage and to organize efforts to resolve it, the Captain remembered the incoming Killer Whales.

"Get me the status on those Killer Whales! SUB CIWS weapons free–engage them now!"

As the Captain issued these orders, another warning came from the duty officer for air defense.

"We've got multiple inbound ballistic vampires again...ten, twenty...now over thirty.

"...now receiving AEW reports of inbound supersonic bandits consistent with TU-22M or Blackjack bombers.

"Many aircraft in two groups approaching from both the west and the northeast!

"Count is up to fifty aircraft in the western group and now thirty-eight aircraft in the northeastern group."

For just a few seconds everything got deathly quite in the CIC. With few anti-air missiles left, with only three ships able to operate their SUB CIWS against the onrushing onslaught, and with damage already sustained, every man in that room knew what these numbers meant.

All eyes were on Captain Thurmond. He didn't take long in replying, and when his reply came, it was defiant, direct and inspiring.

"Okay, time is short. Send this message as follows to CINC CTF 77 and to CINCPAC.

"By God, we have drawn all of their strength into us here at this location. The enemy has been fooled into directing their entire effort at TF 77.3."

Taking the com in his hand and opening a channel to all of the commanders in the task force, he spoke in a voice loud enough to be heard by every man in the combat information center.

"All right, everyone. We're facing an attack that must have been intended for all of CTF 77. The enemy believes that *we* are the entire combined task force. By fooling them, we've accomplished our mission…each and every one of you can be proud of that."

Knowing full well from the threat displays what the likely outcome of the current engagement was likely to be, but not varying in the slightest, Captain Thurmond completed his communication to all of the ships under his command.

"Now we must maintain that pride and give them hell!

"We'll take the best they can throw at us and still come out swinging!

"God bless and preserve each of you and your commands."

September 4, 2009, 05:32 local time
E-22A Osprey over TF 77.3
190 miles south of Rennell Island

Lieutenant Commander Joshua Morgan had just given a SITREP over secure communications to Admiral Styles about the fate of Task Force 77.3. The report had been to the point…but he couldn't keep his emotion out of it.

"Sir, the Hampton Roads, the Townsend, the Port Royal and the Decatur are all…dear God… they're gone, Admiral, destroyed and sunk.

"Each of them fought to the end, hit multiple times by cruise missiles they fought on and destroyed numerous Killer Whales around them……until they were taken out, one after the other, by Killer Whales that got through to them.

"Currently, there are many men in the water, hundreds of them. What rescue operations we can mount are underway…but we need a lot more.

"We have this early warning aircraft, one HV-22 patrol and rescue aircraft, one F-35 from our inner ring CAP and two F-35s left from our barrier CAP currently returning to this position. Of the entire flight wing of the Hampton Roads…that's it.

Joshua could still scarcely believe what his own eyes had beheld. The intensity of the battle was scarcely imaginable, even to a combat veteran of several engagements. It had lasted barely a few minutes.

The remaining aircraft from the CAP had engaged the TU-22 and Blackjack bombers and their escorts. After their earlier engagement against the carrier-based aircraft from the Zenim and the Xia, there had been far too few American aircraft to overcome the Chinese numbers and so the sky had literally filled with cruise missiles. At the same time, another seventy-two Killer Whales were inserted into the water by their ballistic missile carriers only a few miles from the task force.

The first wave of Killer Whales, twenty-seven in number, swept in on the task force as the ships were fighting the scores of cruise missiles. The Port Royal, already dead in the water, took three more cruise missile hits before she was struck simultaneously by three Killer Whales.

Before the smoke from those explosions could clear, four more Killer Whales flew into that maelstrom and exploded, adding to the pall of smoke and debris. When all of that had cleared…the Port Royal was simply gone.

The Townsend and the Decatur suffered similar fates, each of them being attacked by many more LRASD weapons than their defenses could possibly handle…seven for the Townsend and eight for the Decatur. The Townsend had already been rendered a floating and defenseless wreck by the cruise missiles, but the Decatur went down fighting.

The Hampton Roads was able to heroically fight off the five Killer Whales that targeted her from that first batch of ballistic missile delivered weapons. But the cruise missiles scored no less than twelve additional hits on her, setting her ablaze from bow to stern and holing her in six places.

She was just going dead in the water when the last wave of seventy-two Killer Whales rushed in. A part of the Decatur was still afloat above the waves and attracted twelve weapons…but all of the rest, all fifty-seven of them targeted on the Hampton Roads.

It was the most sustained Killer Whale attack on any allied vessel in the war and for over thirty-five seconds huge geysers, explosions and clouds of debris rose in the air every few seconds, as multiple hits occurred on what was left of the vessel under the developing pall of smoke.

As with the Port Royal, but coming as no surprise to the naval aviators who had watched her end, when that awful cloud of smoke drifted far enough away on the wind to allow them to view where their ship had been…the Hampton Roads was gone.

After conferring briefly with his staff, Admiral Styles issued orders to Lieutenant Commander Morgan.

"Commander, you are to render whatever assistance you can to those in the water. Both your and the patrol aircraft are authorized to pick up as many survivors as you can carry and to leave whatever supplies you can.

"But under no circumstances are you to risk your aircraft or those whom you now command. This battle is far from over and your assets are valuable and must not be wasted.

"Am I clear on this?" the Admiral demanded.

Joshua Morgan was brought right back to the here and now by the command tone in the Admiral's voice.

"Aye aye, sir....Loud and clear."

Having achieved the desired result and hearing the discipline and confidence returning to the young officer's voice, the Admiral continued.

"Good. Then as soon as you must, return with the F-35s to this position and you will be taken on board the GWB.

"We have four other Ospreys coming that way at this moment with a large escort...but they are about two hours out. Make sure the people in the water understand and have them prepared to get the most critical personnel on those aircraft when they arrive.

"Tell them to hold on...vessels will try to be in the area within twelve hours."

As the Commander received his orders, he couldn't help but share one last thought with the Task Force commander while he had him on the horn.

"Admiral...you know Captain Thurmond was right."

Admiral Styles had two other ongoing battles to manage...but hearing the emotion and plea in the young man's voice, he decided to loosen a little and break communications protocol for a moment and respond.

"What do you mean son? How was the Captain right?"

Knowing he was possibly out of order…but not being able to help himself in wanting to bring some order…some closure to the horror he had witnessed in the destruction of the entire task force, Morgan continued.

"Sir, he told us our task force should be proud, that we had accomplished our mission…that this huge attack was intended for the entire force and that we had won the day by taking it all upon ourselves."

The Admiral remembered Captain Thurmond's last words over the secure net…and he knew then, as he knew now, that Thurmond and this young Lieutenant Commander were right.

"Son…your Captain was right. You did accomplish the mission…though not as we had planned.

"Know that what your comrades purchased here today will lead to our ultimate victory …and that their loss will be avenged."

As he ended communication with Morgan, Styles thought to himself, "Sometimes the line between victory and defeat can be hard to ascertain, particularly depending on your reference point. Sometimes the successful accomplishment of a mission can bring as much personal and individual tragedy as a bitter defeat."

September 4, 2009, 06:45 local time
Two Miles west of the PLAN Carrier Zenim
240 kilometers northeast of the Santa Cruz Islands

Koa could see the silhouette of the Zenim off to his east, plowing through the waves in the pre-dawn light. Further to the north he observed the smoking Xia, which had been hit at least three times but had not lost headway and was still traveling in formation with the Zenim. With most of the damage occurring on her flight deck and the hangar spaces below it, the Xia was clearly unable to receive any of the aircraft that were now returning to the carriers from their attack on the Americans.

The Zenim, on the other hand, was feverishly conducting flight operations. Koa could see the planes landing…and lined up to land, approaching from the rear of the carrier. At the same time, she was launching other aircraft from positions near the bow as she continued to maintain a heavy combat air patrol over the retreating task force, while accounting for all of the returning aircraft as well.

And it was this task force that had been significantly reduced in numbers over what it had been less than two hours ago.

"Hang on, Jing," Koa said to the man next to him.

"The helicopters will be here soon. It's only a matter of time."

Until thirty minutes ago, Koa had not known Jing. He was a sailor who worked in the laundry facilities aboard the Chongqing who took his duty watch on the after deck around behind the bridge and superstructure. Koa rarely had opportunity to go there and, other than knowing that there were personnel who operated the vast laundry machines, he knew none of them personally.

Until now.

"Comrade, can you see the helicopters?" Jing asked.

"I can't see anything and I don't hear them. I don't know how much longer I can last. My head and eyes hurt and my arm is going numb."

Koa looked at the young man next to him…and he was young. Barely eighteen years of age. There was a dark laceration across his head that angled down over one eye…but had somehow resulted in the loss of vision in both. In addition, his shoulder appeared to be dislocated, on the side where his arm was going numb.

Jing was a new recruit who had come onboard less than three months earlier, during the last visit the Chongqing had made to their home port…when she had been upgraded with the latest sensors, software and weapons systems. It had been during that time that Kao had been able to spend so much time with his parents and had been able to meet his sister's fiancée.

Now here he was in the water in the Coral Sea, surrounded by dozens of other Chinese sailors, holding on to a large piece of wreckage from his ship, the Chongqing, which was now gone…along with so many of his friends.

Soon after Lieutenant Wu had informed him of the approaching engagement, the orders had come down to prepare for launch of their missiles. Within a few seconds the entire battery of vertical launch cells had been fired… and then reloaded and then all of them fired again.

Soon after that, there had been a violent wrenching in the ship as she took a direct hit from an American missile of some sort, followed by several other even more violent wrenchings that threw Koa and every man in his section to the deck, bouncing off whatever protrusions or hard edges they happened to be thrown against. Koa lost count of the times the deck shook and shuddered before he lost consciousness.

When he came to, it was dark in his spaces and the deck was canted at an angle to the port side and towards the aft portion of the ship. Smoke was seeping in and Koa rose to his knees and then to his feet, searching for the emergency lighting.

Finding it, he had switched it on only to discover that all but two of his men were either unconscious or dead. Over the next minute or two he and the other two had awakened and revived those they could. Within another few seconds they had determined who was able to exit their spaces to the open main deck above them.

Koa tried to get out three of the men who had been injured badly and were unconscious and had to be carried. After bringing one of them topside, there had been first one, and then another, tremendous explosion behind them, in the vicinity of one of the large tactical ballistic missile tubes right in front of the bridge and the after deck. Those explosions knocked them all once again to the deck.

Rising to his feet, Koa looked back at the fire and smoke rising from the port side of the ship in that vicinity, and now noticed that the entire bridge was a mass of twisted and ruined metal…either on fire or heavily smoking.

The deck took on a much more pronounced slant to aft and the men looked to Koa for orders. There was no communication with the rest of the ship and several individual sailors could be seen diving overboard.

Koa quickly assessed the situation and issued some orders.

"The ship is sinking….time to abandon!"

Looking at the cant of the deck where they stood and the distance to the water from the side railing, Koa continued.

"Too high to jump from here….move aft, towards the bridge…..there, to where the ship is broken… not as far to the water surface there."

"Follow me."

The men needed no prodding and, as they made their way towards the center of the ship, they gathered more sailors who were coming topside from various hatchways that led below. Those who could speak did so in clipped phrases, stammering of mass confusion and many too injured to get out below decks.

Finally, they made their way to the port side amidships as water began lapping at the main deck. Arriving there, they saw a large piece of floating wreckage of some type not more than five meters away from the ship that looked like it had plenty of room for the fifteen men that now made up Koa's party.

There was a horrendous ripping sound beneath them and it was apparent that the ship was about to break up.

"Okay, quickly, over the side. Swim to that wreckage there."

Turning to a group of three of his own section standing near him, he issued more orders.

"You three…help me with these two injured men and we'll float them over and place them on their backs on top of the wreckage …. there is just enough room for the two of them."

The men needed no more encouragement. Over the side they went, swimming for all they were worth to the wreckage and then lending helping hands as Koa and his three companions got the two injured men there.

Once there, Koa ordered them all to get on the side nearest the ship and begin kicking their feet to move themselves further away. Kicking for all they were worth, they began to move away from the ship, through the oil and other debris that littered the water. They had to push their way through several bodies and five other men, already in the water joined them as they continued on their way.

They had gone no more than another twenty-five meters when there was a violent explosion behind them…the largest they had experienced yet. A strong shock wave blasted across them. Thick acrid smoke engulfed them. Debris and hot metal impacted all around them. Several of the men screamed and one of those injured who was on the wreckage was blown off into the water, sinking beneath the waves. The sea caught fire around them and Koa yelled for them all to kick towards an open space of water another twenty meters to their right which was completely free of flames.

Ducking under the water several times and losing two more men to the flames, they finally made it and looked back in time to see the Chongqing, less than a hundred meters away, lift up high above them to fore and aft, completely broken in two and then slip beneath the waves, accompanied by a shrieking, grinding sound that was mixed with screams, breaking glass and falling metal. It was a sight and sound Koa would remember until the day he died…which at that time seemed like it might be that very day, any minute.

At that point, there were only eleven men holding to the wreckage, along with the single injured man left on top of it. Over the next twenty minutes, over twenty-five other men made their way to the wreckage that Koa and the others were holding to.

One of the last of these had been the injured Jing, who had been assisted there by two other men. They had swum right up to the area where Koa himself was holding on. Speaking over several of the sailors' reluctance, who believed there was no more room for others at their wreckage, Koa had been adamant.

"Quiet, all of you!

"These are our comrades…our countrymen and our shipmates. We will take on all who come to us for help, just as we have made room for you others who joined us here.

"I am the ranking enlisted person here and we will maintain our discipline and our hope.

"Now, make room for these men. If we run out of space, then the most healthy will spell each other in five minute intervals…and I will be the first to do so."

But there had been no need to spell anyone. Over the next thirty minutes, another five men had succumbed to their injuries or fatigue and slipped beneath the waves, despite the best efforts of those around them who tried to hold them up.

In one terrible case, one man who sank beneath the waves grabbed onto his healthy comrade in a death grip and pulled him under with him. There was nothing anyone could do. Again, a gruesome vision that each of them would carry with them and remember for the rest of their lives.

As the ships of the task force moved off, leaving those in the water to their own devices…and leaving them nothing but hope for rescue, Koa began to plan on how to keep these men alive.

Already they had three men on top of the wreckage where there was really only room for two. They were rotating the least injured, who needed time out of the water, into that third position.

Perhaps it was because of his loss of sight, perhaps it was because he simply desired it the most and was somehow attuned to it, but it was Jing who made the first pronouncement.

"Listen…off in that direction," he pointed.

"I hear a helicopter getting closer!"

All eyes looked in the direction Jing was pointing, hoping against hope that he was correct. Their hopes were rewarded as they saw a large Ka-50 helicopter, configured in the search and rescue role, approach them and then hover fifty feet over them.

The three most critically injured were winched up to the helicopter first and then it pivoted in the air, tilted its rotors slightly forward and flew off in the direction of the Zenim. It was soon replaced by another helicopter.

Over the next twenty minutes, using three helicopters shuttling between the wreckage and the Zenim, all of the men in Koa's group of survivors were plucked from the water and transported safely to friendly decks. Koa was the last to leave.

September 5, 2009, 17:30 local time
Task Force Commander's Cabin
PLAN Carrier Zenim
650 kilometers north-northeast of the Santa Cruz Islands

The Chinese were withdrawing north, away from the Coral Sea and away from direct naval intervention of allied operations in support of their invasion of Australia.

Admiral X'in reviewed the last two days' action in his mind.

He believed he had delivered telling blows to the U.S. Navy in the area, but he would not fool himself. It was he who was withdrawing, not the Americans. As telling as his blows may have been-and the complete destruction of an American task force could not be discounted-his own nation's losses had been heavier.

The Admiral discounted some of the boasts from the maritime strike force commanders regarding the size of the American task force that had been destroyed. Some of those reports filtering back to him indicated that multiple American carriers and at least eight support and escort vessels had been sunk...the sea wiped clean of a large American task force.

But the Admiral believed his own returning aircrews more. They indicated that there had been a single American carrier there with three escorts...and that the carrier was not one of the Nimitz or newer CVX class carriers. Instead, it had been one of the smaller Sea Control vessels.

"It's no wonder we wiped them out," thought the Admiral.

"That strike package had been meant to contend with a force four times as large as what they found...and even though we wiped out what we did find, we squandered a great opportunity, both in terms of surprise and in terms of equipment available to be employed."

To the Admiral's credit, he had continued to try to press his advantage, even after the attack he had received from the main American force. That attack had sunk the Chongqing and three of his escorts and damaged the Xia.

Operating under his command, land-based maritime strike aircraft from New Caledonia and Santa Isabel Islands had found and attacked the principle American formation very late in the day of September 4th in conjunction with another TAS ballistic missile LRASD attack coordinated from his retiring vessels. The aircraft were from the same squadrons that had delivered such a decisive blow to the U.S. Task Force that the Admiral and the rest of the Chinese had presumed was the principle American force earlier in the day.

But the American task force was much bigger and much stronger than the smaller blocking force Admiral X'in's efforts had eliminated earlier that same day. What turned out to be three American super carriers and a damaged sea control carrier were capable of establishing an almost unbreakable barrier CAP between themselves and their foes…and they were capable of doing so on several threat axes.

Each arm of the Chinese attack that X'in had ordered had encountered barriers CAPs over two hundred miles out from the carriers, numbering in excess of fifty aircraft each. Before their long range cruise missiles could be launched, the majority of the aircraft had been shot down. Still, because of the significant escort that had traveled with the strike aircraft, sixteen TU-22M aircraft off of New Caledonia and ten Blackjack bombers off of the Santa Isabel Islands had gotten through and successfully launched over fifty cruise missiles at the Americans.

While this was occurring, another ballistic LRASD launch also came in, coordinated with the air attack. But the American task force contained several more DDX destroyers, Burke class Aegis destroyers and Ticonderoga class Aegis cruisers. This meant that there were more TBM standard missiles that could engage the attack…and this Chinese attack consisted of only forty-eight missiles, due to the loss of the Chongqing.

Only twelve of those LRASD devices landed and engaged the American fleet.

Results were unclear…but it appeared that at least one of the American carriers had been severely damaged and that the sea control carrier had possibly been sun, along with three or four of the escort ships.

"And what did we trade for this?" the Admiral asked himself.

Of the five Beijing Class carriers and their eighteen escort and support vessels, only one carrier and five escorts had been able to break through the American submarine force after being badly mauled by large strike forces off of the large American carrier force in the Coral Sea. That much-reduced Chinese force was now escaping westward over the top of the Gulf of Carpenteria, towards the Arafura Sea where they were moving under increasingly friendly and heavy air protection off of New Guinea and out of northern Australia.

"And this task force is escaping first north, and then west towards the Solomon Islands," bemoaned the Admiral.

"Less one TAS and several escort vessels ourselves, and with a badly damaged Mao class carrier."

The Admiral had already reported these results to his high command and had received tentative orders for provisioning and rebuilding an effective strike force. Later, he would plan a new counterattack that would challenge the Americans and their allies at a future date…but at a future place and time that was still wholly undetermined to the Admiral or his superiors.

It was still just too soon.

In the meantime, the allied landings and strengthening of their positions in the southeast portion of Australia around Sydney and along the coast towards Brisbane and Melbourne would continue, as would their steady advance inland.

"They'll also undoubtedly move on New Caledonia and the New Hebrides Islands quickly," thought X'in, "now that we can no longer protect them from the sea and they are left hanging out there."

As he rolled the tactical and strategic picture over in his mind, he began the first tentative planning towards the kernel of a plan that would lead to his next moves.

"Somewhere around the Solomons," he said to himself.

"If we can get the promised help from the Indians and the improved Beijing and the new Mao class carrier groups down here in time…that's where we'll stop them."

September 5, 2009, 18:00 local time
Task force Commander's Cabin
U.S.S. Shanksville
350 Nautical Miles Southeast of Brisbane

Admirals Jerry Styles and Ben Ryan conferred in Styles' cabin as they prepared for the departure of Ryan, the CINCPAC.

He would be going back to New Zealand for two days to confer with the exiled heads of state and then on to Hawaii to prepare for the transfer of his command to his new replacement. Form there, he would fly to Washington, D.C. to report directly to the CNO, the Secretary of Defense, and the President of the United States about the current situation in and around Australia and operations in the Coral Sea. He would then be assuming his new assignment, the role the new Secretary of Defense and the president had asked him to fill…that of the Chairman of the Joint Chiefs of Staff.

Operations around Australia and in the Coral Sea had turned out to be a victorious campaign to date, but they had also become an expensive campaign. In fact, it would prove to be the most expensive successful campaign of the war, in any theater of operation. Oh, there had been more expensive defeats that had been handed to America…like the one on March 15, 2006, that had kicked off the entire Pacific war. But this would be marked as the most expensive victory.

It was an expense that both Styles and Ryan felt personally. Terrance Thurmond had been a close friend of both men, and had been viewed as a rising star throughout the naval high command. He would be sorely missed as would his entire task force and the experienced and loyal personnel who had comprised it.

"When you add the Kitty Hawk, the British carrier and the Canadian carrier to what we have left here in the Coral Sea, we have six carriers still operational here off of Australia. Four super carriers, one large medium-sized carrier and one sea control carrier.

"As I see it, we should keep one of our super carriers, probably the Kitty Hawk, and the Canadian sea control carrier here off the invasion beachheads to support those operations," Admiral Styles said as he pointed out the area on a small map laid out on the conference table.

"Then we can put a strong taskforce of two large super carriers, let's say the Shanksville and the Reagan, here off of Brisbane to support our ground forces' movement to the north and serve as a blocking force to anything the Chinese move into the Coral Sea in the near future.

"That leaves the Bush and the British carrier, the Thatcher, which we will place off of Melbourne to support our offensive down there and also act as a blocking force to the south."

Thinking for just a moment, and then looking at the overall map, placing his right index finger first on the Alfasura Sea and then on the Solomon Islands, the Admiral then continued.

"Ben, the only problem is that I don't believe it will be enough, particularly here to the north. That force off of Brisbane needs to be significantly larger because the Chinese still have heavy forces in the area.

"We don't want to lose what we just won.

"That's why I am requesting that you talk directly to the folks in D.C. on our behalf when you get there…and I am going to presume that you will support this request, Ben, to get at least another two, if not three, carrier battle groups here to us as quickly as possible.

"I'd like to see a CVX and a Hampton Roads class minimally, with a preference for a Nimitz class to augment those two.

Ben Ryan understood where his friend Jerry Styles was coming from. They had lost six sea control carriers and two super carriers in the last three to four weeks.

The Chinese had already shown that two super carriers, like those that would be stationed off of Brisbane, could be overwhelmed with enough Killer Whales, cruise missiles and attack aircraft. And the Chinese had shown a perfect willingness to commit whatever forces were necessary to do just that.

"You and I both know that if that main Chinese attack had fallen on this task force on the morning of the 4th, instead of just on Thurmond…God rest his soul…then we could have been hurt badly.

"Thank God it didn't turn out that way.

"The planning that put Thurmond there may be second guessed in the future…but I know…all of us here know…that it probably saved most of our lives."

Still, the losses they took were horrendous losses by any measure, and they were losses that would be difficult, if not impossible, to sustain either here with existing vessels, or back home.

But the Chinese had lost even more and there was no way they could sustain the rate of attrition that was being inflicted upon them.

Admiral Ryan responded. "I've got your back, Jerry, and will support and pass on the recommendation just as you have stated it.

"But we have to find some way to slow this attrition down on our side and increase it to the Chinese and their allies."

Seeing Jerry's eyes flair at this statement, and understanding the reaction perfectly well, Ben Ryan pressed on while trying to soften what he had to say about the hard cold reality of their position.

"Look, I know we took down over twice the number of carriers and other major combatants, and that we drove these Chinese SOBs out of the area.

"But we still lost eight carriers ourselves, Jerry…and over a dozen major escort vessels. Those are losses we can't afford to sustain.

"We can't continue to trade off twenty thousand American or allied lives for forty thousand Chinese. We need those numbers to be more like no American lives for a hundred thousand Chinese...or something along those lines."

Admiral Styles understood his commander...all of them wanted to end the American attrition and force the enemy to perform all of the heavy casualty counts.

But the enemy wasn't cooperating.

"Ben, thanks for wording it that way. I know I now have the dubious distinction of having won the most costly naval victory in the history of the United States Navy. We drove off the biggest fleet we have ever encountered, and sent them packing, but we paid a horrible price to do it...we both have lost a lot of dear friends and valiant Americans.

"I guess it would be easy to let that fact ruin it all, you know? To somehow make the term *victory* turn into something hollow.

"But that would be true only if you fail to consider the alternative.

"Ben, I know you realize this, but that God-awful alternative– the one the Australians and so many others have had to experience-is something we are not going to allow to continue here in this theater...no second stage...no encore."

Admiral Styles let the silence hang in the air for a moment between them. Once again, the thought came back to him:

"Sometimes the line between victory and defeat can be hard to ascertain, particularly depending on your reference point. Sometimes the successful accomplishment of a mission can bring as much personal and individual tragedy as a bitter defeat."

To him, that thought was like the tune to an old song that you can't get out of your head. Haunting...driving him to ensure that he and all of the commanders under him kept the right perspective, the right reference, so they would always see the defeat of this abject tyranny as victory.

He continued. "You get me those extra carriers, Ben...and their escorts. And you keep working with those folks at China Lake and the other weapons labs to keep getting us the best weapons... And speaking of weapons, when are we going to have our own offensive supercavitating devices?

'We've been in this war for four full years and that's yet to be produced. I keep hearing rumors and comments...but haven't seen anything concrete yet.

"I don't mean to minimize what those folks have done, it's actually phenomenal and bordering on miraculous what they have come up with since the balloons went up and this thing got started.

"It would just be nice to throw something equally or more effective back at these Chinese bastards and their allies.

"Anyhow, you just keep getting me that equipment and the boys willing to run it and fight it...and I will make sure that the Chinese and all of their allies are pushed completely the hell out of the southwest Pacific all the way back through the China Sea to Shanghai!"

Ben looked into his subordinate's eyes...eyes that were at the same time the eyes of a long time friend and compatriot. Admiral Ryan and Jerry Styles knew that Ben was going to be in an important position to help Styles here in the Pacific...but he would also be concerned about every other theater of operation as well..

"Jerry, our own supercavitating weapons are well past the drawing board stage. I can't go into it any further at this point, but you will hear something dramatic about it in the next few months.

"... and I'll get those additional resources for you. I know that the CNO, the Secretary of Defense, and the President all have complete confidence in you...I have complete confidence in you. I know you'll use those resources to accomplish exactly what we have discussed in the manner you have explained.

"Now, I've got to be going…my aircraft is standing by and I don't want to keep the folks back in Christchurch, Pearle or D.C. waiting any longer than necessary."

Chapter 7

"The wilderness and the solitary place shall be glad, and the desert shall rejoice." - Isaiah 35:1

October 2, 2009, 19:07 Mean Time
Bridge of the USSS Gaspra
Approaching the Orbit of Mars

Commander David Lewis, the task force commander of America's first deep space task force, and also the commander of the USSS Gaspra, one of the two frigates in that task force, scanned the status displays.

Things were going according to plan. In fact, they were going extremely well. They would be approaching the halfway point to their destination the week after next, a full six days ahead of the original schedule.

Crewed by six officers and twelve senior enlisted personnel, these spacecraft exemplified the finest qualities of American ingenuity, technology, and perseverance. Each vessel carried two of the same miniature nuclear reactors like the single units that powered each of the corvettes back at Point Conception. As was the case with those vessels, the reactors were used to power the electrical, environmental, laser weaponry, research, and sensory systems carried by the frigates.

But with two reactors, the frigates carried more powerful laser weaponry, communication system, and sensory devices than their corvette cousins. They were also capable of housing more personnel and affording a much larger cargo capacity. They had been designed with just that objective in mind and that capability constituted a large part of their current mission.

The crowning jewel of the American technological breakthroughs, in addition to the SSTO nuclear pulse boosting that allowed these ships to be effective voyagers within the vast distances required for travel within the solar system, was the long-range propulsion system that they employed. That propulsion system consisted of operational solar or light sails for each vessel.

As light particles travel in space, they exert pressure along the path they are traveling. Normally, that pressure cannot be felt or even measured without very sophisticated instrumentation. But if the light source is powerful enough and the sails are adjusted appropriately, and if the surface area upon which the light pressure is being exerted is large enough and has relatively little mass...then all of that pressure cumulatively builds up to a point where it represents a significant force capable of propelling spacecraft.

The sails of the Gaspra and Ida were unbelievably large, covering many hundreds of square miles, but made of high-tech polymer material so light as to amount to the barest wisp of a presence. The sails easily folded up into a relatively small storage area mounted on the exterior of each vessel. Departing the Conception, the sails had been deployed and properly aligned to maximize the pressure from solar radiation, the lasers on the vessels had been properly calibrated with divergent optics to provide additional thrust, and the vessels began to pick up speed in a slow, constant acceleration.

Once the Gaspra and Ida had come under light sail propulsion, they had slowly and steadily increased their velocity through a constant, but slight, acceleration until they were traveling at great speed. Several months at the phenomenal velocity they attained would allow the frigates to cover the distance to their objective in the timeframe allowed for in their mission plan...a distance in excess of 187 million miles.

Without such a propulsion system, the travel time for the two frigates would be measured in years and would be dependent principally upon gravitational and orbital mechanics and the narrow windows of opportunity associated with them. Although with light sails the craft also depended upon orbital mechanics, this method of propulsion afforded the task force much more latitude and flexibility in the travel to its objective and also in contingency planning.

The Gaspra and Ida had reached optimum velocity some weeks ago, and would now maintain it until they reached a point where the frigates would unfurl and stow the forward light sails and then deploy their aft sails in a configuration such that their lasers, calibrated by their computer system to the proper focus and intensity, would be used to slowly brake them until they arrived at their objective. Once arriving at the objective area, they would use conventional retro-rockets to maneuver.

"Current velocity and status, Lieutenant?" the Commander asked the duty officer.

The young man quickly answered.

"Remaining steady at 68,405.5 knots sir. All systems are well within nominal tolerance."

Satisfied, the commander responded as he turned away, "Excellent, keep me posted on any changes or anomalies."

As he made his way towards his cabin, Commander Lewis looked at his watch and saw that it would soon be time to confer with the commander of the other vessel, the USSS Ida. As he considered the various items on the agenda for their regular evening conference, he thought about the irony, or the coincidence…though he personally doubted that it really was a coincidence at all…that had put the two of them out here on this long and critical expedition.

Commander David Lewis of the Gaspra, was the task force commander, and Commander Floyd Clark of the Ida, was the second in command. The entire affair had already been dubbed in unofficial circles as the second great Lewis and Clark expedition.

And, reflecting on the historical parallels, Lewis knew that it was just that...a great undertaking. Just as those early explorers had ventured into a vast and unyielding North American wilderness on behalf of their nation in the early 1800s, this expedition had set forth into the vast and unyielding wilderness of space.

Space was the true last frontier.

If anything, this time, over two hundred and five years later, the expedition was much more critical and urgent for the nation's survival than the first had been. For while that first expedition had contained all of the various aspects of exploration, a relatively small company, potential impact on commerce, trail-blazing and geopolitical intrigue that this expedition carried, it had not been undertaken during a bloody world war where the literal immediate survival of the nation hinged on the outcome of the expedition.

"Those men had followed a river of water...we are following a stream of light," thought the commander as he entered his small cabin and made the request through the communications duty officer to call Clark and patch the video conference through to him, here in his personal quarters.

After a few minutes, there was a soft chime and the handsome dark features of Floyd Clark, a longtime friend and associate of David Lewis, appeared on the screen.

"Hey, David. You're a couple of minutes early. Something come up?"

Lewis looked at his friend and thought of the two long and intense years they and their crews had spent training for this mission. Astronauts, Naval Officers, and close friends, they both knew how much was riding on what they were doing out here passing the orbit of Mars, further than any human had ever ventured into space before.

Though their non-military protocol and bearing in the evening review meetings might suggest otherwise, David knew that they were both tightly focused on the importance and success of their mission…and they both knew, along with all of the crew…that above all else the mission was military in nature.

"Nope, F.L., nothing out of the ordinary. Just thought I would get into the meeting and review the parameters and catch up on what has happened on the Ida today.

"Right now all of our systems here on the Gaspra are nominal; and it looks like we are still a good six days ahead of schedule. That additional solar activity we were briefed on is really paying off.

"As you know, earlier in the day we experienced some fluctuations in particle diffusion on the sail and had to request the system to perform a normal recalibration on one of our lasers.

"That turned out fine and took only a few moments and, as I said, everything is nominal now.

"Outside of that, anything out of the ordinary with you?"

Floyd Langley Clark, known to his friends as F.L., respected and trusted his commanding officer, David Lewis. He knew that the former President, President Weisskopf, the Chairman of the Joint Chiefs, and the Chief of Naval Operations had all been involved directly with the final decision on the command of this task force. As far as he was concerned they had chosen wisely. Over the last two years Floyd had seen for himself the quick wit, the analytical prowess and the unbelievable astute strategic and tactical mind that David Lewis exhibited in action, and he was proud to be serving under him.

"We did have a scrubber act up earlier in the day, but specialist Powers was able to repair it without having to use any of our extra units.

"Outside of that, and our matching your momentary velocity fluctuation as you recalibrated the one laser, everything has been by the books.

"Pretty standard I would say…in fact too standard. Maybe it's time we have another drill."

Commander Lewis smiled broadly at this and Clark knew that the two of them were thinking on the same wave length.

"Exactly what I was thinking, commander.

"Let's say tomorrow morning at oh-two-thirty-five. What shall it be? Fire, enemy action, collision avoidance, major system failure...I'll let you make the call."

This was one of the things Clark liked most about Lewis. He knew how to foster his command and, whenever possible, let them take an idea and make the most of it...and thereby learn the most from it.

"How about a problem that involves a combination of critical issues?"

"What do you think of a system failure coupled with collision avoidance...maybe the need to avoid a small meteorite or debris field in the midst of a couple of laser propulsion failures.

"We could have the Gaspra discover the debris in our path and then, in the middle of the avoidance maneuver, have the Ida suffer the failure while you have to maintain formation and still clear the debris."

Lewis felt good about the plan Clark was proposing. He knew very well that the crew needed to be kept at the top of their game, not only to prepare for the potential reality of such experiences here in space, where there was no one but themselves to look to for assistance, but also for the time when they arrived back in Earth orbit.

He was certain when that time came and they were back in orbit ready to exercise the final portions of their mission, that both vessels would be tested to the max in combat. Commander Lewis knew that both crews had to be honed to a fine edge to prepare for that eventuality.

"I like it, Floyd. I like it a lot.

"Let's get it programmed.

"You and your XO handle the system failure and I'll get Roger to work with me on simulating the debris field.

"We'll make it an unannounced exercise.

"Let's get back together at 2200 hours, all four of us, and see where we're at."

October 20, 2009, 23:25 local time
Muri clan enclave
Gregory Range, South of Cape York Peninsula
Queensland, Australia

The last few years had been the most momentous, the most dangerous and the most event-ridden of any of the clan's collective memory. That memory, passed from father to son, from mother to daughter and from dreamer to dreamer, stretched back to the great *Jukurrpa*, or creation, when the ancestral spirits had arisen from beneath the earth and had given form to the earth, to the mountains, the valleys, the plains, the lakes, the streams and the very stones.

The Europeans had come in the late 1700s and had slowly, but unrelentingly, pushed the original inhabitants of the land aside. Such had been the policy until, beginning in the 1960s, the hearts of the Australian people, as they called themselves, had softened and the same rights and privileges accorded the newcomers in their government and society began to be extended to the original inhabitants, the aborigine peoples.

But the two century takeover, and then reconciliation, by the Europeans paled in comparison to what the Asians had done in the last two to three years.

The new Chinese and Indian inhabitants, like their armies that had swept all before them, had no tolerance of, compassion for, or mercy on anyone other than themselves. They had come with a great vision of filling the land with their own kind, at the expense of all others, European, aborigine, Islander, or any other.

And that is exactly what they had implemented.

It was a simple but ruthless plan: either the former inhabitants served them, or they perished.

The Caucasian and well-to-do Islander Australians were at least given the opportunity to serve the newcomers and have some measure of life and livelihood. The aborigines, from the Muris here in what used to be called northern Queensland, to the Kooni in South Wales, the Nungah, Warlpiri and others, were hardly even regarded as human by the invaders.

Like most of the others, the Muri had chosen to flee to the mountains and the wilderness areas. A few had tried, along with other Australian citizens, to resist.

That resistance continued in many areas of the island continent and invariably led to harsh retribution by CAS military units and citizens alike…many times taking out their vengeance on innocent and unsuspecting aborigine communities that had tried to do nothing more than move out of the way.

Nabalco was a recognized leader in the entire Muri clan. Traditionally the aborigine people did not have a fixed social or religious culture. They had banded together as necessary, with the central societal structure being the family. Elder members of the various families were accorded more respect and deference and usually carried more weight in decision-making. Most groups would generally come to some conclusion based on what the majority of the older individuals had to say.

They were all influenced by dreamers, who were believed to have special access to their ancestors and whose dreams carried significant weight, although there were not official social leadership positions, nor a religion, in the strict definition of those terms. This was simply the traditional lifestyle of the earlier hunter-gatherer aborigine culture.

But the two hundred years of European culture that dominated Australia had changed that somewhat.

Now the clans had those who represented their interests, even though great effort had been taken by the Australian government to integrate the aborigine peoples into society as full citizens. There were still legal and homeland issues that had to be resolved and many aborigines desired to live together–some even practiced the old ways in the more remote regions of the continent.

In seeking those to represent them, the clans had turned most often to educated and loyal people of their own. Nabalco was not only an adult of great stature and bearing, one who had fathered and raised five children with his wife, Ulura…he was also educated in the best Australian schools, having graduated in engineering at Brisbane, and having done his masters work in legal affairs.

Despite his impressive education, he had never forgotten his people or the old ways…and he had passed them on to his children. All of them spoke fluently the dialect of Pama-nyungan that was peculiar to the Muri people.

For this reason most of the Muri people trusted Nabalco. They had done so before the great conflagration and onslaught of the Asians…and they trusted him now.

He had led them to this remote area of the Gregory Mountains and they had established themselves, several hundred of them with their families and a few refugees, living the old life and avoiding the new enemy. Nabalco had used the common knowledge of many and had taught the rest, so that they gave off very little heat or other infrared signature of their existence.

When scouts observed Asian military or civilian activity anywhere close to them, the people simply vanished, taking preselected routes to the north into several separate safe locations deeper into the Cape York Peninsula.

The clan found itself in just such a situation this evening. Nabalco was preparing everyone to leave and make their way to the places of safety that they had used several times.

"The Chinese and Indians are much more active along the major Charter Tower-Cloncurry road, and even the minor wilderness tracks of late.

"You don't have to travel but a few miles to the south to hear their motors and see their aircraft. Military traveling to the east, civilian traffic to the west.

"We've all heard the rumors and seen the couriers and scouts that have passed through. We've put up several of our Kuni and Nungah brothers who were spreading the word. The Amis have landed and taken Sydney, and then moved up to Brisbane and down to Melbourne. They now control almost all of Victoria and New South Wales, and they are pushing the Chinese, Indians and Indonesians into Queensland.

"There's a strong rumor that they have made an amphibious and airborne landing in strength near Rockhampton and are now pushing into the Great Artesian towards Emerald. A large number of U.S. Marines and returning Australian forces are supposedly in this group, and the Asians are fighting them fiercely.

"All of that bears on the decision we have to make this evening.

"Chinese and Indian activity in our own area is at the highest levels since the takeover.

"All of you know this.

"I have seen it, my brothers and sisters. It is only a matter of time before our large clan here is discovered and treated very badly. I believe we must all move to the places of safety that we have used in the past...and that we should stay there until the conflict resolves itself one way or another, communicating regularly with runners and the few radios that we have.

"It will mean we are much smaller in numbers and more vulnerable individually...both to the elements of our mother earth and to the enemy, should they discover us.

"But I believe it is unlikely that they will discover us, because the Cape is an area off their beaten path and one they have shown no interest in colonizing to this point. As they defend what they have already taken, it is not likely that they will infiltrate the more remote areas unless they are forced to run there as a result of defeat.

"If that happens, then they are likely to be small in number and unprepared and that is when they will find us waiting for them.

"These are my own thoughts and feelings. I know Ulura and my sons agree with me, but it is now left open for discussion and a decision of the entire clan.

The discussion continued long into the night, into the early morning hours. Many respected men and women spoke. All of them wanted to avoid direct confrontation with any military force, either from the recognized enemy of the CAS, or from the more friendly allied nations. They had seen too often the result of brushing up against military forces conducting combat operations.

Many of the family leaders were reluctant to separate into smaller groups, and wanted to have the entire group only split up to travel to a new more remote location where they could all again assemble. They felt more secure with their numbers, particularly given the sixty to seventy refugees, most if them white Australian citizens, who were just now getting acclimated to living in the wilderness. They feared having to live in smaller, more austere groups while supporting those refugees, particularly given the more dangerous circumstances they now faced, it having been over eight months since the last time they had briefly had to retreat to their enclaves.

Rightfully, it was pointed out to these individuals that there were no areas that had been scouted on the Cape to this point that were large enough to support them all as a single group. They were also reminded by others that the refugees had even been less capable eight months ago, and yet they had all survived.

To challenge all of this speculation, one of the older and very much respected Muri woman rose in the circle to speak. "But, my brothers and sisters, there were also fewer refugees when we made that move eight months ago. Many of the newer refugees are wholly unprepared for the more difficult living that a small camp will impose upon them.

"And besides, the circumstances were much different.

"Eight months ago we left because the Asians were widening the major highway to the south, and because of the increased activity associated with their construction. We knew that change would be of short duration.

"This time we have no idea what the duration will be–and it is likely that the fighting will spread to this region. Any group too close to that fighting, or caught up in it, is unlikely to be able to support itself or avoid being overwhelmed.

"I believe we must find a larger place, much further north on the Cape and all go there."

The very first hint of lightening lit up the sky when Nabalco prepared to stand and address what had just been said. As he did so, his wife of thirty years gently put her hand on his knee and put just enough pressure there to let him know that he should remain seated.

Thus it was Ulura who stood up to address what the older Muri woman had said.

"Noongi, there would be much wisdom in what you have proposed if we had the time to carry it out…if we had the time to send scouts to find this new place that you speak of, and *then* had the time to devise travel routes to it so that we could all safely come there without notice.

"But there is no longer the time for all of that. We do not know the place and we do not know the route to take to get there.

"We would have to travel in much larger groups which would attract the attention of our enemies and the devices they carry on their airplanes.

"No, I believe we must do as Nabalco has indicated. Let us split up, as we have done before, into our twenty different small groups and make our way to the places we already know are there. Traveling there using the well-planned and well-concealed routes we have already determined.

"If there is any concern for extra refugees, then I say we here in Nabalco's group will take those you are concerned about with our group, in addition to the ones we already have.

"But now it is time to decide. We must rest during the coming day and then be gone with the next night."

When Ulura set down, for several minutes there was a reflective quiet in the assembled group of families…and then, one by one, the various heads of the family groups made it known what they would do.

Fourteen groups would do as Nabalco indicated and make their way to their individual areas of safety. Six groups, over 120 individuals, would travel together to the south and search for a larger place that could accommodate them all.

Several of the less capable or disabled refugees were passed from that larger group to several of the smaller ones. Nabalco's group received four of these refugees in addition to the three they already had taken in. They took them in gladly and prepared them to support themselves, meeting afterwards to arrange the assignments necessary to see them all through to their place of refuge.

The journey would not be easy. Three of the refugees were young children without parents. Two had been adopted by one family and the third, one of the new ones, would now be adopted by another. Another of the new refugees was from the Brisbane area, and had been afflicted with some form of a mental condition that rendered him as senseless as a young child…having lost some of the most basic adult interaction skills. He was also physically disabled and could do little more than hobble slowly, using a cane to support himself.

Nabalco was worried about that one…he would be a severe strain on the group and its ability to reach each evening's travel goal while moving to the new location.

The other two new refugees were both very soft and well-to-do women, who were extremely unacquainted with wilderness living. They seemed willing enough, but both Ulura and Nabalco knew that the rigors of the upcoming trip and then the condition of their remote camp would try these women's good intentions to the breaking point.

It was definitely not a good time to be learning how to *camp*.

By seven o'clock that morning, all the decisions had been made and each group made its way to their various concealed sleeping huts to sleep through the day. They would all be leaving an hour after sundown to make their way to the north.

Most of them slept fitfully. Numerous times planes could be heard in the distance to the south, some prop-driven making their way to the west, but as the day went on, more and more of them were military jet aircraft flying in formation to the east–Chinese and Indian aircraft of all types.

…and while he slept, Nabalco the dreamer, saw in his dreams a foreboding storm wave breaking over the land…over this very spot…devouring and destroying all in its path as it traveled slowly from southeast to northwest.

November 12, 2009, 11:38 local time
Incirlik Air Force Base
Near Adana, Turkey

1st Sergeant Dave Johnson and Security Force Superintendent (SFS) Nick Jackson, of the 159th Security Forces Squadron of the Louisiana Air National Guard, both waited impatiently, along with their commanding officer, Colonel Lee Bowman, for the upcoming meeting. All three of them had arrived here at the new operations center just moments ago in an up-armored M998 HMMV escorted by two of the new M1117A Armored Security Vehicles (ASV), which had been designated ASV+ to distinguish them from the earlier ASV models.

Watching now as the M117As and the M998 took up their positions in a mutually defensive, blocking formation on the new tarmac, the 1st Sergeant couldn't help but think to himself, "The ASV+ sure is a great upgrade to the original M1117. Putting a larger turret on them so they could hold that 25mm chain gun, *and* a TOW missile launcher in addition to the M2 50 and the M19 grenade launcher has really added the kind of firepower we need to cover all of our ground defense bases.

"It's good seeing them there…just makes a guy feel…well, just more secure. Now, if we could just get that AAW variant.

Turning to Nick Jackson, and knowing that Colonel Bowman was hearing every word of what he was saying, the 1st Sergeant commented out loud, "Chief, when are we going to get the air-defense variety of the M1117As we've been promised? It sure would be nice to have a couple of them hanging out here with us as well, don't you think?"

Before the chief could respond, Colonel Bowman, taking the hint, responded for him.

"Chief, explain to the 1st-shirt here that we're being adequately watched over. We have four Navy Hornets above us, four

Patriot batteries up and functioning, and four HUMRAAMs all making sure the boogey man stays away."

Then, turning to the 1st Sergeant and speaking directly to him while continuing to address the Chief…and with a twinkle in his eye, Bowman continued, "But let him know, Chief Jackson, that the air defense M1117s are being unloaded in Adana tomorrow and we'll have them here on the base by the end of the week."

As he finished, the Colonel winked, and then strolled over to the group of individuals where the colonels who commanded the Rangers and the Turkish forces stood.

Chief Jackson wasn't long in responding for himself as the Colonel walked away.

"Well, Dave, you heard the man…sounds like we're in good shape, and those units will be here before you know it."

Johnson was glad to hear it…and appreciated the manner in which the Colonel and his Chief had delivered the message. All of them, Johnson, Jackson and Bowman, along with almost their entire squadron, had trained together as a National Guard unit and had known each other for many years. Their last duty assignment had been in Cuba where the 159th had set up security arrangements at one of the large Cuban air bases right after it had been taken in the fighting.

Nevertheless, with their sterling combat record and with the current offensive in the Mid East, the 159th had been pulled out of Cuba so other, less experienced squadrons could use the now more peaceful assignment in Cuba as a place to learn…while the 159th was assigned to the task force with the critical combat mission of invading the underbelly of Turkey and taking and holding the Incirlik Air Base.

Now they had been on the ground here in Turkey for less than a week, firming up the security situation around the newly reconquered base as the front lines pushed deeper to the north and east into Turkey. All three men were anxious to conduct this meeting and get some very useful pointers from the special guest who was about to pay them a visit.

As they waited, Johnson believed the current security situation at Incirlik was well under control, but he would never underestimate the enemy, or allow his people to overplay their own hand. They still had a regiment of U.S. Army Rangers and an entire battalion of Turkish forces augmenting the perimeter security at the base, guarding against a possible GIR breakthrough should the enemy counterattack and break through allied front lines that were now over fifty miles to the north and to the east. Such a counterattack was still a definite possibility, and allied forces at Incirlik and Adana had to continue to guard against that possibility.

As its first order of business, the 159th Security Forces Squadron had been assigned to handle all of the inner ring security at Incirlik. And that was what these three men were focused upon. Ultimately they would be responsible for the security of the entire base, once the overall tactical situation calmed down further and allowed their forces to accomplish that mission by themselves.

For the time being, they were still experiencing enough GIR air attacks and persistent small arms attacks from groups of GIR soldiers and local Islamic partisans to warrant the additional allied forces. Those GIR ground forces had either gone to ground or been bypassed in the general allied offensive that had landed near Adana and then captured Incirlik three weeks ago. With time, those enemy attacks were decreasing in both number and intensity as the enemy groups were identified, prosecuted and either captured or destroyed.

The base itself, and its rapidly ongoing repair, was serving as a model of Joint Operations effectiveness in the ongoing allied operation. Marine and Air Force engineers, and civil contractors were getting the runways, hangars and control facilities rapidly into working order. The Navy was bringing in more than sufficient fuel and other supplies by ship and was providing air defense over the base from both TBM Aegis ships and carrier aircraft until air operations were possible from the base itself. American, British and other allied intelligence operations were providing a very clear picture of the current overall tactical and strategic picture. And, as he had already covered in his mind, Johnson knew that Army and his own Air Force security personnel, augmented by returning Turkish forces, had local security concerns well in hand.

But, despite their confidence in the current intelligence and security situation, there was nothing like firsthand experience to augment their perceptions and preparedness. The man they were about to meet represented the epitome of firsthand experience for this entire area over the last few years, not only for Incirlik, but all the way across Turkey and up into Armenia and Georgia, when dealing with GIR military forces. He had been doing so, with the barest minimum of resources for almost four years, behind enemy lines.

Amongst American security forces, particularly U.S. Air Force security squadrons, the name of Captain Luke Hanson was something of a legend in this conflict. And David Johnson, Nick Jackson and their commanding officer, Colonel Lee Bowman, all would be meeting that legend today.

In fact, that meeting would occur in just a few moments as all three men saw that the Black Hawk helicopter carrying Hanson was just landing about a hundred yards away at that very moment.

November 12, 2009, 11:41 local time
Incirlik Air Force Base
Near Adana, Turkey

Luke Hanson soaked up the memories as the helicopter flared to a gently descending hover before touching down, allowing him to exit the aircraft with the intelligence and security personnel who had escorted him here.

It was hard to believe he was back at Incirlik, standing on this ground where so many of his friends had been wounded or died, and where he and a few others had narrowly escaped alive in January of 2006…almost four years earlier.

So much had happened in the intervening years as he fought the GIR behind enemy lines. All of those guerilla and partisan experiences had finally culminated almost a year ago with the successful covert operation directed at GIR General Talabari in Tbilisi, Georgia, in November of 2008, when the U.S. CIA operative, Riley Adams, had successfully eliminated the famous GIR general.

That success had been followed by the amazing allied victories later that fall in Alaska, Israel and near Moscow, and then the great breakthrough in Syria into Saudi Arabia and the former Iraq late this summer. Those later breakthroughs had eased pressure on his own partisan forces in Georgia as the enemy armies in those areas, seeing that they were about to be cut off entirely on the Turkish peninsula, streamed to the east to try to thwart the allied advances.

The vast reduction in GRI forces in his area had allowed Hanson to successfully carry out the mission he had been given last month and to make his way south, to meet up with the American, British and Turkish at the beachhead here. That meeting was occurring today, here near Adana, where the allies, using American C-90A transports, huge SSTN amphibious assault submarines, a massive allied naval task force and a plentiful supply of Hail Storm missiles had forced their way ashore. The U.S. and its allies were now pouring more and more men and materiel into a massive pincer on the GIR forces, which were trying to defend their holdings in Turkey and keep American forces out of central Iran.

Reflecting on all that he had experienced in the fighting of the past years leading to this moment, those few months as the calendar turned from 2005 to 2006, were indelibly etched in his memory. Those weeks saw him transform from a regular army officer into a guerilla fighter who built a force of partisans to combat the conquering GIR forces in this part of the world.

Nor had he forgotten his home back in Nebraska, and now, at long last, he was going to be returning there.

But he had one last assignment to fulfill before doing so, and he was looking forward to it. He was here to brief the new security forces on the defense of his old base here at Incirlik, helping them understand how the GIR had been able to defeat the base in early 2006, and then over-run it with their massive forces.

And from that understanding he was hoping to convey to them how they could prevent it from happening in the future.

Approaching the group, he saw a full-bird U.S Air Force Colonel, flanked by a U.S. Army Ranger Colonel and a Turkish Colonel, step forward. The Air Force Colonel addressed him as they warmly shook hands.

"Captain Hanson, I'm Colonel Lee Bowman, commanding the 159th Security Forces Squadron.

"Let me be the first to welcome you back here to Incirlik Air Force Base. You've been away far too long."

After shaking hands, the Colonel made all of the other introductions to the other two Colonels, to SFS Jackson, and to 1st Sergeant David Johnson. Then, just before moving indoors, he halted the entire group and made another announcement.

"Before we proceed with the briefing, Captain, let me just add this so that everyone can be sure to keep their schedules straight.

"You are going to be involved in a special awards ceremony here at the base tomorrow afternoon, before your departure, which will be repeated in Washington, D.C., when you return stateside.

"That ceremony will include the presentation to you of a Silver Star, and an advancement in rank.

"So let me be the first to personally congratulate you, Lieutenant Colonel Hanson. Well done!"

Luke Hanson really didn't know what to say as all of those present shook his hand again and slapped him on the back, wishing him the best. All of this was news to him and came as quite a shock.

Looking around, he caught site of the ASV+ vehicles, standing vigil over their gathering, and he had to stare at them.

"Colonel," he said, as everyone turned their gaze towards the M1117As where Lieutenant Colonel Hanson was looking.

"If I may?"

Colonel Bowman understood very well why Hanson was captivated with the new Armored Security Vehicles. They represented a firepower capability that was a far cry from the capabilities of the V-150 security vehicles that would have been in place here at Incirlik when the base had been overrun and upon which Hanson and his own forces would have had to depend.

"1st-shirt, why don't you accompany the Lieutenant Colonel and explain to him all of the finer points of the ASV+?"

David Johnson gladly complied. "My pleasure, sir."

As the two of them walked over to the nearest vehicle, Johnson found that, for the moment, there was very little to say. The mood just wasn't right for discussion or explanation at this point. Hanson could very well see for himself the strength of this vehicle. As they got close, the vehicle commander climbed out and greeted them both with a friendly smile and a warm handshake.

When Hanson reached the vehicle, he climbed up onto its large front tire and then onto its armored side and stood up on the deck surrounding the turret. He leaned over and thoughtfully, reflectively touched the 25mm gun barrel and put his other hand up on the TOW missile launcher while observing the .50 caliber machine gun and 40mm grenade launcher barrels that also protruded from the turret.

Standing up to his full height again, Hanson slowly turned around and surveyed the view from where he stood.

The 1st Sergeant could see the faraway look in his eyes, and knew that Lee Hanson was recalling the fight that had taken place near here when he had been in charge of the security at Incirlik and had faced overwhelming odds.

"It's a fine piece of equipment, Colonel. I'm sure you guys would have made the most of them in that fight back in 2006."

Hanson was brought back to the present by the 1st Sergeant's comments. Looking down, he smiled as he imagined what he could have done with three or four of these babies.

"1st Sergeant…you are right. It is a fine piece of equipment, and we most assuredly would have made the best of them. They would not have turned the tide in that battle…there were far too many GIR tanks and aircraft for that.

"But we surely would have sold this base at a much stiffer price, and perhaps a few more of us would have made it out. I just hope we've learned in the intervening years to never underestimate the capabilities of our enemies."

And for that, the 1st Sergeant had a most definitive answer.

As Hanson climbed down off the vehicle and they began walking back to the operations building to start the briefing, 1st Sergeant David Johnson put his arm on Hanson's shoulder and replied, "Lieutenant Colonel Hanson, we *have* learned that lesson, over and over and over again over the last four years.

"…and I believe you are going to be very pleasantly surprised and satisfied at just how well we have learned it."

November 21, 2009, 17:16 local time
Anadyr Mountain Range
North of the Kamchatka Peninsula

Sergeant Alan Campbell took stock of his current situation and position. He and his lead platoon were perched at an altitude of over 6,000 feet on a divide that looked down a barren slope into the next drainage. It was snowing and visibility was poor.

Progress had been slow and costly. The Chinese were not about to relinquish any of their positions without a heavy fight, though they were surrounded and cut off. In the three months since Alan had landed further south on the Kamchatka Peninsula and started north, they had been toiling against the elements and fighting the Chinese hard for every inch of ground, facing increasingly cold and blustery weather, facing mass attacks and charges by the Chinese.

But they had made progress, and in all areas.

American forces had pushed up from Magadan despite the massive Chinese air and sea effort to close that logistics point and cut it off. Some of the fiercest prolonged fighting of the war, on the sea, on the ground and in the air had occurred there…and it was still going on. Despite that prolonged Chinese effort, the allied 12th Army that had been assembled in Magadan and had been sent north and east toward the Bering Strait, was now less that eighty miles to Alan's south and west.

The force of which Alan was a part, which had landed on the north central Kamchatka Peninsula and moved north, had gained the high ground in the Anadyr Mountains and pushed the Chinese who were trying to retreat down the Kamchatka, back over those mountains here. Other Chinese forces clung feverishly to the most direct route through those mountains, the superhighway and rail line they had built to make their invasion of Alaska possible…but the joint allied command had circumvented that roadway and had marched overland through the steep mountains to penetrate the range here, where Alan was now positioned.

From this position, they would be able to encircle the Chinese who were defending the roadway and not only pincer them…but also push on towards the major forces that had been trapped by the American crossing of the Bering Strait.

In that area too, the allies had made progress, albeit against more begrudging and fierce opposition by the Chinese. The crossing had been extremely costly, as the Chinese knew it was coming and were prepared for it. But it had been made, and the Chinese had been driven completely out of North America, with the final Chinese organized forces surrendering north of Nome on October 27th, a day that would be long remembered and celebrated in American history.

"We sure celebrated the news of it here," thought Alan as he spotted through his infrared scope. "And we weren't even involved in the action.

"I bet just about every American celebrated that date when they heard of it. I'd love to know how Leon celebrated it over in the land down under."

Thinking of the land down under made Alan wish he were there with his brother…it had to be something approaching warm down there as opposed to this ice cold…and it wasn't even officially winter yet!

Just then Alan spotted movement, a good nine hundred or more yards out, down the slope, moving in his direction.

He checked his scope and made sure it was properly calibrated.

There! One, two, three…many figures now coming out of the fog and clouds that hung close to the mountains here.

"Heads up, men…we've got company coming up the slope," Alan informed his squad, causing them all to sit up and take more careful note from their firing positions.

"Keep your heads down and prepare your positions!"

Alan knew that the rest of the platoon was positioned just below him and he was ready to send a runner over to the LT to apprise him of the situation. The rest of the company was headed this way and if a fight was going to be made, Alan was grateful that he held the high ground.

Just as he thought about dispatching the runner, he noticed the leading figure in the approaching group of soldiers stop–over eight hundred yards out–and aim some sort of scoped device up towards the ridge line where Alan and his men were positioned.

"Get ready, men…prepare to fire…

"No!…hold that…do not fire…hold your fire!"

Alan had seen the flash of light from the device the leading soldier held and he recognized it as the identification sign they were supposed to flash to friendly forces.

"Corporal Lindsey, get over to the LT right now and let him know that it looks like we have some friendly forces headed up out of the next drainage…make sure he understands that. They are to our forward and moving this way and they have flashed a proper ID code.

"Ask him for instructions."

Alan was not taking any chances. He flashed the recognition signal back down the slope, and then yelled for the approaching soldiers to hold their position until he got some type of indication what to do.

The soldiers below him did as he said and a tense wait ensued.

The lieutenant contacted his captain who passed the word back to make contact by sending a few men forward, making sure they were covered.

The lieutenant brought the entire platoon up to the ridge and set up effective covering fire positions, with good overlapping fields of fire. Only then did he send Alan and two privates down to make contact with the advancing group.

As Alan got closer, he hoped that these people really were friendly forces. Hidden by a depression in the slope, and by the clouds, he now noticed as he approached within one hundred yards of the men how many of them there were. Stretching around the corner of the hill and then all the way down into the valley below was a line of several hundred soldiers.

As he got closer, a Captain came forward past his point men, smiling, and reached out to shake his hand, while an individual several soldiers back took a picture.

"Sergeant, I'm Captain Beasley of the Alaska Army National Guard.

"Which way to China?"

Alan Campbell's face broke into a wide grin at the question as he clasped the Captain's hand and shook it vigorously…ending in a warm embrace and a slap on the back as the camera clicked the picture. That picture of American forces linking up in the Anadyr Mountains to the west of the Bering Strait would become as famous as the picture of the American and Russian soldiers shaking hands as they met in Germany in World War II.

For Alan and all of the other Americans, it meant the beginning of the end of their successful campaign in the cold eastern reaches of the Asian continent…something they all looked forward to with anticipation. It would be an end that would spell the ultimate and complete encirclement of almost three million remaining Chinese soldiers in this theater of operations.

Many of the Chinese would fight to the end, and the final surrender would not occur until their numbers had been vastly reduced by Hail Storm missiles, American infantry and armor attacks, and by the elements. That surrender would occur near their last holdout, along the highway they had built to funnel their armies toward Alaska the prior year. It would occur once the sub-zero winter conditions near the Arctic Circle, coupled with the continuing, relentless American attacks and the Chinese lack of fuel and supplies would dictate the absolute futility of their position and the necessity of their unconditional surrender.

December 4, 2009, 21:05 local time
Near the Little Zab River
North of Kirkuk in the former Iraq

General Abduhl Selim had gotten the great Imam to approve all of his plans. He was a little surprised by the approval…but was glad that the Imam was giving him full military leeway in this area that used to be a part of central and northern Iraq.

He had called for the abandonment of Baghdad because it was indefensible against the Americans and their allies. His large forces could hold onto the terrain around Kirkuk and in the mountains to the north, south and east of it…or so he believed.

Ever since his own grand and successful counterattack against the Americans in Syria, his reputation and the esteem and trust that the soldiers held for him had continued to grow. Ultimately that counterattack had failed, but not because of the young general. No, it had failed because older, less capable generals had not held the flanks as they should have.

His southern flank had failed and then folded, and it had taken all of his skill and intuition as a soldier and a leader to achieve a strong fighting withdrawal. But he had accomplished the dignified retreat and saved most of his command after having inflicted severe punishment on the Americans and their Israeli allies.

"I could feel a breakthrough in my grasp," the young general reflected.

"Another thirty kilometers and we would have been on the Golan Heights with all of Israel at our feet."

But it had not turned out that way, and for whatever reason Allah had willed it otherwise.

Since that time they had been forced into one fighting withdrawal after another all across Syria and into Iran. At least in his sectors they had been fighting withdrawals. In other areas further to the south, the withdrawal had turned into a rout…and then a major allied breakthrough as the Americans and the Israelis broke across the former Saudi Arabia and into what had been southern Iraq, threatening and then entering the southwest corner of what had been called Iran before the great Hasan Sayeed had united them all into the Greater Islamic Republic.

There the eastward advance of the enemy had been halted as fierce, fanatical fighting broke out, where the Americans and Israelis were attacked by the GIR military, the militias and the local population. Reports indicated that the carnage was horrendous, but the advance eastward into the GIR had been halted and the enemy had turned north.

That northward turn is what had ultimately concerned Abduhl.

He was covering central and northern areas of the former Iraq, stretching up into Turkey where an avenue had to be kept open for the GIR armies there in Turkey and northward through Armenia and Georgia into the southern parts of the Russian confederation to return and consolidate their defenses here and further east in the mountains.

But it had not worked out that way either.

The Americans and returning Turkish soldiers had landed with amazing swiftness in southern Turkey, bypassing many of Abduhl's defenses along the Syrian-Iraqi border and surprising the GIR commanders in Turkey. It was Abduhl's first experience with the new American T-90 transport and SSTN submarine technology, and it was something he would not forget or fail to factor in to future contingencies. But now those American forces had pushed deep into Turkey and were cutting off many of the returning GIR forces and threatening the western elements of his own.

Abduhl knew he was being forced to withdraw his forces and whatever GIR forces had been able to escape out of Turkey.

"Either we withdraw them, or face having our own positions undermined just like those fools in Turkey," he thought as he continued to analyze the situation.

And having his own carefully positioned forces become undermined was not something the young general was going to allow to happen. That is why he had asked for and received permission from the Imam to evacuate Baghdad and pull back into the mountains into a more defensible position.

Sayeed had carefully considered Selim's plans, made a number of comments that were very relevant to the current tactical situation in his area, and then approved his plans. In so doing, he had given Selim further assurance.

"Hold out there along the borders, in the mountains around Lake Azerbaijan.

"Stop the Americans and their allies there, and I will raise an army of God to come to your assistance and once more drive them back."

Abduhl Selim believed that the Imam, Hasan Sayeed could do just that. Particularly after hearing how the people had fought alongside the Army to halt the incursion near Ahvas. If the Mahdi had the time, he could bring to bear millions of faithful committed to Allah and to Jihad and drive the infidels back out of their lands.

…and perhaps he could do a similar deed here in the mountains…perhaps he could mobilize the people to work with his forces here…to help thwart the Americans and their allies…to fool them into spending their precious Hail Storm missiles.

"Ahkim, contact the divisional commanders.

"I either want them here by 2300 hours, or I want them conferenced in. No excuses. Let them know that it is according to my express orders.

"We have much to discuss."

December 9, 2009, 23:42 local time
Indian Embassy
Krasnoyarsk, Siberia

Ambassador Buhpendra Gavanker locked his desk drawer, turned off and secured his computer, and prepared to go home after another long day conducting the diplomatic duties of his office as the Ambassador of India to Siberia. It had been a long, sixteen-hour day, just like most of his days dealing with the many diplomatic, economic and military issues that were constantly arising.

Sometimes he knew that his wife and children wondered why he had moved them up here to Siberia to be near him when he rarely saw them more than a couple of hours most days. But just having them here, being able to look into the kids' rooms before he went to sleep himself, being able to lay next to his wife…all of that made the pressures and stress bearable…much more so than having them thousands of miles away.

It had taken him a good nine months to call for his family's relocation to Krasnoyarsk, the new capital of Siberia. By that time the fighting had moved much further off to the west, across the Urals, as the Russians continued to fight to preserve Siberia. It was a fight that was ultimately carried into the heart of Russia itself, and right to the gates of Moscow.

By that time, Buhpendra had considered the areas all around the capital safe. During that period he had also felt that it was surely only a matter of time before the western nations conceded and a diplomatic solution to the world war could be achieved because, at the time, the CAS and their allies, the GIR, were victorious on all fronts.

But much had transpired since that time, in the twenty months since he had been appointed to this role on the eve of Siberian independence, and since he had brought his family here nine months later…over a year ago.

"Siberia itself has changed," he thought as he walked out of his office and past the guard station. "The politicians here are just like everywhere else…perhaps they have learned too well. It wasn't six months before they started trading land and resources for recognition and treaties…and personal favors."

To begin with, Siberia had officially stretched from the Ob and Irtysh rivers in the west, to the Pacific Ocean. From the Arctic Ocean in the north, to the border of China and Mongolia in the south. A massive land area, numbering almost forty million inhabitants and a wealth in natural resources that had barely been tapped, despite the several years of the Siberian Economic Development Treaty that had preceded Siberian independence.

Under that treaty, enacted in 2005 between the Russian Federation, the People's Republic of China, and India, Siberia had been opened up to economic resource exploration and development by the vast numbers of workers that India and China could mobilize, as Russia benefited from the hard currency those nations could then pay for the resources they discovered and developed.

The pact had held during the outbreak of hostilities between America and the GIR, and then as the entire CAS, including India, had entered the fight against the United States. Russia played both ends against the middle, stayed out of the fight and prospered immensely.

For two and a half years.

Then Siberia had declared its independence and was immediately recognized by China and India. Russia, seeing how they had been used and taken advantage of, had immediately declared war and joined the fight on the side of the western Allies, on the side of the United States.

But Russia, like America and all of the others arrayed against China, India and the GIR, had continued to be pushed back. Right out of Asia, right out of the western Pacific Ocean, right out of the Middle East, and right out of all of Australia.

It was during this time that Siberia had begun to be partitioned. First, all of the far eastern provinces and areas, from the Lena River system, across the Cherskiy Mountains to the Bering Strait had been sold to China. In return, the Chinese had paid over one hundred billion yuan in hard currency and agreed to provide for the perpetual defense of Siberia.

Within three months of the great *Siberian Purchase* as the Chinese were calling it, a buffer zone was created by mutual agreement that extended from the Ob and Irtysh rivers to the Yenisey River. This region was to remain an official part of Siberia, but was to be autonomous and administered jointly by India and China in two distinct "regions."

What this meant was that many hundreds of thousands of Indian and Chinese immigrants were moved into their respective regions. Ultimately, millions would be moved in and when those populations reached the appropriate percentages, it was clear that the autonomous regions would "vote" to become a part of their mother nations.

Over the ensuing months it became clear what these two actions represented, beyond the obvious fact of adding territory to the nations of China and India. As CAS and GIR armies poured across Europe right to the gates of Moscow and crossed the Bering Strait into North America, right up to the doorstep of Anchorage, Alaska, it became clear that China and India also had intended these two vast regions to be staging areas for their further military conquests.

And they had.

By that point, Buhpendra had marveled at the progress and felt that the war was all but over…that surely Russia, the United States and their allies must sue for peace.

But he had been wrong.

In the last year, the Americans and Russians had used new high technology innovations and an indomitable will to somehow rally their forces, stand their ground and then force the CAS and GIR armies back. Now it was the GIR and CAS forces themselves who were suffering great setbacks.

Now there were occasional air raid warnings in the Siberian capital. No bombs or missiles had fallen yet, but the very fact that the warnings were being broadcast and that the citizens, including Buhpendra's family, were drilling to take shelter, sent shivers down the Ambassador's spine. It would only be a matter of time before the "exercises" became real.

Based on Buhpendra's own intelligence briefings, which he believed that Foreign Minister Patel–a political animal if there ever was one–was doctoring to appear much more positive than they actually were, Buhpendra knew that the military situation was worsening.

Such thoughts about the kinds of political intrigue that individuals like Patel seemed to spawn never failed to remind him of his old friend, Russian General Andrei Nosik. That Russian General's forces had provided security to the work project Buhpendra had managed for India during the days of the Siberian Economic Treaty, before the outbreak of hostilities.

"Now there was a man who did not have a political bone in his body," Gavanker thought, reminiscing about his old friend.

During their many months working together, Andrei had taught Buhpendra how to read between the lines of the contemptible politicians' statements, and how to form friendships and alliances with those who could give a more accurate picture of what was going on.

Buhpendra had put that knowledge to good use since Andrei and his forces were driven out of Siberia. He had read between the lines...and he had friends who could tap into less formal lines of communication that provided a clearer picture of the overall diplomatic and military situation. As a result, the Ambassador knew that the Americans were pressing into Asia in the east, and the Russians were threatening the Ural mountain regions in the west.

"Perhaps it is time to consider a quiet move back to Madras for Eshy and the boys," he thought.

...and he immediately rejected the idea.

"With Patel looking over my shoulder, and having to ask him for the permission and the funds to accomplish such a move, there would be no hope in keeping it quiet," he thought. "...and then it would breed consequences of its own."

"Perhaps I can find a way to speak directly and discreetly with the President," he opined to himself, knowing that KP Narayannen would arrange for his family's safe and unfettered travel back to India if he knew that Buhpendra was concerned for his family's safety and if they were in any kind of imminent danger.

Failing that, Buhpendra Gavanker would not just sit back and wait for the worst. He would prepare a way to ensure his family's safety, while doing what he considered to be his duty to his nation...however he had to go about it.

December 9, 2009, that same time
Field Marshall's Command Headquarters
Kazan, Russia

The briefing was going just as he liked them. Punctual, to the point and with absolutely no hint of what the Americans would call brown-nosing.

Field Marshall Andrei Kosik was not the type of General who led from the rear, or who would ever be comfortable sitting in the plush offices of the Kremlin–and since the destruction of the Kremlin in last year's fighting it wouldn't be possible anyway–rubbing shoulders with political officers and issuing orders that were as much based on how one could advance his career, or impress the President, as they were based on what was best for the Rodina. He had made his feelings and his habits in that regard very clear to President Puten when he had been selected to lead all Russian ground forces in the war against their enemies in the CAS and the GIR.

So here he was, less than fifty miles behind the front lines, working directly with the generals leading the Russian army groups…many of whom would rather be much further behind the lines…and with the generals leading the divisions within those army groups. Planning with the roar of mechanized units in the background and the screech of jet aircraft passing overhead. In an environment where the accountability and responsibility of the decisions made could not only be appreciated, they could be felt and heard…right down to the tips of your boots.

Catching the eye of the American Colonel, who was here as an advisor and as a liaison between the Russian high command and the small but very powerful American light division that was traveling with the central army group, the Russian 23rd Army, the General spoke.

"Colonel Evans, please brief the command staff on the current disposition of your American Hail Storm missiles and the new Patriot batteries your forces have with them.

"Also, if you please, what is the status and planning for getting an American space station platform up over eastern Russia?

"I am interested in the capabilities of the lasers we know are operating from those platforms against Chinese, Indian, or GIR ballistic missiles. The Patriots are great…but they are not a seamless defense. I am hoping that the laser capabilities of those platforms are as effective in the atmosphere as our observers have indicated they are in space."

Colonel Barry Evans had been handpicked for this assignment by the Chief of the U.S. Army, and he had been interviewed by the President of the United States at the time, Norm Weisskopf, immediately before departing for Russia. He had completed his doctorate in advanced Russian studies, held a Masters degree in orbital mechanics and had graduated at the top of his class in mechanical engineering…at West Point.

Bright, engaging, and a natural leader, he was also a proven combat officer who was an expert marksman, and who proudly wore the ribbons and emblems of a qualified and combat-experienced Ranger paratrooper. He had joined General Nosik's staff immediately after the great victory near Moscow last year. He had seen and experienced Nosik's brilliant leadership as the Russian and European armies, gratefully assisted by America's single high-technology, joint services division, pushed the Chinese and Indian masses east towards the Urals, and the GIR armies south towards the Black Sea.

Evans knew that the Field Marshall understood and greatly appreciated the advantage that the American Hail Storm missiles afforded his joint command, and he understood that Nosik also was very capable of making the best use of them. He had seen it over and over again, knowing that the Russian pushed for a higher allotment of the missiles to his effort, but knowing that he would make masterful use of whatever resource he did have.

"Field Marshall, we have just received two hundred of the Block 3 Hail Storm missiles.

"They have a 60 kilometer longer range, are capable of 25% more loiter time over the target area, have enhanced active stealth capabilities, and are now capable of varying their own fire rate and munitions muzzle velocity based on over five hundred pre-programmed target profiles as opposed to the eighty target profiles of Block 2 missiles.

"Three new Patriot Block VIA missile batteries and kits for five upgrades to the Block VIA standard have just arrived here in

Kazan in the last thirty-six hours, flown in by Globe Master transports. This will allow us to complete upgrades to all existing batteries and will give us a total of twenty-four batteries for the Russian theater of operations–enough to cover your entire eastern and southern front–but only enough for single-layer coverage in that wide an area.

"If we want depth, we have to be more picky and look at major and secondary threat axis, and defend in that manner.

"For more area coverage, we are now completing and manning three land-based AEGIS VLS cells around Kazan, although the sites for these missiles are essentially fixed compared to the Patriot batteries.

"They are the latest upgrade and they provide very adequate coverage out to Theater range…of course their effectiveness is greater at closer ranges, and particularly if the area targeted by the enemy is not more than twenty degrees off the azimuth of the location of the battery.

"These three cells now mean that Kazan, Kirov, Gorkiy and Saratov are all covered, in addition to the Moscow coverage already in place. Between these point locations and the Patriot batteries, your forces are amongst the best defended against ballistic missile attack–certainly the equal of any of our other allies–and in many cases, better defended than many of our own forces…admittedly most American forces are in a lower threat environment compared to what we face here."

The Colonel intentionally stopped at this point, knowing that he was not authorized or in a position to go into the Field Marshall's other request…hoping that the good news he had just shared would generate conversation and planning that would help him avoid those questions.

But the Field Marshall did not ask questions only to see them go unanswered.

"This is excellent news, Colonel, and you will have to pass our gratitude and appreciation on to your superiors…particularly your new President, who has impressed us all greatly in a very short time.

"Now please cover the timing and planning for the laser-armed space station and the capabilities of its laser systems as regards atmospheric interception of ballistic missiles."

Andrei Nosik knew that the Colonel did not want to respond…that he did not want to be placed in a situation in which his options were either to disappoint his hosts, with whom he was doing his best to help defeat the common enemy…or to fudge and see if he could get around what undoubtedly were strict orders regarding information about America's new secret weapons.

"Field Marshall, you know that I cannot go into specific details on what little I do know of the space stations, their scheduling and their weapons capability. I do not have the "need to know" for a lot of it…and I am constrained on the rest.

"You also know that I will help you in any way I possibly can to enhance your efforts against our enemies. So I can say this:

"America's National Command Authority, our President, has made it very clear, and very public, that its first order of business is defeating the Chinese gains in the Pacific and bringing direct pressure against the Dragon from that quarter.

"As we clear the sea lanes and increase direct operations against mainland China, they will respond. That will relieve pressure in other areas and weaken the enemy so that our allied forces can exploit those opportunities in their area of operations.

"It is likely that the next station will go up over the Pacific…though there are good arguments favoring positioning over southern Europe or the Mediterranean. I'm certain that your government will make the case diplomatically through the U.S. State Department…and through your own military channels.

"Since I personally represent one of those channels, I will relay your strong preference and the reasons for it."

Again the Colonel stopped short, pausing in the hopes that Nosik would have had enough…and again the Field Marshall would not let him off the hook.

"And what of the laser capability?"

Smiling now because he knew that he would have to find a way to walk the tightrope…and knowing that the Field Marshall understood this and was maneuvering him into doing so, the Colonel continued.

"I cannot share with you the exact performance parameters of the weapons on the Conception station or the new Southern Star station that has been announced to now be operating over Australia.

"I do not know the parameters myself and believe that the numbers of those individuals who do know them is relatively small…and very well compartmentalized.

"However, I do have some expertise in the area myself and I can share with you my own conjecture. The laser capabilities will be based upon the power source, the beam wavelength, and the atmospheric conditions at the time of the shoot.

"Without a truly massive power supply-something probably larger than could fit on a station the size of those in orbit-and unless we inserted multiple stage, high pulse devices into orbit, it is not likely that the lasers will have sufficient strength to reach very deep into the atmosphere and destroy hardened RV (re-entry vehicles) warheads…particularly if there is any cloud cover at all.

"As a result, short of some technological breakthrough in miniaturization that I am unaware of–which is always possible in circumstances like this–I doubt that the current stations are going to be capable of helping us much with ballistic missile attacks here on the ground.

"Now those lasers can be quite effective against long-range ballistic tracks that actually reach near orbital altitudes. In that case, or in self-defense where missiles are entering space to attack them, they probably have effective ranges measured in the many hundreds of miles.

"That is the best information I can share with you regarding the topic. I believe that the Block 3 Hail Storm missiles and our latest Patriot batteries coupled with the AEGIS sites are going to be much more effective for you."

Andrei Nosik knew that the Colonel was right, but believed he could make use of the Space Stations just the same…although not in the way that either Colonel Evans or the Chinese and their allies might envision.

Sun Tsu would best appreciate what Andrei Nosik was considering, and Andrei found that very ironic…and very satisfying.

December 16, 2009, 09:29 EDT
Situation Room, the White House
Washington, D.C.

The Vice President was increasingly confident in the executive team that the President had assembled over the last few months, replacing those who had fallen in the attacks which claimed President Weisskopf. His respect for the new President's leadership abilities grew with each passing day.

Fred Reissinger respected the quiet, resolute and effective job John Bowers had done as the National Security Advisor to President Weisskopf. His regard for Bowers grew as he observed him. Bowers had, at first reluctantly, but very capably, filled the shoes of Alan Reeves as Weisskopf's Vice President after Reeves had been killed in the initial Chinese attacks of March, 2006.

But the esteem and respect he held for Bowers were climbing to their highest levels as a result of how the young President was now conducting the nation's affairs in the absence of Norm Weisskopf. Reissinger knew that the new President's conduct of the war and his adroit hand at the nation's helm increasingly inspired those in the administration as well as their political opponents.

After the tragic death of his friend and President at the hands of their enemies, Fred Reissinger had seriously considered informing the new President that he would serve out his term until January of 2010, and then retire as soon after that date as the President could find a replacement. But before he could find the time alone with the President to deliver that message, John Bowers had come to him and asked him to serve as his own Vice President.

In the midst of the ongoing crisis, with the country still in desperate need of firm and unshakable leadership–and Fred himself being a 110% loyal American patriot–there had been no way Fred Reissinger could refuse. Like almost all of the soldiers who were fighting, Fred knew he was in this thing for the duration, and he willingly acceded to the President's request.

Now, as this special meeting of both the international and Homeland Security teams continued into its third hour, where he and several others were joining the meeting by secure video conference, Fred was once again glad to be surrounded by people of such high caliber, all committed to a calling higher than themselves.

"*Who more than self their country loved,*" were the words that came to his mind.

The President was speaking.

"I can't emphasize to you how critical it is to maintain the pressure and the gains that we have achieved of late.

"The victories have been expensive… but we knew they would be. There are those who will count the expense and perhaps indicate that we should have accepted the Chinese offer in July after all.

"But every person sitting in this room knows that the cost of such an acceptance would have been far higher than what we are paying now. It is a price in terms of trust and faith, in terms of our way of life and in terms of history that this administration was, and will continue to be, unwilling to pay.

"...and in the long run it would have been much more expensive in terms of lives when these rabid enemies came at us again after they were good and rested and in a geo-political and economic position that would have been almost unassailable.

"So we must persevere and continue. And I have to say that we are making good progress. If we can keep it up...if we can maintain it...in another eighteen months or so we will be in a position from which I believe we can dictate the unconditional surrender of our enemies...and they will accept it.

"Jeremy, fill us all in on the latest regarding our second space station launch and in terms of our efforts in space."

Jeremy Stone was an old war horse. He had been a soldier all of his adult life. He viewed his current position as Secretary of Defense as a political position...as a necessary evil. It was necessary because he was irrevocably committed to his nation's foundational premise that the nation's military was always to be under civil command authority. He viewed it as an evil because of the politics that necessarily came along with that premise.

But he was a good soldier and he supported this President completely. He supported his judgment; he supported his maturity; he supported his instincts...his honor and his integrity. He knew that John Bowers was open to good counsel and that he sought it in his decision-making. And he knew he, Jeremy Stone, could impart some of that counsel to the President.

Knowing this–not in a vainglorious manner, but simply in understanding the applicability and need for his own experience–Jeremy had agreed to serve as Secretary of Defense. That acceptance had then opened the door for Admiral Ben Ryan to be promoted to the post of Chairman of the Joint Chiefs, which he had just vacated.

"Mr. President, the launch and assembly have gone according to schedule, but not without opposition. The Chinese continue to try to bring both the USSS Conception and the USSS Southern Star down, launching considerable attacks at them both. But they have failed in their attempts, and the Southern Star is on station and keeping a watchful eye over the entire Australian theater of operations.

"As long as the Chinese continue to use their kinetic weapons, launched from ground, and as long as they use long-range missiles as they have done, we feel confident that both stations will weather the storm. An added benefit is that the Chinese are expending substantial resources and effort, which they would otherwise apply somewhere else.

"They know that these stations are returning to us the tremendous advantage of having space-based surveillance where they do not. Our advantage is not yet as widespread as it was prior to 2006…but we'll get there. And each new piece of information that we obtain is making a huge difference in our opportunities for success.

"It's just too bad that we are still five months out from the next launch, and then three more before the one after that. But that is the way it is. Anything we launch that does not have the level of defense that these craft have is going to be most likely shot down before it can arrive on station and perform whatever function we establish for it.

"But regret is the most useless of emotions…" the Secretary observed, with a tone bordering on pensiveness.

The President took Secretary Stone's brief pause as an opportunity to interject.

"What about the status of the decision as to where the next station will be? Fill everyone here in on that."

The new Secretary of Defense was happy to speak to this issue in front of the entire group. There was a political aspect to this that he wanted to encourage, and he felt that he could accomplish that here.

"Well, Mr. President, the decision has boiled down to two principle contenders for our attention: one over the central Pacific where we can obtain oblique coverage all the way to the Philippines and Japanese Islands, and the other over the Eastern Mediterranean, where we can obliquely cover Moscow to Tehran and down into North Africa.

"There are significant diplomatic and political efforts being exerted to influence the decision. State will have to be involved with the decision…but I see those as our two most advantageous choices."

The President caught the inference and felt he knew where Stone was going with it.

"Jeremy, explain to the group what the most important military consideration is for the location of this next station in terms of prosecuting the war effort?"

The old General silently thanked God that the President had responded in this way…it was exactly what he hoped for and it allowed him to cut through to the heart of the matter.

"Mr. President, China is by far the greatest threat to our forces and our nation. Putting that bird over the Pacific is what will help us hurt and push back the Chinese the most."

There was no pause. There was no equivocation.

"Then that probably makes the decision for us. Short of something more compelling, the next station will go up over the Pacific," the President responded, without hesitation.

"Anyone have a different take than the one the Secretary of Defense has just shared?

"Other opinions? Fred? ... Sam?"

The President knew that Fred Reissinger and the new Secretary of State, Sam Loper, might have diplomatic reasons to consider a different alternative and he wanted to make sure that they had a chance to air them.

In fact, Fred Reissinger, as the former Secretary of State, could think of several reasons that allies, particularly Russia, Israel and perhaps the United Kingdom, would give for parking a station over the eastern Mediterranean, and they were based on more than diplomatic concerns.

Speaking from his secure location at Camp David, the Vice President addressed the meeting. "Mr. President, the liberation of Turkey there on Sayeed's doorstep would occur more surely and quickly if a station were located there...and the Russian offensive against the Chinese would benefit greatly as well."

Seeing Sam Loper, the new Secretary of State, sitting near the National Security Advisor, Fred asked, "Sam, what do you think?"

Sam had been Fred Reissinger's recommendation when the President had asked him who he thought should replace him. After meeting with Sam and reviewing his background, the President had come to the same conclusion. Loper had a distinguished career of over twenty-three years working within the State Department, spending well over half of that time in the field, particularly in eastern European nations and the nations of the Mid East.

"Mr. President, Russia, Israel, and the exiled government of Turkey...which by the way has taken up offices in Adana in the last five days...along with several of our European allies, notably Germany...have all contacted us directly over this issue. They are all expressing their strong desire to have our next space station positioned over the eastern Mediterranean.

"They all feel that the result of having such a strategic military advantage in the area, coupled with our Hail Storm missile technology and our growing naval advantage, would result in a much more rapid defeat the Greater Islamic Republic.

"In Russia's case, they feel that a breakthrough in the Urals would accomplish the same thing we are seeking to do in the Pacific…with much the same results.

"They feel that that if we can continue to make gains in Australia using the most recent station, and then make some gains in the central Pacific with our growing allied strength there until the next station is positioned, we will quickly reach a point with either the GIR defeated, or a Russian breakthrough into Siberia, where the CAS has to fight against our vastly superior forces on both their eastern and western borders."

The President carefully considered this alternative. He had requested that all scenarios be played out in the war colleges to determine whether a U.S. focus on China would end the war more quickly and with less loss of life…or whether a focused effort on the GIR or Siberia would make the desired outcome occur more quickly.

"Jeremy, do you and Ben have anything to say to these comments from our allies in Europe and the Mid East, and the requests and recommendations they are making?"

Ben Ryan, who had only a few days earlier arrived in Washington after making a smooth transition of CINCPAC to his successor, indicated he did have something to say and Jeremy Stone nodded for him to go ahead.

"Mr. President, Mr. Vice President, and Mr. Secretary of State…with all due respect to our allies. As dangerous as the cumulative power of the GIR is, and as dangerous as India's masses and technical capabilities are, it is clear that the Chinese are our most serious adversary, both quantitatively and qualitatively.

"We simply must apply maximum pressure against the Chinese while we continue our efforts in the Mid East, in Africa, in Central and South America and in helping our allies in Europe. The best place to do that is in the Pacific with the triple axis approach we are conducting.

"The greater threat we pose to the Chinese, the more resources they will be forced to turn towards us and the less they will be able to export to their allies. Make no mistake–despite the capabilities and resources of the GIR and India, the most serious technological threats are represented by what they are receiving in the way of exports and license builds from the Chinese.

"We see this over and over again on the battlefield…on land, in the air, and on the sea.

"I cannot emphasize enough, from a military perspective, how critical it is to maintain the pressure on the Chinese in the Pacific…to keep them from having the time or the resources to either further consolidate their holdings or to develop effective counters against the advantages we are beginning to bring to bear.

"Those are my thoughts."

Jeremy Stone had listened to his subordinate and friend carefully. He was content to let the words Ben Ryan had spoken stand pretty much stand for him as well. A few words, well spoken, sometimes created the greatest impact. So he simply added his own closing comments to Ben's well-chosen words.

"Mr. President, I concur with Ben. He has summed up our wisest choice, and he has done so very succinctly and very well.

"The GIR and India are capable of putting up stiff fights against us. China has already shown that, if we give her the time, if we allow her to build her resources, if we do not keep increasing pressure on her–she is still capable of defeating us.

"I agree that the best place that either we or our allies can apply the pressure is in the Pacific."

The President did not take long to consider the alternatives. He was determined and felt that America must press the advantage against their principle antagonists, the Chinese, without pause.

"Jeremy and Ben, I agree.

"Proceed with the necessary orders and planning to put this next bird up over the central Pacific.

"Fred, work with Sam to explain this delicate, difficult decision to our allies and then make the firm commitment to them that the fourth one will go up over the eastern Med. This assignment requires your time and wise attention. Our allies need to fully understand our reasoning here.

"In fact, unless I miss my guess, by that time, they will probably be asking us to advance the location out over southern Siberia, Arabia or the Indian Ocean. I believe our allies will make those kinds of gains in any case.

The President then turned to his National Security Advisor, Bill Hendrickson.

"Bill, I know you've been working heavily with Secretary Stone's people and with NASA. Please give us a briefing about how L&CII is proceeding."

By L&CII, the President was referring to the new acronym that had been universally adopted by both the national and military leadership for the deep space mission out beyond Mars, what was now being called Lewis and Clark Expedition II.

"Mr. President, the mission is now eight days ahead of schedule in terms of the initial flight time. They are well over halfway to their objective and are now well beyond the orbit of Mars.

"We expect that they will be on station by mid-February, and will then spend two to three months gathering material, testing it and then preparing for their return trip to earth.

"At that point, if their return voyage goes as well as the outbound trip, we can expect them back at Point Conception with their cargo by early autumn of next year. Once there, after another six to eight weeks of final calibration and material forming, they should be able to begin the planned..."

As the National Security Advisor continued, a number of the people in attendance couldn't help but notice that discussions of this nature seemed so surreal. Despite the fact that they had planned for, worked for and had visions of this day for several years, now that it was actually happening it almost seemed like a dream. The perfecting of the laser technology, the miniaturization of the powerful nuclear plants, the nuclear pulse SSTO boosting, and particularly the light sail propulsion–all developed under the tightest iron clad secrecy–had been topics for science fiction novels to this point in history. Now all that had once been mere educated scientific conjecture had become scientific reality. It was a large concept to swallow, and it served to make them all extremely proud of the American scientific community.

John Bowers was amazed by the achievement, and he saw a visionary potential for it beyond the current circumstances. Without them realizing exactly what his full intentions were at this point, he was already working with the budgetary and oversight committees in Congress, the scientific and business communities, and with NASA to develop the groundwork that would bring that vision to fruition.

Norm Weisskopf had wisely embraced this bold, expensive. and risky scheme as an avenue to end the war more quickly and convincingly. Now John Bowers was going to take the ball the former President had handed him and not only make sure that the critical and paramount military goal was achieved...he was also going to make sure that the United States continued to use the proven technology to press further outward into space after the war.

As far as he was concerned, it was well past time that America and the free world push on towards the full scientific and economic development of space. He felt inspired to move towards establishing a permanent presence on the moon, and then on Mars and Phobos–perhaps one day even on the distant Galilean satellites.

It was inspiration…planning and dreaming on a grand scale.

"But it is inspiration whose realization must wait on the more pressing issues that lie before us," he thought as Bill Hendrickson continued.

"Everything in its turn. We can perhaps plan and prepare to one degree or another for some of these far reaching goals now…but we will not begin to accomplish them until we rid the world of these rogue regimes and the hell they have created here on earth.

"…and when we do, perhaps then we can gaze outward and begin to move in that direction with the other sovereign, independent constitutional Republics of this earth."

Those thoughts crystallized the President's thinking…and his commitment. In a flash of enlightenment, he understood what he had to do, and how he was going to go about doing it.

At the end of Bill Hendrickson's briefing, the meeting was opened for discussion. It was an upbeat discussion, full of optimism and hope…full of a spirit of accomplishment and an almost boundless horizon for American ingenuity.

The President bided his time during the discussion, listening to all of the comments and recommendations. Most of the participants were already aware of the President's basic position regarding the space program, not only for its impact in the war effort, but his general longer-term desires.

But the plans were no longer general in nature. The President had made an epoch decision in the course of this meeting, one that would entail a monumental goal and challenge to the American people…indeed, to all of the free peoples of the world.

President Bowers decided that now was the time to share his vision with the members of his security council.

He motioned to get everyone's attention.

"This has been a great discussion…stimulating, uplifting and enlightening. With our freedoms and vitality, with our faith and the support of Providence, there is nothing worthwhile that we cannot accomplish.

"Let me just outline to you another decision I have been seriously contemplating during this morning's meeting, in addition to the one regarding the placement of the next space station.

"It is a decision that would couple our ultimate victory in this conflict with even more far-reaching effects afterwards.

"The decision that I am contemplating making as the President of the United States of America is this.

"At the conclusion of this war, I want us to seriously consider and move towards committing our nation to a far-reaching goal in space research and exploration that will establish a basic identity, purpose and challenge for our people. After this war is won, and in conjunction with the research, development and manufacturing efforts we will have made to win it, we will then proceed to not only maintain those efforts, we will use a large portion of the mobilization of our production, manpower and technology infrastructure to accelerate them.

"I know that during the reconstruction and rebuilding efforts that we will be expending on behalf of our allies and other people of the world, this will be a monumental effort, but as a nation I feel we should make the firm commitment to have a permanent, manned installation on the moon by the year 2015, followed by a permanent manned installation on Mars by the year 2020. By permanent I mean something more than just habitable but dependant on constant resupply from Earth. By permanent I mean installations that are self-sustaining in terms of basic air, water and food supply.

"I see the decade of the 2020s as a decade in which mankind, led by the free and principled leadership of the United States, moves out into the solar system...to the asteroids and the Saturn and Jupiter systems to develop the wealth of information and resources that lie there waiting for us.

"I believe it is another of America's manifest destinies...that our solar system, and space in general, beckon to us just as the great American west beckoned more than two centuries ago.

"Americans have always been a people who yearn to discover what God has created...what is simply out there *waiting to be discovered*...and to *use* those discoveries for the benefit of all mankind. That is one of the noble characteristics that has separated us from other civilizations. I believe that, once we have defeated the evil that is represented by our adversaries in this war, it is incumbent upon us to use the technological advances that we have obtained in our war efforts in a more historically positive and constructive way.

"By committing ourselves to this enterprise we will take the will and the drive with which we are prosecuting this war effort and further apply it towards expanding into space. In so doing, I believe we shall see miraculous strides forward in our lifetimes...and our children or grandchildren will inherit the stars.

"Such an enterprise will allow us, along with our allies, to extend the true free market that we shall have established amongst freedom and peace loving sovereign nations here on earth, and advance it into space.

"Some might claim that I am putting the cart before the horse by envisioning such achievements even before we have been victorious in this war effort. But I want all of you to know that what I am envisioning is evidence of two things: my confidence that we and our allies will eventually prevail, and my belief that we will use our uniquely American ingenuity and goodness to turn the scientific components of a once horrific global situation into promise for the future of all mankind.

"This presidency and this administration, if nothing else, will be marked by two great accomplishments.

"First and foremost, we shall focus all of our energies towards bring this war to a successful and victorious conclusion…and we shall achieve this goal. This has been the most horrific and widespread war in mankind's history. In winning it…in completing the work begun by Norm Weisskopf, we will make the world once again safe for liberty and republican minded governments everywhere.

"Second, following that triumph, and utilizing the capabilities associated with achieving it, we will initiate mankind's drive into space, with America's principled leadership and example pointing the way in what will be an unprecedented, historic, and tremendously positive effort that will serve to further unite the free nations of the earth..

"Our current efforts in space are rightly meant to lead us to victory over our enemies' tyrannical regimes. Regimes who would destroy all peace, who would eradicate all freedom and who would forever extinguish the ability to achieve any worthwhile prosperity based on the true and enduring values of individual liberty, responsibility, and freedom governed by individual moral restraint.

"…and those efforts *shall* accomplish that aim, which will end with the eradication of those regimes and their abettors from the face of the earth.

"As we proceed down that path, I wanted you to know exactly what my long term view includes. In addition to winning the war and helping to rebuild all that has been lost…it will most definitely include the types of commitments I have shared with you here at the end of our meeting. Please keep those critical commitments in mind as we move forward. We will discuss them with greater and greater frequency, and in more and more detail as we progress towards victory, and as circumstance warrant it.

"Again, I thank each of you for your part in this meeting."

Chapter 8

"A man, Sir, should keep his friendships in constant repair." - Samuel Johnson

Christmas Day, 2009
Presidential Suite
Brasilia, Brazil

Maldenado picked up the extension, surprised at the unannounced and unscheduled call from John Bowers, the President of the United States. She hoped that nothing had gone terribly wrong in the war effort. In the few seconds before she had picked up the call, her advisors had not alluded to anything of that sort…at least nothing that current intelligence was aware of.

But you never knew.

"Yes, this is Henrietta Maldenado, Mr. President. It is a surprise to hear from you…a pleasant one, I trust.

"Well, thank you very much, Mr. President. Merry Christmas to you as well.

"It is wonderful to speak to you, and I will convey those wishes and thoughts on to my entire cabinet and the people of Brazil.

"Yes.

"That is correct, Mr. President, and thank you for making mention of it. We take a great pride in our troops and their accomplishments in the foreign deployments we have made outside of South America, in Africa, and in Australia as well.

"It is.

"Yes, things are going well here on the continent also. Not as quickly as we would like in Argentina after the Chinese influx of troops there, but ahead of our projections in Colombia and Venezuela.

"Thank you.

"You know, I must say that, in addition to the overwhelming numbers you are providing in Australia and in Africa and elsewhere in the world, your efforts in Panama, now that the Canal Zone is once again in American hands, have truly bolstered us. The ability to now place much more pressure on the enemy from the north in Colombia and your special forces' achievements in Venezuela have been nothing short of extraordinary.

"Oh, no need, Mr. President.

"Believe me, those sentiments come directly from the field, Mr. President and are conveyed through me. Please pass them on to your own military leaders and particularly those in Panama, Colombia and Venezuela.

"Yes, I understand. I will.

"Before we finish, I must also convey to you the thanks of all of the Brazilian people for you, your government's, and your people's generosity to our people here in Brazil. The food, the equipment, the weaponry, and the technical assistance in rebuilding and improving areas torn by this war have been God-sent…and we thank you all for being the instrument in His hands.

"Why thank you, John. God bless you and your people as well.

"Once again, Merry Christmas.

"Goodbye."

As she hung up the phone, she was amazed at the time that the President of the United States had taken with her personally.

There at the end, he had addressed her by name, as a friend–as an equal partner in this fight. There was a unique combination of strength, warmth and humility in his demeanor. And she would never forget the effect it had on her. It was a trait that apparently Norm Weisskopf had either passed on, or had sought in his Vice President, and Henrietta was comforted that John Bowers possessed a genuine warmth and thoughtfulness just as innately as his remarkable predecessor.

…and, thinking now on its impact on her, she decided to pass it on. Picking up the phone she had just used, she contacted her own Chief of Staff.

"Alfonso, please schedule three calls for this morning.

"I know they are not on my schedule, but I am asking you to put them there. About fifteen minutes each.

"I want to speak to the Presidents of Peru, Chile, and Ecuador this morning."

Christmas Day, 2009
Presidential Dahka
Near Klin, outside of Moscow

Vladimyr Puten thought back on the call he had received from John Bowers as he played with his grandchildren in this warm, comfortable and secure retreat deep in the forest outside of Moscow. The call had been unscheduled and unannounced…but not entirely unexpected.

"The Americans are very sentimental about such things during this season," the President thought, "and well they should be.

"Their faith has sustained them throughout their history, and has helped sustain others.

"Despite the years of mistrust, antipathy and 'cold' warfare…that faith is helping to sustain us during this conflict as well."

And he had to admit, since Communism had been overthrown over twenty years ago, the traditional feelings of goodwill and faith at this time of year, so long suppressed by the Communist party…had blossomed again and were very evident all over Russia.

"In fact, if anything, the sentimentality here is even stronger," he reflected. "We never reached a point before this war began where the season could be as commercialized as it had become in the United States."

Just the same, the call had been pleasant, even refreshing, at a time when the rigors and concerns of all-out war still completely occupied him, as the leader of the Russian Federation.

In Puten's eyes, John Bowers was shaping up to be a very capable leader. He had great vitality due to his relative youth, and he was driven…at least as driven as Weisskopf had been, and that was saying a lot.

As he reflected on the call, he was amazed at how friendly and how personable the President had come across to him. The call had, in fact, been a personal one…not laden with the usual formal speech of diplomacy or negotiations.

And yet, Puten realized that John Bowers had accomplished some important diplomacy and negotiating during the call. He had reaffirmed America's intentions with respect to their space station deployment–intentions that were not aligned with what the Russian Federation had desired. He had reassured the Russian President regarding America's unwavering support for the Rodina, promising specific quantities of more support troops, weapons systems, food, agricultural equipment, and technical assistance.

"And he had done it all with a call that I will always remember as a wish for me and my own family to enjoy a 'Merry Christmas'...amazing!" concluded the Russian President.

And as it had done with Henrietta Maldenado, the call inspired Vladimyr Puten to make several calls of his own...to pass on the faith, good cheer and commitment of friendship and support from one allied leader to another.

Christmas Day, 2009, 19:00 EDT
The Oval Office
The White House, Washington, D.C.

After a day of talking–of contacting all of the major allied leaders and extending them the heartfelt feelings and wishes of the season, and then bolstering them with the firm assurances of America's support–the President prepared to make his most important address, to the American people.

Through most of his life, he had never thought of himself as much of a public speaker. Oh, he could issue the orders and directives necessary to fulfill whatever goals his superiors in the military or civilian life had outlined for him. And he was strong at developing and implementing the plans necessary to accomplish those directives.

But, until he had been appointed into high public office, he had not been required to speak in front of large numbers of people.

Then, starting with his appointment as the National Security Advisor to President Weisskopf in 2005, all of that had begun to change. He had tried to avoid public appearances as much as possible, but with world conditions degrading, the responsibilities of his office increasingly required him to articulate the administration's positions on national security via television news shows, radio talk shows and at public events.

As Vice President, his spoken words were increasingly in demand, particularly as America had suffered so many setbacks in the early years of the war. In addition, President Weisskopf's plan for using the leadership to rally the morale of the American people continued to this day, in the face of persistent enemy attacks.

While John Bowers was still a rather reluctant public speaker, believing that he lacked a natural flair for it, reality belied his own feelings on the matter. He was inspiring in his sincerity in communicating his thoughts and his goals in a compelling, heartfelt manner. If asked how he so smoothly transitioned from a *behind-the-scenes* man into an *in-the-public-view* man, he would simply state that somehow God had filled in the gaps and given voice to his thoughts and that accounted for the changes.

And perhaps He had.

Either way, as the cameras came on, and the President looked into the one directly in front of his desk, he knew he was looking into the heart and soul of America and of free people everywhere as he started his Christmas speech.

"Good evening my fellow Americans, and good evening to all of our friends and allies watching throughout the world.

"Merry Christmas to each of you, and a particular wish for a Merry Christmas to all of our military service personnel stationed throughout the world on this special day. For all of us, no matter what our role, I trust that, even in the current hardships of war that we all face, the spirit of the Christmas season abides with all. That the great example of selflessness, sharing, giving, healing, unity, perseverance, and sacrifice fills your hearts as it does my own, and that of my family.

"Tonight I bring you a message based upon those traditional and foundational Christmas principles. It is a message filled with hope and progress in this war, and one filled with the promise of a bright future that we can now glimpse on the far horizon.

"Though the dark clouds and rough seas still make the journey perilous, I am confident that we are steadily progressing toward the thin line of light along the horizon dispelling the storms of these past many years.

"Let me share with you why I believe this.

"Tonight, except for a few miles just north of the juncture of the Isthmus of Panama and South America, all of Central America had been freed of the tyranny of Chinese and CAS forces. Although the locks have been destroyed by the retreating Chinese forces, the Panama Canal is once again firmly in American hands, and it will remain that way perpetually.

"Tonight I can say to you that the Caribbean has been cleared of enemy forces. Cuba has been completely pacified, her people freed from dictatorial oppressions, and her leaders brought to American justice. Along with other prominent terrorist leaders who have already been captured and sentenced in American military tribunals, those leaders will have their sentences carried out on January 1st of the coming year, less than a week away. All other Chinese and other enemy forces and facilities in the Bahamas have been defeated and occupied by American forces.

"In South America the war effort is progressing favorably. Venezuela has been completely cut off from resupply or reinforcement by our air, land and sea forces, and Venezuelan, Chinese and remaining Panamanian forces there are now confined to rough terrain and dense jungle areas along the northeastern coast. American, Colombian, and Brazilian forces have them surrounded there. In Colombia, enemy forces are fractured, but continue fighting fiercely in pockets in the densely forested highlands, but they are without hope of assistance from either CAS or CASAS forces.

"The only area of South America where enemy forces continue to maintain any advantage is in Argentina. Brazilian and other allied South American forces have been thwarted from making headway there since the Chinese shifted their major South American focus to that region. Over eight hundred thousand Chinese troops, some from northern sections of the continent and others who arrived there in Chinese convoys and aircraft, reinforced and bolstered Argentine forces to the point of stopping Brazilian, Ecuadorian, and Peruvian advances, and in many areas, throwing them back.

"Tonight I am announcing the formation of a large American expeditionary force to assist the Brazilians in defeating the last vestiges of Chinese power and tyranny in the Americas in Argentina. We will continue to assist our freedom loving friends and allies in South America until that task is accomplished, and their lands are once again free of this blight that threatens the peace, prosperity, and liberty of all people.

"In Africa, the three-year aim of allied forces of driving a pincer at the underside of GIR and Chinese forces that have been assaulting Israel from Egypt has finally been realized. Using a coalition of free African states, coupled with Brazilian, American, and English forces, we have broken through enemy defense forces in Chad and driven hard up under the principle GIR forces in Egypt. At the same time, joint Israeli, American, and English forces have broken through enemy defenses in the Sinai and have now retaken the Suez Canal and crossed over into Egypt. Five days ago these two allied forces met and joined together one hundred miles south of Cairo on the Nile River, successfully splitting enemy forces in the area. At this hour, GIR forces are in retreat across the western desert of Egypt toward Libya. while Chinese forces are retreating to the south towards Ethiopia.

"In Asia, the Chinese invasion of Alaska has been repulsed and Chinese forces in far eastern Siberia have now been defeated. It has been a costly campaign and we still must deal with the entire southern two-thirds of the Kamchatka Peninsula. At Magadan, where a large portion of our forces staged, though Chinese attacks are continuing there on a frequent basis, the tide of battle has turned. The original purpose of our invasion of Magadan has been realized. Now the large forces that have steadily built up there, coupled with those pouring out of Alaska, will focus on consolidating the strong foothold we have established on the mainland of Asia. Once that consolidation is accomplished, we will extend our foothold to the east to threaten the Chinese homeland directly. It will be a threat the Chinese cannot ignore.

"My fellow Americans, tonight I am proud to be able to announce that in Australia, allied forces from America, England, Australia, and the many exiled nations of the Pacific and Asia are making steady, hard-fought progress against monumental numbers of Chinese and Indian forces. We are liberating the continent, but it is not an easy fight, and it is not yet accomplished. Enemy military forces are being bolstered by a tenacious citizens' militia comprised of millions of Indian and Chinese immigrants who have been given land in the area, brutally displacing the former and rightful inhabitants. The further north and eastward we push, the more difficult the battles become as those inhabitants now occupying the land have lived on it for two to three years and considered it all the more their own.

"Well, that land is not their own. And we say to these people that they will have to relinquish it and lay down their arms or be treated as enemy combatants. Despite their resistance, with our space-based surveillance, and with a plentiful supply of Hail Storm missiles coming off of our production lines, along with all of the other implements of modern warfare, we are steadily pushing the enemy back. As of tonight, the line of advance extends from Townsville on the northwestern coast, across the Dividing range to Hughenden, from there on a line south across the Great Artesian Basin and to the west of the Grey Range to the Darling River in New South Wales and from there, following the Darling River to the coast, where our forces have just finished liberating Ardelaid in South Australia. Over 20% of Australia is once again free. Before long, all of Australia will be freed from the oppressive yoke of tyranny.

"In Europe, hard fought progress is also being made. European Union armies, assisted by our own forces, have driven the GIR out of the Balkans and are now fighting fiercely along the western borders of Greece against Greek and GIR forces. All of central Europe has been liberated all the way to the Ural mountains where Russian, European and American forces are preparing for a great offensive against that natural defensive barrier that Chinese and Indian troops have strengthened into what they are calling the Ural line. They will soon find that such a static defense, manned by the forces of oppression, cannot hold against the forces of liberty.

"Other Russian and European forces have pushed to the south, pushing GIR forces, who are attempting to retreat to the south in an effort to support their forces in the Middle East. Our allies are now about to break through GIR defenses in Georgia and threaten GIR Turkey from the north.

"In the Middle East, American, Israeli, and English forces have defeated GIR armed forces in Syria and Saudi Arabia, cutting off the southern Arabian Peninsula and penetrating deeply into the former Iraq. American and exiled Turkish forces have established a strong foothold in Turkey around Adana and have progressed to the north and east of there, entering Iraq on the north near Mosul. GIR forces have retreated from Baghdad and now allied forces from the south and American forces from the north have linked up there in the former Iraqi capital where many of the citizens have welcomed us, and are looking forward to the institutions of a democratic republic being once again instituted amongst them. Our forces are now facing stiff resistance in the mountainous regions of northeastern Iraq all the way down to the Persian Gulf along all approaches into the heart of the GIR, the former Iran.

"My fellow citizens, these are all tremendous gains and have all been made in the year that has passed since the great military victories at Anchorage, Moscow, and in Israel. The actual gains in Australia have been made over the last four months.

"I must add that all of this is also occurring only a little more than a year since the miraculous moral victory that we experienced here in America, when we turned our nation's course away from the culture of death that had reigned for over thirty-five years and re-embraced life and the moral foundations of our heritage.

At that time, President Weisskopf urged America to remember the more important moral victory because it lays the groundwork for all other victories and gives them meaning. I have memorized a portion of his words from that speech and would like to recite them to you this evening. I believe that they should be written on every American's heart and soul.

"As much as we must remember those victories, let us remember even more the date of October 12th, 2008, Columbus Day, a true day of discovery, a day of self discovery, when an even more important focal point in the history of our nation and our people was reached. Through the Supreme Court ruling of that day, the legal sanction of the evil growing in our own hearts was dealt an even more stunning blow.

"As a result. I am compelled to believe that Providence is once again smiling on these United States, and that we are now not only in a position to physically go forward in this monumental struggle…we are prepared to do so in our own hearts.

"What our great, late President Norm Weisskopf said at the time was true. His words were true when he uttered them, and they will remain true eternally. That is the nature of truth. Despite what others might believe, time and circumstance do not erode its meaning, significance, impact and value. If anything, they serve to reiterate them.

"Those words Norm Weisskopf spoke have turned out to be prophetic when considered in light of what has happened in the ensuing twelve months. Our continued knowledge and acceptance of those truths have reflected in our actions and in our success. Here we are, a year later, and all of our gains bode very well for our cause and give reason for great hope. Hopes for similar gains over the next year's time. Hopes for a brighter world for tomorrow, of that thin line we now see on the horizon breaking forth with clear skies and bright sunlight upon the entire world…the light of peace, truth, and liberty.

"Let us use that hope, that commitment to truth, to fuel our drive towards the light. Let us always remember that our gains have come at great cost. Hundreds of thousands of allied military personnel are dead along with uncounted numbers of civilians. Even though they have been greatly diminished, there are continuing acts of terror inside of America. One of those cowardly terrorist acts killed our beloved president and members of his cabinet right here in Washington, D.C.

"But, in the face of this, and as a result of our hopes, Americans and allied peoples all over the world are making the sacrifices necessary and enduring these hardships with a will. The hearts and souls of free peoples everywhere have been tested, tried and purified in the forge of persecution and the unrelenting mortal opposition of an enemy committed to the destruction of our freedoms, our way of life and our very lives.

"Their wicked crusade has caused us to look deep within ourselves and tap the strength and faith existing in our innermost being. And now that we've returned to those roots, there is no end to the good we can accomplish once we have defeated this monstrous evil.

"Let us go forward, secure in the knowledge of our standing with one another and before God. We are fighting for the right; we are fighting for liberty; we are fighting for moral compassion and the unalienable rights of all mankind.

"And we shall prevail, so help us God.

"Merry Christmas to you all, and may God continue to bless the United States of America."

January 1, 2010, 06:42 CDT
The Lazy H Ranch
Outside of Montague, Texas

It was a cold morning in north-central Texas. The temperature was hovering around twenty degrees, and the wind was out of the north under cloudy skies that reflected the few lights shining in the town of Montague, eight miles to the southwest. There were occasional flakes of snow in the air, and the forecast called for light snow later in the morning.

Jess Simmons was loving it.

He had left Cindy asleep in the bed and gotten up at 4:30 AM to come and take a look at the tractor. "Taking a look" had turned into a complete check-up and rundown of its operating condition. By 6:15 he had gotten the beast started and was letting her warm up there in the barn while he did a few daily chores.

His leg was feeling great, despite the limp.

He wondered if Cindy was up yet, whether the rumbling of the old Case tractor here in the barn had awakened her.

"If I know her, she was up by six and will have breakfast for me before I can get this thing out of the barn and into the fields," he thought as he prepared to climb up on the tractor.

Sure enough, as he drove the tractor out of the barn and started down the gravel road that to the fields they owned on the south side of their property, as he passed the house, a light appeared in the doorway as Cindy opened the door and waved him in.

Jess left the tractor idling and climbed down off of it. It was a little awkward for him with his leg, but he was able to get down from the Case safely. He had been practicing for over a week, looking forward to the day he would take the tractor out and get some of the necessary work done to maintain his fields through the winter.

Today was that day...but not until after he had eaten a hearty breakfast prepared by Cindy.

"Oh man, what's that I smell?" he asked, as he walked through the door and caught a whiff of the aroma coming out of the kitchen.

"Smells like thick sausage gravy over homemade biscuits."

Cindy already had the places set and the food on the table when he walked into the kitchen.

"Biscuits and gravy with some scrambled eggs and orange juice, to be exact," she said with a warm morning smile, as he sat down.

After a blessing on the food, which Jess asked Cindy to say, he dug right in and began eating.

"It must be twenty degrees or less out there this morning, so this is really hitting the spot, sweetheart. Thanks."

Cindy ate her own food and watched as her husband literally devoured his. She was happy to see him applying himself to working on the ranch. The war had kept him away for a long time, and there had been some doubt at first as to how much he would be able to do. But he had always loved ranch work and he was determined to be able to mind his own "place."

She would have liked him to take a little more time, but knew him well enough to know that he would push the envelope as soon as he felt he was ready. He always had; it was one of the qualities that had made him such a successful National Guard officer--the ability to know when you were prepared to push the limit, and then to be able to do it successfully.

And apparently today was the day he was prepared to push the envelope here on the ranch.

Thinking about his service in the National Guard caused her to remember something she had wanted to ask him.

"Jess, did you finish that letter to Abraham?"

Cindy was referring to General Abraham Eshkol of the IDF. He had worked with Jess extensively when Jess had served in Israel, first as an advisor to the IDF, and then, later, when he was on active duty there. They had become close friends and the Eshkols had provided a second home to Jess whenever he was on leave in the area.

In the course of the warfare, Abraham had been promoted from Colonel to General and was now fighting with American and other allied forces in the former Iraq. Jess had received a letter from Abraham late last week and had mentioned to Cindy after they both had read it that it was important that he reply soon.

Cindy knew how he felt. She had recently sent a lengthy response to Elizabeth Trevor, letting her and her husband Joe know how Jess was doing and again thanking them for the six weeks they had here on the Lazy H. They had been a tremendous help to both Cindy and Jess in preparing for Jess's return, and then assisting as he rehabilitated to a point where he could get around on his own.

"Not yet, honey. Later today or maybe tomorrow morning after turning over that stubble field, depending on how well the Case works…and how well my leg holds up.

"I owe him a detailed report on my condition…and I also owe one to Marty and to General Donovan. May even mention working on the tractor today.

"I also want to respond to the SITREP Abraham gave me about what is going on over there in the Middle East, and encourage him and let him know how much faith we have in him and what they are doing over there."

Jess became quiet and contemplative for a moment.

General Abraham Ishkol had conveyed to him the success they had experienced since Jess had been seriously wounded and transported back to the United States. Knowing that operational security was paramount, and realizing that anything of any tactical or strategic importance would be edited out, Abraham had still been able to convey the essence of the situation.

Like anyone else, Jess worried over the safety of his friend. But he also understood the risks of military life, and particularly of combat. He had experienced them himself for several years, culminating when he was shot down and severely wounded. He and Cindy had both also experienced it in the most poignant way possible with the loss of their son, Billy.

As Jess now knew, from his friend's letter, from other reports he had received from General Andrew Donovan, from news reports, and from the President's Christmas message, not long after the start of the battle that had injured Jess, the leading elements of the GIR counterattack had punched completely through American and Israeli defenses. That breakthrough had carried GIR forces all the way past Damascus to the very foot of the Golan Heights where Jess had spent so much time. In that position, the GIR forces had endangered the entire northern portion of allied operations in the area and were threatening to break through into Israel itself.

Then, one flank of the GIR forces had collapsed under pressure from US forces that had maneuvered northward, along the coast of Lebanon, and attacked GIR forces just south of Homs. That battle had resulted in the failure of the entire GIR counterattack. With the major forces that had penetrated through Damascus in danger of being encircled, all of the GIR forces had fallen back rapidly to their original positions, before the counterattack had started.

And allied forces had then pushed them back much further beyond those positions.

Using a vastly replenished supply of Hail Storm missiles and with all available reserves being thrown into the battle, allied forces repulsed GIR forces all along the front. They quickly penetrated into the former Iraq, and well into Saudi Arabia. What had looked like a potential defeat had been turned into a successful offensive of tremendous proportions. And it had been turned around in the space of a few short weeks.

Now things had slowed down. After initial success in southern Iran, Allied forces were being held firmly there by reinforced GIR armies and a belligerent population. In the mountainous regions of the northeastern portions of Iraq, the same young general who had masterminded the GIR counterattack in Syria, General Abduhl Selim, was conducting effective defensive operations against allied forces. Abraham and the other allied commanders in that area were having a tough time rooting him out.

"They have a lot of fighting and hardship to go through before they crack that GIR egg…but with our forces on the borders of Iran, at least victory in sight now."

Cindy reached across the table and put her hand on her husband's arm.

"Jess, those capable men and the good Lord are going to see to it that all of that happens. Both of us have complete faith in that.

"Right now, I'm just grateful you're home safe.

"Our family has given everything we have to it," she said with her eyes welling up, the memories of Billy forever intertwined with any mention of the war.

"And I can honestly say that…if presented with the same conditions again…despite the loss and heartache, I know we would do nothing differently. But I'm glad you're home and that you're rehabilitating here where I can keep an eye on you.

"No offense to Andrew Donovan, Abraham, Marty and the others, but the Simmons have borne a heavy price. What we need for you now is healing that comes from the tender loving care that you are getting here at home, and from the therapy you are receiving every minute you work on that old Case tractor."

As Jess lifted the last forkful of biscuits and gravy to his mouth, he stared into his wife's moist eyes. In his mind he thanked God and his lucky stars for this wonderful woman, who had suffered so much and who came through it all strong and dedicated.

"Honey…I can think of no place I would rather be than right here with you.

"I want you to know…I believe you know that it's always been that way, even when I was called away and had to go. It's that way even when I feel this war would be over sooner if I'd be back over there doing my part.

"I know I can't do that now and I have accepted it…and I am grateful to have you here…taking care of me.

"It's the same with Andrew, Abraham and Marty. They all look forward to the time that they can each be back home with their own families, and I pray God will grant them each that opportunity soon, so they can feel the great joy and contentment that I feel.

"But, right now," he said as he chewed and swallowed that last bite of breakfast, and then stood up and hurriedly washed it down with the last of his orange juice, "the Case and that southern stubble field are in need of my attention, and I can't keep them waiting any longer."

As Cindy smiled and shook her head, she started picking up the dishes. With a smile on his face which radiated his love for her and the excitement he felt about getting back on the tractor, Jess came over and gave her a warm hug and then opened the door and went out into the warmth of the Texas cold.

January 5, 2010, 22:55 local time
Pham Residence
Secure Housing Unit, COSTIND Conversion Operations
Tianjin, China

The family gathering was somber as Lu Pham, his wife, Song, their daughter Chiang, and their new son-in-law, Hua Jianying, reflected on the latest news about Kao.

After being rescued by the Chinese helicopter, Kao and the men from the Chongqing had been safely bought aboard the Zenim as it retreated north and westward, past the Solomon Islands. While in the infirmary there, Koa had developed a pulmonary infection, falling gravely ill. The pneumonia only worsened his serious condition attributable to the oily water he had swallowed and the burns he had suffered both on the ship and later while in the water.

As a member of the Politburo and the executive council, Lu had been able to access the latest information…had even spoken with Admiral Xia about his son and received word back that his condition had worsened and that he had been airlifted to the best medical facilities the Chinese had within distance of the aircraft carrier at the time, in Rabaul.

Since that time, the information had been no better. The doctors considered Kao too sick to be transported, otherwise he would already be back in Beijing receiving the best care available in all of China and its holdings.

"Well," Lu said to the entire family as they sat around the low table in the family room of their home, "I have received permission to make a trip to Rabaul, and Song can come with me if we feel it's necessary. "I will be conducting official state business in New Guinea and at various other locations on the return trip.

"We wanted to talk about this, discuss it together, and see what you and Hua think, Chiang."

Chiang held her husband's hand and considered it. But before she could make a comment, her mother, Song, spoke up. "Chiang, before you and Hua share your thoughts, I just want to make sure everyone knows how I feel."

Lu immediately interjected, "Song, I'm sorry…I took it for granted that everyone would…please, go ahead and forgive me for being presumptuous."

Song reached over and took Lu's hand while looking at him. She knew he had a lot on his mind and was under intense pressure…more so in his role in the Politburo where he was expected to continue overseeing and managing the technical side of weapons development, but also on the political side, an area that he had always avoided…even disdained. Now, of necessity, he had to deal with it and he had to do so deftly.

"It's all right, Lu. I meant nothing by this. I know you understand and it is easy to take things for granted. I do it all the time. I just want to make sure Chiang and Hua know how I feel."

She then turned back to her daughter and son-in-law.

"Chiang…Hua, your father tends to be extremely positive about things. He has always been an optimist.

"Coupled with his drive to produce the expected results, it is his optimism that has made him successful…not only as an engineer, but as a hero of our adopted homeland, of your homeland, Hua. It is also helping him in his role in the politburo…although I constantly tell him that he must remain careful because not all leaders are like him…some will use his positive attitude against him.

"Nevertheless, he is being very optimistic about Kao now. The fact is, your brother…Hua, your brother-in-law, is very near death.

"I have prevailed on your father to seek and to obtain permission for this trip. I could not bear him dying there, so far away, alone. I want to be with him.

"If, as your father hopes, he recovers...then we will be there to help him through. If not, then we will be there in his last moments to comfort him and to give him the dignity of being surrounded by those he loves as he dies. Then, afterwards, we will bring him home."

As Song said this, she found she could not go on. A vision of her wonderfully handsome son, who had been so full of life, who would make a special and precious husband and father, suddenly eclipsed all else in her consciousness. The thought of life without him was too much to bear and contemplate...and so she broke off talking and the entire room was silent for a few moments.

Chiang broke that silence.

"Mother and father, I only wish I could go with you!"

Turning to Hua, she looked at him imploringly.

"Hua, do you think I should put in a request at work...would they approve it?

"Would there be any negative repercussions?"

Hua had come to love and respect this entire family that had made China their home and done so much for his nation. He was impressed with Lu's achievements and recognized him as a People's hero...not because of the association and opportunities it might open to him, but because he genuinely hailed and revered what Lu had accomplished. He respected Kao and knew of the upbringing he must have had to be so willing to fight for China, his adopted home.

Most of all, he was in love with Chiang...this marvelously talented and beautiful woman who was as driven as her father.

Letting go of her hand, he used his other hand to gently place his finger under her chin and raise it up so she was looking at him. He had never seen her like this...and it touched his heart to see her emotions and love for her family.

"Chiang, of course you should put in a request.

"I know you do not consider such things….and I know that you would not seek favor or advancement as a result of such things…and I know that you eschew anyone who would use their position to seek favor or advancement. But I promise you, with your father being a Hero of the People's Republic, and with his recent advancement not only onto the Politburo, but onto the Executive Council at the express request of the President… there will not be a problem.

"My guess is your supervisors and their managers will jump at the chance to make sure your schedule is arranged so that you can make this trip as easy as possible. They probably will suggest that you make sure your father knows who it was that approved the trip.

"If I could come with you I would, but unfortunately the campaign for mayor here in Beijing will not wait, and the vote will come in March, whether I am here or not.

"From what your mother is saying, you may well find yourself over in that part of the world until that time. My only regret will be that we are so far apart for so long."

Chiang threw her arms around Hua and hugged him, smiling at her parents as she did so.

"Father, Mother, would you mind? Can I come with you?"

Song's answer was immediate. "Of course you can, Chiang. I know that your brother will be helped by your being there. It will brighten up his mood considerably and we all know that a person's mental attitude is an important part of his health."

Lu was a little slower in responding. After a few seconds, Chiang's smile faded a little, expecting that there was some obstacle.

"Chiang, I too want you to be there. I know it will help Kao. But I have some reservations. The area is near the combat zone. Australia has been invaded by the Americans and their allies, and there is a great battle raging there now.

"Rabaul is a critical staging area for our forces in defending Australia, and in defending approaches to our homeland from the southwest Pacific.

"There will be danger and I think we should carefully consider it before making that decision. I have a hard enough time accepting your mother on this trip because of the danger. But, as you know, she is headstrong and has insisted."

Smiling now, Chiang quickly responded to her father. "And I am my mother's daughter, father…and just as headstrong. Just ask Hua."

Hua lowered his eyes sheepishly, smiling while shaking his head in clear agreement with the obvious.

And Lu knew his daughter…and also knew when he had been soundly defeated and over-ridden.

"All right, all right!" he said, raising his hands in a mock attempt to ward off a fictional attack. "I had to point out the dangers. But I know we all love Kao as much as he loves us and are willing to take those risks.

"Besides, we will be accompanied by an elite, combined arms security brigade whom the President informs me are the absolute best in the business. We will have aircraft, troops, and even a specially outfitted destroyer at our disposal.

"I'll meet with the executive committee day after tomorrow and should know the final travel schedule then."

January 14, 2010, 20:12 MDT
Boise International Airport
Boise, Idaho

Geneva Campbell was a little worried because Alan's plane was now more than twelve minutes late…but she was not overly concerned. A few minutes late was not at all unusual from what the others who were also waiting on the plane had said.

"I've waited months and months to see my son," she told one woman who waiting for her husband. "I suppose I can wait another few minutes."

Several of the others, when they discovered that she was waiting for a Marine who had been serving in Siberia, thanked her for her son's service to the country. They also thanked her for raising her son in such a fashion that he would want to serve.

One older gentleman, upon hearing that Alan was in the Corps, came over and sat with Geneva while she waited. It seemed he was a veteran, a Marine himself, who had served his first tour of duty in Vietnam in 1972, and had served his last one during Desert Storm in 1991.

So it was, when Alan came walking off the aircraft, wearing his dress uniform, there were applause from the people standing there waiting for him...first from the few Geneva had been able to talk to, and then spreading to almost everyone in that section of the concourse. Somewhat unsettled by all of the attention, Alan walked up to his mother and gave her a big hug.

When he was finished, the older gentleman touched him on the shoulder, got his attention and shook his hand.

"Sergeant, I want to thank you on behalf of myself and my family, for your service to our Republic...to our nation and our freedoms.

"From this old gunny, all I can say is, *Semper Fi!*"

Alan knew immediately that he was talking to another Marine. He introduced himself as Master Gunnery Sergeant Jason Gwinn and, as others shook his hand and voiced their thanks, Alan and his mother waited while the old gunnery sergeant met his wife and then made introductions.

The four of them then walked down the concourse together discussing their families, the progress of the war and the conditions in America. All of them agreed that the overall experience had brought everyone together as Americans like no other event in their memory, despite the hardships and sacrifices…or perhaps because of them. One example of this rediscovered togetherness was that there were very few, if any, hyphenated Americans now…just Americans. If someone tried to identify themselves or another as such, they were almost universally corrected with a simple, *"You mean American, don't you?"*

Alan had not considered himself an *"African-American"* since he couldn't remember when. Whites, blacks, browns, reds, and every other variety of citizen were working together as Americans in this conflict, fighting together…dying together. There just wasn't time or inclination for the vast majority of Americans to worry about such foolishness when they were fighting for their very survival.

"And that means there never really was any time to worry about it," Alan realized as the conversation continued.

When the Gunny heard that Alan's brother was Leon Campbell, he stopped in the middle of the hallway and again shook both Alan's and Geneva's hands. He knew all about Leon's exploits and his citation. He made a point of knowing all of the Marine Corps Medal of Honor winners and had not put the Campbells' names together here in Boise, Idaho, until Alan mentioned it.

"I can't tell you what a pleasure it is to meet the brother and mother of a Medal of Honor winner…and to see the younger brother following in his brother's footsteps," he said.

"God bless you. God bless you all."

As the four of them exited the terminal building, they parted as the best of newfound friends and shared addresses and phone numbers. The gunny lived only about twenty-five miles away in a small town called Emmett, where he and his wife had retired.

"We live up on the bench on the north side of town," he told them.

"A beautiful rural American town, rooted in agriculture with its values and principles rooted firmly in God's green earth, where they live the parable of the harvest every day…you reap what you sow. One day when you get married and start having kids, think about coming out here…great place to raise a family."

"In the meantime, Alan, you, your mother, your brother Leon, and any of your family or friends are welcome out at our place anytime. I know Melba will cook you up a fine meal…and we can go out in my back pasture, that runs clears up against the butte, and shoot my Barretts .50 cal. rifle and talk about old times."

Both Geneva and Alan thanked Jason Gwinn graciously and indicated they would take him up on his gracious invitation at least once while Alan was on leave…and more often after the war. Alan was certain that Leon would want to meet Gunny as well.

All of it was almost overwhelming. As they got into the car, Alan spoke to his mother across the car. "What a neat thing, Mom, to come home to a spontaneous welcome like this.

"When I walked off the plane, I thought you must have arranged all of that or something."

Geneva smiled, knowing how it seemed, but also grateful for the people who had so spontaneously responded to her son's homecoming. It was like something you read about, but never really expect to happen to you.

After they had gotten into the car and as they were putting on their seatbelts, she responded, "I know. I was worried when your plane was late and started asking some of the people waiting if all of this was normal…if I should be concerned.

"They were all so nice and began to get excited when they heard that one of our boys was coming home on leave on that flight.

Then I began to worry about what you would think of all of the attention, that it might be embarrassing.

"But, Alan, all of those folks, all on their own, were anxious to welcome you home. To welcome anyone home who has been fighting in this war.

"...and the Gwinns were sure special, now weren't they? I believe you boys have found a friend for life."

Leaving the airport, they got onto Interstate Highway 84, and traveled west towards the expressway connector that led towards downtown Boise and their home off of Orchard Avenue.

Alan sat in contemplation for most of the ten minute ride, thinking about his experiences, about his home and conditions here in America and the realities he had witnessed in Africa and Siberia. As they exited the freeway and turned onto Orchard, he tried to articulate his feelings as best he could to his mother.

"Mom, you know, over the last year I have a learned a lot...seen a lot. I thought I had made some big changes in the years preceding my war experience, what with us moving here to Idaho from the ghetto in Chicago and all.

"But now I realize that all of that was just setting the stage.

"We are so lucky...so blessed in this country, Mom! I don't think there's another place on this planet, based on what I have seen, where a family could do what we did. Where there is so much opportunity if people will just make the effort to work hard and pursue it. They got to just look past all of that bickering and social squabbling...all of those people trying to keep others penned up in stereotypes, buying their votes.

"I'll tell you this, Mom. Ain't none of that on the battlefield...and from what I can see, there's not much of it here at home anymore either."

Geneva cherished the change she had seen in her sons over the last few years associated with their move to Idaho…but particularly since they both had gone into the Marines, been trained, and been out in the world.

"Alan, your Papa, God rest his soul, he knew these things all along. He used to talk in much the same way you are now, using many of the same words to express many of the same thoughts…you're more like him than you know.

"Anyhow, he would get into some real heated discussions, and even into some trouble with the local politicians and leaders, back there in Chicago.

"That's why I was so touched by the experiences Leon had when he was coming out of that coma. I know he saw Jerome, your father, there in Heaven, or whatever place Leon was visiting while he was unconscious. I know he is there waiting for each of us.

"I know he would be proud of you both, Alan.

"As terrible and dangerous as this war has been, it has brought most Americans to the point where they are looking past all of that previous foolishness and looking instead at what they can become with the freedoms we enjoy…and how they can help others. As much as I look forward to the end of this war, to when you boys can be safe back home and starting families of your own…and as much as I ache over the terrible losses, I am grateful for the change in the people and I am grateful that we are making progress and beating these monsters who would take it all away from us and away from everyone on the planet."

Alan was surprised at the length of his mother's statement and the passion with which she spoke…and he was proud of her. She embodied the principles they were talking about and she had tried her best to pass them on to her sons. It was clear to him now, more than ever, that both his Mom and Dad were solid–rock solid–people and Americans, and he was so proud to be their son.

"Well, I have to tell you, Mom, we've still got a long and hard fight ahead of us. Those people have been indoctrinated in what it is they believe and they fight us tooth and nail. But we are winning, Mom, and pushing them back.

"I believe that, as soon as they finally realize that we are not going to make peace, that we are taking this all the way to Beijing…and as soon as the large portions of the people in the nations that they are subjugating to make their machine work, as well as citizens of their own countries…realize that that God-awful machine is vulnerable and breaking down, I believe we are going to have a lot of help finishing these tyrants off.

"We've just got one heck of a long road, a long difficult march, before we get there.

"But enough of all of this philosophy and war talk…let's move on to what's really important this evening.

"What you got on the stove for your boy, huh? What's for supper?"

February 11, 02:05, local time
124 Kilometers South of Vladivostok
The Sea of Japan

The large convoy was moving north, towards the petroleum terminals and docks at Vladivostok. Five supertankers, eight large container ships and six smaller transports escorted by two Jiangwei II frigates, a Luda III class destroyer, and a single Luhu destroyer.

The Jiangwei frigates and the Luhu destroyer had all been upgraded to the latest sonar, radar and defensive weapons suite that the Chinese offered and they were formidable vessels for escort duty. Both the Luhu and the Luda were outfitted with four LRASD weapons each, suited for use against any enemy submarines that might penetrate the four corner defensive formation they were using to defend the tight formation of tankers, container vessels, and transports they were shepherding.

The box was sixteen kilometers across, sixteen kilometers between escorting vessels on each corner, with the merchant vessels in a tighter formation in the middle that was four kilometers across. The entire group was under constant air coverage from patrol craft operating out of Vladivostok.

Suddenly, without warning, the Luhu destroyer blew up in a huge and terrible explosion that ripped vertically across its midsection and literally tore the entire ship in two. Within seconds, the other leading escort, one of the Jiangwei II frigates, also exploded with deafening *BOOM!* that echoed across the entire formation.

Warning messages were immediately communicated to all vessels and aircraft...though none of them needed the official messages to understand that they were under attack on this clear night. The light, smoke, and debris from the explosions were visible to all. One Badger patrol aircraft saw the first two explosions clearly from its altitude of twenty thousand feet at a distance of over forty kilometers.

Within another ten seconds more horrific explosions cascaded through the formation of ships being escorted. Each of the tankers was hit twice and blew up. Three of the container ships and two of the cargo vessels all exploded in a similar fashion. The worst explosions were aboard the tankers as their huge cargoes of petroleum products were complete ignited by the initial detonations that assaulted them

From above, an SU-24 Fencer maritime patrol aircraft was in a position to see the assault on the inner group of merchant vessels before the wave of explosions engulfed them. Later, they reported seeing what appeared to be the slightest hint of several underwater streaks approaching the vessels, becoming more apparent and more resolute as they approached the ships, culminating in the tremendous explosions that racked the vessels. The streaks were coming at the formation of ships from over one hundred and eighty degrees to their front, spread out to hit each of the ships that had been attacked.

Within ten minutes the attack was over except for the continued blaring of the warning klaxons from those vessels that had not been hit. There had been no hint of any approaching weapons on the sonar of any of the escorting ships. Outside of the report from the single patrol aircraft, there had been no visible sighting of the impending disaster.

The ships scattered and completed their journey into Vladivostok during the rest of the early morning hours, the last two ships limping into port near noon, having been damaged from the proximity of the explosions of two of the tankers and the debris that had rained down upon them.

Chinese naval analysts immediately began to pore over the data from the surviving ships, the eyewitness reports and the data from patrol aircraft that had been over the scene. Within twenty-four hours, they had reached an initial conclusion and passed the report on to COSTIND and to the higher level officials who had gotten word of the attack and were demanding answers.

February 13, 2010, 17:36, local time
Captain's Quarters, USS Jimmy Carter
400 miles west of Hakodate, Japan

The Chinese analysts had come to the conclusion that America had finally employed some sort of offensive, supercavitating weapon of their own, and they had been right. The propulsion system and the material that the weapon was either made out of, or coated with, was a mystery to the Chinese. But the signs of the rapid approach and the terrible explosions were clear evidence.

Captain Simon Thompson was sitting in his cabin, completing the final after action report for the attack he had conducted on that large Chinese convoy. It had been successful beyond his hopes or imagination. For once, there had been no return fire. The devices had worked as advertised and had left little trail of their approach.

"Even if the Chinese had shot down the azimuth of what little trail those weapons left," he thought, "they would have come up completely empty-handed.

"I'll bet they figured they were attacked by three or more boats…and that they have no idea from what distance the attacks had occurred."

But Captain Thompson knew all of those things.

America's newest naval weapons system, the submarine-launched Mk-77, had just received its baptism of fire and it had operated almost completely flawlessly.

Thompson had released eighteen of the weapons. Only one of them had failed to operate and had sunk to the bottom of the Sea of Japan. The other seventeen had performed flawlessly.

Programmable from aboard ship either before launch, or after launch as long as the control wiring remained attached, the long, sleek supercavitating torpedoes were stealthy, capable of loiter, and capable of making their attacks from almost anywhere on the compass. And, with the new synthetic fuel products that had been developed specifically for them, in either conventional or rocket-propelled mode they left very little evidence of their presence.

"That is, until just before they strike home," thought the Captain as he continued to type in the details of the attack.

Running towards their target at an extreme depth, up to one thousand five hundred feet, or loitering at that same depth, the weapons attacked at a steep angle from beneath. That angle was of course programmable, but since the trail of the weapon would become visible on the surface after the weapon passed through a depth of fifty feet, the designers presumed that most attacks would utilize the deep attack approach.

Which is exactly what Captain Thompson had ordered.

Their warheads were a wonder. The plastic explosive packed into the warhead kept the weight down but was capable of producing the equivalent of up to three-quarters of a ton of TNT. The yield and certain characteristics of how the explosion penetrated the side of the target vessel were also programmable and could be adjusted for maximum effect against various types of targets.

The maximum range was over one hundred and twenty miles, but that was also variable depending on the loiter time, the target acquisition and approach parameters that could be programmed into the microelectronic brain of each weapon. Under full rocket power, the weapon had a range of almost fifteen miles and could reach speeds in excess of five hundred knots.

The Jimmy Carter had fired these weapons from a range of more than seventy miles. The Chinese never saw or heard the Jimmy Carter, and she had been well off the azimuth of any of the terminal attack bearings of any of the devices.

"…and we fired them right out of our standard torpedo tubes," the Captain emphasized to himself.

"Just a little longer than an ADCAP Mk-48, about the same weight…but a lot meaner looking and a whole lot more wallop," he concluded as he finished the report.

His last statement, after a summary of the vessels sunk, the effect of the explosions as measured through his own passive detection gear, and the report on the failure of the one device, was adamant and to the point.

"In summary, the initial combat test of the Mk-77 Supercavitating Weapons Systems (SCWS) has been an unqualified success."

"It is the recommendation of this command that we outfit all Sea Wolf, Virginia, and remaining LA Class boats with a full offensive complement of these weapons.

"That would include:

22 Mk-77 SCWS

8 Mk-48 ADCAPs

8 Mk-50s

12 Tomahawk SLCMs

"The Alaska class SSTNs and the Ohio class SSGNs should also carry a reduced number of these weapons for self-defense purposes against either surface or submerged threats."

Epilogue

March 4, 2010, 18:47 Mean Time
Bridge of the USSS Gaspra
In orbit around Ceres
The Asteroid Belt

David Lewis watched as his team brought another piece of the asteroid up into orbit and secured it to the train he was building. That team consisted of six specialists working with the Frigate's lander and the mining and cabling equipment that had been brought into space for just this purpose.

They had arrived in orbit around Ceres, the largest asteroid in the asteroid belt, almost two weeks earlier and had immediately set about their task with a will. This forty-ton rock was the third that the team operating off of the Gaspra had cut out of the massive hulk of Ceres which was a little less than a third the size of Earth's moon. The team operating off of the USSS Ida, Floyd Clark's vessel, was a little behind the Gaspra operation and was completing its second excavation and transport into orbit during this shift.

The material was a dark, rocky material called carbonaceous chrondrite, similar in appearance and substance to what made up many meteorites. Because of this, Ceres was classified generally as a Class M asteroid, but it was a special Class M, and the special nature of its composition is what had brought the Gaspra and Ida here, to Ceres, for this mission. Ceres' material had registered on the spectro-analyzers from Earth as being somewhat harder and less porous to other forms of carbonaceous chrondrite. Tests performed when they first arrived proved this to be the case, which made it an excellent choice for material for their purposes. Over the next six weeks they intended to cut out a total of forty of these rocks, twenty per vessel, and place them in orbit in chains behind the Gaspra and Ida for transport back to Earth.

Commander Lewis had his communications specialist contact Commander Clark on the Ida once he saw that the eighth rock was finally secured in position in the chain.

"F.L., this is Lewis. We have number four in position and I am going to have my team start the preparatory work for cutting out number five on this shift. What's keeping you guys?

"We're going to be two up on you in another few days if you're not careful. Over."

It didn't take very long for Clark's witty response to be communicated back to the Gaspra.

"I roger that, Gaspra.

"What can I say? Some folks prefer fast and loose…others prefer slow and steady. We'll finish number three today, but will not get started on four until next shift. Each and every one of them will be within allowed tolerance of composition and mass. We intend to keep it that way and finish within the schedule of the mission.

"Over."

Commander Lewis responded.

"OK…We have four of the same.

"As to fast and loose versus slow and steady…once in a while you meet a team that is fast and steady. That's us."

"All chatter aside, I want to finish ahead of schedule if I can so we can take some extra time on our visit to Pallas inbound. It's a little further out of the way than your secondary objective, Vesta, and I want to ensure that we have sufficient time for a thorough study.

"So, we'll target a departure date of Gaspra on April 10th or 11th if things continue to proceed this well. If we get approval, we'll have to alter the mission plan accordingly.

"We'll plan on keeping the same inbound rendezvous point and schedule in accordance with the current plan. That means we'll meet just inside of the orbit of Mars.

"Please come up with an altered communication plan to conform with that objective and get it back to me ASAP.

"Over."

Clark knew that Lewis was excited about the prospect of more exploration; it was in his nature, and he wanted to get as much benefit out of the mission as possible while they were out here.

But Clark also had a feeling that the Joint Chiefs and the NCA would want to get those rocks back into Earth orbit as soon as possible, particularly if it was discovered that there was any slack whatsoever in the schedule.

"Wilco, Commander. We'll get an altered plan outlining the communication and other objectives that you have outlined to you by 0900 hours tomorrow.

"But, if I may, you might find that command wants us to expedite things and cut out the secondary targets altogether if we have enough rocks and any extra time.

"Satellite photos of Australia and the latest SITREP show things proceeding faster than expected there. We've punched through Chinese lines in the Channel Country and are driving on Alice Springs. It looks like a large force of Chinese has been cut off on the Cape York Peninsula, and that the CAS is making a massive resupply or evacuation effort there.

"If we have that kind of success elsewhere, they may want to move the timetable for our operation up. If they do, I bet they'll order us home quicker and forgo the secondary research objectives.

"Just the same, we'll get that plan to you as advertised.

"Over."

"I read you loud and clear on that, Ida," Lewis replied. "At least we'll give them the option to enhance the research objective…they can decide from there. I'll look for your plan around 0900 tomorrow.

"Gaspra, out."

April 15, 2010, 11:20 Local Time
Executive Council Chambers
Politburo, Beijing, China

President Jien Zemin expected good news. He and the rest of this committee needed good news, and he demanded good news on behalf of himself and his nation. And today was the day he expected COSTIND to deliver.

"General Hunbaio, please proceed with your report."

General Hunbaio was aware of his leader's discomfort and expectations…and he was painfully aware of the reasons for it. Lately, from near earth space, to the oceans, and on land, Chinese fortunes, and those of her allies had been faring badly. After so many years of success…after so much territory won…it was hard to take the setbacks and reversals. Hard militarily and hard politically.

Ultimately, if the setbacks were not arrested, they would lead to doubts, and doubts would lead to questioning, and questioning would lead to disaffection, and disaffection would lead to unrest, and ultimately rebellion. Chinese leaders had walked a razor's edge in modern times since the Long March of Mao and the cultural revolution. It was the same razor's edge that imperial Chinese leaders had been forced to walk for many millennia.

Now Jien Zemin could see that edge on the near horizon and he did not like it. He was depending on Hunbaio and his people, like

Lu Pham, to come up with something to counter the Americans, and once again place China and her allies in the leading role in this war. In the role from whose vantage point she could dictate the pace and the flavor of this conflict and its ultimate outcome.

For almost four full years the Chinese had done precisely that. Everything had gone as Jien and his inner cadre, including the General himself, had planned and predicted it would go in conducting the war effort. But everyone in this room knew that, over the last year, the Chinese and their allies had somehow lost their grip on the pivotal role and were now relegated to principally reacting defensively to their enemy's initiatives.

Hunbaio knew that this was an unacceptable position, both militarily and politically, and he knew that something extraordinary was required. Something that could challenge the new technologies and advantages that the Americans were coming up with. Something to once again throw them off balance so China could regain the initiative, pass it on to their allies and retake all that had been lost.

And General Hunbaio believed that he had just the information that the President was looking for. "Mr. President, I have some extremely good news. We have completed the final atmospheric testing of our new Dragon Spirit prototype craft, in the Altyn Tagh region near Lenghu. This is a very secret and very remote facility employing our highest technology and most advanced defensive systems. The nearest thing it could be compared to is the Americans skunk works in Nevada.

"Initial feedback on the tests indicates that the six prototypes were completely successful in all of their operational tests within the atmosphere, exceeding expectations in several critical areas, including particle weapon tests, maneuverability, and electronic warfare.

"Beginning in May, they will be tested in space, using special SSTO orbits that keep them well clear of the American space stations for the time being, although at that point their existence will become obvious to the Americans and their allies.

"Production builds have already begun in anticipation of a successful battery of space-based tests. This decision was made on my own authority, Mr. President, with input from Admiral Lu Pham and from Sung Hsu, a leading manufacturing technologist who has spent years working with Admiral Lu.

"It became clear from their input that, barring any unforeseen catastrophic problems, we would be able to retrofit any minor adjustments to the units of the initial production run after analyzing and adjusting the design as required based on the atmospheric and space-based tests.

"I am happy to say that, based on the atmospheric tests that we have just completed, there will be no alterations required. We expect to be able to produce five of these craft per month beginning in April, Mr. President."

Jien Zemin was ecstatic. This was precisely the type of report he had hoped for. He also respected and appreciated Hunbaio's initiative and risk in ordering the production runs. Success in the testing put him, and the program, in a position to make a tremendous difference in a shorter period of time, probably saving many weeks, if not months, on the schedule.

"This *is* excellent news, General. I commend you on the successful tests and on your own initiative…"

As he said this, Zenim turned and faced the video conference screen directly, speaking to Lu Pham who was attending the meeting from facilities in Rabaul.

"…and the use of your very capable employees…and I am speaking of you Admiral Lu…regarding the production schedule.

"Now, here is my directive.

"We shall not perform the initial space-based tests using the hyperbolic orbits you have described. The reasons for deleting these tests are not technical; they are political and they are military, and they are well worth the risk we take in doing so.

"Our sources in the United Kingdom and in Russia indicate that the next American space station will be launched into orbit over the central Pacific in early to mid-May of this year. Its presence there, as is the case with their other two stations, is completely unacceptable.

"They have damaged us significantly in Australia with their Southern Star station, and any similar presence over the central Pacific will allow them to accelerate their offensive operations against us with a much greater chance of success.

"I am ordering you, General Hunbaio, to work directly with the PLA and our space defense forces to see to it that the space-based test of the Dragon's Spirit craft in May is a combat test. You, along with General Hsua'ba, are authorized to plan a mission to intercept the new American space craft after they are launched and while they enter orbit to build their new station.

"Plan immediate follow on missions, presuming a success in the first, against the American Southern Star station and then against the American Conception station. I want them all brought down, and I want their destruction to be as visible and evident as possible over Australia and America.

"In addition, I want production rates for these craft doubled by June so that it is we, the People's Republic of China, who exert a complete and uncontested control over space by July of this year and on into the foreseeable future.

"We shall see how the American leaders and those of their allies enjoy defeat and helplessness in space, just as they have sought to exert those same conditions on us.

"They shall soon find that we are not helpless…no, not helpless or defeated at all."

The End of Volume IV.

Maps and Illustrations

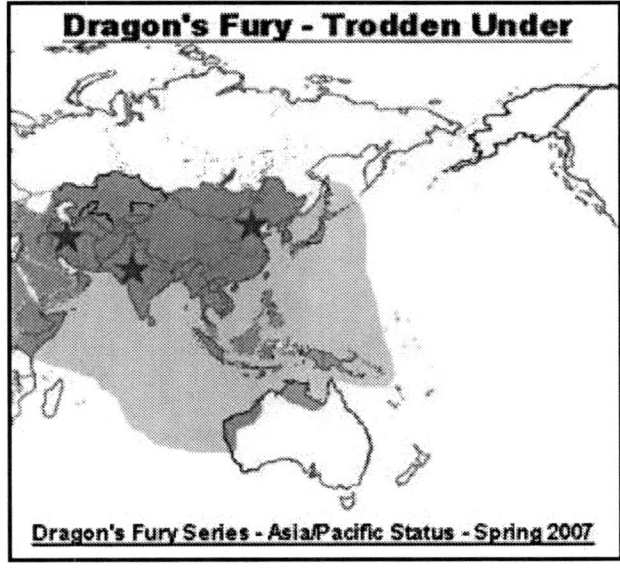

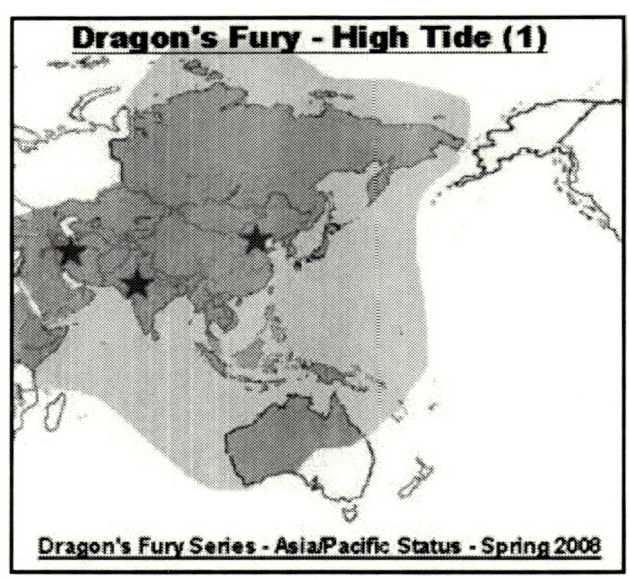

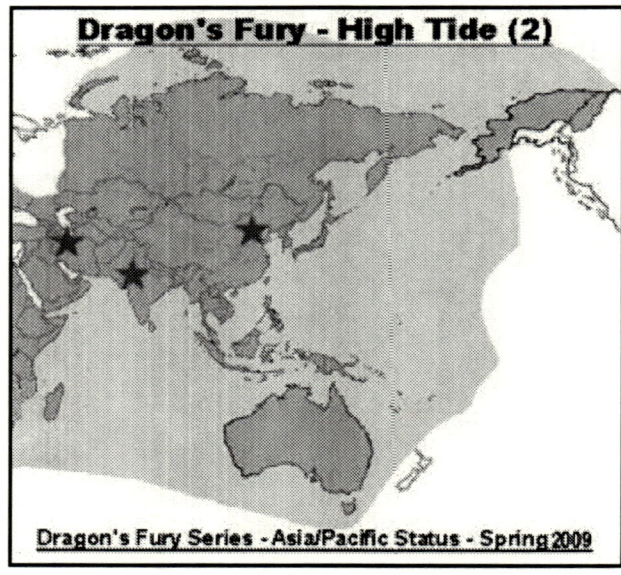

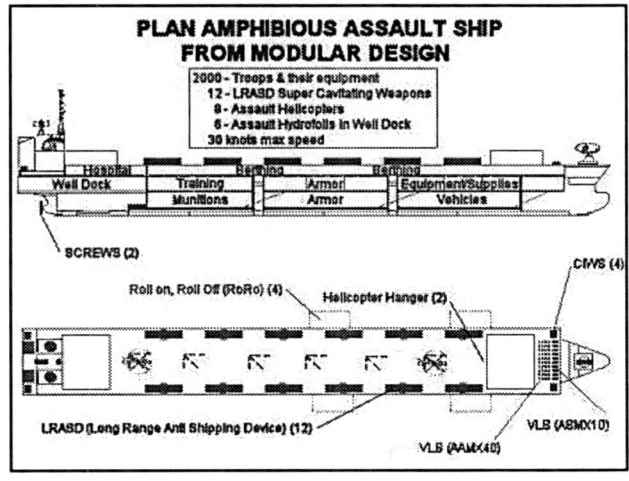

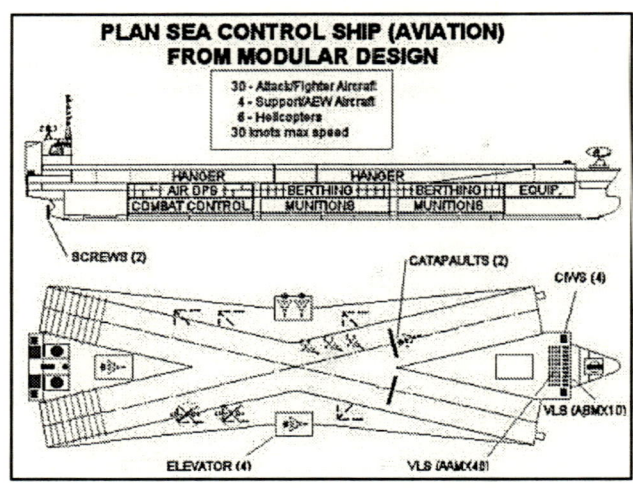

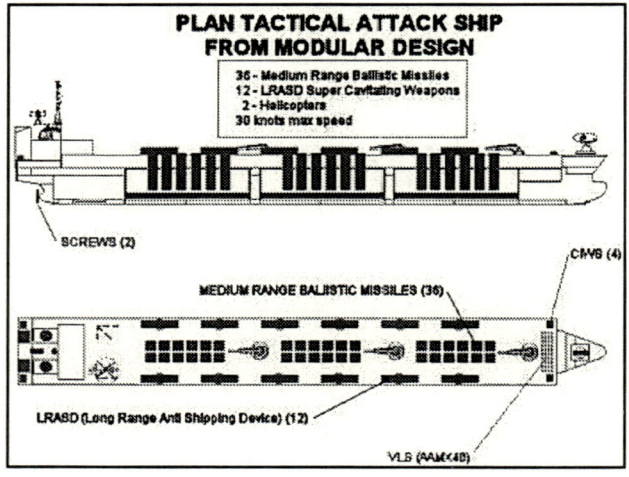

Glossary of Terms and Acronyms

TERM/ACRONYM	DEFINITION
AAW	Anti-Aircraft Warfare
Abrams	Premier main battle tank designated M1A1. (U.S.)
ABM	Anti-Ballistic Missile
ABS	American Broadcasting System
ADCAP	Advanced Capability
AEGIS	An advanced phased array radar system for acquiring, tracking and engaging airborne targets (U.S. Navy)
AH-64	Most capable western attack helicopter called Apache (U.S.)
ALCM	Air Launched Cruise Missile
ALRAAM	Advanced Long Range Anti-Aircraft Missile
AMRAAM	Advanced Medium Range Air to Air Missile
Apache	Most capable western attack helicopter designated AH-64 (U.S.)
APS	Armored Personnel Carrier
APSRON	Afloat Pre-positioning Ship Squadron (U.S. Navy)
ARCM	Anti-Radiation Cruise Missile
ASAT	Anti-Satellite
ASDS	Advanced SEAL Delivery System
ASROC	Anti-Submarine Rocket assisted torpedo
ASV	Armored Security Vehicle designated M1117A
ASW	Anti-Submarine Warfare
ATO	Asian Theater of Operations
AV-8B+	VTOL or STOL fighter-bomber used by U.S. Marines called Harrier. (U.S.)
Avenger	AAW variant of HMMWV carrying Stinger missiles. (U.S.)
AWACS	Airborne warning and command aircraft
B-1B	Advanced supersonic, Long range bomber called Lancer or Bone (U.S.)
B-2	Sub-sonic, long range stealth strike bomber called Spirit (U.S.)
Backfire	Supersonic, long range Russian strike aircraft, exported and license built designated TU-22M. (Red China, India)
Badger	Older, subsonic, 1970's vintage Russian strike aircraft export designated TU-16(Red China, India, GIR)
Bandit	Enemy Aircraft
BATF	Bureau of Alcohol, Tobacco and Firearms (U.S.)

TERM/ACRONYM	DEFINITION
BDA	Bomb or Battle Damage Assessment
Bear	Older, prop-driven Russian reconnaissance & ASW aircraft designated TU-142. Exported and license built. (India)
BMD	Ballistic Missile Defense
BRITREP	British Representative
Buddy Stores	Refueling tanks
C-90A	Huge surface-wave lift transport aircraft developed by the U.S.
CANTFOR	Canadian Task Force
CAP	Combat Air Patrol
CAS	Coalition of Asian States
CBC	Continental Broadcasting Company
CBG	Carrier Battle Group
CBT	Carrier Battle Task Force
CENTCOM	Central Command (U.S.)
CIA	Central Intelligence Agency (U.S.)
CIC	Combat Information Center
CINC	Commander in Chief
CINCCENT	Commander in Chief Central (U.S.)
CINCPAC	Commander in Chief Pacific (U.S.)
CIR	Council on International Relations
CIWS	Close in Weapons System
CNO	Chief of Naval Operations (U.S.)
CO	Commanding Officer
Comanche	Advanced, stealthy recon/attack helicopter. RAH-66 (U.S.)
Condition Zebra	Watertight combat threat condition for naval vessels.
CONUS	Continental United States
COSAS	Coalition of South American States
COSCO	China Ocean-going Ship Company
COSTIND	Commission of Science, Technology & Industry for National Defense (Red China).
CTF	Combined Task Force
CVN, CVX	Nuclear Powered Aircraft Carrier, CVX is the latest generation
DDG	Guided Missile Destroyer
DDH	Large helicopter carrying destroyer
DDX	Advanced Guided Missiles Destroyer (U.S.)
DNC	Democratic National Committee
DOE	Department of Energy (U.S.)
Dragon's Fury	Chinese operation in March 2006 to ambush the U,S, 7th Fleet.

TERM/ACRONYM	DEFINITION
E-2C	Naval Airborne Early Warning and Command aircraft called Hawkeye. (U.S.)
E-3	Air Force warning and command aircraft called Sentry. (U.S., U.K., Japan)
Eagle	High performance, supersonic fighter aircraft designated F-15C. (U.S.)
ELINT	Electronic Intelligence
EMCOMM	Electronic Emissions and Communications
EMP	Electromagnetic Pulse
EMT	Emergency Medical Technician
ETO	European Theater of Operations
EU	European Union
EW	Electronic Warfare
F/A-18E	Most modern, supersonic, high-performance naval fighter/attack aircraft called Super Hornet. (U.S.)
F/A-18F	Two seat attack/strike/EW version of F/A-18E. (U.S.)
F-14D	Latest upgrade (early 90's) of supersonic, high performance, long range, 1970's carrier based fighter/bomber called Tomcat (U.S.)
F-15	High performance, supersonic fighter aircraft called Eagle (U.S.)
F-15E	Two-seat strike version of F-15C aircraft called Strike Eagle (U.S.)
F-16	Highly maneuverable fighter/bomber called Falcon or Viper (U.S. and allies)
F-22	Advanced, stealthy, high performance fighter, the Raptor (U.S.)
F-35	New, very advanced, multi-service fighter-bomber called the Joint Strike Fighter. STOL and VTOL. (U.S. and allies)
Falcon	Highly maneuverable fighter/bomber, F-16 (U.S. and allies)
FBC-7	Long range strike aircraft (Red China)
FBI	Federal Bureau of Investigation (U.S.)
FEMA	Federal Emergency Management Agency (U.S.)
Fencer	Long Range Strike Aircraft called designated SU-24 (China. GIR and India)
FFG	Guided Missiles Frigate
Flanker	Advanced Russian fighter/bomber exported and license built designated SU-30. (Red China, GIR, India)
Foxbat	High speed, 1970's vintage Russian export interceptor designated MIG-25. (North Korea, GIR).
FTP	File Transfer Protocol

TERM/ACRONYM	DEFINITION
Fulcrum	High performance Russian export and license built fighter bomber designated MIG-29 (Red China, India, GIR)
GIR	Greater Islamic Republic
Global Sentinel	High altitude, long endurance unmanned aerial vehicle. (U.S.)
GOA	Government Office of Accounting
GPS	Global Positioning System
HARM	High-speed Anti-Radiation Missile
Harrier	VTOL or STOL fighter bomber used by U.S. Marines and U.S. allies designated AV-8B+ (U.S.)
Hawkeye	Naval Airborne Early Warning and Command aircraft designated E-2C. (U.S., Taiwan, Japan, France)
HELLFIRE	Laser guided anti-tank or surface missile (U.S.)
HGP	Human Genome Project
HMMWV	High Mobility Multipurpose Wheeled Vehicle
HR-7	Hyper-velocity, exo-atmosphere reconnaissance and surveillance aircraft called the Thunder Dart. (U.S.)
HUMRAMM	AAW variant of HMMWV carrying ground-launched AMRAAM missiles. (U.S.)
ICBM	Intercontinental Ballistic Missile (Nuclear)
IDF	Israeli Defense Force, or Indigenous Defense Fighter (ROC)
IFF	Identification Friend or Foe designator
IFV	Infantry Fighting Vehicle
INS	Immigration and Naturalization Service
J-10	Advanced fighter/interceptor/attack aircraft. (Red China)
JGI	Joint Genome Institute (U.S.)
JH-7	Long range interceptor aircraft (Red China)
JMSDF	Japanese Maritime Self Defense Force
JSF	Joint Strike Fighter (U.S.)
JSOW	Joint Standoff Weapon
JSTAR	Battlefield management aircraft using synthetic aperture radar and advanced processing (U.S.)
KEDS	Kinetic Energy Defense System (On board U.S. Space Ships)
KFOR	Korean Forces
KS-2(+)	Advanced surface to air missile, Plus (+) variety has similar characteristics to Patriot. (Red China)
KS-3	Advanced version of the KS-2+ missile capable of TMD (Red China)
KV	Kill Vehicle
Lancer	Advanced supersonic, long-range bomber, the B-1B (U.S.)

TERM/ACRONYM	DEFINITION
LAWS	Light Armor Weapon System
LAX	Los Angeles International Airport
LCU	Landing Craft Utility
LRASD	Long Range Anti-Shipping Device
LWS	Laser Weapon System (Aboard U.S. Space Ships)
M1117A	New generation Armored Security Vehicle (U.S.)
M1A1	Premier main battle tank called Abrams. (U.S.)
Mach	Designation for the speed of sound
MAD	Mutually Assured Destruction
Mk-77 SCWS	New American Supercavitating Torpedo system
MLRS	Multiple Launch Rocket System
MEB	Marine Expeditionary Brigade (U.S.)
MEU	Marine Expeditionary Unit (U.S.)
MFD, MFCD	Multi Function Display, Multi Function Color Display
MIG-25	High speed, 1970's vintage, Russian exported interceptor called Foxbat. (North Korea, GIR).
MIG-29	High performance Russian export and license built fighter bomber called Fulcrum (Red China, India, GIR)
MOS	Military Occupational Specialty
MPSRON	Maritime Pre-positioning Ship Squadron (U.S. Navy)
MUAS	Miniature Underwater All-aspect Surveillance Devices
NAFTA	North American Free Trade Agreement
NAS	National Academy of Sciences (U.S.)
NASA	National Aeronautical and Space Administration
NATO	North Atlantic Treaty Organization
NCA	National Command Authority (The President of the United States)
NCO	Non-Commissioned Officer in the military
NEW	National Endowment for Women
NGO	Non-Governmental Organization (Affiliated with the United Nations)
NHGRI	National Health Genome Research Institute (U.S.)
NIH	National Institute of Health (U.S.)
NORAD	North American Air Defense Command (U.S. and Canada)
NORCOM	Northern Command (U.S.)
NRO	National Reconnaissance Office (U.S.)
NSA	National Security Advisor or Agency (U.S.)
OIC	Officer in Charge

TERM/ACRONYM	DEFINITION
OPLAN	Operation Plan
Orion	Turbo prop ASW, Recon & strike aircraft designate P-3C (U.S. and allies)
P-3C	Turbo prop ASW, Recon & strike aircraft called Orion (U.S. and allies)
Patriot Missile	Land based, long range, anti-aircraft missile system.
PCRM	Poly-carbon Reactive Mesh defense for U.S. Space Ships
PDWE	Pulse Detonation Wave Engine
Peacekeeper APC	Highly exported APC armed with .50 cal. machine gun. (U.S.)
Pervador	New high speed, high altitude, reconnaissance and surveillance aircraft designated SR-77. Replaced the SR-71 Blackbird. (U.S.)
Phoenix	Long range air to air missile designated AIM-54 (U.S.)
PKF	Patriotic Kurdistan Front
PLA	People's Liberation Army (Red China)
PLAN	People's Liberation Army Navy
POC	Point of Contact
PRC	People's Republic of China (Red China)
PTO	Pacific Theater of Operations
RAH-66	Advanced, stealthy recon/attack helicopter called Comanche (U.S.)
RAM	Rolling Airframe Missile
Raptor	Most advanced, stealthy, high performance air superiority fighter aircraft designated F-22 (U.S.)
ROC	Republic of China (Taiwan)
ROC(AF) (N)	Republic of China Air Force or Navy
RORO	Roll On Roll Off transport ship
RPG	Rocket Propelled Grenade
R&R	Rest and relaxation
RTB	Return to Base
RV	Re-entry Vehicle
SAC	Strategic Air Command or Special Agent in Charge
SAG	Surface Action Group
Sea Flanker	Navy version of SU-30 called designated SU-33. (Red China, India)
Sea Sparrow	Medium range, ship launched radar guided anti-missile missile. (U.S.)
SEAL	Sea, Air & Land Special Forces (U.S. Navy)
SECDEF	Secretary of Defense (U.S.)

TERM/ACRONYM	DEFINITION
Sentry	Air Force warning and command aircraft designated E-3. (U.S., U.K., Japan)
SFOD-D	Special Forces Operation Detachment - Delta
SFS	Security Force Superintendent
Sidewinder	Advanced all aspect short-range air to air missile designated AIM-9X (U.S.)
SITREP	Situation Report
SLCM	Ship or Submarine Launched Cruise Missile
SPAEGIS	Space-born version of the AEGIS weapon's system
Spirit	Stealthy, sub-sonic, long-range bomber designated B-2 (U.S.)
SR-77	New high speed, high altitude recon and surveillance aircraft called the Pervador. Replaced the SR-71 Blackbird. (U.S.)
SSBN	Nuclear Powered Ballistic Missile Submarine carrying ICBM's.
SSGN	Nuclear Powered Guided Missile Submarine carrying SLCM's.
SSN	Nuclear powered attack submarine
SSTN	Large nuclear powered transport submarines (U.S.)
SSTO	Single Stage to Orbit Space launch
Standard Missile	Long range U.S. anti-air missile. Advance used for TMD.
Stinger missile	Short range, all aspect, self-guided anti-air missile. Shoulder, vehicle, helicopter, aircraft or ship fired. (U.S. & allies)
STOL	Short Take-off and Landing
Strike Eagle	Two-seat strike version of F-15C aircraft designated F-15E (U.S.)
SU-24	Long Range Strike Aircraft called Fencer (Red China. GIR and India)
SU-30	Advanced Russian fighter/bomber exported and license built called Flanker. (Red China, GIR, India)
SU-33	Naval version of SU-30 called Sea Flanker. (Red China, India)
SU-35	Two seat strike/radar suppression/EW version of SU-30 aircraft. (Red China)
SUBT CIWS	Sub-surface Threat Close in Weapons System
Super Hornet	Most modern, supersonic, high performance naval fighter/attack aircraft designated F/A-18 E (U.S.)
SUV	Sport Utility Vehicle
SWAT	Special Weapons and Tactics (Police)
T-72	1980's variety main battle tank employed by GIR and CAS.
T-80	1990's variety main battle tank employed by GIR and CAS.
Tango	Military term for a terrorist

TERM/ACRONYM	DEFINITION
TAS	Tactical Assault Ship (Red China)
Ta shih	Chinese anti-stealth sensor, acquisition and fire control system.
TF	Task Force
Thunder Dart	Hyper-velocity, exo-atmosphere reconnaissance and surveillance aircraft designated HR-7. (U.S.)
Threat Condition Zebra	Watertight combat threat condition for naval vessels.
TMD	Theater Missile Defense
Tomcat	Supersonic, high performance, long range, 1970's carrier based fighter/bomber designated F-14D (U.S.)
Top Dome	Russian provided radar system for advanced surface vessels. (Red China)
Top Plate	Russian radar system for advanced surface vessels. (PRC)
TOW	Wire guided anti-tank missile
TU-16	Older, subsonic 1970's vintage Russian strike aircraft called Badger (Red China, India, GIR)
TU-22M	Supersonic, long range Russian strike aircraft, exported and license built called Backfire (Red China, India)
TU-142	Older, prop-driven Russian reconnaissance & ASW aircraft called Bear Exported and license built. (India)
UAE	United Arab Emirates
UAV	Unmanned Aerial Vehicle
UEDF	Unified European Defense Force
USCGS	United States Coast Guard Ship
USFK	United States Forces Korea
V-150	Highly exported APC armed with a 20mm cannon used by U.S. Air Force security. (U.S. and allies)
VLF	Very Low Frequency
VLS	Vertical Launch System
VTOL	Vertical Take-off and Landing
WMD	Weapons of Mass Destruction
WNN	World News Network
XO	Executive Officer

About the Author

Jeff Head is a 47 year-old father of five children living in southwest Idaho. He and his wife of 25 years are the proud grandparents of three grandchildren. He has worked as a designer, engineer and consultant in the defense, nuclear power, and computer industries. Among others, he has worked on the A-7 aircraft project, the San Onofre nuclear power project, the Multiple Launch Rocket System, and the Theater High Altitude Air Defense System.

While working as a director at Structural Dynamics Research Corporation, Mr. Head was involved in efforts at the Thiokol Corporation Strategic Operations Division to improve operations in the years following the shuttle Challenger disaster. As a result of that effort, in 1992 Mr. Head was presented a Vice President's award from Thiokol Strategic Operations for his team's efforts.

Since 1995, in both a program management and consulting role, Mr. Head has traveled extensively overseas on behalf of U.S. firms to establish manufacturing and development operations in the Far East, India, and Eastern Europe.

Mr. Head has also been involved in several civic events including the "Klamath Basin Water Crisis" in Oregon in 2001. In August of 2002, Mr. Head accepted a "Person of the Year" award resulting from his involvement at Klamath Falls and work associated with his 9-11web site, "The Attack on America".

In 2003 Mr. Head was presented a National Leadership Award and selected as an Honorary Chairman from Idaho for the Business Advisory Council to the National Republican Congressional Committee by the Majority Leader.

Mr. Head is also very active in his Church and involved with the Boy Scouts of America, helping with rafting trips and winter camps in the mountains of southwest Idaho.

Printed in the United Kingdom
by Lightning Source UK Ltd.
124656UK00001BA/8/A